"Do you ever miss it? Home?"

Ben shook his head. "No."

"I do, every day," she murmured. "It's like an ache."

"Still in the thrall of the exotic?"

Tavy steeled herself against the unwanted emotion. She did not want to go back, to remember everything, no matter what the temptation.

"It was not like that. Perhaps at first. But then I—"

He walked toward her. Something shimmered in his eyes. Something that made her heart stumble and her knees turn liquid.

"I—" She struggled for breath, but he seemed not to breathe at all, his body a rigid wall.

"You?"

"I miss—"

His hands came up to either side of her face but not touching, his arms locked and jaw hard. His gaze scanned her features, fraught and fast. His chest rose hard.

With every mote of skin and blood sparking and alive from his nearness, Tavy panicked. She stepped back.

Ben grasped her wrist, pulled her forward, and joined their mouths.

Romances by Katharine Ashe

IN THE ARMS OF A MARQUESS
CAPTURED BY A ROGUE LORD
SWEPT AWAY BY A KISS
A LADY'S WISH

IN THE
ARMS
OF A
MARQUESS

KATHARINE ASHE

AVON
An Imprint of HarperCollinsPublishers

AVON BOOKS
An Imprint of HarperCollins*Publishers*
10 East 53rd Street
New York, New York 10022-5299

Copyright © 2011 by Katharine Brophy Dubois
Excerpt from *When a Scot Loves a Lady* copyright © 2012 by Katharine Brophy Dubois
K.I.S.S. and Teal is a trademark of the Ovarian Cancer National Alliance.
ISBN 978-0-06-196565-4
www.avonromance.com

First Avon Books mass market printing: September 2011

Avon Trademark Reg. U.S. Pat. Off. and in Other Countries, Marca Registrada, Hecho en U.S.A.
HarperCollins® is a registered trademark of HarperCollins Publishers.

Printed in the U.S.A.

10 9 8 7 6 5 4 3 2 1

*To the writers whose work inspires, teaches
and strengthens me—
The light within me bows to the light within you.*

*And to my mother, Georgann Brophy.
Thank you, great lady and cherished friend.*

Never attack a tiger on foot . . . for if you fail to kill him, he will certainly kill you.
                    —*Walter Campbell,* My Indian Journal

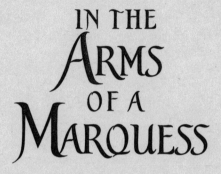

IN THE
Arms
OF A
Marquess

Prologue

Madras, 1812

Beneath a thick coating of sun, the port bazaar seethed with heat lifting off the ground in waves striated with dust. Pungent human bodies packed the street, dark-skinned, clad in white, yellow, and orange, working, shouting, begging, jostling. Music throttled the air, tinny pipe and the twang of plucked strings, harried and intricate. The young English miss, wrapped in wools that had seemed eminently practical on board ship, stewed like a trussed hare in a pot of boiling broth.

Yet none of it dulled the sparkle of wonder in her brown eyes or stilled the quick breaths escaping her lips. After years of dreaming, then months of shipboard anticipation, she was finally here.

India.

Her uncle hurried the servants, snapping phrases at them in their language, ugly from his tongue but beautiful, *colorful* in the mouths of passing natives, a babble of incred-

ible sound. Beads of sweat trickled under her tight collar
and inside her gloves. She clutched her reticule under her
arm and wrenched the gloves from her damp fingers, eyes
alive, seeking everywhere, drinking in the sights.

Beneath awnings spread nearly to the center of the
street, tables laden with market goods spilled into the
narrow pedestrian passageway. Bins of vegetables, nuts,
grains, and beans the hues of primroses, gardenias, vio-
lets, and moss competed for space with spools of fabrics
in brilliant colors, shining silk and supple cottons, and
barrels and clayware vats and bottles glistening with dark
liquids. Vendors shouted and customers bickered, trading
coins. A pair of skin-and-bones children, brown as dirt,
darted between, a fruit seller hollering after them. The
music grew louder from ahead, saturating the heavy air.

It was a marketplace such as she had never seen, chaotic
and fluid so far beyond the market her mother frequented
in London that it stole the breath from her young breast.

Behind the makeshift shops, buildings rose to modest
height in impressive English elegance laced with exotic
detail. Flanking the harbor the massive Fort St. George
dwarfed them all, the presence of England so ponder-
ously established upon this vast continent.

"I could not bring the carriage closer." Uncle George
turned and shook his head, his brow wrinkling. "And a
chair is not to be found today. But the carriage is not far,
just beyond the *bazir.* You there," he ordered one of the servants, "run ahead and alert the coachman of our approach."

The servant disappeared into the crowd.

The girl hoped the carriage was still very far away
indeed. Nothing, not all of her reading and studying
and every picture plate and oil painting she could see in
London, had prepared her for the bone-rattling heat, the
overwhelming scents of tangy, intoxicating spices mingled with unwashed humanity, or the sight of so many

people, so much life, so much movement and color all on a single street.

After nearly sixteen years of life she had finally arrived in heaven.

Someone beside her stumbled, knocking into her, and she fell back, catching her knee on a crate. She stepped forward, but her dress clung, snagged on a jutting nail. Dropping her gloves onto the dirt-packed street, she tugged on the skirt. Her uncle's hat was barely visible yards away, the servant gone. She yanked at the hem. It tore.

A tall man moved close. His thin lips curved into a grin, fist on his belt where a jewel-handled blade jutted in an arc from his loose trousers.

Her heart lurched.

Uncle George shouted for her as he pressed back through the crowd, but it flowed the opposite direction, pushing him away. The tall man drew forth the dagger and gestured with it. Someone gripped her upper arm. She whirled around. A swarthy face loomed inches from hers.

"Uncle!" she screamed, but the music seemed to swell, swallowing her cry.

"Come easy, *memsahib*, and you will not be harmed." The dark man's voice seemed sorrowful, belying his grip.

"No." She struggled. "Unhand me!"

The man's head jerked aside, his eyes opening to show the whites all around. He released her and dropped back. Just as abruptly, the tall native sheathed his dagger, his wary gaze fixed over her shoulder.

She tried to turn. Big hands cinched her waist, a voice behind her snapped terse foreign words, and then in the King's English at her ear, "You are safe. Now up you go," and he lifted her aloft.

With an *oomph* shot from her lungs, she landed upon a horse's back. She gripped its tawny mane as the animal's master vaulted into the saddle behind her. She teetered, but a strong arm wrapped around her and a long flash of silver arced over her head. The horse, a large white muscular animal, pressed forward.

She caught up her breath. "Sir—"

"Your uncle's carriage is ahead a short distance. Allow me to escort you there."

He slid his sword into its sheath at his hip, and her gaze followed the action. Sleek with muscle beneath fine leather breeches, his thighs flanked her behind, holding her steady like his arm tight around her middle. An arm clad in extraordinarily fine linen.

Her heart pounded. She twisted her chin over her shoulder and her gaze shot up.

"Sir, I must—"

Her protest died.

Eyes like polished ebony, long-lashed, warm and gently lazy, glinted down at her from beneath straight brows and a careless fall of black hair. His mouth curved up at one corner, a crease forming in his bronzed cheek.

"You must loosen your grip upon my horse's mane," he said softly, a hint of music in his gentleman's perfect English, "or you will come away with a handful of hair, and he with a frightful bald spot." A flash of white teeth animated a quick, boyish grin.

Why, despite his broad shoulders and splendid mount, he could not be very much older than she, perhaps only by a few years. And he was laughing at her, albeit nicely.

"I—" She pried her fingers open then grabbed at the silver-encased pommel digging into her thigh. The crowd seemed to part before them, but he was not watching their path. He was watching her, from very few inches away. Fewer inches than she had ever been separated from any man.

"I—" Words would not form upon her thick tongue, certainly a first. A whiff of scent tangled in her nostrils, leather and fresh linen and something else. Something subtle, like sandalwood but spicier, and . . . *wonderful.* Her palms went unaccountably damp.

"You?" His steady gaze gently smiled.

"I— I have torn my dress."

His glance flickered to her thighs jammed between his knee and the animal's withers, paused, then slowly traced her legs from hip to foot, and back again. She ceased breathing, every inch of skin beneath her gown tingling where his gaze passed.

He returned his regard to her. His eyes glimmered with laughter, but his shapely mouth slid into a serious line.

"I daresay you have."

His grip on the reins shifted and he averted his face as he turned the horse's direction. A glimpse of man's neck showed above his cravat. She dragged her attention away, fixing on his hand beneath her ribs. It was a man's hand, large and powerful, grasping the leathers with practiced ease, an enormous gold tiger's head ring on one finger, ruby eyes flashing.

Perhaps he was rather a bit older than her, after all.

Tickles fluttered in her belly. And somewhat lower. She blinked.

The noise and closeness of the bazaar fell away, in its place open street, clean shop fronts, a pair of English officers like those she had traveled with all the way to India, and finally a carriage, her uncle's servant standing before it.

"Your destination." In one smooth movement her rescuer dismounted and drew her off the horse. She wavered, gulping breath. He ducked his head to peer beneath her bonnet brim. "Have your bearings now?"

She nodded, mouth dry. His hands slipped away from her waist, and he put his foot in the stirrup and mounted. Taking up the reins, he gestured behind her as his horse's head swung around.

"Your uncle arrives."

Uncle George shoved from the crowd into the cross street, his brow taut. He peered at the horseman, frowned, and strode forward.

The young man's watchful gaze remained upon her.

"Sir." She sounded oddly breathless. "Thank you for your assistance."

He bowed from the saddle, his gold-embroidered waistcoat and the hilt of his sword sparkling in the sun falling in slanting rays behind him.

"It was my great honor." His mouth quirked into a grin and the horse pranced a half circle. "Welcome to India, *shalabha*." The beast wheeled away, stirring up a cloud of dusty street. She stared through the cloud. When the dust settled, he was gone.

"Dear lord, niece, I thought I'd lost you." Uncle George gripped her hands, then cinched her arm under his and drew her toward the carriage. "Why didn't you keep up? Are you unharmed? What did he want of you?"

"He rescued me. I snagged my dress and a pair of cutpurses accosted me, just as on a London street. It was fantastic." And terrifying. Momentarily. "But he frightened them off." Even though he certainly was not much bigger than either of the thieves, although he was quite tall. "He had the horse, however. A very fine horse. And a sword. A sword must count for more than a dagger, after all."

"A dagger? Good God. Those men were not cutpurses. The *bazir* is not safe for Englishwomen. You may not go there again. Do you understand?"

"Yes, Uncle," she said, shifting her gaze between him and the servant. The men exchanged peculiar looks. Uncle George handed her up the carriage steps. She settled into the seat, her heartbeat slowing but her limbs suddenly shaky.

"Uncle George, who was that young man?"

"His uncle owns the villa beside your brother-in-law's house," he said in short tones.

"Oh." She was still two years from being out in society, but her sister's husband, Sir St. John, always said the rules were rather more relaxed in the East Indies than at home. And the community of English traders in this part of India was quite small. If she and her rescuer were neighbors, she would certainly meet him again soon. Her stomach jittered with anticipation.

Uncle George climbed in and closed the door. Beyond the open sash, the *bazir* teemed with people, vibrancy, and sound. She worried her lip between her teeth and a shiver of delayed relief glistened through her. It would be lovely to return and explore the stands and shops, the next time much more carefully, now that she knew villains lurked about. Fortunately, so did dashing young English gentlemen.

"Uncle, what does *shalabha* mean?"

Chapter 1

HORIZON. That circle which seems to bound our view, or limit our prospect, either at sea or on land.
—*Falconer's* Dictionary of the Marine

Madras, 1821

Miss Octavia Pierce came fully into her looks at the advanced age of five-and-twenty, several thousand miles away from England and in the midst of a monsoon.

Lounging in a shadowed parlor, hand wrapped around the stem of a fan in an attempt to stir the moisture laden air, her elder sister, Alethea, noticed the softening of Octavia's sharp jaw, the gentler curve of lips no doubt due to less biting upon them, and the lengthening of fine, red-gold hair that should never have been cut short to suit fashion. She noted too the elegant, stiff set of her sister's slender shoulders, the once-wild chestnut brows now plucked into perfect submission, the smooth cheeks and rather too temperate brown eyes.

"Tavy," Alethea said, "when did you stop laughing aloud?"

Octavia's gaze remained on the letter in her hand. "What on earth are you talking about? I still laugh aloud." The sheet of foolscap was crossed and recrossed with their mother's spindly scrawl. Her brow beetled.

"No, you do not. I wonder when it happened."

"During some monsoon over the past eight and a half years, I daresay." Tavy glanced up again. "This is the third time this week you have asked me some silly question like that, Thea. The rain has sunk you into the dismals. Would you like me to fetch a glass of tea for you? Cook made some with mint and fennel this morning."

"You have become a beauty, Octavia."

Tavy lowered the letter. "Oh. You've gone batty."

"You have. Look at your elegant gown straight from Paris, your shining hair, your lovely figure. And it is not only your appearance. Everyone in Madras adores you."

"They pretend to because I am the only one who tells the truth around here, and they are all afraid I will tell the truth about them someday too. Behind my back, they crucify me." She wrinkled her nose. "Now, you are making me ill with this line of commentary. Cease." She put a hand to the shuttered window and pressed it open to allow in more light along with a whorl of damp air. Returning her attention to the letter, she took her lower lip between her teeth. "Thea, what did you write to Mama about me most recently?"

Agitated chatter an octave higher than either woman's voice erupted from the banister along the covered porch. Tavy extended her arm through the open window and a tiny black and brown ball of fur and limbs streaked up it, settling atop her shoulder.

"Hello, Lal. You are back early. Did you find anything tasty in Lady Doreé's kitchen today?" She stroked the monkey as it curled its spindly arms around her neck, and glanced at her sister again. "What did you write, Thea?"

"She asked me how you were getting along."

"She asked why I am not yet married."

Alethea's fanning slowed. "It is time to go home, sister."

Tavy stilled, not allowing her reaction to show—the jump in her pulse, the frisson of panic across her shoulders. Her sister was correct in one respect. She had grown nearly expert at hiding her emotions. On the outside.

"Why now? Finally?"

"There is malaria in the old quarter."

"There has been malaria in the old quarter before, and the new. We did not leave then."

Alethea's palm slipped over her abdomen. "This time I have greater reason for caution."

Tavy's mouth popped open. Alethea smiled, hazel eyes sparkling. Tavy threw herself across the chamber and her arms about her sister.

"Finally. Oh, finally." She pulled back, gazing with delight and wonder at Alethea's lap. "When did you know?"

"March."

"March?" she exclaimed. "And you did not tell me? But that would explain St. John's distraction lately. Well, more than his usual distraction."

"After so many years, it seems too good to be true."

Tavy grasped her sister's hands. "I am so, so very happy for you. For St. John. For me! I shall be an aunt. How positively lovely. But you will have this baby on board ship."

"Perhaps. The doctor is coming along, and we will make few stops. St. John is seeing to the arrangements now. There is something to be said for one's husband having influence over a number of fast vessels." Alethea's gaze sobered. "You will not mind going home?"

Tavy stood and moved toward the window again, an odd restlessness slipping through her. She reached to her shoulder, and Lal curled his tail around her fingers, a comforting gesture. But she did not need comforting, she reminded herself firmly. She had always known she would someday go home.

"When Father allowed me to come to India, it was only to be for a year or two, living with Aunt Imene and Uncle George," she said with forced lightness. "That I remained so much longer after you and St. John came astounds me as well as anyone."

Alethea took up the letter Tavy had set down on the sofa. "I see Marcus Crispin has been awarded a title."

"For his service in that Singapore affair." Tavy told herself not to chew on her thumbnail then did so anyway, cringing when her sister's gaze narrowed.

"He called upon Papa?"

"I shall have to marry him now." Her shoulders jerked in a peculiar little spasm. The monkey grasped her ear for balance, clicking its tongue.

Alethea's head came up. "Have to?"

Tavy pursed her lips. "It is one thing to be a spinster here in Madras, where my brother-in-law is the highest Company official for miles and miles and I can do whatever I like."

"And quite another to be one back home," Alethea supplied.

"A mere 'miss,' receiving an offer from a bona fide lord of the realm, a baron for heaven's sake. I wonder if he truly means to wait for me to return, as he told Papa?" She lifted her brows but the effort cost her. A sliver of discomfort worked its way between her eyes to the base of her neck.

"But you do admire him, don't you?"

"Marcus Crispin? Intelligent, handsome, successful?

Oh, and charming." Tavy waved an airy hand as though it did not concern her in the least, an affectation she had years ago intentionally adopted that now seemed as natural as breathing. "I certainly admire him. Who wouldn't?" She stared out at the heat rising in the garden.

"You are not hoping for more than admiration?"

Tavy shot a sympathetic smile toward her sister, turning again to the window before Alethea saw it fade.

"Thea, your happiness with St. John is all I could wish for. But love matches are not for everyone." Her gaze lingered upon the banyan tree at the back of the garden, its trunk enormous and branches spreading. She drew in a deep breath and turned away. "Marcus Crispin is a fine man. I believe I can be happy with him."

No response met her for a time.

"We will sail for London in a month," her sister finally said. "It should be a comfortable journey if all goes smoothly."

The trip in the other direction years earlier still lingered in Tavy's memory with all the delicious vibrancy of a girl's fantastical memory, the months of shipboard adventure and pauses at ports along the way. With her young heart full of excitement, her dreams finally coming true, everything had sparkled.

She stroked the monkey's tail curled around her palm and her gaze traveled across the chamber. The cloud cover parted briefly, and motes of dust wandered through the dappled sun sprinkling through the shutters. Palm branches brushed against the veranda outside, dark and dripping with moisture. The heat-filled air stealing from the kitchen wing was redolent of cardamom, citrus, and myriad other subtle aromas.

A shallow breath stole from her lungs.

"I will miss this. I will miss India."

But deep in the pit of her belly a tingle of nerves stirred, hidden for so long and so thoroughly it should have by all rights vanished by now. A frisson of awareness best left buried but reawakened, as persistent as on each day the London journals arrived in Madras, months out of date, welcome nonetheless by the English residents hungry for *on dits*. Tavy searched those journals, her face slightly averted and eyes narrowed as though to fool herself into believing she was not searching at all. Merely glancing. Only curious of the old news that often seemed so irrelevant in this world apart from England.

Three times her searches had been rewarded. Three breath-stopping, painful times in nearly seven years.

Those instances had almost made her afraid to pretend not to search the next time the journals arrived. Almost. But each month she pretended again, and each month the announcement she awaited did not appear. Nor did she hear it gossiped amongst Madras society, English or natives.

He had not yet wed.

Now, however, the journals would print her own betrothal announcement. And when she became the baroness of Crispin, she would stop pretending not to search. It was far past time, and she was not the person she had once been. The girl who cared about that expected announcement no longer existed.

She lifted her gaze. Her sister's thoughtful regard was trained on her, oddly sorrowful. Tavy's throat thickened. She shook off the sensation. Too much rain made her maudlin too. In the morning she would walk to the bazaar to work out her fidgets and say goodbye to her friends there.

"I hope you will live with us in town instead of with Mama and Papa," Alethea said. "St. John's aunt, Lady Fitzwarren, can introduce you into society."

"I would like that." Tavy moved toward the parlor doors to the terrace. "In the meantime, I shall begin packing the house," she said with purpose. "You mustn't strain your-self. Leave it all to me."

"Thank you, dearest. Octavia?"

She glanced back.

"Is this acceptable to you?"

"Of course. Why wouldn't it be?" She passed out onto the veranda.

A man sat against the wall beneath the broad awning, cap drawn over his dark face, his loose cotton trousers, shirt, and long tunic neat as a pin.

"You have no doubt heard the news already, Abha." She curled into a chair. Lal leapt from her shoulder to the win-dowsill. Droplets of rain pattered from edge of the roof to the tiled floor.

Abha pushed the cap back on his bald pate. He was a large man, thickset and heavy-eyed, with an Oriental flat-ness to his cheeks and brow. When her uncle hired him on her eighteenth birthday, Tavy thought it excessive to keep a servant principally to attend her when she went about Madras. But Abha had remained even after Uncle George left for Bengal.

"Thank you," she said.

"For what do you thank me now, *memsahib*?" he rum-bled.

"For putting up with me for so many years. In case I should forget to thank you later when everyone is busy getting ready to depart, I wanted to do so now. Or perhaps simply twice. Will you go now to work for my uncle in Calcutta?"

"I will go to London."

Tavy sat up straight. "Has my brother-in-law asked you?"

Abha did not respond. He often did not when she asked questions to which the answers seemed obvious. To him, at least.

Tavy shook her head. "London is not like Madras. Englishwomen are not kidnapped and held for ransom there, and I am not royalty. Far from it. I can go to the shops or call upon my friends with only a maid."

He put a thick palm on the ground and pushed himself up to stand, silent as jungle birds at the onset of a storm.

"Well, you won't like it, I daresay," she said. "It is horridly gray and cold. Sometimes, at least."

He moved toward the kitchen entrance.

"Abha, you cannot come. India is your home."

He halted and looked over his bulky shoulder. "As it is yours, *memsahib*." He disappeared around the side of the house.

Lal landed on Tavy's shoulder and pressed his tiny hand against her cheek.

"You smell of rosewater." She stroked him beneath the chin. "You have been in our neighbor's kitchen, after all."

He clucked his tongue.

"Lal, will you come to London and stay with me when I become Lady Crispin?" Tavy's gaze strayed to the wall between the garden and the neighboring villa. Vines twined around the gate, especially thick where they tangled about the rusted latch. Her heart beat hard and fast. "You see," her voice dimmed to a whisper, "except for Abha, I will not know anybody else there."

Chapter 2

To IMPRESS. Where no other adequate mode can be substituted, the law of imperious necessity must be complied with.

—Falconer's Dictionary of the Marine

Cavendish Square

I have no need to hear the details, Creighton." Benjirou Doreé, Fifth Marquess of Doreé, set his elbow atop the broad mahogany desk, closed his eyes, and pinched the bridge of his nose between a manicured thumb and forefinger. "Indeed, I would rather know nothing about it at all." He looked up and lifted a single black brow. "As I have told you ten score times. No, I must correct myself. Twelve score. But perhaps your memory fails." His smooth voice seemed unperturbed.

His secretary knew better than to trust in that tone. While the marquess remained deceptively calm, his black eyes saw everything and his mind never rested. It had been this way ever since Creighton came to work for him seven years ago. A man of Lord Doreé's wealth and power had no other choice, even if he liked to pretend otherwise.

Of course, everyone knew of that wealth, but few in English society knew of the power. For the sake of the projects the marquess pursued, that was best.

"My lord," Creighton murmured, "I would review the matter with Lord Ashford were he here. But he has not yet returned from France—"

"And damn him for it and leaving this to me."

"Very good, sir."

The marquess glanced at his secretary's poker face. He had, after all, hired Creighton after a night of cards in which the fellow won a pony from a veritable sharp.

The tug of a grin loosened the knot in Ben's jaw, but the tension in his shoulders persisted. He rolled his gaze to the massive, gilt-framed canvas across the chamber. Afternoon sunlight striped his study in lines of gold and shadow, like the great beast depicted in the painting. But the portrait of the tiger remained fully in the dark. As always.

"Have you already inspected this—" He glanced at the papers Creighton laid before him. "—*Eastern Promise*?"

"Partially. The master was off visiting his family, and the quartermaster wouldn't allow us belowdecks."

"You suspect they are hiding something. Faults in the hull, or cargo?"

"Either." Creighton's brow crinkled. "Or neither. The pratique-master gave it a clean pass."

Ben flashed his secretary a look suggesting his opinion of the honesty of quarantine officials. "A man has no need to protect himself from prying eyes when he has nothing to hide, Creighton."

"Quite so, my lord." Creighton's puddle-brown eyes glimmered and his narrow chest puffed out. Ben nearly rolled his eyes again. He should never pontificate; his secretary enjoyed it far too much. Devoted fool. Excellent employee.

"Sir, atop I did see some evidence of human—"

"Enough." Ben took up his pen and scratched his signature onto a bank check. He pushed it across the desk and stood. "Take Sully with you." Creighton was a tough man of business, but the former dockworker and his crew of miscreants who served Ben's interests in other capacities were tough in quite another manner. "Allow the quartermaster no more than thirty minutes to clear out his crew and their personal effects."

"But, sir, don't you wish to see the vessel for your—"

"No." Ben's voice was unyielding. "If you find illegal goods aboard her, incinerate them. If she proves unseaworthy, scrap her for materials and find another vessel to serve our current needs." He gazed steadily at his secretary. "Now, Creighton, leave before I become inordinately displeased that you have disturbed my leisure in this manner again."

One corner of Creighton's mouth quivered, but nothing more. Wise man.

"Right, my lord." Creighton pulled an envelope from the collection of papers in his satchel. "This arrived at the office today."

Ben barely glanced at the sealed missive before slipping it into his waistcoat pocket. He picked up the sword he'd set upon the table when he entered his study, hands perfectly steady despite the familiar uneven rhythm of his heart.

Every three months like clockwork such a letter arrived, brought across half the world along the fastest routes. A punishment he willingly self-inflicted, it was the sole remnant of the single reckless moment of his life. A moment in which he had lived entirely for himself.

Gripping the hilt of the épeé, he strode through his

house. A liveried footman opened a door into a broad, high-ceilinged chamber.

"Bothersome business matters. My apologies, Styles." He drew on his fencing glove.

The gentleman standing by the rack of glittering swords chuckled, a sound of open camaraderie.

"I wish I had that particular bother." He took a weapon from the collection. "How much did you net this quarter, Doreé? Ten thousand? Fifteen?"

"You know I never concern myself with that."

"You merely live lavishly on the proceeds." Styles gestured to the elegant fencing chamber Ben had converted the ballroom into after he succeeded to the title six and a half years earlier and had the whole house gutted. His father had been enamored of India, and his town residence reflected that. Just as his third son did, in his very person.

The opulent style had not suited Ben.

"Just so," he murmured.

"Come now, give over," Styles cajoled. "We have been friends far too long for you to continue denying your extraordinary influence at India House. And I think it's about more than all those manufactories and plantations and whatnot you own over there. Your family connections give you an unfair advantage over the rest of us struggling traders, don't they?"

Not the advantage any of them imagined.

"I am a mere proprietor in the East India Company, just as you. No particular advantage to speak of." Ben studied his former schoolmate from behind lowered lids. Walker Styles came from an old Suffolk family ennobled in the era of Queen Elizabeth. His aristocratic pallor, blue eyes, and narrow, elegant frame were proof of it. The latter also happened to make him a devilishly fine fencing partner. And his sharp competitive edge kept Ben on his toes.

Ben swiped his blade through the air.

The baron cocked a brow beneath an artfully arranged thatch of straw-colored hair. "Are you certain you don't thoroughly control those fellows over at Leadenhall Street, despite your lack of apparent involvement?"

"Good God, quite certain," Ben lied as smoothly as he had been taught as a boy. "There are those at Whitehall and Westminster who would be horrified at the mere suggestion of such a thing."

"You are just like your brothers, Ben, all honorable self-deprecation. Jack of course was not so close-mouthed, the good-natured sod." Styles laughed, digging a familiar burrow of grief through Ben. He still could not bear to hear his half brothers spoken of casually, even by the one man who had been as close to them as he himself.

"So be it." The baron lifted his blade in salute. "The secret of your empire is safe with me, whatever it is."

L'Empire de la Justice—the name Ben's uncle had given it. An empire born of his uncle's education in France in the years before the Revolution, nurtured by his horror over the massacre at Mysore, and supported by a vast fortune in cotton, spices, and saltpeter. Groomed his whole young life to someday rule it, for years Ben had danced like a puppet on strings at his uncle's insistence in service to that empire. As the progeny of a lord, even a third son and foreign-born, he had entrée into certain sectors of European society that his Indian uncle never would.

His uncle hadn't any idea what that entrée had truly entailed. Or he hadn't cared.

But for seven years now Ben had been master of the empire that operated below the notice of polite society and most governments. And he was no longer a third son. Other men, like his associate Ashford, now did the dirty work.

His steel tip clicked on the polished floor.

"Allez," Styles announced.

The play remained light at first, then grew more intense. But it lasted little time, no longer than it took Ben to disarm his friend.

Styles flexed his wrist, breathing heavily from his exertions. "I must learn that useful little maneuver."

"In the normal course of things, you haven't any need of it." Ben wiped his face with a cloth and racked his sword.

Styles's eyes flashed. "You haven't either."

"I will always have need of such skill, Walker. Your longtime loyalty blinds you to that, I think."

"Humanity is a savage lot, Ben." The baron's voice was tight, his brow uncustomarily clouded.

"Perhaps. But exceptions to the rule do exist." He extended his hand. With a moment's hesitation, Styles clasped it. Blue-veined ivory met bronze.

Styles's palm slid away. "Is it to be the theater for you tonight?"

"Lady Constance insists that I escort her."

"Apron-led fool."

"You could ferry her about instead. She has been hinting at it for months now, or haven't you noticed?"

"I'm not yet ready for parson's mousetrap." Styles smoothed a fingertip along the flat of his blade. "And she is meant to be a marchioness."

Ben did not respond. His understanding with Constance Read was no one's business but his and Constance's alone. If the *haut ton* believed them to be set on marriage, let it. After the fire, gossips had whispered it was even more suitable that she wed him rather than the man she had been betrothed to from the cradle. With Jack Doreé in the grave, an alliance between the heiress of a Scottish duke's East Indies fortune and a wealthy half-Indian peer seemed destined.

Savage humanity, indeed.

"I will be heading over to Hauterive's later tonight."

Styles's tone was a shade too casual. "Join me after you see Lady Constance home?"

Ben buttoned his waistcoat. "You know I don't care for that sort of sport any longer."

"That's right. You prefer swords and horses to cards and dice now. But Hauterive's offers more than dice."

"Allow me to recall." Ben smoothed a hand over his coat and straightened his cravat. "Drunken lords, unhappily married ladies, and sharps hoping to have their way with both? Yet more reasons not to accompany you." He walked toward the door.

Styles grinned. "You sang quite a different tune, once."

"A man changes." Recklessness could cause that. Standing beside a pile of ashes could too.

The baron clapped him upon the back. "If you reconsider, you know where I will be."

Unease prickled across Ben's shoulders as he watched his friend move off along the corridor. Styles had encouraged him to return to their old haunt before, but never so insistently. But Ben hadn't any interest in renewing his university days—rather, nights. He had never wished to live those nights in the first place. Duty and blood had guided him then. Always, then.

His hand moved to his waistcoat pocket and he withdrew the letter. He scanned the missive and his breathing slowed.

She was in England.

Long ago, he had ceased anticipating this day with any feeling whatsoever. It should not now take him by surprise. But for a moment he could not move.

Drawing in a cool breath, he walked into the parlor to the hearth. His hand extended over the grate. The flames seemed to reach forward, urging. His fingertips gripped the paper. As planned, this would be the last such note he received.

Jaw tightening anew, he cast the letter within. Fire licked at its edges for an uncertain instant then consumed it in a breath.

Without another glance, Ben went to change clothing for the evening. He was no longer twenty-two and just up from university, no longer the boy his uncle had controlled from four thousand miles away then again from the grave. In the intervening seven years he had fought and struggled in quite a different manner from the back-alley brawls Styles still seemed to enjoy. That moment, the brief slice of eternity when he had known her, might as well have been a lifetime ago.

"She is an Original." The lady garbed in turquoise taffeta and turban with an ostrich feather poking from the nest lifted her lorgnette and nodded sententiously. "Tell everyone you heard me say it first."

"Sally Jersey said it already, only yesterday morning at Kew when Lord Crispin escorted the girl there."

"No. She came to my notice before that."

"I am certain you wish she had, darling."

"She is hardly a girl," a third matronly voice interjected. "Five-and-twenty, I understand, and brown as a berry."

"The East Indian sun will do that," the first pronounced dismissively. "I call it charmingly sun-touched. Enormously elegant."

"And refined."

"And what taste! Did you see the gown she wore to Lady Alverston's fete? Silver tulle over emerald silk, with mother of pearl and diamonds sewn into the sleeves. I have never seen its like."

"Her sister's husband is despicably wealthy from his East Indies interests."

"And her coiffure—"

"Divine. I daresay I've seen nothing so smart in years.

I would arrange my Penelope's hair just like it, but of course it would not do for brown. Miss Pierce's hair is entirely unique."

"And *natural.*"

"She may be over the marriageable age, but she has the most maidenly address."

"They say she keeps a monkey. *And* she has ridden an elephant."

"Good gracious, how adventuresome."

In the shadow of a potted palm, Tavy sipped her glass of orangeat, wishing it were black tea laced with cane syrup and cardamom. Theatergoers wandered about enjoying themselves. The play was diverting enough, but outside it was gray, London in late September just as she remembered it. And cold, just like her hands and feet and humor.

Tavy wished for sun and heat and Lal sitting upon her shoulder playing with her hair as she read, both of them ensconced in a hammock woven of soft hemp. Instead, she had carriage rides in the crowded park, supper parties, thin tea, and endless wide-eyed commentary. English society just as in Madras, simply lots more of it.

Tavy's stomach tightened, her surroundings closing in like a cage. Albeit a pretty one.

"Have you truly ridden an elephant?"

She swiveled and met a smiling gaze. Stunning in a gown of midnight silk threaded with silver, sable tresses bound atop her head with sapphire combs, the lady had an air about her of Continental fashion.

Tavy lifted her brows. "I wish I had. Yet somehow the rumor is rife."

"Do not allow anything they say to affect you. In a few weeks they will have entirely forgotten they said it. I ought to know."

"Thank you, I think. Are we acquainted?"

"I feel as though we are." The lady extended a gloved hand, her eyes warm. "I am Valerie Ashford and your sister has for years been my fondest correspondent. I know more about you, perhaps, than you would wish." A laugh like honey spilled from her lips, and she leaned forward to kiss Tavy on both cheeks in European style. The gesture warmed Tavy. Momentarily.

"I am honored, my lady." She curtsied, but the viscountess clucked and drew her up.

"Where is your sister? I only arrived in town today from the countryside and intend to call upon her tomorrow. Tell me she is well."

"Very well, I am happy to report. At home with the baby. She cannot tear herself away."

"No fond new mother can. But why are you standing in this corner all alone? You should be surrounded by eager gentlemen." Valerie drew her from behind the palm into the light of the corridor. "With whom have you come here?"

"Lady Fitzwarren. She went searching out her friends, I believe."

"She is delightfully eccentric. And I can see from the twinkle in your eyes that you know that. No doubt you rub along famously together."

"I like her quite a lot."

"Of course you do. Goodness, you *are* lovely, just as all the gossips say. Have they seen you smile like that, I wonder? Probably not. You were hiding, after all." Her gaze sparkled, then fixed over Tavy's shoulder. She lowered her voice. "Now who is this handsome gentleman approaching? I do not believe I am acquainted with him but he seems to know you."

Tavy's heart made a tiny thud as she turned. She met a pair of amiable hazel eyes and her insides righted themselves.

Foolish nerves.

Lord Crispin bowed neatly, his smile ever so pleasing beneath a long, aristocratic nose, clear brow, and thick sepia-colored hair. Tavy made the introductions, glancing at his finery. He always dressed with understated style, up to the stare but never beyond it. Neither nabob nor pink, dandy or dowd. Perfect Marcus Crispin.

"Delighted, Lady Ashford." He bowed. "The praise of your beauty is not overdone." His voice reflected the appreciative glint in his gaze. Tavy had seen that glint turn dozens of ladies giddy, occasionally even gentlemen. Marcus Crispin had not collected a comfortable fortune in trade and won a peerage by failing to use his charm and good looks to advantage.

"I understand you have spent time in the East Indies, like my friend here." The viscountess touched Tavy's arm in the gesture of an intimate.

"Indeed," the baron replied. "It was the most fortunate coincidence that Miss Pierce and I became acquainted there." He smiled at Tavy.

Valerie's gaze darted between them then returned to the baron. "And how did you find that country, my lord?"

"The climate is dreadfully insalubrious, and the Hindustanis often fractious. But, if I may entertain a crude topic in the presence of ladies, the business is excellent. If one can cozen the natives in just the correct manner." His offered a confiding smile.

Tavy's neck felt hot and a bit sticky.

"Really?" Lady Ashford seemed intrigued. "In what manner exactly does one cozen the natives? Do tell, my lord."

Tavy's attention slipped away. In the weeks since her return, she had heard him expound upon his ten months in India to any number of people. His narrative rarely altered, although he always delivered it with charming animation. She should be proud to be on his arm so often, this handsome, successful gentleman whom everyone seemed to know was courting her.

Throat tight, she scanned the glittering crowd. Unfamiliar face upon unfamiliar face, fashionable ladies and gentlemen, diverting conversation.

She missed home, and the outer shell of measured, elegant propriety she had struggled so hard to affect over the past seven years had finally burrowed beneath the skin. Her heart felt chill, just like the dreary English autumn.

A flicker of the spirited girl she had once been, locked so neatly away, cried out in protest. She shushed it.

Clearly she required diversion. Whenever she had the blue devils in Madras she invented projects. Perhaps a project would help her now. Quite a large one.

The bell rang to announce the third act. Tavy turned toward the box and her gaze arrested.

In a cluster of people close by, a gentleman stood with his back to her. His black hair glistened in the chandelier light, short at the nape of his neck meeting a snowy white cravat. His broad shoulders were encased in a black coat fit perfectly to his lean, muscular form, his long legs in elegant buff trousers. On his left hand, a thick flash of gold sparkled, his skin warm-toned, like golden sand at sunset on the Equator.

Stillness washed through Tavy.

Panic swiftly replaced it, rushing from the soles of her feet to her legs and twining into her chest in hot little darts.

She had suspected she would see him eventually. Indeed, she expected it. But suddenly it seemed too soon. She was not yet ready. A few more weeks in society, after she gained her bearings, and she might be. Or possibly never.

But she could not tear her gaze from him. It clung, quivering with the fear of looking and the even greater fear of looking away. Without her willing it, it consumed every line of his body, every lock of hair and detail of the only man she had ever particularly cared to stare at.

His head turned slightly, his face averted from his companions, as though he had become aware of being watched. Tavy's blood seemed to fuse to her bones. How well she had memorized that profile, square jaw, high cheekbones, straight nose, the careless fall of ebony hair over his brow.

His shoulders shifted, turned, and his gaze met hers.

Nothing showed in it, nothing of surprise or even recognition in the languid black eyes. He looked at her for a moment then returned his attention to his friends.

Tavy blinked, a shudder of heat and alternate cold coursing through her, so internal, so deep, it buried itself before it was able to come to the surface.

Then numbness. No feeling at all.

She assessed her heartbeat as though from a distance. Even. Calm. Her breathing regular. After seven years of wondering and waiting, it was an astoundingly anticlimactic finale. But it was a finale, at least. She now had something to write in the margins of her Falconer's *Dictionary of the Marine*, both bible and diary to her since her fifteenth birthday. Perhaps under the heading "To Disembark."

She pulled in a thin breath and shifted her regard to his companions, several elegantly arrayed gentlemen suitable for a marquess's acquaintance, and a statuesque blonde with a good deal of cleavage decorating the bodice of her modish gown. The lady lifted a fawn-gloved hand and rested it upon his sleeve, and her gaze spanned the space to Tavy.

Tavy stared into the wide blue eyes. She was beautiful, all warm golden glory, luscious lips, and voluptuous curves. As gorgeous as her handsome escort. A perfect pair.

It must be the Scottish duke's daughter. Lady Constance Read.

"May I escort you to your boxes, ladies?" Lord Crispin's voice pulled her back.

"My party is just over there." Lady Ashford squeezed Tavy's fingers. "Octavia, I will call upon you tomorrow." She moved away.

The baron took Tavy's arm. "Are you enjoying the play?"

"The scenery is—" She flicked her gaze around, but the elegant party had gone. "It is interesting, my lord."

"Miss Pierce, will you do me the honor of calling me by my given name?"

"If you wish, Marcus. We have been friends for two years, after all."

"Octavia— May I call you Octavia?"

"Yes." He already had.

"Octavia, I hope to be more than friends."

"Thank you, Marcus. I know. My father told me, of course."

"Of course." He chuckled. "You are priceless." He patted her hand and led her into Lady Fitzwarren's box. The dowager had not yet returned. Marcus's brow beetled. "I don't like to leave you here alone."

Octavia took another slow breath, this time of intention.

"Why don't you sit with us for the remainder of the play?" she said. "I am certain Lady Fitzwarren would be happy for your company."

"Would you?" His eyes glimmered with confidence. Life married to this man could suit her. She would have the freedom to do whatever she wished as a married woman, and an inestimable companion.

"I enjoy your company, Marcus. I quite like you, in fact." The words felt strange on her tongue. But she did like him.

He squeezed her fingers. "I will bid my party *adieu* and return shortly."

Alone, Tavy glanced at the unruly crowd in the pit, avoiding the boxes above. Apparently the fashionable set never remained through an entire play. Of course, she didn't know anyone amongst that set, so really it did not signify where she looked.

She folded her damp hands, heart pattering behind her ribs. Like a caged bird's wings. Her skin felt hot all over now and uncomfortably tight. Some sort of delayed reaction, no doubt. It had been seven years, after all. Quite a long time. Quite a foolishly long time.

Voices came from the other side of the partition, hushed and urgent, Marcus and another man. The conversation of the rowdies in the pit below had reached a clamor. As she'd done in the *bazir* and society parties in Madras for years, Tavy tried to focus upon the furtive conversation.

"I will not," Marcus said. "I signed it once before because of our agreement—"

"And you'd better again, milord," a scratchy voice replied, "assurin' that ship leaves wi'out inspection, or you know what'll happen to—"

"Don't think you can threaten me." Marcus's voice crept higher.

"I just did, milord. You'd better agree or I'll be visitin' you at home the next time."

"You would not dare."

"Wouldn't I?"

Footsteps sounded and Marcus appeared beside her.

"My apologies. I was detained by an acquaintance." His face looked oddly blotched.

"Marcus, is everything all right?"

"Certainly." He chuckled uncomfortably. "Especially now that I am with you."

"I heard some of your conversation just now. It sounded like that man was threatening you."

"Of course not. Octavia, I have a great many business associates, just as St. John. Some are less genteel than others, I'm afraid. But this is nothing to concern you, merely a typical transaction. Men's business."

He patted her hand. For the second time that evening, Tavy had the urge to remove her fingers from beneath his and throw her gaze across the theater.

The actors retook the stage, and she pinned her attention to them until the applause ended and Marcus escorted her to the carriage waiting along the crowded block.

"There you are, dear girl." Lady Fitzwarren's multiple chins bounced, her violet taffeta skirts billowing as she strode toward them at a clip far too rapid for a woman of her ample girth. "Crispin, you are gracious to see my charge to our carriage."

He handed the dowager up, a rumbling fit of coughs and snuffles accompanying her ascent. She waved a scented kerchief and settled onto the squabs.

"You must join our party at Vauxhall tomorrow evening."

"Thank you, ma'am." He smiled, but the expression did not reach his eyes, and his gaze shifted about the street. Gaslights burned amber halos across the pavement, heavy mist swirling about the people departing the theater like ghosts in a dream.

"Marcus," Tavy said quietly, "won't you tell me what distresses you?"

"My dear," his brows knit, "if we are to get along well together you must leave the minor unpleasantries of business to me and content yourself with being beautiful and charming." He took her hand. "Simply having you by my side relieves all foolish displeasures, I assure you."

Tavy nodded, but conviction settled. This could be her project. Marcus had trouble with a dishonest man of business. He would not share the problem with her. But if her future lay with him, she must do what she could to help. And she was fortunate to be perhaps the single lady in London who knew where best to seek assistance with this sort of challenge.

A frisson of old doubt mingled with new certainty glistened up her spine. Pushing the sensation away, she took a step up, lifted her gaze past his shoulder, and her breath failed.

As though it were yesterday and not a lifetime ago, in a street crowded with market stalls instead of carriages, bathed in sun rather than misty midnight rain, Lord Benjirou Doreé stood at a distance, watching her. Perfect, clear awareness shone in his dark eyes.

She stared back and his regard did not falter.

"Why do you keep that man in your service?"

She dragged her gaze away and followed Marcus's up to the coachman's box where Abha sat beside Lady Fitzwarren's groom.

"He—" Tavy caught up her breath. "He has been with me for years."

"It is unseemly for a lady to go about London with a manservant of that sort."

She slid her fingers free. "Thank you, my lord. I will take that under advisement. Good evening." She stepped into the carriage. The baron bowed and shut the door. Tavy sat back and closed her eyes, fingers clamped about her reticule.

"What a splendid outing," Lady Fitzwarren exclaimed. "I daresay I've never met with so many friends at one theater production. I'm simply exhausted from talking." She chuckled liberally. "But you wouldn't know a thing about that, you are such a demure lady now. Don't remember you being like this when you were a girl. How you used to kick up a lark wherever I took you and St. John's sisters about town. Must be that horrid East Indian sun. Bakes a girl's head until she ain't got two thoughts in it to rub together." She cracked a laugh, then her voice sobered. "Or perhaps it was that awful Imene Stack. Wretched woman. Don't know why your mother let her have the care of you, though it ain't charitable to speak ill of the dead, of course."

Tavy bit her lip and reached for Lady Fitzwarren's fingers.

"Thank you," she whispered. "Thank you for all those larks years ago."

Taffeta rustled. The dowager surrounded her hands.

"Dear girl—"

"It was not the East Indian sun." She could not open her eyes. The image behind them was too fresh yet far too familiar. "Although it may have had something to do with Aunt Imene." Her lashes parted and she met the dowager's concerned gaze. "But I think perhaps I am through with it now."

"Through with what, dear girl?"

Tavy smiled hesitantly. "Pretending."

Chapter 3

MAGNETISM. The quality or constitution of a body . . .
a transient power, capable of being produced, destroyed,
or restored.

— *Falconer's* Dictionary of the Marine

W ho was that lady last evening at the theater,
Ben?"
He turned from the drawing room window.
"Which lady, Constance? I spoke with several. Lady
March, Alverston's wife, the Countess of Savege. I be-
lieve you are acquainted with them all."

Constance tilted her head, the diamonds threaded
through her hair-ribbon glinting.

"You did not speak with her." Her light brogue lilted
across the chamber. "But you may as well have. A great
deal was communicated in that exchange of glances, I
think."

He returned his gaze to the street traffic. Tradesmen
mostly, thin at this early hour.

"I haven't the foggiest what you are hinting at, as is often the case, my dear."

She made a clicking sound of displeasure with her tongue.

"Communicating with me like one of your prized horses, Connie?" he drawled. "I am flattered. Truly."

"Don't patronize me. We have known each other far too long."

"Then you should be aware that I do not wish to continue in this line of conversation." He turned to her. "Disappointed Styles did not show last night?"

She tightened her lips and her forehead wrinkled.

"Very becoming." Ben lifted a brow. "Hold your face in that manner for long and it will stick." He moved away from the window to the pianoforte and sat at the bench. "Play a duet with me, will you?"

"After that comment? Absolutely not. You sound like you are thirteen again."

"You bring out the best in me."

She chuckled, moving toward him, and draped a hand over his shoulder.

"Are you certain we should not marry, Ben? It would be so much easier than—"

"Yes, Constance." He spread his fingers and touched the keys.

"C minor. Amusing," she murmured. "But I daresay it is best that at least one of us is strong."

"I daresay." He played another chord. Strong was not the correct word. He stood up and started toward the door. "You will be late for your breakfast party." He paused and gestured for her to follow.

"How welcome you make me feel." She came forward. "Yes, I am late. Please, won't you accompany me?"

"Constance, you cannot continue using me like a crutch. A man has his limits."

"Not many when it comes to me," she said with a pretty shrug. "Admit it."

He nodded. "But I still will not accompany you. I have business to attend to this morning, and you must face the gorgons on your own."

She laughed, a tinkling sound full of high nerves and warmth. "Wretch."

He allowed himself a slight smile but could not hold it. He turned toward the door. A woman stood upon the threshold, the footman beside her.

"Miss Pierce," the servant announced, and withdrew.

Just as she had done twice the previous night, she met his gaze squarely now, her wide brown eyes direct. Ben remembered this the best about her—her forthright approach, entirely unlike what he had known of English-women before her, a female devoid of subterfuge, secrecy, and manipulative lies. Or so he had thought for a time.

Otherwise her appearance was wholly altered. Her fashionable gown of icy blue, hair swept into an elegant arrangement, rigid posture, and the straight line of her mouth held little resemblance to the girl he had known. Especially her mouth.

"How do you do, Miss Pierce?" Constance moved forward and shook her hand. "I am Constance Read. I am pleased to make your acquaintance but must beg your pardon now as I am late for an engagement elsewhere." She cast Ben a glance, murmured, "My lord," and left the room with less fanfare than Ben had seen her do anything in his memory.

He met Octavia's gaze.

"Hello, Benjirou." Her voice was cool, another alteration.

"It is Ben now."

"Really?" she remarked as though singularly disinterested. "Have you changed it?"

"It is the name I go by."

"I see. But I suppose everyone calls you Doreé." Her gaze flickered about the lavishly appointed chamber. He followed it. No trace of his father's obsession with India lingered in this place, a dwelling entirely designed to lend consequence to the most English of English lords. Ben's eldest brother, Jack, would have been proud. But then, he had always been proud of Ben, regardless.

"What brings you to my home this morning, Miss Pierce?"

"Then it is clearly Doreé for me as well."

"Do you have a particular purpose in calling, madam, or are you conducting some sort of study on names?"

"I see you are quite as droll as ever." She drew off her gloves and folded them between her slender hands. "I have come here to ask for your help."

He allowed no flicker of surprise to show upon his face. But he should not be surprised. People applied to him for help every day. Never in his drawing room, however, and rarely beautiful women. Her lips were dusky pink, her skin like cream. She was the same all over, he knew, dusky pink and cream.

Her eyes narrowed. "A friend of mine is in some sort of trouble having to do with trade to the East Indies. Clandestine trade, I believe."

Of course.

"A friend?"

"A gentleman. A friend of my family, rather."

"Then I suspect you should be applying to your brother-in-law for aid."

"I cannot. I do not believe St. John would be able to deal with this."

"And how do you imagine I can be of assistance to this gentleman if his own friends cannot?"

"I know that your—" She paused. "—*business* interests are quite broad."

"Do you?" He leaned back against the piano and crossed his arms loosely.

"Yes. One cannot live yards away from a person's house for years without learning something of what goes on there. Anyway, it is common speculation in Madras amongst the permanent residents."

The natives, she meant.

"Is it?" Ben turned his attention to the view beyond the window again. "Fascinating how mythology serves the imagination of the ignorant, isn't it?"

"Mythology?" She stepped forward then halted, as though she had not meant to advance. "Eighteen months ago a band of sepoys defected from the army and stirred up trouble for hours throughout the city before they were apprehended. But I suspect you know that, and that you also know how they threatened every Englishman's house in Madras except yours."

Slowly he returned his gaze to hers.

"You recall," he said smoothly, "that my mother, aunt, and cousins residing in that house are Indian."

"Grenville Fletcher's wife is Indian, but the rebels set fire to his property," she retorted. "He of course is quite a minor trader, but—"

"And your brother-in-law's home? He is hardly an unimportant figure in Madras. Was his house also targeted?" He already knew. This was a foolish gamble. He should end this conversation now.

"No." Her brow troubled. "But the proximity to yours must have deterred them."

"It must have," he placated.

She stepped forward again, her gaze firm.

"You cannot throw me off with this. I know what I know, and I have nowhere else to turn. A man threatened Lord Crispin last night, a man of low speech. He was attempting blackmail, I think. I need assistance to discover who he is and what he wants."

"Madam, I fear you labor under erroneous notions concerning my involvement with such persons, although I certainly thank you for the compliment. Perhaps you should ask Lord Crispin himself?" He tilted his head as though suggesting the obvious. But she had never been slow-witted. She had come to him because she knew. A hot, insistent pressure began beneath Ben's ribs and threaded across his chest.

The fine line of her jaw set. "Denying your business will not make it nonexistent."

"I have little to do with those matters, and less interest. My employees deal with India House here in London, and others abroad."

"You know I am not talking about the East India Company." Her breasts rose upon a short, jagged inhalation, a hint of color staining her smooth cheeks. But her carriage remained erect, her chin level. She was frustrated, but in perfect control of her emotions. Nothing remained in this cool, exquisite woman of the laughing, feeling girl he remembered. But then, nothing remained of the youth who had known that girl for a brief, time-out-of-place moment. *Almost nothing.*

"I am afraid, Miss Pierce, that as this conversation fails to progress, we must remain at a stalemate." He pushed away from the piano. "The footman will see you out."

Her eyes flashed, then the look faltered and she blinked rapidly. Her lips parted, color rising full in her cheeks. Desire, thick and hard like Ben hadn't felt in years, ground in his gut.

"Is that all?" she said. "Am I to be dismissed without any consideration whatsoever?"

He moved across the chamber toward her. Her gaze held, widening only slightly as he neared. He halted close and her scent filled his senses, Indian roses, sweet and musky. Sunlight slanting through the windows danced upon her soft skin and in her hair the color of fire opals. In seven years she had matured into her beauty, and it sat like a mantle of royalty upon her, rendering her untouchable, distant.

All the better.

"Miss Pierce," he said evenly, "you have intruded upon me at home, accused me of consorting with low characters, and suggested that I am in the habit of lying. What more than dismissal do you imagine I owe you?"

A tiny breath of sound escaped her lips. He looked, and cursed himself for not being man enough to look away.

Her mouth tightened into a line again, and he lifted his gaze to her eyes. They were shuttered once more.

"How foolish of me," she said. "Of course, I am no one. You owe me nothing." She turned and strode from the chamber.

He stood motionless for an interval that might have been one minute or thirty. Finally he ran a palm over his face and stepped into the corridor. The footman did not so much as blink.

"Samuel, send word to the stable to have my horse saddled and brought around."

"Yes, my lord." He moved off toward the rear of the house. Ben hadn't the need to instruct him not to repeat anything she had said. His employees knew him well, each of them loyal and discreet.

One, however, he would have a word with. She mustn't come to his house again. But perhaps he had already taken care of that problem himself.

She should not have come.

"Home, please, Abha," Tavy threw over her shoulder. She could not speed quickly enough down the steps of the imposing mansion. What had she been thinking? He might have a network of spies and underlings involved in clandestine business throughout India, England, and the whole world for all she knew, not to mention a fleet of ships. That did not make him her only resource for helping Marcus.

Abha closed the carriage door and they jolted into motion.

Tavy dropped her face into her hands. Dear Lord, what a fool she still was. She had come for the worst reason. For Marcus, yes, but more for herself.

Years ago she had convinced herself there had been nothing between them, that she invented the warmth in his watchful gaze, even her own profound reaction to him, his pull upon her from someplace inside that left her breathless. She had been so young, so naïve and full of imagination. Just a girl.

Now she knew she had not invented it.

His voice was wonderfully rich, deep and almost musical, beautiful—more beautiful even than she remembered it. And he seemed taller, broader, his shoulders filled out and square jaw firmer, the slightest creases about his mouth and brow. He was no longer the young man she had been infatuated with. He was a titled lord, power and strength in his very stance. But his eyes were the same, black, long-lashed, languid and intense at once.

A shiver ran along her spine, curling into her belly.

She pressed the heels of her palms to her eyes. The heat in the pit of her stomach and the ache of longing in her chest, both dormant for so long, stirred the moment he had spoken. He merely looked at her and she was eighteen again, in the garden crying for him.

She threw back her head and sucked in a deep breath. All these years—*years*—should have taught her.

The carriage halted before her sister's town house. Tavy smoothed her hair and straightened her shoulders. Abha let down the step.

"Abha, this afternoon I should like you to accompany me to visit Sir St. John at his office at the docks."

Lines gathered upon his high, flat brow. *"Memsahib*, is this wise?"

"You needn't come if you don't like it." She climbed from the carriage. "I am perfectly able to go searching out a shady character on my own. No one else seems to wish to help me, after all." She strode into the house.

In the upstairs parlor, Lady Ashford sat beside Tavy's sister, both cooing over the bundle in Alethea's arms. It was a cozy scene and peaceful, unencumbered with high emotion. Tavy drew a steadying breath and smiled despite the roiling inside her.

"How is my nephew this morning?"

"Hello, Octavia dear." Valerie extended her hand to squeeze Tavy's. "He is perfectly precious."

"Do you think so?" Alethea tucked a corner of swaddling around the sleeping infant, hazel eyes misty. After nine years awaiting the miracle in her arms, Tavy could not blame her. Alethea was such a sensible person, much more so than she herself, who had spent her childhood dreaming of traveling the world, especially of seeing India, her head constantly in the clouds. Alethea deserved her mistiness now, and Tavy must settle back into the measured temper she had so carefully cultivated over the past seven years.

"It is not merely a mother's fondness?" Alethea asked.

"Or a father's?" St. John entered the chamber and briefly passed his hand across the back of his wife's thick chestnut locks. He often did that, touched Alethea in some subtle way as though conveying his attachment to her with the gesture. Each time Tavy saw it her throat thickened.

"You will always see your son as beautiful and perfect, unless he is being horrid, like mine at the moment," Valerie said on a laugh. "Steven has been detained in Paris and will not return this week as planned. Max is threatening to stow away upon the first ship that will put him into Calais and reunite him with his father more quickly."

"Precocious for eight," St. John commented. "Send him to me and I will find him a berth upon a comfortable vessel."

The viscountess grinned. "You are all kindness, sir, but when I wish for your help, I will ask for it."

St. John's fair good looks and phlegmatic air belied a thoughtful man of business. But when Alethea had entered her confinement while they were still aboard ship sailing north along the Spanish coast, strain had shown on his brow and in his blue eyes. Now he gazed upon his wife and newborn son with evident pleasure, the tension of so many months entirely erased.

"It has been an age since we last saw Steven." Alethea stroked her son's tiny fingers. "Just before we left for India, if I recall."

"Which puts me in mind of an errand I must do now." Valerie clasped Tavy's hand again. "Octavia, I am having a supper party on Friday. Only a few close friends. I cannot hope to persuade your sister and Sir St. John to leave this tiny treasure for an entire evening, but you must come even so."

"I would be delighted."

"Splendid. Tomorrow I will take you driving in my carriage. But for now I must be off." The viscountess pecked Alethea upon both cheeks, cast a smile at St. John, and departed.

Tavy bent and touched her lips to her nephew's brow, then her sister's.

"I have letters to write. If you need me I will be in the downstairs parlor." She left her brother-in-law and sister to their private happiness.

Lal perched atop the stair rail awaiting her. She placed her forefinger inside the monkey's gentle grip.

"St. John's joy is too new," she whispered, "his heart so thoroughly bound to them that in the middle of his busy day he is here at home."

The capuchin tilted his small black and tan head as though considering.

"I cannot ask him to help Marcus. I must leave my family out of this."

Footsteps sounded in the foyer below. Lal clucked his tongue and scurried down the banister. Marcus appeared. Lal barked a comment and went stiff.

An odd frisson of relief stole through her. "What a lovely surprise, Marcus."

"I hope not too great of a surprise." He watched as she descended, his handsome face shaping into a smile. He had laughing eyes, somewhat heavy in shape but bright in expression, and always pleased when he looked at her, except briefly at the theater.

"Not too great. I expected to see you today or tomorrow."

"You did." It was not a question, but he looked at her in that way he sometimes did, as though he expected her to say something clever or flirtatious rather than the truth. So it went with everyone she had ever known. Nearly.

"Won't you join me in the parlor for tea?" She moved toward the door. "I was on my way there to do correspondence."

"Missing your connections in Madras?"

"I am." But she could not write letters to the fishmonger or fruit seller or rice merchant. "I used to be great bows with St. John's half sisters." She rang for tea. "They are both in the country with their children and families now, but we still correspond."

He followed her to the sofa.

"Do you look forward to that sort of domestic life yourself?"

Tavy smiled. "I have had that domestic life for years, Marcus, in India with my family."

"Not your own establishment."

"No." Unmarried Company officials and army officers

were in short supply in Madras's small English community. Several had tried to convince Tavy to relinquish the comfort and autonomy she enjoyed in Alethea's home. But a husband might have made her leave India whenever he desired.

But now she was in England, and Marcus was a friend.

"Octavia, you know how I admire you."

"I do, Marcus. You have been unfailingly kind and attentive since we became acquainted in Madras, and again since I stepped off ship three weeks ago. I cannot see that as anything but admiration."

He shook his head. "You never say what I expect."

"I beg your pardon. My mother always says my tongue goes before my thoughts. But really they go at quite the same moment, which can be inconvenient at times."

"Octavia, may I have the honor of your hand in marriage?"

She regarded him carefully then stood and moved to the window. The day without seemed to be clearing, thin striations of pale blue in the gray canopy.

"A fortnight ago—no—in fact, yesterday afternoon I would not have hesitated to accept your offer." She turned to face him. "But last night I heard something with which I cannot be comfortable."

He approached her. "I am overjoyed to hear that only a small matter deters you in accepting me."

"I do not believe it is a small matter. That man was trying to blackmail you, wasn't he?"

"My dear," he took her hands, "I assure you he meant only to encourage me to complete a negotiation I did not agree with. But I have already decided to take my business elsewhere and have informed him of that. You needn't be concerned."

"Really? You seemed quite overset about it last night."

"I was irritated that he disturbed my enjoyment of your

company. Octavia, I have waited over a year to bring my suit to you. Will you have me wait longer?"

She looked into his green-gray eyes, convivial on the surface, but a shadow lurked.

"I beg your pardon, Marcus, but I don't know that I trust you on this matter. I think you are not telling me everything, and that cannot be a good place to begin a marriage."

"Octavia—"

"I only wish to help, you know, whatever it is. I could, but not if you will not be honest with me."

He released her hands and took a half step back. "If this is all that inhibits you from accepting, I cannot take it as a refusal."

"And that is another thing. I haven't asked before because it would have seemed precipitate, but why are you so set on marrying me? There must be any number of ladies who could make you an inestimable bride."

He chuckled and shook his head again, his handsome face wreathed in a rueful smile.

"You do know how to depress a man's confidence, don't you?"

Tavy laughed, despite herself. "Not intentionally, and I truly doubt your confidence is pricked by my hesitation."

"Then a list you shall have. You have intelligence and steadiness of character. You understand the work I am engaged in. We enjoy each other's company." He traced a fingertip along her cheek. "And you are a beautiful woman. I would be proud to have you at my side."

His touch moved nothing within her, not even a hint of the craving the mere sound of Benjirou Doreé's voice did. But she liked Marcus, and he seemed attached to her for all the reasons that would make him a good husband.

She ignored the unease gathering at the base of her spine. She would be a fool to refuse such a suitor, and she was through with foolishness.

"Then I ask you for more time. Forgive me, but I do not feel entirely in charity with you now, Marcus. If I were to accept you at this moment I would not be true to either of us."

"The moment would be tainted? Your romantic sensibilities are stronger than I had imagined." He smiled. "How much time do you wish?"

She frowned. "Aren't you irritated with me?"

"Why would I be?"

"Well," she floundered. "It is only that it may require several weeks for me to—"

"Weeks?"

She laughed at his pained look, then she sobered. "But I have given you my reply. If you cannot accept it, I will not fault you for withdrawing your offer."

"As always, you are steady and straightforward. I could not withdraw my offer." He gave her his most winning smile. "We will do well together, Octavia." He took her hand and lifted it to his lips. "Now I will leave you to your monkey and letter writing and be off to Leadenhall Street. Good day, my dear."

Lal entered the parlor as soon as Marcus departed, jumping up to Tavy's shoulder and patting her hair. Tavy went to the window and watched the baron's carriage down the street. She had surprised herself in refusing him. But her instinct for honesty had only failed once in her life. In this case her emotions were not deeply engaged, nor her baser nature. The girl who once allowed dreams of adventure to color her perception of men was, after all, long gone.

Chapter 4

To LABOUR. To roll or pitch heavily in a turbulent sea.
—*Falconer's* Dictionary of the Marine

"Other fellows run around here in a heat these days, Doreé, but you always seem so at ease." Styles cocked a curious brow. The corridor of the East India Company's London headquarters bubbled with activity, traders moving from one chamber to another, one deal to another. "Why is that?"

"I suppose I have no desire to draw attention."

"Then you should not look as confident here as the king ensconced at Carlton House." The baron laughed.

"I should hurry along as well, do you think?" The East India Company and its desperate attempts to stay afloat beneath the pressure of Parliament's finicky rule meant little to Ben. His fortune had never depended upon the Company's successes, nor his principal endeavors. He maintained an active membership for the sake of connections and appearances only.

"Court's in session, don't you know, Doreé," a gentleman announced as they approached the Directors' Court Room. "G'day, Styles." He nodded. "Trapper's hearing. Lost a bundle in that Bengal fiasco. Going in to gawk at the poor sod?"

Ben lowered his lids. "Never."

The man's face puckered, his thick brows tilting downward.

Styles laughed. "Doreé rarely minces words, Nathans. You ought to know that by now."

"Don't know that you've got cause to chortle at me, Styles," Lord Nathans grumbled. "Didn't see so clearly with that Nepal venture, did you?"

Ben turned to his friend. "Nepal, Styles? How positively intrepid of you."

Styles's blue eyes narrowed. "Not all of us can be universally successful. Some of us occasionally make mistakes."

Nathans chuckled, a sound halfway between relieved and self-satisfied. "Well, I'm popping in to see Trapper try to salvage the wreckage. P'raps I'll buy him a bottle after, to cheer up the old fellow."

"Good of you," Ben murmured. A few years over forty, George Nathans had the thick carriage of a man a decade older and all the bluff conceit of the worst sort of middlebrow Englishman involved in eastern trade. The king had recently awarded him a peerage, alongside his partner, another prosperous private trader turned Company lackey, for work they'd done smoothing the sea path to Singapore.

Nathans's business partner was Marcus Crispin.

"By the by, Nathans," Ben said, "I am having a few friends out to the house next week for some shooting. Care to join us? Just a handful of Company men. You are welcome to bring Lady Nathans along, of course. How a man could bear to be separated from such a beautiful wife I cannot imagine."

Nathans's square face reddened, but his eyes looked eager. Cantonese tea had made him rich as Croesus, but his father had been a haberdasher, and his title was spanking new.

"Well, I'm glad for the invitation, Doreé," Nathans blustered. "Don't mind if I do."

"Capital. Friday, then."

Nathans bowed and went into the hearing.

Styles turned to Ben, brows high. "Thought you didn't care for entertaining."

"I must have altered my feelings on the matter." Ben started toward the exit.

"Don't I merit an invitation as well?"

"Do you wish one?"

"I haven't been to Fellsbourne since—well, since the funeral." He cast Ben a questioning look. "Sometimes I wonder if you ever go there yourself."

"I have had little occasion to." Until now. Despite himself. But old habits were difficult to lay aside.

"If you wish to change government policy concerning trade in the East Indies, why don't you do it in the Lords? You've got the seat. You don't need to knuckle around with nonentities to drum up support. Step into your father's footsteps." Styles's voice prodded.

"I have no interest in politics. You know that."

"So you insist. But then why this shooting party of Company men? And, for God's sake, Nathans? His wife is good *ton*, but the fellow is a horrid Cit."

"Perhaps. But I am particularly ill suited to throw stones." Ben's gaze passed over an oil painting hanging on a nearby wall of a great, shaggy lion subduing a thick-shouldered tiger. The striped animal, longer and larger than its opponent, nevertheless lay prone beneath the king of beasts. "And perhaps I am inspired to know my competition."

"Competition?" The baron's eyes seemed to spark.

"*Adieu*, Styles."

Ben passed through the front door onto the portico. The Company's headquarters, built in Greek revival style to disguise its purpose in austere, classical costume, rose like a depressive shadow from the narrow street. Behind the striated Ionic columns and pediment stuffed with symbolic statuary, gold changed hands over kegs of saltpeter and barrels of cotton piece goods, bushels of opium and stacks upon stacks of tea bricks. But no London bypasser would know that from its exterior. It looked like a temple.

Ben moved from the porch, leaving the ponderous weight of India House behind him. The street was clogged with mud after the morning rain, but in front of the building straw was piled in ample supply to facilitate passage. The gentlemen-traders of the East India Company, struggling against the censure of high society, must not be seen to muddy their boots.

He pressed a coin into a stable boy's hand and rode through the City toward Blackwall Village where the East India Docks spread across acres of planking and water. Before the massive wall that surrounded the quay, warehouses loomed, sentinels of Britain's mercantile power upon the seas. Beyond, a forest of masts rose above the hubbub of business. Seamen strained at capstan poles, hauling aboard the produce of English manufacturers and mines—woolens, bullion, copper—and from the East, spices, tea, silk, and porcelain to be sold on the Continent and in America. Gulls circled masts and blanketed sails, alighting upon spars and barrels stacked along the boards awaiting transfer onto carts, their strident cries cutting the air.

Ben's gaze slid over the nearest vessel, a hulking three-masted East Indiaman suited to the rough seas of the Cape of Good Hope. His secretary stood amidships beside a dockworker, gesturing aft to a pile of crates.

Creighton caught Ben's gaze, dismissed the lumper, and moved toward the rail. Ben climbed the gangplank serrated with shafts of sunlight slanting through the rigging.

"Good day, my lord. This is the *Eastern Promise*."

"Show me."

He followed his secretary down into the belly of the vessel, the air growing close as they descended. Upon the low-slung berth deck, Creighton moved forward to the infirmary. He folded his hands behind his back and his brow furrowed, gaze fixed on the detritus stuffed into the foremost corner of the surgeon's quarters.

"So you see, my lord."

"I do."

Human hair clogged the crevice. Straight, curly, red, brown, blond, some black. In considerable quantity.

"Too long for bilge rats," Creighton muttered.

Ben tilted his gaze aside to his employee.

"Of all the moments for you to insert a note of levity into your work—and perhaps, Creighton, it may be the first in my memory—this is an odd one."

"Forgive me, sir. I have nothing else to say. I'm afraid this has left me quite speechless."

"The former master had no explanation?"

"None, sir. Said he never saw it."

"The surgeon?"

"Gone to America last week, unfortunately."

"What do you believe to be its origin?"

Creighton shook his head.

"Captain's fancy?" Ben suggested.

"I've seen some strange treasures, sailors being what they are."

Ben drew in a long breath. "Clean it out, then forget about it."

"My lord—"

"I will look into it."

Creighton's eyes brightened. "I say, sir, that's very good of y—"

"If you praise me for taking up this small task, Creighton, I will fire you."

Ben retraced their passage up four flights of narrow steps to the main deck, his secretary following. A twelve-hundred-ton ship, broad-bellied and cleanly built from her three sturdy masts and fifty guns to her sparkling decks, the *Eastern Promise* was as fine a merchant vessel as could be seen docked anywhere in the world.

"Creighton, who brought your attention to this ship? Lord Ashford?"

"No, sir. I had a tip through the regular channels. Since you were looking for a third vessel to send down to Tunis with the others, I inquired after it."

Ben endeavored to loosen his jaw muscles. First mysterious hair, now the need to ask the sorts of questions he typically left to his secretary's discretion.

"From whom have I purchased her?"

"A Frenchman we've done good business with in the past. He took her off her previous owner six months ago in Calais."

"Only six months? That is brief to own a ship like this."

"He's an honest man. Had another vessel founder off the Cape filled to the gunwales with goods intended for Bombay. He needed the cash."

"And we needed the ship."

Creighton flipped open a leather folio and scanned the top page. "She'll be ready to put to sea within the month. The tea will take a fine price in Marseilles." His face grew impressively blank once again. The cargo of tea masked

the vessel's true function, to trawl the Barbary Coast in
search of pirate ships with holds full of human ballast.
Ben had kept Creighton on for seven years precisely because of his consistent failure to emote over the principal
project he oversaw, the destruction of slaving vessels and
conveyance of their cargo to safe ports. Men involved in
the slave trade tended toward pride, then greed, when
they met with success. Creighton never showed a hint of
either vice.

His only vice, in fact, seemed to be in continually
hoping for his employer's greater involvement in his business. If he had any idea what Ben was currently planning,
he would be in alt.

"Fine," Ben replied.

"The muskets and cannonry Lord Ashford took off that
privateer last month arrived in Portsmouth. Shall I see to
their storage?"

"Too likely to go astray."

"I'll have them sent to the foundry to be melted down."

Ben's gaze strayed to the Union Jack hoisted high upon
the mizzenmast, bright blue, white, and red against the
pale sky. Beside it the colors of his front company flapped
dully in the slight breeze, brown and white stripes with a
gold slash through the center. That company made him a
healthy income he then used to fund other shadowy and
considerably more controversial causes.

A weary crease shaped his brow. Styles imagined he
had an interest in politics, perhaps that he was trying to
work his way into society's good graces by pleasing his
fellow lords and tradesmen at once.

Ben's old friend hadn't any idea of the truth. For seven
years, even longer, Ben had worn the secret of his life's
work like an invisible yoke about his neck.

"Sir," Creighton said, "about that letter you dictated to
me yesterday, to the governor of Madras . . ."

"Complete it, allowing for the transfer of funds to the army if he agrees to the terms."

"Yes, my lord. And the Malta issue?"

"It may work itself out without interference, and we will not know for some time yet."

His secretary scribbled upon the ledger.

"Creighton, I need you to pen some invitations."

Creighton's head snapped up. "Invitations?"

"A dozen or so, for a sennight of shooting at Fellsbourne."

"Shooting."

Ben leveled a clear stare at his employee.

Creighton cleared his throat. "Of course, sir. To whom should I send them?"

"The Leadenhall Street set, but exclusively titled men. Nathans, Styles, Crispin, the others. Include their wives." He turned toward the gangplank.

"I don't believe there's more than a handful of lords involved with the Company at this time."

"It is a modest group indeed." All fairly well known to each other. All with business interests in the same far distant waters and upon the same eastern coasts. All with fortunes to lose should Parliament decide to further tighten its control over Company purse strings and trade practices. Since the bill of 1813, government had been holding the ribbons, driving the Company in a new direction. Some proprietors chafed at the bit, remembering days not long past when Company officials acted independently of Whitehall and made a hefty profit any way they saw fit.

A man who saw his business autonomy dwindling might have any number of reasons for blackmailing a fellow trader who was also a lord and had a voice in Parliament.

"And, Creighton, make certain St. John Pennworthy and Abel Gosworth are on the list."

"Mustn't be the only gentleman there whose fortune is stable, my lord?" Creighton's face shone with pride.

Ben made his way to his horse, and home to change clothing for Lady Ashford's gathering. A few hours in the company of clear-minded people was just the thing he needed to prepare himself for the journey into his old manner of living he was about to embark upon with this house party. All for a woman who meant nothing to him any longer.

Sometimes the sense of responsibility that had been hammered into him from childhood astounded even him.

Tavy dressed for the evening then held Jacob while a maid arranged Alethea's hair. She handed the infant into her sister's snug embrace, who then handed him into Nurse's arms with teary eyes. St. John met them at the carriage.

The street before the Viscount and Viscountess of Ashford's town residence was lined with elegant vehicles.

"I thought Valerie said it would be a small party." Alethea chuckled as St. John handed her out. "Didn't she, Octavia?"

"I—I hardly know." Tavy's heart raced. The curricle parked beside them bore upon its sleek, black door a crest she knew better than any other noble family's. It had adorned the carriages of their next-door neighbors in Madras.

She laid a hand on her brow. "Thea, I feel a megrim coming on. Would you mind very much if I went home now and sent the carriage back for you?" She despised herself for being craven, but she could be brave later. Dear Lord, was this how it would be now? Would she always wish to flee from him?

"Lady Ashford is expecting you, Tavy. She told me so most particularly this morning when she called."

"Oh, of course. My discomfort will no doubt pass," she mumbled and avoided Alethea's curious gaze.

Inside, dozens of people filled the drawing room and adjacent library. Tavy's gaze darted about. The Marquess of Doreé was not present. Perhaps she had imagined his crest on that vehicle, further proof that she needed diversion from unprofitable thoughts.

"Octavia, you are stunning." Valerie bussed her on both cheeks then stepped back to survey her gown. "Gold suits you beautifully. Thin as tissue and quite daring. Parisian design but Indian silk, I think, or Chinese?"

"Indian." Always. She was an open book, if anyone ever cared to read it. Marcus Crispin did, of course, but with the cover merely ajar.

"That puts me in mind of someone you will be delighted to meet." Valerie grasped Tavy's arm and drew her toward the library. Books lined the recessed shelves from floor to ceiling. Mementos of Lord and Lady Ashford's travels decorated tables and walls—a beaded mask, a pair of alabaster elephants, a model ship. Tavy glanced away from the shelves and her pulse ground to a halt.

"You and he were neighbors of a sort in Madras," Valerie said as Tavy's regard met the secret preoccupation of her thoughts for the past three weeks. And seven years. "Octavia, may I present to you the Marquess of Doreé? Oh, how lovely, clearly you have already met."

Met. Laughed. Touched. Fell into sweet ecstasy.

Tavy barely managed to rise from her curtsy on jellied knees. After his unkindness at his house, she had not imagined merely encountering him in society could distress her.

Her imagination had not served her well.

He bowed, all elegant grace. "Good evening, ma'am."

"The two of you must chat about Madras, old times, what have you," Valerie said. "Ah, someone has opened up the pianoforte. How delightful. We will have dancing. Do you think dancing before supper is simply too rustic?"

"Of course not, m'dear." Lady Fitzwarren's round swell of a personage shuffled close, garbed in magnificent puce taffeta and peacock feathers. "Dancing at any hour is to be recommended for health and good spirits. Hello, Doreé. Met my niece yet? Of course you have. As handsome as a body can stare, you must know all the pretty girls even if their mamas don't give you the time of day." She tapped the tip of her fan on his coat. Black, the same as before, like the rest of his garments save his snowy white linens. Gone, apparently, were the splendid waistcoats of his youth.

"Miss Pierce and I are indeed acquainted." He bowed again, this time to the dowager countess. "And I thank you for the undeserved compliment."

"Undeserved? Pretty airs and false modesty disguise all sorts of depravities, Doreé. Don't cultivate them too assiduously or those mamas might come looking for you after all."

Valerie chuckled. The corner of his mouth crept up, a grin of sheer masculine ease. Tavy lost her breath.

"*Your* mama, Octavia," the dowager stated, "is a widgeon of course. Always has been. Like her brother, George. Daresay you know the fellow, Doreé, though he's still in the East Indies these days, ain't he?"

"We must have dancing," Valerie announced with a clap. "Mellicent, I know you will not dance, so do come turn pages for Miss Foster. Despite her talent she is missing every twelfth bar, what with having to do it herself, the poor dear." She led the countess away.

Tavy met the marquess's gaze. His eyes were quite, quite dark, without a hint of the pleasure in them that he had shown the dowager and viscountess.

She shoved back her shoulders. "Can you bring yourself to speak with me civilly, sir? Because if you cannot I am perfectly happy to walk away now and leave you to other company." Rather, to run. Except that her joints seemed frozen. A violin's bright twitter joined the piano-forte's perambulations.

The slightest crease appeared in his cheek.

"Would you care to dance, Miss Pierce?"

Tavy frowned. "Can you?"

"Yes, the scoundrel who consorts with low characters can dance."

"I meant, of course, can you bring yourself to speak to me civilly?"

"Ah. And the implication is entirely different in that case." His tone had altered. Almost—*almost*—it seemed to tease. A tiny thrill of something sweet and forbidden passed through Tavy. She ordered herself not to trust it.

"I did not imply any such thing." She attempted an indifferent air. "I only wonder that if we are to continually meet in society you will repeat the manner in which you spoke to me at your house."

"It is unlikely we will meet."

A knot formed in her stomach. "Why not?"

"I rarely go about in society."

"I see." Sticky nausea clawed at the knot. "Too dedicated to—to *more enjoyable* pursuits?"

"No. But forgive me for repeating myself. I recall already once informing you of that."

Tavy's breath stalled. Around her, the music and voices fell away and she was once again in the *bazir*, in a sea of people yet only able to see him. Silence enveloped them, his black eyes unreadable.

"Come now," he finally said. "I cannot stand here with my hand outstretched indefinitely. People will begin to comment."

"I don't particularly care what people say. And frankly I do not think I can take your hand."

"You will be obliged to if we dance." He seemed entirely unperturbed. "The set is forming."

Two lines of guests stretched along the length of the drawing room, the pair of them at the head by the library door. Panic slithered through Tavy, the same she had felt at the theater when she first saw him. With brutal will, she shut out the memories.

"Very well." She placed her fingertips upon his palm.

And her world halted.

Then began again, with a great lurch and considerably more color and sound and thorough agitation than in far too long.

He guided her into place and released her to take his spot with perfect ease as he had always done everything. Until that night. The night when ease had become hunger.

Tavy barely managed the patterns, calling upon years of practice to make her way through the steps without disgracing herself, aware of little but her shaking fingers and her partner. Clearly, her mother was not the only widgeon in the family.

"Why don't you go about in society?"

The pattern separated them. They came back together at the lead of a line of dancers. He drew her forward.

"Why don't you?" she repeated.

"I have only a modest acquaintance in town."

"That is impossible," for a peer, an East India Company proprietor, and an enormously wealthy man. "I do not believe it."

"Whether you believe it or not has little effect upon the truth."

She bit her lip. "So I see you cannot be civil after all."

"Not when you continually plague me with impertinent questions. No, apparently."

Her gaze darted to him. He faced forward, but the dent had reappeared in his cheek. Tavy's heart sped.

"I merely wondered."

"I cannot fathom why you ask when you clearly know

all the answers already," he said with a brief glance at her and a lift of one black brow. He released her and they parted.

He had spoken to her as though they knew one another. As though it had not been seven long years and one horrid drawing room conversation since their last meeting. She watched him through the other dancers, allowing herself to stare now. She didn't know why she should not. Every other woman must, when confronted with such masculine perfection.

"I came to you the other day because I haven't any answers," she said when the dance brought them together again. "Or, at least, very few."

He grasped her hand and drew her to a halt, the other dancers continuing around them. Tavy's blood seemed to wash through her veins like monsoon rain.

"Oftentimes, Miss Pierce, that is for the best." Double lines appeared between his brows.

"What are you saying?" Her fingers shook in his. She could do nothing for it. His black gaze held hers but she had no desire to look away. She should. She must. This was a mistake, this familiarity, this strange intimacy that was not intimacy at all, the memories scratching to be set free from imprisonment.

"Here now, Doreé," a gentleman said at her shoulder. "You are disturbing the pattern with this flirtation."

The marquess released her into the other gentleman's hold. Breathless, Tavy looked up into bright blue eyes, amusement writ across a finely handsome face capped with yellow-gold hair. He guided her into the steps.

"I give my friend credit for excellent taste," he said, scanning her face.

Tavy ducked her head. Her cheeks burned. She willed herself to calm. No man ever flustered her. Not even him, then. *Especially* not him. She would not begin now. If this was what renewed acquaintance with him meant, she did not welcome it.

When the dance brought her back to her partner, she met his gaze firmly and curtsied.

"My lord."

"Madam." He bowed, his look benign. The moment had passed, just as seven years earlier. She would not let it happen again.

She moved away, her steps measured, only the base of her spine warm, and the palm of her hand where his fingertips had rested briefly and perhaps—she tried to ignore the sensation—not entirely steadily either.

Tavy could not rest. She paced her bedchamber like a panther in a cage at the Calcutta menagerie. Finally despairing of sleep, she threw on a wrapper and climbed the stairs to the nursery. Her sister stood at the door, garbed in a night rail, a thick chestnut braid trailing down her back. Tavy smiled at the bundle of linen in the crib then the bundle of new-mother nerves leaning as far into the darkened chamber as possible without crossing the threshold. She stole up beside Alethea and curled an arm around her sister's soft waist.

"You cannot tear yourself away, can you?" she whispered.

Alethea leaned her cheek on Tavy's shoulder.

"It is like I felt about St. John at the beginning. But now he and I are so well known to one another, I feel him with me even when he is absent."

Tavy's throat tightened. "Jacob is so new. Your love is only just beginning."

"New and enormous and unsteady, and yet so certain. It is like falling in love all over again, but different."

Tavy could not speak. Emotion pressed at her chest, thick and hard.

Her sister lifted her head. "Octavia, are you unwell?"

"I am fine. Truly."

Alethea's brow creased. "How was your outing to the museum with Lord Crispin today?"

"Quite pleasant." She barely recalled it. A single dance had erased all else. "He is a charming companion."

"I daresay." Her sister's tone led, but Tavy would not follow. After a moment Alethea turned her regard back into the nursery. "St. John has received a rather singular invitation."

"Singular?"

"The Marquess of Doreé is hosting a shooting party at Fellsbourne in several days and has invited St. John."

Tavy's heart turned about.

"I suppose it is about time," she said with impressive steadiness, "after the way Lady Doreé ignored you for so many years when she lived right next door. Perhaps the marquess is trying to make up for their rudeness."

Alethea frowned. "You know it was nothing of the sort."

Tavy knew now, although she hadn't always. High-caste native women never socialized with the English in Madras, no matter whom they had once been married to and what name they bore. The community of proprietors of the Company and their wives was an intimate one, but it did not embrace Indian women, even ladies.

"Then what is so singular about the invitation?"

"Lord Doreé never entertains, and he is only peripherally involved in the Company, really. But this must be a Company gathering. He and St. John are well enough acquainted, of course, the number of proprietors of secure means and title as small as it is. Still, we have never socialized with him."

"Never?"

"Some years ago, before we joined you in India, we did invite him to a dinner party or two, but he declined our invitations."

Of course he did. "Perhaps he is an eccentric. They say very wealthy men can be peculiar."

"Yes." Alethea cast her a sidelong glance. "They say that about my husband as well."

"But you don't care a whit about it. Neither does St. John. Perhaps Lord Doreé is the same." Tavy tried to smile, but her lips quivered. She had never spoken of him aloud before, except that one morning, to her aunt.

"Perhaps," Alethea considered.

"He was at Lady Ashford's party tonight."

Alethea's head came around. "Really? St. John and I left early, of course. Did you—"

"We spoke."

"Good heavens. What is he like?"

"He was civil." And beautiful. And confusing. And everything she had feared. And she could barely breathe thinking of it.

"St. John says he seems a perfectly unexceptionable person, despite his great fortune and recluse ways. But you know, it is a trial to try to wrest detailed commentary from my husband. He does not see people in quite the same way most do." Alethea shrugged and smiled, her eyes tender.

"St. John is a good man." Tavy squeezed her sister's hand. "And isn't it lovely that you can remain at home happily with me and Jacob while he goes to discover the mystery of this shooting party?"

"There is the trouble. I was included in the invitation."

"To a shooting party?" The heart thump rattled her again, pleasure mingling with discomfort beneath her ribs. Sheer foolishness she must learn to control. Again.

"Odd, isn't it? But there you have it. The marquess must be an eccentric, after all." Alethea chuckled. "Although he is rather young for one. I do not think he is above thirty."

Thirty in December.

"Well, you needn't go." Tavy's throat stuck. "St. John will understand."

"But I feel that I should. If other wives are to be there, I cannot leave St. John alone. It would not be fair to him."

Tavy's gaze swung to her sister's. "Jacob is only—"

"A month old, I know. I will not abandon him, of course."

"Alethea, you can barely part with him for five minutes yet you expect to leave him with Nurse during hours of entertainment?"

"Not exactly." Her sister's green-gray eyes entreated.

Tavy's stomach tightened. "Thea, I—"

"Nurse will be there, and she is quite good, but I would be so much more comfortable if you were with me."

"You will have St. John." Her heart raced, the panic spreading beneath her skin much thicker than before. "You do not need me. This is ridiculous."

"Rather, it is my wretched nerves. St. John will be out and about with the gentlemen, and I am torn between my loyalty to him and this perfect little creature. If you come, my absence amongst the wives at times will not be so marked, and I will not be so distressed."

Tavy peered at her sister's pleading eyes and a surge of warmth rose in her, overpowering the alarm. She drew in a breath and slid her arm around Alethea's waist again.

"You recovered so swiftly from your confinement, I think we all have forgotten how recent it was, and how difficult the journey was for you."

"Then you will come?"

"I will if you wish it."

His party could prove useful. She could not ask the gentlemen point-blank if they knew Marcus's black-mailer. But traders' wives sometimes knew more than their husbands realized. Merely sister to a trader, Tavy herself knew more about the Marquess of Doreé than any of them would even begin to imagine.

But that meant nothing in any way that mattered. She would go to his house but she would avoid conversation with him, thereby avoiding confusion. And if every time she caught a glimpse of him her heartbeat sped and her blood warmed, that would simply be her punishment for being such a fool once.

Ben took his head between his hands and tried to focus on the rough surface of the table inches from his face. To no success. The clamor of coarse male voices and equally unrefined female ejaculations combined with the agitated sawing of a fiddle racketed through his brain, halting thought.

But dulled thought was precisely what he had sought here. He couldn't remember how he ended up on a bench surrounded by dockworkers and sailors, nor could he really recall anything for quite some hours, except the desperate need to forget. He scrubbed his hands over his face and sank them into his hair, the haze thickening.

"Poor ducky." A woman's cool, callused fingers passed over his brow. "I'll wager you ain't been in such a state in a month of me pa's sober days. Not here, leastways."

"Does she truly not understand, Lil?" he uttered to the tabletop. "Could she be so naïve, or is it lies?"

"Who's that, love?"

He swung his head around and made out the moll's rounded features. "She has no idea."

"Then she's a fool, whoever she is." Lil pursed her full lips and ran her hand down his neck and back. "Forget about her and come give Lily a cuddle." She twined her arm around his waist.

He shook his head. "I've been trying to forget for years. Can't seem to. But thank you for the invitation."

"Always the gentleman." She smelled of ale and some-thing cloyingly sweet, sorghum sugar, perhaps. But her heart was good. He remembered that about her from years back. Ben tried to smile and failed.

"If she's noddy enough to put you off, she don't de-serve you, duck. But there's quality females for you." Lil shrugged, her bosom threatening to tip over her tight-laced bodice. A brawl brewed across the gin house, shouts and gruff insults. Ben wrapped his hand around the bottle of Blue Ruin and lifted it to his lips.

"There there, ducky. Ain't you had enough already?"

"I daresay he has, Lil."

Ben slewed his gaze up. Styles hovered beside the table, swaying from side to side. Or perhaps that was the gin.

"Aw," Lil scowled, lips tight. "Come to take his lord-ship away and I've not yet got what I came over here for."

"What's that?" Styles murmured with a smile.

"What I'll not be giving the likes of you ever again." She glared.

Styles's grin faded.

Ben shook his head. He'd certainly drunk too much.

Lil leaned to his ear and slid a hand along his thigh. "Come on, love. I'll take your mind off that bit o' prim-and-proper for half price."

A chuckle cracked in his tight chest. "Still generous, but never too generous. You give a man hope in the hon-esty of women, Lil."

"You're a peculiar cove, but I likes you. Always did. She don't know what she's missing." Beneath the table she ran her hand over his crotch, lingering, then pulled away and stood up. With another dark look at the baron, she moved off through the crowd.

"What've you done to fall into Lil's bad graces, Styles?" Ben pushed the bottle away and pressed his palms to the sticky table.

"No doubt she's on her high horse since you are here. She always liked you quite a bit better than me."

Ben glanced up and Styles's gaze came around to meet him, shuttered. Peculiar. Unlike him.

Definitely the drink.

Ben pushed onto his feet. His clogged head spun.

Styles laid a hand on his shoulder. "I'll take you to Hauterive's. Why you came in here when the company down the street would welcome you, I haven't the slightest. Glad I came upon you, though."

"No. I'm for home." Ben started toward the door.

"You disappeared from Lady Ashford's party so swiftly I hadn't an idea of it until you were gone. If I'd have known you were heading here I would have dissuaded you."

"Couldn't have." Ben pushed through the lollers at the tavern's entry and headed toward the mews down the alley with bleary eyes but houndlike precision. If he hadn't trekked this path hundreds of times in his university days, he would be lost now. Lost in London's hells and lost in confounded memories, neither of which locations he particularly wished to be.

"Who was that girl you were dancing with, the one that looked like an Irish Athena, all sublime figure and eyes of soft steel?"

Ben blinked to shut out the image of Octavia's body wrapped in the shimmering gown, her soft lips, pinkened cheeks, and the sensation of her trembling fingers within his. But behind his lids the image was even stronger, and his hand still felt hot where hers had lain.

"Good God, Walker," he grunted, "you and Constance would make a perfect pair, both of you curious as a couple of magpies."

"Lady Constance asked about the girl too? Is she jealous?"

"Only of your paramours."

"Then the lady at Ashford's is a paramour?"

Ben shook his head, his stomach rolling. "Not mine." Not any longer.

He moved across the street in unsteady strides.

But why not? No one controlled his destiny now. His life was his own. Why not seduce a beautiful, deceitful woman, a woman whose flavor yet remained upon his tongue? Why not take pleasure where he wished?

Because he could not then and still could not believe in her deceit, although he had tried to convince himself of it again and again. To absolve himself of guilt.

He stumbled into the stable and pressed his face into his horse's satiny neck. Taking to the bottle tonight had been a mistake. He needed clarity. A pitcher of icy water over his head would do it, just as her smile had earlier, so brief it seemed she didn't even know she smiled, washing his vision clear for an instant as it always had.

Drunken idiocy.

He pulled his horse from the stall, jammed his foot into the stirrup and climbed aboard the big black mare. He reached into his pocket to toss a coin toward the stable lad.

"Home, Kali." If he made it to Cavendish Square without falling off his horse or prey to footpads, it would be by the grace of God, Allah, and Vishnu combined.

"Lady Carmichael was asking after you with great interest not an hour ago," Styles called after him.

"Lady Carmichael can take her interest and put it where it will give her the most pleasure." Ben pressed his knees into the mare's sides.

The wealthy, stunning widow Carmichael had been a habitué of Hauterive's years earlier, when Ben frequented the exclusive gaming club. She hadn't made any secret to Ben what she wanted from him. Guided by a young man's lust and his uncle's directive, he had given it to her. But away from Hauterive's, amongst polite society, the lady never once acknowledged their acquaintance, not even after he acceded to the title.

He rubbed a hand over his face, Kali's heavy hooves sinking into the street. The night hung thick with mist and soot, just like Ben's head.

He didn't give a damn about Lady Carmichael. A hundred such perfumed and petted females could seek him out and he still wouldn't be interested. Lil's businesslike honesty appealed to him much more, if not the particulars of what she had to offer.

But Ben didn't want a woman. Like an idiot schoolboy drunk on his first bottle of brandy, he wanted a fantasy. He wanted the past. The past in which, for a few precious moments, he had willfully forgotten how the weight of the world seemed to rest upon shoulders far too young to carry it.

Chapter 5

ROACHING A SAIL. A term used by sailmakers to signify the allowance made for the beauty in the appearance of a sail.

—*Falconer's* Dictionary of the Marine

Waking at midday to a pounding head and mouth apparently filled with cotton lint, Ben shaved, dressed, and poured a cup of coffee into the tin bucket that was his stomach. In the stable his saddle horse, sleek-headed and strong-withered, met him with a wicker.

"My apologies for last night, old girl." He ran his hand along her ebony neck. "But you made it home despite me. The gods were kind this time, it seems."

She turned her face to him and he imagined compassion in her deep brown eyes.

"I shan't do it again, I promise." He moved to the tack room, where a groom sat polishing a harness. "Saddle

Kali for the road, and have the traveling carriage readied to go to Fellsbourne. Samuel and Singh will ride in it."

Despite Styles's skepticism, Ben visited his principal estate at harvest time and whenever else his steward needed him. Perched upon an offshoot of the Thames, its bulk nestled at the edge of a forest of oak, pine, ash, and walnut, Fellsbourne was the single place in England Ben felt thoroughly at home. Memories lingered there, all good, of holidays from school spent with his brothers riding, shooting, practicing swordplay, and getting into trouble with the butler and housekeeper—like all hot-blooded English boys of the nobility. They'd been largely alone there, free to do what they wished, only the three of them and sometimes Walker Styles.

Ben's father had spent little time at the estate, busy in Parliament, living in town in the exotic retreat he had created twenty-five miles away from the grave of his first wife. It was her death in childbirth that had driven him to travel four thousand miles, seeking comfort. There, in India, he discovered a beautiful native maiden with a brother eager to make a lasting alliance with an English lord. A love match, some tittered. A scandal, everyone else gossiped. A failure of a marriage that propelled the marquess back west in less than a year.

Eleven years later he finally sent for his son.

The October afternoon shone cool and mild when Ben set off from London, and the road was short. He arrived at Fellsbourne as its granite and limestone mass glowed in the amber glory of the waning sun, its ancient crenellations and modern windows tipped with gold. Depositing Kali with a servant, he turned from the house and made his way across the green.

Beside the little Elizabethan chapel, free standing in a cluster of ancient trees, a wall enclosed the family cemetery. Ben stepped into the carefully tended plot of tombstones to the newest. Three massive white marble slabs stretched across the turf. The dates etched upon his father's and eldest brother Jack's tombs were a mere two months later than Arthur's, the middle brother.

Burying Jack and his father had been Ben's first act as the Marquess of Doreé. Trained as a child to the dangers of spying, the complexities of eastern trade and Indian power struggles, the harsh realities of war, and the responsibility of hundreds of people who would someday be in his employ, the funeral had seemed oddly pure and simple, his grief profound yet clean.

He walked back around the house. A carriage stood in the drive. Constance descended from it with the aid of a footman.

She came forward upon light feet. "Do you mind that I have appeared without warning, or asking?"

He took her outstretched hand. "You know you are always welcome here." He drew her toward the stair to the front entrance.

"Your butler in town told me you were here. He said you intend to make a week's stay of it. Whatever for?"

"I have invited several acquaintances here upon business."

"Always business."

In the foyer, he removed her cloak and passed it to a footman. Her cheeks were rose-hued, her vibrant gaze skittering away from him.

"Come and have a cup of tea. You must be weary after your journey."

"Oh, it was nothing, a short ride, of course." In the parlor she drew away, moving to the window facing the north side of the house. "Did you already visit their graves?"

"You know me well."

She pivoted. "Of course I do. But I do not understand why you do that. It is mawkish."

"You should try it sometime." But he knew she would not visit Jack's grave. He didn't think she ever had.

Her high brow furrowed. "Do not tease me, Ben. I don't think I will like it just now."

"Constance, why are you here?"

She trailed her fingertips along the windowsill, the movements agitated.

"I need distraction. I have had a wretched several days, and must put myself back to rights. Please let me stay. You will need a hostess anyway when your guests arrive."

"You have not brought Mrs. Josephs, I see."

"What do I need with a companion when I have your company?"

"I hardly need enumerate the reasons."

"When does the party begin?"

"In two days."

"Until then I will play least-in-sight and no one will even know I have been here but you."

"And the servants. And the villagers who hear it from the servants. You are being unwise, my dear."

"I don't care." Her voice was brittle. "I don't care if my reputation is ruined and I never marry. Does that satisfy you?"

"Not if I am the reason for it, however innocently." He moved to the sidebar and poured himself a glass of claret. "Styles is coming."

The color drained from her cheeks. "How lovely. It will be a pleasure to see him, and in any case if I find the company tiresome I shall simply dash back to London, if I wish."

"Constance—"

"No." She came to him, hands outstretched to grasp his. "Do not let us be bothered by anything. You are the single spot of sanity in my life, and I shan't allow you to ruin that."

Ben studied her face, the beauty who had awaited her first season with feverish joy because during it she would finally marry the man she had been betrothed to since birth. The man she had adored as only a warmhearted, sentimental girl could, and whose life ended in flames mere weeks before the wedding.

"Fate is a wretched master, is it not, Ben?" she whispered as though reading his thoughts. "Aha, now I have made you smile, although I am not certain why. But I am glad of it. I don't think I have seen that in weeks."

"I suspect that is not true, but I will not argue the point." He drew away and set down his glass. "Now, if you will excuse me, I am off to write a note to your Mrs. Josephs, and to instruct Samuel and the carriage to convey her hither. Will she come in the middle of the night?"

"The middle of the night?" Constance laughed. "I thought you wished to fend off gossip."

Ben smiled again and went to the door. "I will see you at dinner."

"You will be weary of my fidgets by the time the others arrive," she said behind him. "Weary of your responsibility to me."

"Never, my dear."

Ben had recently made the rounds of the estate during harvest time. But he did so again, now without his steward, glad to be abroad and his mind occupied. Constance rode alongside the first day, but after that remained within, reading, she claimed.

He left the arrangements for his guests to his housekeeper, only conferring with his gamekeeper to assure that the armory was straightened, the fowling pieces cleaned and polished, the dogs well rested. It was a peculiar comfort to play his lordly role, despite the familiar tension that always accompanied a charade like the one he now orchestrated. But he might as well provide the gentlemen with a bit of sport while he got what he sought from them.

Rising early, he took Kali out to the river in the chill morning, then back along the inland route across newly cleared fields. As he approached the house, a traveling coach trundled down the drive.

Ben pulled off his gloves and hat as he mounted the mansion's front steps. A gentleman and lady stood in the foyer, removing their coats, footmen seeing to the luggage about them.

"Well, well, Doreé," Nathans blustered, cheeks red. "Splendid place you have here."

Ben bowed. "Welcome, Lord Nathans." He turned to the man's wife. "Lady Nathans."

The baroness narrowed her emerald eyes and extended a lily-white hand.

"Lord Doreé," she purred through bow-shaped lips, short chestnut curls framing a face accustomed to being admired. "We are delighted to be here."

Ben bowed over her fingers. "The honor is all mine, ma'am." He turned to his butler. "Mr. Scott, have tea set out in the blue parlor, please."

Nathans peered about the broad-ceilinged foyer, bending his neck to the dome above, frescoed with Baroque figures of Greek gods—Zeus with Hera at his side, flanked by a warlike Ares, and a graceful Pallas Athena amidst opulent clouds. Years earlier Jack had seen to restorations. Despite their father's obsession, no hint of Brahma or Shiva could now be found in the hallowed halls of Fellsbourne.

Ben looked at Lady Nathans. Her sharp, underfed gaze was trained upon him.

"May I offer you refreshment after your long journey?" he said, allowing his gaze to slip to the well-filled bodice of her traveling gown. Her ruby lips crept into a cat's smile.

Nathans swiveled around. "Just the thing, Doreé. Don't mind if we do. Splendid lodgings you have here, I say. Splendid. Positively top drawer."

"Forgive me," Ben said mildly, "but I have just now come in from riding and must do away with my dust. Samuel will see you to the parlor." He gestured toward the footman. Nathans followed, his lady sliding Ben a half-lidded glance before taking her husband's arm and moving off.

Ben released a weary breath. It seemed too easy. Marcus Crispin's business partner had a wife looking for mischief. He needn't have invited them all here. He probably could have gotten the information he sought in a single night in London. But that was not how he intended to pursue matters now. He hadn't operated in that manner since his uncle was still alive.

He had not forgotten how to, though. And now he had paved that path in case it should be needed.

He started toward the stairs.

"My lord," his butler said, "Sir St. John's carriage arrived in advance of Lord Nathans. The lady appeared interested in the house, so Mrs. Scott offered a tour in your absence."

"Thank you, Mr. Scott. Where might I find them?"

"I suspect by now they will have reached the east wing, sir."

Ben changed his direction, heading along the corridor to the public chambers. His housekeeper's voice became audible as he crossed into the drawing room. He stopped short.

Octavia stood on the opposite side of the chamber in a pool of pale sunlight, her hair lit with a sprinkling of gold, face averted. A gown of winter white caressed her gentle curves and long slender legs, rendering her like the sylphlike image of Athena in the clouds, shoulders back, her stance perfectly at ease. The goddess come to life.

In his house.

Again.

"My lord." His housekeeper's voice came to him as though through cotton wadding. "The gentleman and his lady have retired to their chambers with the infant. I was showing Miss here the portrait of your brothers."

Octavia's head came around, her lips parted, brown eyes wide with honest dismay, and Ben knew himself to be, upon this occasion, thoroughly abandoned by all the gods.

"Good day, Miss Pierce." He bowed.

"Lord Doreé." Tavy could say nothing else, nor bring her shaking legs to manage a curtsy. She had not imagined she would meet him first alone at his house, or alone at all.

He was, impossibly, even more handsome than four nights ago at Lady Ashford's, garbed now in clothing suited to the country, a loose coat, burgundy waistcoat, breeches that hugged his lean, muscular thighs, and top boots sprinkled with mud, a pair of gloves in one hand. His ebony hair was tousled as though he had just removed a hat, his face aglow from riding and his languid black eyes bright.

"It is quite a good likeness," he said in an odd tone.

She could not form words. Or, apparently, thoughts.

He gestured behind her. "The portrait. My brothers were but twelve and thirteen at the time, but the artist captured them well."

Tavy's tongue would not unstick from the roof of her mouth. The housekeeper rescued her.

"How well I remember it. Masters Jack and Arthur

could not be still through the sitting, fidgeting about like boys will do, like you all did once you came to live here, if you don't mind me saying so, sir."

"Not at all, Mrs. Scott." He smiled. "Has Miss Pierce yet seen the gallery?"

"No, my lord. We were to go there next."

"Allow me to complete the tour, then. Lord and Lady Nathans have arrived and I suspect they would be best served by your capable ministrations."

Mrs. Scott curtsied and departed. A pause ensued during which Tavy's heart beat uncomfortably like the wings of a hummingbird and they stared at one another. Finally he filled the silence.

"The gallery offers a number of fine works." His voice still sounded peculiar, but he moved toward the door in easy strides, motioning for her to precede him. "Including several of royals who visited Fellsbourne in one century or another."

She tried to wet her lips enough to speak. "How interesting." She stepped from the drawing room into a chamber lined with marble statuary.

"My father did not have a taste for European art," he said close behind her, sending a skitter of nerves glistening along her spine. "My eldest brother expanded this collection. He was quite fond of classical subjects."

"I see." She did not pause to study the pieces, catching only a glimpse of a reclining Gaul, his impressive musculature covered by a minuscule loincloth, and an amorous Cupid and Psyche locked in an embrace in which the god's hand rested upon his lady's breast.

Tavy squeezed her eyes shut. This could not be happening. How could she have agreed to this? Any of it?

Cheeks aflame, she strode to the opposite door. It opened onto a ballroom. Pristine white walls rose to the second story, a carved balustrade running its length offering a view from above. A chandelier draped from the whitewashed ceiling, hundreds of tiny crystals reflecting the sunlight filtering through the windows, sparkling upon floorboards like a thousand diamonds. It was a spectacular chamber, but in all its glory, cold as ice.

She turned. He stood at the threshold, watching her.

"I beg your pardon," she said quickly. "I am sorry to intrude on your party. You did not invite me and I cannot imagine that—"

"You needn't be sorry."

"My sister begged me to accompany them. With their son so new, you see, she is quite anxious and requires a great deal of comforting. I could not refuse her."

"You are welcome here."

Her throat went dry. "I am?"

He nodded.

Of course. Why would it matter to him whether she was in his house or in Timbuktu? He hadn't cared for her whereabouts for seven years. He certainly would not care now, as his calm demeanor suggested. The anxious anticipation Tavy had nursed for days abruptly deflated, leaving only the awful, humming awareness of his presence.

He did not advance into the chamber, but his gaze remained steady upon her. Tavy's heartbeat sped, her hands damp. She should have remained in London. She could not bear this, the memory of wanting him beside the newness of knowing him again so perfunctorily. And he was not making it any easier on her, his black eyes intense and distant at once.

She turned away, searching for words in the heavy swags of white and silver fabric framing the floor-to-ceiling windows. Elegant, all of it. So cold. So English.

"Do you ever miss it?" Her quiet voice echoed across the ballroom. "Home?" Stomach tightening, she glanced over her shoulder.

He shook his head, twin lines appearing between his brows. "No."

Outside the windows, the park stretched toward a copse of trees, their leaves mottled with the ripening of autumn, so unlike the tropical paradise she had lived in for nearly a decade.

"I do, every day," she murmured. "It is like an ache."

"Still in the thrall of the exotic, *shalabha*?"

She pivoted around. He stood very still, the word lingering between them, the nickname he had given her in another lifetime, but said so differently. Not warm and playful as she remembered it, instead now with a sharp edge. His eyes were dark as coal, and wary.

Or perhaps warning.

Tavy steeled herself against the sinuous pressure of unwanted emotion rising in her. She did not want to go back, to remember everything, no matter what the temptation. She wanted to pretend that he was the stranger he seemed now, that she knew no more of him than his reputation and position in society.

She *did not* know him. She never had. She needn't pretend.

"No." Her voice cracked, words escaping despite her will. "It was not like that. Perhaps at first. But then I—" Her throat was parched. The empty space between them stretched like layers of mistrust.

He walked toward her.

Fear rushed through her, wholly primal, and she balanced on her toes, ready to flee. He halted within inches and Tavy had to force herself not to retreat, dragging up her gaze to his handsome face. Awareness that he was a stranger flooded her anew, a man, tall and more solid than when she had known him, with tiny lines about the corners of his mouth that had not been there before, his brow severe.

But something shimmered in his eyes behind the shadows shrouding the black. Something she used to see there when he called her by that pet name. Something that now, just as then, made her heart stumble and her knees turn liquid.

"I—" She struggled for breath, but he seemed not to breathe at all, his body a rigid wall.

"You?"

"I miss—"

His hands came up to either side of her face but not touching, as though he did not wish to do it, his arms locked and jaw hard. Like a silent dance he shaped the air around her, spreading warmth upon her skin that penetrated then stole beneath. His gaze scanned her features, fraught and fast. His chest rose hard.

With every mote of skin and blood sparking and alive from his nearness, Tavy panicked. She stepped back.

Ben grasped her wrist, pulled her forward, and joined their mouths.

Chapter 6

WIND. As the sun, in moving from east to west, heats the air more immediately under him, the air to the eastward is constantly rushing towards the west to restore the equilibrium.

—*Falconer's* Dictionary of the Marine

He held her so firmly Tavy could not resist. But she had no will to. There was nothing hesitant in their meeting, nothing shy or uncertain. He pressed his mouth against hers and she met him eagerly. Firm commanding lips, hot mouth, and strong hands controlled her and she let it happen, let the heat of his skin and the taste of him sink into her. He felt wonderful, hard and male and beautiful. And familiar. *Him.*

He lifted his head. His mouth hovered above hers, his black eyes seeking.

As though in a dream, Tavy laid her palm upon his chest and leaned forward.

He tilted her head back, slid his thumb along her jaw,

and pressed her mouth open. She gulped in a breath and
he covered her gasp. She melted, lost to his tongue tracing
her tender flesh and tasting her lips, caressing, coaxing
her to respond. She pushed up onto her toes to meet him
more fully. His hand tightened at the nape of her neck,
holding her close, and she drank in the taut texture of his
skin, the flavor of his mouth, ripe apples, rich wine and
desire. The delicious, warm scent of him she had buried
so deep enveloped her now like a fantasy.

His hands slid down the sides of her neck to her shoulders, covering her in a sweet blanket of sensation, and
she spread her fingers on his shirtfront. His body was
firm muscle under the linen. Not a dream but flesh and
blood—warm, real man beneath her hands. Heat tangled
between her legs. Without allowing herself to think, she
pressed her sensitive breasts to his chest.

A shudder seemed to pass through him. He pulled her
close and heaven descended, his body against hers, his
mouth governing the parting of her lips, the cadence of
her very breaths. He paused, then took her lower lip between his and lightly sucked. She sighed, a breathy sound
of pleasure she could not withhold. His tongue dipped
inside her, then again, twining delicious satisfaction
and need together. As though he had a world of time, he
played with her ache gently, teasing her soft dampness,
mounting her need until she clung to him, fingers digging into his ribs. In the haze of desire, she imagined he
wanted this, to make her want him, that he was kissing
her this way to force her need. He swept her tongue and
lips, giving her just enough of what she craved until she
was breathless for more of him, more of his touch and his
hands upon her. Her skin was alive, her breasts tight, her
breaths short.

Then, for a moment, he fit his lips to hers and kissed
her fully, sealing their mouths in pleasure, making them

one. Time, pain, hurt fell away. No man except Ben had ever kissed her this way, as though giving her pleasure and slaking his thirst were one in the same. As though he could not stop.

He strafed the corner of her mouth, her jaw, and the tender skin beneath her ear. Tavy's legs barely held her up. Ben gripped her arms tight, pressed his cheek to hers, and his voice came deep and rough.

"Why are you here?"

She drew away, struggling to order her thoughts amidst the tangle of emotion.

"I told you, my sister—"

He dragged her back against him and whispered over her mouth, "In England." He kissed her again, as though he must, as though he had to touch her as much as she needed to fill herself with the sensation of him after so long.

He broke away abruptly. "Why did you return?" The words were a condemnation.

Tavy's chest constricted. She pulled from his grasp and stumbled back, pressing her hand across her mouth. His breaths came unevenly like hers, but the muscles in his jaw looked hard, his eyes wells of blackness.

"I did not wish to." Her voice cracked. "I would never have left India if my family had not."

Footsteps sounded at the door. Tavy whirled around. A footman stood upon the threshold.

"My lord, more guests have arrived," he said hurriedly as a gentleman came into view behind him.

Marcus paused in the doorway then strode forward.

"Ah, there you are, my dear. Good day, Doreé. Your housekeeper sent me looking for you. She said you were giving my fiancée a tour of your impressive castle. What an attractive chamber." He glanced around, bowed to his host, and grasped Tavy's hands. "You suit it beautifully, my lady." He lifted her fingers and kissed them.

Ice lodged in the pit of Tavy's belly, spreading like frost into her hot cheeks and trembling hands. She drew out of his grasp, heart pounding, and sought Ben's gaze.

His languid eyes were cold, his beautiful mouth a line. He met her regard like a stranger, and the binding around Tavy's heart that she had tied there so carefully seven years ago seemed to tear apart.

No. *God, no.* Not again.

She grabbed onto speech, forming words from desperation.

"How was your journey, Lord Crispin?"

Marcus seemed not to note anything amiss. "Swift. I am sorry I could not travel with you. I had a business matter to see to this morning." He turned to the marquess and smiled conspiratorially. "Don't be cagey about it, Doreé. You have business in mind this week, I suspect. I saw Nathans in the parlor, and Gosworth's carriage pulled up a minute ago. Having the Bengal Club out as well, I daresay?"

"I haven't any such august plans, my lord. Merely a bit of shooting," Ben said with casual ease. "But perhaps we should postpone discussion of that until later. I am certain your fiancée hasn't the least interest in weapons and birds. Now, if you will excuse me, I must be off to change before more of my guests arrive."

He bent and retrieved his gloves from the floor, Marcus's gaze following the action carefully.

Ben bowed. "Madam." Without a flicker of his dark gaze, he strode from the ballroom.

"What were you doing with that fellow, Octavia?" Behind her, Marcus's voice had lost its friendly animation.

Her throat and stomach burned, melting the ice in a flash. Hands gripped into fists, she turned to him on leaden limbs.

"He is our host, Marcus, not a fellow."

He seemed to study her cheeks, then her mouth. "You should not have been alone in his company."

Her insides hurt. No, she should not have been alone with him. No.

"He offered a tour of his house. It is impressive." Her tone splintered. "But that is hardly at issue here. Marcus, I am not your fiancée. I believe I made that clear the other day. Why did you say what you did, and call me that?"

"You will be my lady soon enough." He reached for her hands, his smile reappearing. Tavy backed away, her body shaking, shock and anger running in tandem through her.

"I have not yet given you my reply."

"Doreé is not to be trusted." His grin disappeared again and something unsettling lit his gaze. Something that looked peculiarly like the panic she had felt earlier. "You are a beautiful woman and—"

"No." She thrust up a palm. "I cannot hear this." She hurried toward the door, heat prickling behind her eyes. Dear God, she didn't even know where her bedchamber was in this vast place. Pressing back on tears, she hurried toward the entrance hall.

"Octavia, wait. I do not wish to distress you, but you must know the way of it."

The butler stood in the foyer.

"Sir, could you direct me to my quarters?"

The servant glanced over her shoulder at the baron approaching, and gestured her toward the stairs. She barely saw the corridors he led her through. Inside her bedchamber, she snapped the bolt across the door and moved to the elegant dressing table.

She met her reflection in the glass then dropped her face into her hands. A shuddering breath escaped her. But the tears, so hot behind her eyes minutes earlier, would not come. Instead, memory did, hard and fast with a well-ing up of thick heat in her chest, as she had not allowed for years. Now, with the sensation of his touch so fresh, the feeling of his body against hers, his hands and mouth upon her skin, she could no longer resist.

Marcus called her beautiful, but on the cusp of her eighteenth birthday she had not been anything of the sort. An awkward girl, too lanky and uncomfortable in her new woman's shape, still she hadn't much cared about that, only about being released from the cage of proper English girlhood to explore the world she had lived in for nearly two years yet had not been allowed to experience.

Aunt Imene took her to tea amongst the English ladies, always making certain to comment on her poor looks, pointing out how lovely Alethea had been at that age and tut-tutting Tavy's lack of grace and fashion. Going mad with confinement, Tavy mostly ignored her gaoler. Instead she begged her uncle to take her along when he did errands about town. He complied, but he never allowed her out of the carriage. Enveloped in humid heat, she stared through windows at the world just beyond her reach, the color and beauty she had dreamt of for so many years but was not permitted to touch.

Then Aunt Imene suffered a fever. During her lengthy recovery, with help from discreet servants with whom Tavy had made friends in her two years of incarceration, finally she escaped to the market. Always she stole away at the hottest part of the day when the English and high-caste Indians all reclined upon their fanned verandas.

Lingering over a shopkeeper's wares on one of those escapes, drawing the scents of spiced fruit into her nostrils and shaded by her parasol, she met him for the second time.

"No longer in need of rescuing, *shalabha*?"

Warmth shivered along Tavy's shoulders. She turned and her gaze traveled up a perfectly proportioned male chest encased in a bright blue and gold waistcoat of the finest silk only an Indian prince would wear.

But Lord Benjirou Doreé was exactly that now, a mercantile prince. His uncle had died of fever months earlier, and when his heir returned to India from university in England, Tavy heard news from the servants. She had wondered whether the English were discussing it too, the spectacular funeral that filled the streets, the blazing white procession through Madras to mourn its lost son, friend to peasants, princes, Mughals, soldiers, and Company officials alike. There must be talk. After all, the Indian manufacturer's heir was an English nobleman, the son of a peer.

His black eyes glinted with gentle pleasure as he gazed down at her, one hand slung casually over the edge of the shop awning beneath which she stood. He was twenty-two, with the sleek grace of a tiger and the confident carriage of a young lord.

"Oh, no," she said breezily, brushing an errant wisp of hair from her brow with quivering fingers. "Now I am the one who does the rescuing."

His mouth curved into a slow smile. "Do you often find the need?"

"All the time, I daresay." She waved her hand about. "Why, just the other day Mrs. Fletcher tripped over a stack of tea bricks and fell flat upon her face on the baker's stoop. I was obliged to pass smelling salts beneath her nose at least thrice before she revived."

"How unfortunate for her," he said solemnly, but a small crescent-shaped dent appeared in his cheek. He had beautiful skin, the color of firelight glinting off teakwood, or polished bronze. His features were neither English nor Indian, but a melding of both only a master artist could have invented—lean cheeks that lent him the air of an aesthete, square jaw, aristocratically straight nose, and ink-black hair worn considerably too long for a student at Cambridge. Tavy had never seen the Marquess of Doreé and rarely his second wife, who was always thoroughly wrapped in sumptuous saris and flowing veils when she left her villa next door. She supposed they both must be quite handsome to have produced such a son.

She nodded gravely. "It was dreadful. But she recovered remarkably well when Mr. Fletcher threatened to hire a pair of sepoys to carry her back to the house hammock-style."

He cocked a single brow, its abrupt downward angle accentuating the wonderfully languid dip of his eyes.

"Sounds like a beastly fellow."

"Would you have treated her better?"

"With the respect a lady always deserves." His tone seemed so sincere. And oddly caressing. Tavy's knees felt gelatinous.

Everyone in the port town knew Benjirou Doreé was a wild young man, keeping late nights near the docks with his childhood friends even now after his uncle's death. Rumors of his reputation at university back in England, all revolving around fighting and women, filtered to her through the servants who overheard much because, like she, they were invisible even while standing right beside an Englishman.

This wild young Englishman, however, was still technically a stranger.

Foolish propriety. What was the use in living four thousand miles from London if one could not occasionally break the rules? She sucked in breath and extended a gloved hand for him to shake.

"I am Octavia Pierce."

The corner of his beautiful mouth lifted again. He bent, curled her fingers around his, and raised them to his lips, his gaze never leaving hers.

"I know who you are, *shalabha*." He brushed a kiss upon her knuckles and released her hand.

Her stomach careened against her lungs. "They say you are quite wild."

"Do they say it convincingly?"

She stared. Then laughed.

He quirked a grin. "Well I wouldn't wish to make so much effort all for nothing."

She giggled, trying to rein in her delight. Aunt Imene called her overexuberance her greatest fault. Tavy suspected her mother and father had agreed to send her abroad for the same reason. They loved her, but she was far too plain spoken for their comfort, and she laughed aloud far too often.

"All for nothing? But I suppose it must be enjoyable, after all, I mean to say, er—whatever it is you do that makes the gossips chatter."

His expression sobered. "No."

"No, it is not enjoyable?"

He shook his head, furrows forming in his brow beneath the fall of satiny dark locks.

"Then—" Her heart beat peculiarly quick. She had the uncanny sense that he had revealed to her a secret, something no one else knew. But that was a ridiculous notion. "Then what do you do for enjoyment?"

His gaze scanned her face, sliding along her neck and shoulders then lifting to her eyes again. "I am enjoying myself now."

Tingles of pleasure skittered up the insides of her legs—of all places. Her fingers tightened around the stem of her parasol.

"You know, I am not yet out in society, not until next month, at least, when I turn eighteen. I haven't any idea how to flirt."

His ebony eyes sparkled. "That makes two of us."

"Really?"

"I only speak the truth."

"Then I will make certain to only ask you questions for which the answer is indisputably pleasing."

"Ah, but I will be fashioning all my speech so that it pleases you."

She laughed. "That is absurd. Whatever for?"

He stepped forward, closing the space between them to much less than was strictly proper. "Because," he said in a quiet voice, his gaze fixed on her mouth, "I admire your smile and wish to see it often."

Her lips quivered. "It?"

He lifted his gaze to hers, gloriously dark. "You."

After that day he was at the bazaar each time she went there, twice the first week, then again the following, and after that. She shopped and he walked along beside her, commenting on her purchases and sampling foodstuffs as she recommended and occasionally required.

"You know, Genghis Khan had a royal taster to test for poison slipped into his dinner by assassins," he said mildly as he discarded the remains of a mango she demanded he try before she purchased any.

"How convenient for him."

"Tasters, I should say. He had many enemies."

"Emperors often do. Lucky for you I am just a lowly nobody."

He slanted her an unreadable look. "Lucky for me, indeed."

They spoke of everything and nothing, of India and war and of passing, insubstantial matters—the varieties of flowers for sale, the unlikelihood that the sari mender's husband had moved an inch from his sleeping-slouch in the corner of the shop since the previous week, the obvious mistake the Anglican vicar's wife had made in attaching faux robin eggs to her hat brim. Tavy never asked him of his family or the society he kept, and he never asked of hers. There seemed to be no need.

"He won," he murmured as they stepped away from a particularly spirited barter she had engaged in with a spice vendor.

"Yes, I know."

"Then why do you look so pleased?"

"Because last week I told him I would let him win today."

A crease dented his cheek, a look of frank admiration upon his handsome face. "Remind me to ask for the same consideration should the need ever arise."

Tavy laughed. "I will."

His gaze seemed to still in hers, then to grow warm. His smile slipped away. Tavy's throat went dry.

He moved off and she followed, unable to tear her gaze from his lean, muscular form, hints of the leashed energy beneath his skin revealed in the careless grace of his every action, a young, beautiful man at once sublimely at ease and restless in his body. He wore European clothing with cavalier elegance and eastern flare, expensive trousers and boots, soft-as-silk linen shirts of pristine white, fantastically gold-embroidered waistcoats, and a ring upon his left hand, a large gold tiger's head with ruby eyes. Lord Benjirou Doreé was art and nature combined to perfection.

Pausing at the nut seller's stand, he palmed a handful of almonds from a barrel-sized sack. He proffered them to her, the thick gold band glinting between his fingers as he leaned back against a table.

She shook her head. "You never purchase anything."

"I have no need." He withdrew his hand and slipped an almond between his lips, his eyes watchful upon her.

"And yet here you are so often, and always precisely when I am."

"Perhaps a coincidence."

"I doubt it. Unless, of course, you simply spend entire days here."

He smiled.

"Perhaps," she said, ducking her chin but still meeting his gaze, "we should make an appointment for the next occasion, so that you will not be obliged to guess." Her heart pounded.

They met the following day as planned, in the hottest heat of the afternoon. They wandered from stall to stall, laughing and tasting the vendors' offerings—spiced pistachio cakes, chapatis, and sugar-coated delicacies.

That afternoon he kissed her for the first time. She hadn't known she longed for him to until he did. But when in the deep shadow of an awning behind the falconry he touched her cheek, ducked his head and brushed his lips against hers, everything in her awakened. Then she wanted nothing else but more.

He drew back, gazed at her for a long, silent moment then smiled gently. They walked on. She hardly knew of what they spoke or if they spoke at all until they parted, as always, just beyond the market entrance.

That night in her bed Tavy burned, feverish beyond the heat of the August night, her body and heart filled with strange, strong yearnings.

The next day the house was in chaos readying her birthday celebration, her formal introduction into society. Tavy floated through the hours in hazy anticipation of seeing him again, imagining how he would ask her to dance, his black eyes glimmering with quiet pleasure as they always did when he looked at her. She dressed with care she had never before taken in her appearance, donning a simple white gown with pearled beads on the bodice, and arranging her hair elegantly, all in a daze of excitement.

The party went on, and on, and still he did not arrive.

Near midnight, heart in a heated twist, she approached her aunt and asked if Lady Doreé had sent word she could not attend.

"That family was not invited," Aunt Imene replied, face gaunt from her long convalescence.

Confusion flooded Tavy's young, earnest breast.

"They were on the list," she said through a tight throat. "You asked who I wished to attend and I gave you a list."

"I altered it as I saw fit."

"Oh, of course, you did not invite them because they are in mourning," she said, her disappointment heavy.

"I did not invite them because you may not associate with them. You do not fully understand matters, but now that you are out in society you will learn. Tonight, however, we will not discuss it."

Face flaming with mingled shame and fury, Tavy barely made it into the garden before tears spilled onto her cheeks. Pressing her face into her palms, she leaned against the vast spreading banyan tree and sobbed.

"Someone forget to bring a gift?" a soft, deep voice came through the darkness.

She whirled around. Ben stood a yard away, his mouth curved into a gentle arc at one side, eyes teasing. Tavy's knees turned to jelly.

"N-No. I—I only—" She could not grin in response. She could not even speak. He was here. He had come and her world seemed suddenly complete and bottomless again at once.

He stepped closer, tilting his head curiously.

"You look a bit unsteady. Too much birthday champagne, *shalabha*?"

"None." Her intoxication came solely from him, his gaze, his nearness.

She should have anticipated this. She had dreamed about him from that moment two years earlier when he swept her onto his horse, rescuing her. Over the past weeks she had merely pretended otherwise, and his lovely, undemanding companionship lulled her into familiarity.

But there was nothing familiar about the heat he stirred now in every corner of her body as he gazed at her and his smile faded.

He reached forward and ever so lightly brushed the moisture from her face with his thumb. His hand lingered, fingertips light upon her jaw. Holding her breath, Tavy leaned her cheek into his palm. She stared at his beautiful sensitive mouth, unable to look higher to his eyes to discover what she feared, that her longing was alone, that he did not feel it too.

"What has made you weep, *shalabha*?" His voice soothed, but the agitation in her blood would not be stilled.

"I wanted you to come," she whispered. "To be here tonight. But my aunt—"

"I am here now." His other hand came around her face, tilting it up. The onyx depths of his eyes seemed lit from within, sparks dancing there as bright as the yearning inside her.

She placed her palm upon his chest. He took in a quick breath, his heartbeat fast beneath her hand. Inside Tavy something seemed to open, to shimmer with yearning.

She whispered, "Kiss me again."

His gaze dropped to her mouth, and he slid the pad of his thumb over her lower lip. She felt it all the way to her toes. He lowered his head and touched his mouth to hers.

Sweet, sweet heaven, was this what it was to kiss a man one was in love with? Like jumping off a cliff and coming home both at once. He lifted his mouth and her entire being rushed to the place where his breath feathered across her lips. His shoulders rose in a heavy inhalation.

"Octavia, I—"

"Again." She trembled. "Please."

He did, bending to her and kissing her softly, repeatedly, and she melted. He felt familiar and new at the same moment, his strong hands, his scent and texture. She offered her lips and he teased them gently, as though still hesitant. But inside her a spark ignited, growing and expanding as he touched her with beautiful tenderness, holding her face in his hands like the finest porcelain he feared to break.

She wanted to touch him too. She laid her hands upon his arms. Beneath the finely woven linen he was hard and contoured, like nothing she had ever felt, and a wash of sensation rushed through her, funneling from her chest in a V-shape downward. Her lips parted on a breath of surprise.

He brought their bodies together and pressed her lips open with the pressure of his. His heat poured into her, his long, lean frame against her, and the kiss changed. She felt him at the edges of her mouth, touching her inside, and she got drunk with it. He licked at the inner line of her lips, using his tongue as though he were tasting her, kissing like he might shortly eat her, and Tavy gave up all pretense of modesty. She followed, letting him touch her so intimately, widening her lips so he could do it more, her body rushing with sensations wholly foreign and dazzling. She had never imagined a kiss could be like this, hot and all consuming, mouths and bodies fitting to each other as though fashioned to be one, completely on fire.

He kissed her throat, her jaw, and lips again, their breaths mingling fast and mouths hungry. She clutched at his shoulders, needing to be closer, hot and aching everywhere, frantic in her skin.

He grasped her arms and pressed his cheek to hers. His chest moved hard against her breasts, his body rigid as though with hard-fought control.

"I will call upon your uncle in the morning." His voice was rough. His hand slipped up to her neck, sinking into her hair to cradle her head, and it seemed that his fingers trembled, but she shook so hard it must be her. "May I?"

"*Yes*. Oh, yes." Her heart slammed against her ribs like it would break through. "But don't go yet." She twined her arms about his neck and went onto her toes, sliding her body along his and feeling him everywhere, taut, sleek muscle against her thighs and hips and the sensitive tips of her breasts. He gripped her hard beneath the arms, pulled her against his chest and covered her mouth.

He kissed her deep, then deeper with each stroke of his tongue inside her. His hands sought and her body shivered, pleasure in each caress. Somewhere in the recesses of her awareness she knew she should not be doing this, but his touch generated a craving in her young body as wonderful as it was alarming, and she could not stop. She wanted more. More of his hands on her waist and hips, more of the heat of his mouth, more of his big, hard maleness against her.

"*Shalabha,*" he said against her neck, his voice husky, perfect. "Let me touch you."

She didn't know what he meant. He was already touching her in places no man ever had, not even her dancing master who had once showed her the rudimentary maneuvers of the waltz. But she wanted him to continue doing it, as he was now, caressing the sensitive skin of her throat with his wonderful mouth, the sensation echoing between her legs where she was indescribably warm.

"Yes," she uttered. "Touch me more."

His hand slid between them and over her breast. Tavy thought she would die, the pleasure that assailed her was so intense. If this was what men and women did together in private, she finally understood the focused stares and whispered comments of the adults she had spied on for years. Ben cupped her breast, squeezed gently, and she ached so deep inside it took her breath. It hurt, but good, a throbbing pain that seemed to call for relief. His fingertips slipped along her skin above her bodice, skittering warmth across her bare flesh, then his thumb stole beneath the fabric.

She gasped into his mouth. He caressed her gently, then more firmly, and Tavy's world exploded in a shimmering cascade of desire. It had to be desire. He touched her and she wanted to be inside him, perfectly fused. But she wanted him to continue touching her too. She sank her fingers into his hair and welcomed his tongue exploring her mouth as his hand made her squirm. Her nipple was so tight it felt as though it would burst. A sound came from her throat, a moan of pleasure, surprising her. His other hand pressed into the small of her back, trapping her hips against his.

He groaned and it seemed like frustration and pleasure mingled, and his mouth moved to her throat, hot and wet, his fingers caressing harder. Tavy arched her neck. It felt so good, almost like relief to press against him, their bellies flat against one another, and at the same time it heightened her ache. His thigh came between hers and a sharp tug jerked inside her, delicious and shocking.

She breathed his name. He kissed her shoulder, drawing her sleeve down, then caressing above her bodice along the line of her gown. "Kiss me," she uttered, not really knowing her own words, thought gone in the torrent of sensations, of heat and him and aching need. "Kiss me."

With alarmingly agile fingers he unfastened the hooks of her gown and drew down the bodice, sliding the fabric off her shoulders and along her arms. In a haze she let him do it, and to loosen the laces of her petticoat and corset until they sagged forward. The hard tips of her breasts stood out beneath her thin silk shift, damp from the heat and sticking to her skin. Her heavy breaths strained the fabric.

"Please," she whispered, seeking his eyes, so dark they looked entirely black. She was dizzy from lack of breath and his gaze upon her body. "Please, kiss me."

He put his mouth on hers, sucked her tongue into him and covered her breasts with his hands. In a moment her shift was open and his palms covered her, hot, smooth, holding her perfectly. She moaned, his thumbs passing over her nipples so lightly she wanted to die. But heaven could not be any better, this deluge of longing satisfied and still growing stronger with each caress.

He bent and licked her breast.

"Unh—" A gasp swallowed her ecstatic utterance. She gripped his shoulders as he teased her nipple with his lips, circling and caressing, then biting lightly on the peak. He sank her in pleasure and she held him close. The pressure of his kiss was enormous and she wanted it to go on forever. She struggled to breathe, moving herself against his thigh, the feelings in her body more than she could bear, her actions out of her control.

He kissed between her breasts and her neck, her lips again. She met him fervently, hungry for his mouth that had touched her so intimately.

"You are beautiful." His hands slid over her hips, gathering her skirts and shifting over her behind. He stilled. His palms curved over her, his breathing hard.

Earlier, dusk had sweltered and Tavy had not donned stockings or drawers, as she often did not. Aunt Imene never noticed, and her gown was perfectly demure without either. Now there was nothing between Ben's hands and the skin of her thigh and buttock. He shifted his hold, smoothing over her flesh, and she nearly swooned.

"Oh," she whispered, barely a sound, and clutched at his waistcoat.

He pressed her back against the huge tree, dropped to his knees and pushed her gown to her hips. He locked her gaze with his bright eyes and touched her between her legs.

Reality ground to a halt and something else frightening and wonderful took its place. She was hot and felt liquid, and a beautiful man was kneeling before her with his hands where she had never imagined a man's hands could be. He stroked, and Tavy nearly choked on her own rapture. She dissolved, her legs going weak. He set her knee against his shoulder, wrapped his grip around her thigh, and his intense gaze held hers as he gave her the most sublime pleasure with his hand. Her breaths came faster, his caresses soft and steady. Inside, just beyond where he touched her, something built, thickened and shivered, then withdrew only to rise again. She whimpered, needing him, wanting him kissing her, her fingers gripping the striated bark of the banyan tree, her breasts aching so fiercely. Her eyelids fluttered, and she saw his eyes fevered. Then he leaned forward and put his mouth on her.

He kissed her, and Tavy's body came apart, a wave of pleasure seizing her, washing up then slamming down again. His tongue stroked, wet and firm yet wonderfully soft, pulling her under, submerging her in the sweetest delirium, rippling within her flesh in one after another shower of hot gratification. She made sounds she did not recognize. She shook, weak and in shock, exalted and thoroughly ashamed. Ashamed, because the instant the sensations subsided she wanted more.

Ben pressed his mouth to the inside of her thigh and Tavy dragged air into her lungs. He stood, letting her skirts fall, and curved his hands around her hips. She stared at him in awe, the songs of cicadas and crickets surrounding her, a distant macaw's cry, the heavy heat of the night and silver moonlight shining in his hair like in a dream.

She grabbed his waistcoat, pulling him close, and he kissed her and held her against him. After everything, it seemed absurd that his hand spread on the small of her back gave her such enormous pleasure.

"Ben, I—"

He caught her utterance with his mouth then murmured in a low, beautiful voice, "Hush, *shalabha*. No words." He stroked the side of her breast, then her hair, and she trembled. But his kiss seemed to retreat now, and his body was stiff with tension, like the tension still simmering in her despite how good she felt.

"I want to—" she stammered. "Can I do something to—to make you feel like you made me feel?"

His chest constricted in a taut chuckle. He brushed a stray lock from her cheek and shook his head.

"Not tonight, my—"

"Take your hands off of my niece."

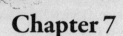

Chapter 7

END-FOR-END. A reversal of the disposition of any thing is turning it end-for-end.
                    —Falconer's Dictionary of the Marine

Aunt Imene's gravelly voice came from three yards away.

Tavy grabbed at her shift, pulling it across her breasts. Heat flooded her face as she scrabbled for her bodice. With unhurried care, Ben slipped each of her hands into the sleeves and drew her garments up, then stepped back.

"Aunt," she choked, gripping her clothing together at her back.

"Be quiet. Your guests asked after you, so I came searching. How was I to know you were cavorting like a doxy with a—" She spluttered and raked Ben with a contemptuous sneer. "Get out of here."

Tavy gasped. But he did not even look at her aunt. His

black eyes glinted in the moonlight, questioning. Tavy nodded and whispered, "Tomorrow."

Finally he glanced at her aunt, hardness forming around his perfect mouth. Then he turned and disappeared through the gate between their houses. Tavy had to restrain herself from running after him.

"You are a disgrace, Octavia," her aunt ground out.

Tavy pivoted. "Aunt Imene, I—"

"Do not speak." She strode forward, jerked her around, and roughly fastened her garments. She stepped away and her harsh gaze slid over Tavy. "Go in by the servants' entrance to your bedchamber. Your guests must be content with learning that you have contracted a megrim." She strode off, her posture stiff.

Tavy stared through the darkness toward the garden gate, her pulse fast. Then she did as she was told.

She did not sleep. The hours until dawn were a sublime heaven spent remembering over and over again his touch, his eyes, and what he had done to her.

As the sun crept above the horizon, over ships anchored in the bay and warehouses and the massive fort, then filtered onto the neighborhoods and into Tavy's bedchamber window, she dressed in her most demure morning gown and arranged her hair neatly. Her cheeks were flushed, eyes bright, and she felt different inside and out, like a woman, and she wanted to look that way for him.

No one yet had come to the breakfast parlor. Nerves too high to allow her to stomach food, she went onto the veranda and paced, but as slowly as she could. She was no longer a child. She must control her actions now. *Some* of her actions. She closed her eyes, warm at the recollection of Ben's mouth touching her intimately.

"What are you doing out here?" Aunt Imene crossed the veranda. "Come inside and take your breakfast."

"Aunt." Tavy clasped her hands. "I beg your pardon for leaving the party last night."

Her aunt stared at her, lips a thin line of disapproval.

"Did you arrange that assignation, Octavia?"

Tavy's eyes went wide. "No!" But guilt nipped at her. She had met him in secret so many times. "I like him." *Like* did not come close to describing what she felt. But she could not share those feelings with her aunt before she shared them with him.

"Yes, and he knows that now, doesn't he?"

"Why shouldn't he? He likes me too."

"You may not take up with that man."

"I didn't say anything about 'taking up with him.' He is a gentleman, Aunt Imene, and I am a lady."

"Neither of you looked the parts last night."

Tavy's cheeks flamed. She hadn't felt very much like a lady, pressed up against the banyan tree. She'd felt like a dervish afire, a star being set ablaze for the first time by the hand of the creator, like the doxy her aunt accused her of being.

She wanted to feel that way again. With him. Many more times.

"He intends to pay his formal addresses to me," she said a little breathlessly. "He is coming to speak with Uncle this morning."

"No." Her aunt's narrow face set like stone.

"No? What do you mean by no?"

"He may not."

Tavy blinked. "Why not?"

"He is unsuitable."

"He is the son of a marquess. He could not be much more suitable, Aunt, certainly not for Miss Nobody without even looks to recommend me."

"Do not be foolish," Aunt Imene said tightly. "He is one of *them*, Octavia. Now, that will be all."

"No, it will not be all. He has just come down from

Cambridge. Before that he was at Eton." She ticked off on her fingers. "His father is not the wealthiest man in England, but certainly not pockets-to-let by any means, and everyone knows he has inherited a fine income from his uncle's business. And furthermore—"

"He is not acceptable." Her aunt's voice cut.

Tavy stared. Her fingers and toes, unaccountably, began to tremble. Why not the rest of her, she could not fathom. But her chest felt suffocated.

"His father is a marquess," she repeated dumbly.

"And barely acknowledges him."

"That is not true."

"Are you so certain of that?"

"No. Of course not. I read the same months-old rags you do and they never—" She halted. She could hardly tell her aunt that for nearly two years she had scoured those journals for mention of him. She jutted out her pointy jaw. "Lord Doreé must acknowledge him in society."

Her aunt shook her head. "I told your parents this time abroad would harm you. You are too impetuous for this country to have a worthwhile effect upon you." She strode toward the parlor door, stiff skirts rustling with purpose. "I intend to write to your father about this immediately. He will call you home and that will be an end to it."

"Good." The trembling crept into her arms and legs and her lower lip. She bit down to still it. "Benjirou will no doubt return to England soon. He can call upon Papa and Mama there, and they will see that you are wrong."

Imene rounded upon her. "You foolish girl. Who do you think you are to question me?" Her eyes flashed. "It makes no difference that his father wed his mother legally, a scandal when it occurred, although you are too young to know it." She punched the air with a poker-straight finger. "His name means nothing to society, nor does his education. He knows that perfectly well. Why do you think he seduced you?"

Tavy gaped, scrabbling for words to cover up the ugly one. *Seduced?*

"You know perfectly well why," her aunt said before she could respond. "He saw how gullible and desperate for a man's attention you are and thought to attach himself to a respectable family if he could."

"No." She barely managed the single syllable. "It was not like that." Was it? The expression of disgust on her aunt's face swirled nausea through her. Doubt followed, prickling and sticky.

Lucky for me, indeed, he had said.

"Your naïveté is suitable for a girl your age," her aunt said, less sharply now. "But it does you no credit in these matters. It is a good thing I happened upon you. He is far from the equal of his half brothers. To be associated with him would only denigrate your family and bring condemnation upon you greater than you can imagine."

Tavy's throat closed. She forced away doubt, forced herself to think the way her aunt would.

"Aunt Imene, he is the son of a peer. I could not do better for myself, even given his reputation."

"You are infatuated with him because you see him as exotic. You have always shown a misguided interest in things a proper English girl should hold at a distance. But your penchant for adventure has served you poorly this time. I am relieved I stopped you from making a greater mistake before it was too late."

"Aunt—"

"You will learn to listen to those who wish the best for you. And you—" She stabbed her finger toward the garden. Tavy pivoted. Ben stood in the ochre morning light, one foot upon the step from the garden as though arrested in his arrival. His jaw was taut, his eyes glittering with anger. Tavy's heart spun.

"You," her aunt continued as though the words could

poison, "you are not welcome here. If you so much as glance at my niece again, I will have you arrested for battery. I know what you intended, but I have found out your game in time, thank God. You will not inveigle your way into my niece's bed or polite society, no matter how prettily you have seduced her."

Tavy gasped. Ben did not speak.

She pressed a palm to her stomach. His gaze followed the action then lifted to hers, hard as polished steel. Completely foreign.

Her certainty wavered, then beneath his cold regard crumbled.

"Is it true?" she asked, realizing more with each moment what a fool she had been. To imagine he might like her—silly, babbling, awkward—that he might truly want her—plain, unnoticeable, all elbows and knees and freckles. It now seemed ludicrous.

They had always met in secret, outside the notice of her aunt and uncle and the rest of English society. She had not questioned it. She *encouraged* it. He was her adventure, and she knew it was wrong. He never called upon her at home and she absolutely loved that. She adored having the clandestine company of a man of questionable reputation. A handsome, charming, reckless young man who seemed nevertheless to command the respect of every native in Madras.

How foolish could she have been? How blind? For what else would a man like him want a girl like her?

"Of course it is true," her aunt spat out, gesturing to the garden gate. "Why else would he come here like this? He knows he cannot enter through the front door."

"Is it as she says?" Tavy uttered, but his eyes already told her. They were blank, as she had never seen them. "It is, isn't it?"

"It must be." His voice sounded nothing like him.

"Young man," her aunt said stonily, "if you do not remove your person from this property I will have the guard summoned."

His eyes flickered with anger again for an instant, then coldness. Without another glance at Tavy, he turned and walked away.

He did not return, although she waited, lying upon her bed, weeping, knowing she could not have been so mistaken in him, then knowing that she was the naïve fool her aunt claimed.

The following afternoon her aunt and uncle closed up the house and took her north. Uncle George, it seemed, had business he was obliged to attend to in distant Calcutta. Tavy waited for her aunt to redouble the condemnation, but she behaved as though nothing at all had passed.

Uncle George, however, changed. Before, he had been kindly neglectful. Now he grew diffident, treating her with an odd, distant respect. Tavy didn't know what her aunt had told him, but she could not help wondering if Ben had spoken to her uncle that morning instead of Aunt Imene, whether matters would have gone differently.

Six months later when they returned to Madras, Ben was gone. It was only then that Tavy learned how his uncle's death had left him the wealthiest Englishman in India, and amongst the wealthiest natives. She also learned what he had not told her, what perhaps her aunt had not even known. His future was already set.

"He is a veritable Midas," a gossiping matron said at tea in the vice-governor's home.

The matron's companion tittered. "He is expected to make some Indian princess a handsome prince."

But he did not. Upon his return to England, only two months after his second brother fell beneath cannon blast at Waterloo, his father and eldest brother perished in a fire that burnt down the family hunting box and killed six servants in their beds. Alongside the death notices the London journal printed the information—as though an afterthought—that the new marquess was expected to marry the heiress his eldest brother had been betrothed to since childhood, the daughter of a recluse Scottish duke who had made his fortune in East Indies trade.

No more Indian princess bride. Benjirou Doreé was a Lord of the Realm now. As such, he was expected to wed as one.

Tavy cried herself to sleep that night a final time, but never again. The young man she had fallen in love with— beautiful, laughing, kind—was no longer. He had disappeared the moment he walked away from her in the garden that morning, leaving her heart torn open. The new Marquess of Doreé, so high above her touch he might as well be a god, meant nothing to her.

Chapter 8

Two dozen guests gathered in the drawing room before dinner. Until their host entered, Tavy only had attention for one.

Lady Constance Read was stunning, and not only because of her natural beauty. When she entered the chamber, her smile and golden spirits seemed to fill it with warmth, her wide, luxuriantly lashed eyes dancing with sincere pleasure to see friends and meet new acquaintances. Tavy wanted to hate her immediately. But since she had never hated anyone, including her Aunt Imene—whom she successfully resisted despising for three full years while living with her—she certainly could not begin with charming, vivacious Lady Constance.

Moving around the room as she greeted people, the heiress finally came to Tavy.

"Dear Miss Pierce, how lovely to see you again." She reached for her hand.

Tavy stared, speechless, then dropped into a curtsy. Lady Constance remembered her. Then again, it seemed unlikely that unmarried ladies often visited the Marquess of Doreé's town residence by themselves. Except, of course, Lady Constance.

But her smile now seemed so genuine, and Tavy found herself smiling back.

"It seems, Miss Pierce," she leaned in and hushed her voice, "that you and I are the only husbandless ladies present at this dull business gathering, for of course that is why everyone is here, although our host will not admit it." She glanced about with a furtive air. "I propose that the very moment we find the company unendurable, we dash off to the village together to shop, or perhaps shut ourselves in a cozy parlor with a stack of lending library novels and read aloud to one another."

Tavy could not help but laugh. Lady Constance was precisely her age, with the appearance of a goddess and the character, apparently, of a girl not yet out of the schoolroom. She, obviously, had not struggled for years to quash that girl. Or if she had, she'd done a poor job of it.

Tavy nodded gravely. "It is always best to have a plan."

A twinkle lit the beauty's eyes, and just like that, despite herself, Tavy gave over her affection. It would no doubt prove horridly inconvenient when he married her. But she had never been very wise in that way.

Tavy was reminded precisely how unwise immediately. Ben entered the drawing room and his gaze came to her and Lady Constance. Shivers of heat and cold passed through her.

"Miss Pierce," Lady Constance said, "may I call you by your given name? My father says I am always wretchedly overfamiliar, but may I tell you a secret?"

Tavy nodded, her stomach tight.

"I feel terribly out of place here amongst all these Company people and would be grateful for a friend." Her gaze flickered about the chamber, a fretful light in it for a moment.

"My name is Octavia."

"Lovely. And you will dispense with the title and simply call me Constance. Ben calls me Connie when he is unhappy with me, but I do not care for that at all."

"I cannot imagine that he is unhappy with you often," she managed, swallowing back a wretched lump in her throat. He had kissed her, in his house, with this beautiful woman beneath his roof. It had been the best and worst thing Tavy experienced in seven years. Marcus, the man who had proposed marriage to her, possibly knew. But only now did she feel like a betrayer.

"Oh, well, no. You are correct." Lady Constance smiled, but not as brightly. "He is very patient with me."

The butler announced dinner. Marcus approached, a blithe smile upon his face, and drew Tavy's hand through his elbow.

"Lady Constance, may I take you in to dinner upon the arm that my fiancèe does not occupy?"

Constance's gaze slewed to Tavy, her winged brows lifted.

"Thank you, Lord Crispin. And may I congratulate you, Miss Pierce, on your betrothal?"

Tavy could say nothing. Marcus pressed his elbow to his side, trapping her fingers against him like he was trapping her into marriage with these public statements. He wished to force her hand. Perhaps he feared she would discover the secret of his blackmailer and refuse him.

Her gaze darted about the chamber as guests headed toward dinner. Amidst the ten titled proprietors of the East India Company, at least one must have information that could lead her to answers about Marcus's blackmailer.

Their wives were a mixed lot, some tradesmen's daughters, others like Lady Nathans impoverished noble daughters sold to the highest bidder during their come-out seasons. Tavy would interview them all and discover information to confront Marcus, either to help or refuse him. And if a refusal made her into a jilt in the eyes of society, that must be the price she paid for once again giving a man her trust.

Tavy tasted dinner, but her stomach would not unwind. At the foot of the table, Lady Constance rose, and Tavy welcomed the ladies' retirement. Slipping onto the sofa beside her sister in the drawing room, she watched Constance move to the pianoforte and draw back the lid.

"Why do you suppose Lady Constance and Lord Doreé are not yet married?" Alethea whispered. "I understand it has been some time since they were expected to wed, and she must be quite a few seasons out of the schoolroom."

"I suppose one is not truly on-the-shelf when one is nearly spoken for," Tavy murmured as the gentlemen entered the drawing room from their port. Ben came last, beside the man who had spoken to Tavy during the dance at Lady Ashford's. Lord Styles spoke with an easy smile. The marquess's hands were clasped behind his back as he listened. His gaze shifted to Lady Constance at the piano and then he went to her.

"Will you play for us, Lord Doreé?" Lady Nathans said in the perpetually silky tones Tavy had already learned to dislike. "I understand you have a marvelous talent."

Ben cast her a glance, smiling slightly, and seated himself beside the goddess at the instrument.

"Schubert, my lord?" Lady Constance inquired.

He nodded. "As you wish."

They played beautifully. Tavy tried to drag her gaze away but could not.

"They are a gorgeous pair," Alethea whispered.

A gorgeous pair, indeed, ideally suited, her golden beauty, his dark perfection. Why weren't they wed?

Perhaps because he was a faithless cur who left women crying for him four thousand miles away then years later kissed them like he would swallow them whole? Because with a woman like Constance Read waiting faithfully to marry him, why hurry matters when other opportunities beckoned?

Tavy's gaze slipped to Priscilla Nathans. The glint in the lady's emerald eyes as she watched Ben was positively proprietary. A woman would not look at a man that way unless she had reason for confidence in his attentions.

In the seven years since her abrupt initiation into sensual pleasure, Tavy had educated herself about such matters, eavesdropping more assiduously than ever, still listening at doors and cracks but with a more mature interest. She had learned one important lesson through these endeavors: Ladies like Priscilla Nathans were not uncommon, and gentlemen who took advantage of them apparently did so without hesitation or shame.

"Octavia?"

"Hm?"

"Has Lord Crispin come to the point yet?"

Tavy jerked out of her unpleasant reverie. She peered at her sister.

"Why do you ask?"

"St. John heard Lady Constance congratulate you upon your betrothal. Are you betrothed?" Alethea's soft hazel eyes held no condemnation. Tavy's stomach tightened.

"He offered. I requested more time to consider it and he accepted that. But today he told two people that I am his fiancée."

"You have not yet given him your answer?"

Tavy shook her head.

"Why not?"

Because she did not want Marcus Crispin. She wanted

hot, stolen kisses from a beautiful man who had broken her young heart, whose faithlessness had taught her to mistrust and encouraged her to do away with the foolish impetuosities of girlhood in order to become restrained and respectable.

But Tavy did not wish to be restrained and respectable. She never had, even less so now that her daily relief from that restrained respectability—the tropical paradise she adored—was so distant.

"I do not love him," she whispered, barely aware of her words.

"I thought you did not require a love match."

Tavy's throat closed. She raised her gaze to the source of the music. The marquess's head was bent, his hands upon the keys graceful, as they had once been upon her. He glanced up and met her stare. Then he looked away, tilting his head toward the woman at his side. His lips moved in speech, and Lady Constance's mouth curved into a smile.

"I do not," Tavy replied.

"Then perhaps you should consider accepting his suit."

Tavy swiveled on her seat, seeking out Marcus across the drawing room. His gaze rested on her. He stood.

"Ladies and gentleman." He tapped his signet ring to the crystal goblet in his hand. "I would like to share with you tonight the greatest joy a man can claim. Miss Pierce has consented to be my bride."

Only years of hiding her true emotions allowed Tavy to accept his hand when he moved to her, and to stand and nod graciously in acknowledgment of the well wishes. But she could not look at her betrothed. Instead, her gaze went to the Marquess of Doreé. He glanced to the door and gestured to the butler.

St. John shook Marcus's hand. "Felicitations, my lord."

"I am a happy man, indeed." Marcus covered her fingers on his arm and smiled at her warmly. Alethea kissed her on the cheek but said nothing.

The butler appeared with champagne.

"Doreé, you old sentimentalist," Lord Nathans chortled, drinking down his glassful in a swallow. His bushy brows peaked. "Damn fine vintage."

"Please, my lord," Lady Nathans admonished her husband, then turned her gaze on Ben as she set crimson lips to crystal. "A true gentleman always knows how to please his guests."

"To the health of the bride and groom," Lord Gosworth said, lifting his champagne, and the others followed, except their host, who did not drink. Tavy could not make herself look away from Ben. At his side, Lady Constance touched his arm. He grasped the stem of his glass and, like Lord Nathans, took the draught whole.

After that Tavy could not look at him again.

As soon as she could, she escaped with Alethea to the nursery. Jacob slept the sleep of the innocent. Tavy squeezed her sister's hand in parting and went to her bedchamber anticipating the opposite for herself.

She drew her bedchamber door shut and closed her eyes. "My innocence is a thing of the past, Lal."

But no soft patter of footsteps met her, no tiny comforting hands upon her face or hair. Lal was still in London with Abha, and she was talking to herself.

But Tavy already knew she had gone mad. Or perhaps only wicked. In a single day she had engaged in more deception than in seven years, and it had only required Benjirou Doreé in her life again to do so.

She breathed a weary sigh and studied the pale green and gold paper on the walls and the canopy bed draped in filmy fabric. The elegant dressing table and mirror shone with modest gilt accents. She slipped off her shoes, and the rug beneath her stockinged feet felt soft as butter. Everything was understated, tasteful, comfortable, just as the rest of the house.

"It is a lovely chamber," she whispered. Mad, certainly. "Perhaps Lady Constance decorated it."

She put her hand upon her brow.

She pulled the bell and her maid came to braid her hair and stir the coals in the grate. When she left, Tavy knelt before the hearth, tucked her linen night rail around her bared feet, and stared into the lapping fire.

A scratch sounded at the door, her sister wishing for conversation she could not yet engage in, no doubt. She opened it. Candlelight shone upon the strong planes of Marcus's face, the glimmer in his eyes thoroughly contrite.

"Can you forgive me?"

"For wishing to marry me so determinedly that you cannot wait for my assent before announcing it to the world?"

He released a strained laugh and shook his head.

"You are a treasure. I never have anxiety that you will not tell me what you are thinking."

"I am glad you appreciate that. Because I am thinking that you do not seem to know a jot about the way to a woman's heart."

His brow furrowed.

"Marcus, I am angrier than I have ever been with anyone." Except one person, but that anger had been laced with grief. "You have shown a lack of respect for me. I do not know how you could imagine that would entice me to accept you."

"Allow me to make it up to you." He grasped her hand. A lock of dark hair fell over his brow. Tavy had the unsettling instinct to smooth it away in a comforting gesture. For all his presumption, he had been a loyal friend in India and since her return to England.

"You can tell me the truth about the blackmailer. I think there is more to it than you have said."

"I cannot speak of it at this time, but I will tell you eventually, I promise. My dear, let us forget about this and renew the friendship we have always enjoyed. This quarrel mars what should be a celebration." His gaze was so sincere. Marcus always looked directly into her eyes. He never looked at her the way Ben did, first at her eyes, then all of her, then at her mouth, before returning his gaze to hers. Marcus's gaze did not turn her inside out.

That had to be for the best. If what she learned about the blackmailer was unacceptable, her heart would not suffer for it.

"Octavia?"

She seemed to be staring at his neckcloth.

"Marcus, what if I told everyone that you invented our betrothal?"

"You would not."

"How do you know that?"

"Because you would not wish to see me hurt or humiliated. I know that about you." He leaned forward and touched his lips to her brow, a gentle, brief caress.

Was this what one was supposed to feel for one's husband, a mild tenderness mingled with frustration and a sense of inevitability? Alethea and St. John's bond seemed the exception. The married pairs at Fellsbourne bore this out, most of them business arrangements between people with little in common. Only cherubic little Lady Gosworth seemed happy in her marriage, her husband gruffly appreciative of her. At least with a husband like Marcus, she would not find the need to seek out other gentlemanly company like Priscilla Nathans did.

Voices sounded in the corridor. Marcus looked toward them. Tavy tugged her hand away and stepped back across the threshold.

He banded his arms around her, pulled her forward and clamped his mouth over hers.

Astonishment shut out all else for an instant. Then she became aware of his lips urging hers to respond, his hands gripping her back and head, her breasts smashed against his big, firm chest. She had a quick impression of the scent of bergamot lotion and his skill at kissing as she flattened her palms against his shoulders and pushed.

A gentleman cleared his throat in the corridor.

Marcus released her. Tavy crossed her arms over her thinly garbed chest and swiveled her head. Lord Styles and the Marquess of Doreé stood two yards away.

"Ma'am." Lord Styles bowed. He turned his regard upon Marcus. "Don't blame you in the least, Crispin, stealing a march on the wedding day." He twirled the chain of a quizzing glass around his index finger. "But do you mind if Doreé and I pass along to our chambers before you continue?"

Ben's languid gaze slipped from Marcus to her, the black depths expressionless.

Tavy jerked back into her chamber and snapped the door shut. Pressing her palms to her burning cheeks, she leaned her brow against the panel. Shame enveloped her. Not because she had been caught embracing a man to whom she was not yet married. Not because anything in that embrace had stirred desire in her. Not even because she had been discovered by a man she had been kissing only hours earlier—enthusiastically, *hungrily*.

He was her weakness. Even as the moisture from Marcus's kiss still lingered upon her lips, warmth bloomed in her the moment she saw Ben. Not a moment earlier. Being kissed by another man only increased her desire for him.

"Perhaps," she whispered to the empty chamber, "I am a great deal more like Priscilla Nathans than I care to admit."

Chapter 9

DECOY. A strategem employed by a ship of war to betray a vessel of inferior force into an incautious pursuit, til she has drawn within the range of cannon.
—Falconer's Dictionary of the Marine

Ben tamped wads of paper into the Manton's double muzzles and braced the fowling piece against his shoulder. His spaniels darted through the brush, rousing birds from hiding with a flurry of soft flapping like loose sails in an easy wind. He took aim and fired, the stock jerking against muscle and bone. Two birds dropped.

"Bloody well done, Doreé." The Earl of Gosworth splashed through an ankle-deep puddle to bypass him. Ahead, beaters smacked at shrubs and patches of undergrowth with paddles, stirring prey into flight. Farther off, gunshot ricocheted beneath the heavy overhanging clouds.

Ben shouldered his weapon and began walking, his

boots sinking into mud. He despised birding, or hunting of any sort. He had hunted enough men to make the pursuit of dumb beasts less than enthralling. He preferred sport with a sword in his hand or a horse beneath him. And today especially he did not care for the opportunity to be alone with his thoughts.

Styles moved up beside him, the tails of his duster fluttering through the grass, his fowling piece gripped jauntily in his hand.

"Gosworth is wagering ten pounds on Crispin throttling Nathans before they can complete the Singapore deal," he commented, following Ben toward the rise beyond the thistle bed to higher, less soggy ground. On the other side of the patch, Lord Nathans gestured with his weapon, shouting for his partner to hurry along. Styles snorted. "That Cit is a thorough boor."

"Crispin seems like a reasonable enough man," Ben replied. "I suspect he would not have gone into partnership with Nathans if he weren't able to keep a cool head about him."

"Perhaps he reserves all his heated moments for the lovely Miss Pierce, hm?" Styles chuckled and switched his gun to his other hand.

Ben glanced at the single-barrel weapon his friend preferred despite its cumbersome length. Leaving the house at dawn earlier, he had offered one of his finer guns, but Styles declined.

Oftentimes a man did not always know what was best for him.

Ben halted on the hilltop, the dogs circling around him. His land stretched beyond in strips of brown fields and copses of trees turned gold, crimson, and sienna. Styles drew a flask from his waistcoat and filled his shot cup, the aroma of brandy stealing through the chill air. He threw back the drink then proffered the flask. Ben shook his head.

"Your brother consumed at least three of these every

time he went out shooting," Styles said. "He got me and Arthur drunk as emperors once, boasting that a man could not take a shot without taking a shot both before and after."

Ben nodded. He had heard the story plenty of times.

"We were all three of us shot to the wind," Styles continued. "Jack staggered back to the house, of course, calling for a cart to retrieve us from the field. But the cart stuck in a brier patch. Arthur and I woke up the next morning scratched on every surface of our skin. You were lucky you weren't there, Ben. You must have been in the Indies."

"Indeed, I was." Just before his twentieth birthday, when his uncle summoned him home to discuss the business, this time man-to-man.

Home.

During that visit Ben had rescued an English girl from a pair of kidnappers hoping to win a quick ransom payment. Afterward he had returned to the market and dealt with the thieves as he dealt with all swine. But months later, occasionally, deep in his cups at Hauterive's, staring at a hand of cards or into a demi-rep's jaded eyes, he had thought of that girl with the wide unspoiled stare and the beautifully long legs, and wondered how India was treating her.

Two years later when he encountered her again in India then returned to England, he had not left her fate to idle wondering.

"Have you gotten what you hoped from this little gathering yet?" Styles swallowed a second finger of brandy.

Ben turned away from the view of his estate, blocked in any case by the vision in his mind of her eyes before he kissed her yesterday. He'd been a fool to succumb to his desire. He should have known better. But he had always been a fool with Octavia Pierce. And for her.

"Styles, have you had any business with Nathans your-self?"

His friend's brows rose. "You are after Nathans, then?"

"Have you?"

Styles shook his head. "Singapore does not interest me."

"Why not? There is good money to be had along that route to Canton."

Styles dropped his shot cup into his pocket. "I am occupied with other affairs."

"Still fixed on Nepal?" Ben asked casually. "You won't get far there, my friend. Those natives are not impressed by English woolens."

"No. I've given up on that." A strange light entered the baron's blue eyes.

"Keeping things closer to home, I daresay? You have not been east in nearly a decade."

"Neither have you." Styles's gaze narrowed. "Not since you acceded to the title."

"I have not found the need." Ben started along the ridge of the hill. Below, Nathans cavorted like a green lad over a brace of pigeons. Gosworth joined the gentlemen heading over the rise, including Marcus Crispin. Crispin cast a glance over his shoulder at his partner down in the brush then went along with the others.

He should send the whole lot of them back to London after lunch. She was set to marry Crispin. Her concerns about the blackmailer must be allayed.

But a persistent unease scratched at him. The night before, when he and Styles encountered Baron Crispin and his betrothed in the corridor, she had been resisting the embrace. And when he released her and turned to them, Crispin's determined gaze fixed on Styles—not on him, the man Crispin had found his fiancée alone with earlier that day, her porcelain cheeks and the ivory column of her neck flushed, her beautiful lips bruised from his kisses.

Crispin was no idiot. In the ballroom Ben had seen the snap of his gaze, the proprietary grasp of her arm to make it clear to whom she belonged. But last night outside her bedchamber, that passionate embrace had been for Styles's benefit. Not his. And she had not been privy to her fiancée's purpose.

Ben would know why.

The wives of the proprietors of the East India Company present at Fellsbourne might be married to milliners, modistes, and jewelers, for all they discussed their husbands' businesses. Their interests seemed to lie entirely in the current season's fashions and in society ladies unwise enough to dress in last season's.

Tavy sat in a windowed corner of a parlor elegantly appointed in ivory and cobalt blue silk, her embroidery forgotten in her lap, and gazed at the gray day without, listening now with desultory attention to the conversation of Lady Gosworth, Priscilla Nathans, and the other wives. Somewhere far off in the corridors of Fellsbourne, Alethea napped with Jacob, an excellent choice of afternoon activities indeed, as it happened.

"Isn't this a cozy picture?" Lady Constance said from the doorway. Resplendent in peach silk and pearls, she moved into the chamber with smiles for each lady.

"Have you any news of the gentlemen's return, Lady Constance?" the Countess of Gosworth asked, her round cheeks dimpling.

"Yes, do tell," Lady Nathans purred. "Has our host enticed our husbands to the farthest reaches of the estate to find the perfect birds?"

"Oh, I doubt it," Constance said with an unaffected shrug of graceful shoulders. "Lord Doreé dislikes shooting, and probably wishes he were here with you lovely ladies instead." Her gaze glittered on the chestnut-haired coquet for a purposeful moment, then shifted directly to Tavy.

"He dislikes shooting?" one of the ladies trilled. "Who ever heard of such a thing?"

"Anybody who might be listening," came the vocal rejoinder. Lady Fitzwarren stood in the doorway behind Constance, her bulk encapsulated in a fantastic constellation of violet organza and lilac silk.

"Lady Fitzwarren, how do you do?" Constance said delightedly and grasped the dowager's lavender-gloved fingers.

Tavy leapt up and went to them.

"Afternoon." Lady Fitzwarren took in all the women in the chamber with the greeting, then brought her open gaze to Tavy. "Octavia, you look peaked, especially with Lady Constance beside you for comparison."

Constance laughed. "Come now. Octavia is as lovely as can stare. And," she added sotto voce, "there are those here who can and do stare."

"I have no doubt of that whatsoever." Lady Fitzwarren took Tavy's arm. "Come with me, child. You may join us, Lady Constance."

"It is good to see you, Lady Fitzwarren," Tavy said uncertainly. "But what are you doing here?"

"You called me Aunt Mellicent when you were a girl. May as well do so now."

"But what *are* you doing here, Aunt Mellicent?"

The dowager dragged Tavy into the drawing room. Constance took up a position at the door.

"You needn't be shy, Lady Constance," the dowager said bracingly. "There will be no secrets passed about here. Come have a seat. Does Dorée's cook make an edible poppy cake? I've had a hankering for a fine poppy cake for a fortnight now and ordered my own Griffin to bake up a batch for tea today. But after I received Alethea's note, I hadn't time to taste a one."

"My sister sent you a note? Whatever for?"

"She thought I should know that you betrothed yourself to Marcus Crispin. I don't blame her for it, of course. Your parents have been angling in that direction for months." She fixed Tavy with a direct stare. "Well, why did you do it?"

"I beg your pardon, Octavia." Constance spoke before Tavy could open her mouth. "I did not mean to suggest last evening that married ladies are dull bores."

"At the time you suggested it, I was not precisely betrothed, actually." It felt unreasonably good to admit that aloud. Too good.

"Aha." Lady Fitzwarren snapped her fleshy fingers. "I knew it."

"How could you have known that, Aunt Mellicent?"

"Suspected it, rather."

"But he is a perfectly unexceptionable gentleman, and you have been present on nearly all the occasions I have been in company with him since I returned to London."

"Precisely." Lady Fitzwarren turned to Constance. "Why aren't you and that handsome marquess wed yet?"

Tavy's stomach hollowed out. She could claim a sudden megrim and flee. But she must hear of their plans eventually. The sooner the better. Then perhaps her foolish imaginings would finally cease. Lord knew she hadn't the strength to cease them through her own will. Like Priscilla Nathans and Lady Gosworth, she had spent the majority of the day wondering when the gentlemen would return. Her betrothed had nothing to do with her anticipation.

She had never kissed two men in a single day. Or year. Marcus's embrace had left her furious and frustrated, and she was still piqued with him for it. But Ben's kiss . . . Hot, delicious little eddies wound through her at the mere thought of it.

Constance smiled. "One reason we are not wed, my lady, is that he has not offered for me."

"Which suggests there are other reasons as well."

"It does, indeed." The heiress's eyes glimmered.

Tavy struggled to appear only mildly interested.

"Has he got a host of lightskirts at his beck and call, or a flamboyant Bird of Paradise you cannot abide?" Lady Fitzwarren demanded.

"Oh, that certainly is not my place to say." Constance's eyes danced.

"I haven't heard that he has either, so you needn't be coy, missy, and I suspect you wouldn't be if he did," the dowager responded with a satisfied nod. "Good." She returned her regard to Tavy. "I thought you told me you were through with pretending. How long have you been betrothed to Crispin and how long will you make him wait before you jilt him?"

Tavy sputtered. "Jilt him? Aunt—"

"Don't try to cozen me, Octavia. I knew you when you were all spots and elbows, long before you put on airs."

"My lady," Constance interjected softly, "I believe Octavia was as surprised by Lord Crispin's announcement of their betrothal as—well—as I was. Perhaps she is only now determining how she may proceed."

"Well, you've got a sensible head on your shoulders, after all, don't you, young lady?"

"I have my moments."

"Moments in which your beauty eclipses the sun, moon, and stars combined, dearest Lady Constance?" Lord Styles drawled as he entered the chamber. "Innumerable, I daresay."

A flicker of displeasure passed across Constance's eyes so swiftly Tavy nearly missed it.

"Afternoon, ladies." Lord Gosworth entered, Ben and Marcus behind.

Marcus moved to Tavy and lifted her hand to his lips. "What a relief from the wilds of nature." He offered a charming smile for all. "Feminine beauty and grace to please a man's weary eye."

"Young flatterer," the dowager scowled.

Tavy tugged her hand away.

"Good heavens." Constance frowned. "What are you doing, tromping in here in all of your dirt and smelling of gunpowder?"

Lord Styles gestured toward the sideboard. "Nasty day out. Need a belly warmer before a hot bath, don't you know." He splashed amber liquid into glasses and passed them to the earl and Marcus. Ben went to the dowager.

"Lady Fitzwarren, it is a pleasure to welcome you to Fellsbourne." He bowed, as elegant as ever in mud-spattered boots and long coat, his broad shoulders emphasized by the capes and his handsome face flushed from the cold. Tavy dragged her gaze away.

"Don't ask what brings me here, Doreé, for I won't tell." The dowager tsked her tongue. "But I knew you wouldn't mind if I showed up uninvited. Your *pater* and I were fond friends, and I spent plenty a day at his whist table—that is, when he wasn't off proposing bills. It's more than a shame he didn't live to force that East Indies reform through to success. Fell apart without him leading the charge."

"It would have put things back the way they were before." Lord Gosworth nodded his head regretfully. "With Parliament's hands in every nook of the Company's business, a man can't sell a teaspoonful of tea without a pack of idiot lords telling him what to do, not to mention our august monarch."

Lady Fitzwarren harumphed. "It was too bad you were abroad when that bill fell through, Abel. After Doreé, you might just have had the support to see it passed."

"Perhaps, Mellicent," Lord Gosworth replied. "But I will speak plainly. What my fellow lords—present company excepted, of course—what my fellow lords know about trade in Hindustan they could fit inside their stays. Don't know why we don't all just hang the Company and go out on our own. What, what, Crispin? You were independent before Prinny pushed you into joining up with the Company. The rest of us were all in it years ago before that damn bill. But why did you take this fool's plunge, lad?"

"I always say it is best to be in the company of successful men." Marcus grinned and lifted his glass in salute.

Lord Styles grunted. "You've got it wrong, Gosworth. The Company's better off with Parliament's oversight. Keeps eastern wealth in the hands of those of us born to control it. It is in Britain's interests." He swung his glass to his lips and gulped the contents. Tavy had the distinct impression that he was already foxed, although he masked it well. But gentlemen often drank a great deal when they hunted. Lord Gosworth and Marcus looked less than clear-eyed.

But not Ben. He set his glass on the sideboard without tasting it.

"Gentlemen," he said as a footman entered with a tray, "I suggest we leave the ladies to their tea."

"M'wife's probably looking for me anyway," Lord Gosworth said pleasantly and departed.

"Until dinner then, *mesdames*." Marcus made a pretty leg and went out with the earl.

"I won't be chased away from the whiskey so soon." Lord Styles cast Constance a pointed look, a sliver edge to his laughing tone. "Can't see why you are allowing it in your own house, Doreé. You've never been the sort to flee in the face of a woman's scorn."

Tavy's stomach tightened.

"No," Ben said. Tavy knew she should turn her gaze away, but she did not and he met it, as she hoped and feared. "I never have."

Then—because she was for all intents and purposes betrothed to another man, who was right to trust in her public loyalty to him even if it chafed beyond endurance, and also because apparently she had lost her talent at dissembling lately—she dropped her gaze until the Marquess of Doreé and his companion left.

Later in her bedchamber, for the first time in years, she wept. She wept for what she never had, yet still lost years earlier. She wept for her friends—Alethea, Lady Fitzwarren, even perhaps Constance—who seemed to hope more for her than she did. And she wept for the girl that once had the courage to defy convention for the sake of dreams, who now feared being hurt again more than settling for mediocrity.

Chapter 10

To PRIME A FIRE-SHIP. To lay the train and get her in readiness for being set on fire.
— *Falconer's* Dictionary of the Marine

After nearly three decades of denying most of his desires, Ben's resistance to temptation was crumbling. Each time she lifted her liquid gaze to him across a room full of people, he was twenty-two again, fantasizing about peeling the clothing from her lovely curves and making her body come alive to him, as he had done so briefly in that moonlit garden.

But she was another man's. It didn't need Crispin's proprietary gestures and words to bear that home. She was the portrait of a composed society lady, just as she had been in Ben's house in town, so different from that girl who for a moment had resurfaced in the ballroom. And she was loyal. When Crispin beckoned, she answered. When he touched her, she modestly allowed it. When he praised her amidst the company, she lowered her gaze.

She did not speak to Ben. But she looked at him. Often. And it was unraveling him.

She could not deny the pull between them any more than he could. But given her betrothal, her purpose was clear to him now. Like Lady Nathans and all the other females Ben preferred to ignore, she wanted to misbehave with him, a man on the edge of society, within it but forever foreign.

The trouble with Octavia Pierce was that he wanted to misbehave with her too.

"In a brown study again, darling?" Constance settled herself upon the garden bench beside him, twirling a listless rose between her fingers. Ben looked up from the book in his hands.

"Seeking a moment's privacy, which you have now effectively ended." He closed the volume and set it on the wrought-iron seat. "Your posy is wilted. Or hadn't you noticed?"

She looked uncustomarily blowsy, the brilliant blue of the sky reflected in her overbright eyes, her cheeks stained with pink.

"They are all inside playing cards."

"While you are out picking dead flowers."

She rolled her eyes. "I abhor cards."

"Then don't play." Ben reached for his book again. She stalled his hand.

"How can you be here when your guests are all within? Almost all of them. Several went to the lake for a stroll."

"Why didn't you, then, if you are so displeased with indoor activities?"

"You are wasting time." Impatience tinted her voice. "Isn't this supposed to be a business gathering? Can you not complete your business and let us all go back to town?"

"Constance, you may return to town any time you like. Nothing holds you here."

She leapt up and spun away from the bench. "I enjoy some of the company. Especially Miss Pierce. Quite a bit. She is forthright and kind and quietly clever, and I think she and I could become great friends if it weren't for that bothersome Lord Crispin constantly demanding her attention."

"Hm. Bored and jealous. An ill-favored combination."

"Don't be silly. I am not jealous." She darted him a sharp look. "Are you?"

Ben stood and pocketed his book.

"You know, Connie, you make an excellent point about the purpose of this gathering. As I still have work to do along those lines, I beg you to excuse me now." He moved along the garden path toward the house.

"I don't know why you will not talk to me," she called after him, flouncing onto the bench anew. "And now you are irritated with me."

He strode along the slate walk toward the formal garden, another of Jack's renovations in anticipation of the estate someday becoming his. Even as a young man, Ben's eldest brother had a fondness for English order.

He entered beneath the long, low trellised walkway and paused. In the shade of the vine-covered path stood a woman. The woman he wanted.

At the sound of his footfalls on gravel she turned. The contemplative smile on her lips faded.

"Good day, my lord."

"Is it?" he replied without thought, without wisdom.

"The sky is clear and the sun bright. But now I hardly know whether the day is good after all."

She remained still as he moved toward her. She had never run away, and she would not now. Of this, he was certain.

"Does it require more than fine weather to render a day acceptable to you, Miss Pierce?"

"Why do you do that—speak to me as though we are

strangers even when no one else is present?" She paused. "Except perhaps briefly at Lady Ashford's party."

He scanned her face. He had been wrong to relegate her girlhood entirely to the past. The slight sharpness of her chin was still there, the faintest dusting of freckles on the bridge of her nose, the single red-gold lock that escaped her chignon to dangle over her temple. Spellbinding details of a woman he once thought he knew but never did.

"I was under the impression that we are, in fact, strangers," he replied.

Her gaze retreated, twisting something uncertain inside Ben.

Mistaken uncertainty. She was like all the others. He must believe that.

"Strangers, you see," he added, "do not bother telling each other pertinent personal information."

"What do you mean?"

He lifted a brow.

"I did not—" She took a tight breath. "It was not my information to share at that time."

"If not yours, then whose, I wonder? Or does he like to be the showman, drawing the attention to himself as he did when he made the announcement in such grand style?"

"You were the one to call for champagne. What was that, gracious hosting or mockery?" The corners of her lips grew taut. Ben could soften them with barely a touch, he knew. Her mouth had always mesmerized him, mobile when she spoke her mind, exquisite when she smiled, and sweet as honey when he kissed her. Until it turned hot. Then it was beyond him to describe the things he imagined that mouth doing to him.

"Would it matter which?" He tried to rein in his thoughts, to no avail.

"I do not know, precisely. I have not quite decided, but you do not make it easy." Her gaze dropped to his lips.

"Thinking to trade up, were you?" he murmured, the rough quality of his voice unsurprising to him. "Crispin is only a baron, after all."

"No. *No.*" A look of horror suffused her features. "You kissed *me.*"

"You wanted me to." He stepped toward her. "You want me to again."

"No. Yes." She backed against a trellis post, a thin ray of light setting her hair aglow like the sky at sunset. "Yes, I did want you to kiss me. That does not make me a criminal. It only makes me—" She broke off, her gaze running across his chest and shoulders. "—rash."

"It makes you a liar, *shalabha.*"

"Don't call me that. I know it makes me a liar, and I am not happy with myself."

"Would it bother him to know you are kissing other men?"

"Of course it would. And I am not kissing other men, in the plural."

A hot finger of warning pressed at Ben's spine, but he took another step, closing the distance between them.

"Does he care so much for you, then?"

Her lips were parted. She pulled in audible breaths, but her shoulders were back, her chin high.

"He said he does."

"Do you return his sentiments?"

"That is none of your business."

The heat intensified, grabbing at Ben's gut and spreading. He flattened a palm on the post beside her head.

"Then you do not."

"That is not what I said. What are you doing? Don't kiss me again." Her lashes fanned, her breasts lifting upon short inhalations to press at the edge of her gown, beautiful swells of woman. He bent his head.

"Please do not," she whispered. "I may have changed my mind about wanting you to kiss me."

"Walk away."

Her gaze swam. "What?"

"You are not bound to that trellis." Her scent filled his senses, Indian roses like he hadn't known in years, rich and wild, moonlight in a garden and a girl in his arms he could not touch enough. "Walk away now."

"I want to, but m-my legs—"

"Losing your courage?" He slid his hand over her hip and she exhaled a sharp sound. His palm moved along her thigh, his blood pounding. This was insanity. She belonged to another man. She was soft, slender, her gown tangling in his fingers like it had that night, driving him mad, only to find nothing beneath but her. Pure beauty. At that moment in the tropical garden with his hands on her damp, satin skin, doubt had seeped into his pleasure. But he had wanted her too much to listen to the warning.

"No." Her whisper was barely audible.

"Then walk away."

"I cannot." Her tone pleaded. "My knees are too unsteady. I will fall. But you could be a gentleman."

"I could." He brushed his cheek against hers, her trembling beauty working through him like strong wine. "But why would I?" He touched his lips to the spot of feminine grace beneath her ear where she was softest silk.

He had not remembered poorly. She was perfect, her scent, her flavor, the intoxicating caress of her quick breaths against his skin. "You want this." He trailed the tip of his tongue along the delicate sinew of her neck. She did not resist. Instead, she tilted her head back to allow him closer, a light sigh fluttering her throat. "And, I have been here before." He covered her breast with his hand.

A hard breath escaped her. Feeling her was torture, the supple shape of her fitting to his palm like he was meant to have her body in his hands.

"And here," he murmured, and slipped his thumb be-

neath her chemise, passing it across her nipple. She
gasped and arched her shoulders as her body tightened
for him, intoxicatingly rough with velvet all around. He
stroked the peak with slow strokes, wanting to take it into
his mouth, wanting to taste her again. Sliding his hand
along her flat belly, he slipped it between her legs. "And
here."

She moaned and sank into his touch. Ben curved his
palm around the back of her neck and brought their
mouths together. She opened to him, her lips and thighs,
inviting him to touch her as he wished. He stroked into
her wet mouth and with his hand cupped her. She was soft
and supple and warm, accepting his caresses. He traced
his fingertips along her flesh, and through the fabric felt
her grow taut; passionate woman so easily aroused.

"Ben." She grasped his arms.

He massaged her, kissing her throat, tasting the heady
flavor of her skin with lingering ease. He could remain
here with his hands on her, drinking her in and knowing
he was giving her pleasure, for an eternity. But he was
hard. He'd been hard since he kissed her in the ballroom.
And he needed more. He swept his hands to her behind,
spread his fingers and dragged her against him.

It was, perhaps, a mistake. She whimpered and clutched
at his coat, meeting his kisses with hot, eager forays of
her tongue. Wiggling in his hold, she pressed her hips
against his and moaned softly.

Ben's vision blurred. He held her tight to him and she
did not pull away. Instead she pulled him in, fitting her
body to his, her thighs and belly and breasts molding to
him as she gave her mouth, and he sought there what he
wanted with his tongue, needing to be inside her. She
gripped his shoulders then his neck and she seemed to
struggle for breaths. She broke free with a gasp but he
followed her, claiming her again, and she met him with a

fervor that rocked him. Because it seemed so unrehearsed and genuine, like on that night long ago. Like no other woman he had known.

With effort he left her lips to trail kisses along her jaw, seeking sanity, but she was beautiful here too, smooth and perfect everywhere, and he did not want to stop. Heat pounded in his chest and groin but doubt clamored in his head.

"You are being unfaithful to your betrothed," he murmured.

She did not respond immediately.

"It's you," she finally whispered.

He went still, only his heartbeats battering a quick tempo. "Because of who I am."

"Of course."

Ben's chest constricted. He released her and stepped back.

"It is unfortunate for you then, madam, that I have had enough women like you to last me a lifetime."

Her eyes were pools of dazed astonishment, her lips swollen and hair loose where his fingers had twined through it. Blast it, she did not look like those other women. She looked hurt and shocked—this woman who kissed a man who was not her betrothed as though she were free to do so—and he could look no longer.

He moved toward the trellis's exit.

"Damn you, Benjirou Doreé. Damn you!" she shouted after him like a Madras dockworker.

He paused, half turned from her. "Damning me for your own transgressions? Then as well as now, I suspect."

"I waited for you."

He knew he must move or speak, but he could not.

"I did. I actually waited for you, somehow imagining you would return. I was such a fool. I should have known better. I should have realized you knew it was wrong, meeting like that in secret."

He struggled for steadiness.

"Lie to yourself," he finally said, a lifetime of control assuring the indifference of his tone. "Lie to the both of us, as you wish. Then as now, it is all the same to me." He strode from beneath the trellis.

It had to be all the same, lies and truth. For seven years he had nursed regret and anger, pretending he had forgotten, but it was there all along. It could not be undone now with a few words, especially not when her hand bore another man's ring. But the warmth of the afternoon sun beat down upon him like a curse, like the golden tropical days he had spent in her company.

He remembered like it was yesterday.

Returning to his house that morning after it all—after the night and her body in his hands, after her aunt's scorn and her own wide-eyed accusation—he told his mother and aunt his intentions. The objections of Octavia's aunt meant nothing to him. Her uncle, George Stack, a trader for the East India Company, knew well enough the influence Ben's uncle had wielded with natives and Englishmen alike, and now Ben himself. Her guardian would not deny Ben his wishes. He would have her if she would have him.

But even as he spoke the words, he knew. He'd known from the first, when intrigued became enchanted, then enchanted lost. She was not part of the plan for him, and he would suffer for the weakness he had allowed himself.

Tears streaming down her Brahmin face, his aunt begged him to reconsider. The potential for disaster was too great so soon after his uncle's death. According to her husband's last wish, she had not thrown herself upon the funeral pyre as customary, and many of his native business associates were unhappy with this breach of tradition. They claimed that the family had become too western and could not be trusted. As well, if Ben took an English wife, he would lose his allies amongst the Mughal princes.

"Remember the treaties your uncle negotiated, the peace he established between rivals," his aunt entreated. "All that would be for naught if you do such a reckless thing at this fragile time, Benjirou. You will lose everything my husband spent his life building."

Then his mother came to him, urging him to think of his family, his cousins, their husbands and children. He would put them all in danger. Would he not reconsider this decision? Ben stared at their pleading faces, and the weight of his destiny descended upon him like an avalanche. They did not demand. They asked. It was his choice to make. At twenty-two, he alone commanded the fates of hundreds. His life had never been entirely his own. Now it was not at all.

"Benji," his mother had said softly. "What of this girl?"

"What of her?"

"Do you know her?"

He knew her laughter, her smile, her fearless directness. He knew that when he was with her, he felt at once vital and at peace, and when he was not he only wanted to be with her again. He knew that the flavor of her lips and her hands on him made him mad with need.

"Do you know what is truly in her heart?" she asked. "Would it be worth all that could be lost if you someday discover her lust for status and wealth to have been powerful enough for her to put aside other concerns?"

Other concerns . . . The Indian blood that ran through his veins and shadowed his skin, that for years had made his life hell amongst the blue-blooded, pink-hued sons of Britain.

But she had a penchant for the exotic, her aunt had said. He should have guessed that. Even at that young age he had already had more than his share of women who took an extra thrill in being with him, believing themselves especially wicked. Women who wanted to feel and appear wicked even more than they wanted pleasure. He had used that to his uncle's advantage, and the pleasure he got from those encounters was great. The pain was greater still.

Something had told him Octavia was not one of those women—her clear gaze, her unselfconscious enjoyment of the simplest pleasures, the eager innocence of her touch. Still, she believed what her aunt said of him. He had seen it in her eyes, heard it in her voice. She believed the worst because she had no reason not to.

"No." The word came from his throat rough. "It would not be worth it."

He got his horse and went out to the cotton fields that day, needing the distance from his family and space to come to terms with what he must do. But the next morning, despite all, he called at her house.

"You are not welcome here." Her aunt barred the door as though he were a barbarian who would storm through if hindered.

"By you, or your niece?"

Her nostrils flared. "She does not wish to see you again."

"Then she should tell me so herself."

"She told *me* so in no uncertain terms, sirrah. She said she was mistaken in encouraging you to imagine she had any particular attachment to you." Her gaze raked him with distaste, as though he did not even merit disdain. For nearly a decade Ben had been the recipient of such appraisals from his schoolmates, even his masters at university. He thought he had become accustomed to it.

"Then good day, madam." He bowed, mounted his horse, and rode to her uncle's warehouse office.

Stack met him with a wary, anxious face that suggested he knew perfectly well Ben's position in Madras. Ben spoke to him briefly and clearly, and without awaiting a reply departed. He would not be gainsaid in this matter.

That afternoon, a half-Japanese manservant presented himself for work at the Madras home of Mr. George Stack. The Englishman employed the native without question. When the family departed for Bengal the following morning, the new manservant went with them. Thereafter, every three months, a letter arrived for Ben wherever he was. Like clockwork.

Even then he never wondered if what his mother and her aunt had said about Octavia was true. He had not wondered until she came to his house with a fiancée then kissed him anyway. Until she became a player in a game between wealthy men, at least one with something to hide.

Perhaps Crispin's possessiveness had to do with Styles. Something Ben did not wish to consider. But he knew he must. He needed to learn the truth, and he needed it to justify his suspicions. Because if it was not her fault that matters had gone as they had seven years ago, then it was his. And that simply could not be.

Chapter 11

To SINK. To force a vessel under the surface of the water.
— *Falconer's* Dictionary of the Marine

The following day Ben set off with his gentlemen guests for another interminable morning of spraying birdshot at flying targets.

"Up to my ears in contested lading bills," Lord Gosworth grumbled, pouring iron pellets down his gun barrels.

"You and I both." Lord Crispin watched the earl load his weapon. "Still, soon as I am back in town I'll be stopping in at Tattersall's for a new set of carriage horses." He turned to Ben. "Do you know of any fine animals coming up for auction, Doreé?"

Ben lifted a brow. "Only what anyone might."

Crispin grinned. "Always seeming to know news of the trade before anyone else does not qualify you as generally omniscient, is that it?"

Ben studied the man. The baron was roughly his own

age, well set up, and he never showed himself poorly amongst ladies or gentlemen. Nothing flickered in his gaze now, no hint of secrecy, guilt, or even ire.

"I am humbled by your praise, sir, if praise is intended."

"Of course it is. If I had half your blunt, Doreé, I'd be a happy man indeed."

"Got yourself a pretty little girl there." Gosworth set the gun cock to his shoulder. "Should be perfectly happy already."

Crispin blinked. Twice.

Wings pounded the air. The earl fired, the blast echoing across the field. A bird dropped.

"Fine shot, my good man!" Nathans shouted from a distance, saluting with his gun. "Fine shot."

"Fool of a novice," Lord Gosworth mumbled. "He'll get himself killed waving his piece around like a schoolboy." He moved toward his prize.

Crispin's gaze seemed to struggle for focus. He looked straight at Ben, his regard uncustomarily cloudy. Ben's breath slowed. As a boy he had been taught to recognize the moment of weakness in his adversary, and to take advantage of it.

"Lord Crispin," he said quietly, "may I assist you in any way?"

Crispin's brow pleated. "I— No." He looked toward his partner. "Nathans, you know. Not accustomed to gentlemanly sport." But his tone lacked conviction, and his brow remained beetled.

Ben nodded, and continued after the earl toward the thicket.

After dinner, he encouraged the gentlemen to enjoy a round of billiards, instructing the footman to maintain full glasses. Conversation turned to business. Lord Gosworth complained of tea smugglers undercutting the profits of honest traders, drawing round agreement. Someone mentioned recent opposition in Parliament, another the blasted missionaries poking their noses into everything. Crispin remained subdued.

Pennworthy took his leave early, preoccupied with his wife and colicky infant. The others bade good-night at intervals until finally only Nathans remained, as Ben had hoped. He invited him to the library nestled in a far corner of the house and ladled brandy into him until the man finally fell upon the divan with a mighty snort.

Ben poured himself a drink—his first of the evening—and sipped it pensively, watching the bluff fellow snore and despising himself for what he was about to do.

He set Samuel to guard outside the library door and made his way to the other end of the house. Lady Nathans reclined in the drawing room, alone, where according to Ben's servants she had been every night until late. Waiting for him or some other lucky fellow.

"Your husband, it seems," he leaned his shoulder against the doorpost, "has some trouble holding his liquor."

She barely batted a lash. "But you haven't, apparently, my lord?" She unfolded herself from the sofa with feline sinuousness, assessing him from brow to toe. Appreciation shone in her narrow emerald gaze, and clear intentionality. "How convenient for you."

He laid aside his regret. For the moment. "For both of us, my lady."

She moved toward him, a studied *provocatrice*.

"He mentioned something before he dropped off." Ben mimicked intimacy with his tone. "A matter preying upon his mind lately concerning his partner."

She halted inches away, the unmistakable scents of Parisian perfume and promiscuous female twining in his nostrils.

"Oh, no, that is impossible. My husband hasn't any

mind upon which a matter might prey." She slid the tip
of her tongue along the berry-red curve of her lower lip.

"You are harsh on him, I think." He allowed his gaze to
dip to her bosom covered by a thin gown more suited to
London than the countryside.

"But, you see, he is rather harsh on me." She tilted her
chin up, her chestnut curls glistening in the candlelight.
"In one particularly unpleasant manner."

"What manner is that?"

She traced a fingertip along the lapel of his coat to
his waist. "He has no idea how to please a woman." She
paused and her tongue darted out again to moisten her
lips. "Carnally."

Her actions and words roused nothing in him, neither
desire nor surprise. Women like Priscilla Nathans had
always spoken to him in this manner, as though he understood bestial nature better than civility.

"Pity for him," he murmured.

"Pity for me," she replied, her fingers descending.
"Until this moment." She cupped his groin.

Ben reached down and smoothly lifted her hand away.

"This moment would no doubt be better enjoyed in a
more private location, my lady."

Her bosom rose upon a breath, her jeweled eyes glistening with triumph.

"Abigail Carmichael said you could not be enticed
these days, but I told her I could move you."

Not yet. Not even the slightest bit. Dear God, he was
out of practice. But he had always been able to perform
upon demand. Like the trained animal they imagined
him to be.

"Let us see about that, shall we?" he replied.

She pressed her breast to his arm as they ascended the
stairs. The corridor stretched dark save for a lamp set at
the far end. She opened her bedchamber door. Within,

coals simmered upon the grate, a pair of candles illuminating the bed table. The maid had recently visited; they would not be disturbed. But suddenly Ben could not wait to complete his task, and the blatant appetite in the woman's eyes told him he might rush matters without forfeiting his goal.

"Tell me," he said just above her lips, "of the nature of your husband's partnership with Marcus Crispin."

Her eyes narrowed. She took his hand and placed it upon her breast. Her lashes fluttered.

"What do you wish to know, my lord?"

Relief skidded through him. She understood the game. He stroked and she smiled in victory.

"What motive would a man have to blackmail Crispin?"

She guided his hand to cool, smooth skin above her bodice, then beneath the garments.

"But one, I should say." She tilted her head back and her eyes slitted. Ben gave her what she desired, but his mind went to Octavia's soft skin beneath his hands, her wide, needy gaze, and his body stirred in response. Finally.

"What is that?" Imagining Octavia while touching another woman turned his stomach. He withdrew his hand, gripped the coquette's waist and bent to set his mouth upon her neck. By any standard Priscilla Nathans was stunning. That should suffice.

"A ship," she breathed, sliding her hand low once more. "A cargo. Always the same."

"The same?"

"As two years ago." She grasped his cock.

His jaw tightened. "Illegal goods?"

"What else? Come inside now." Her voice was thick with desire. "Now." She drew him within. The door clicked shut and she reached to lock it.

"No."

Her fingers paused upon the key. Her thin brows lifted.

He moved behind her, covered her hand on the lock, and rounded her waist.

"I must know what cargo." He stroked up to the heavy swell of her breast, barely brushing it. "Exactly."

"And you will not remain unless I tell you." She had probably been playing this game for years already. "What if I don't know?"

"Then you will learn it."

"If I do?"

He moved around her to the door, allowing a lazy look in his eyes as he scanned her body.

"Then, my dear Lady Nathans, you will have what Lady Carmichael does not."

Her eyes glittered, her breaths fast. Ben stepped into the corridor and shut the door behind him. Leaning back against the wall, he inhaled a shuddering breath and willed his stomach to cease churning.

He could not. Not tonight or any other night, and not only because of the cuckolded tosspot in his library. He could not do it because of the woman sleeping elsewhere in his house. Not even *for* her sake. It felt too much like a betrayal. A betrayal of a woman who should mean nothing to him yet for whom he designed his every action and word.

He scrubbed a hand across his face. If he had truly left behind those days of bowing to his uncle's will, he must leave them all behind. She was marrying another man and yet she kissed him with a hunger equal to his, like Priscilla Nathans giving herself to him while the man she owed her loyalty to slept nearby.

He pushed away from the door, disgust roiling through his gut, for the woman he had just left panting, for the one he wanted, and for himself most of all. For years he had avoided this tangle of regret and desire by avoiding anything that would remind him of the young man he had once been. He lived quietly on the peripheries of society, and damn it, he'd been happy. At least content.

Then Octavia Pierce stepped back into his life.

He strode down the corridor, blind, but not from the dim lighting. Blind, confused, and angry because after seven years he was a puppet once more dancing to another's tune. But there was no puppet master at whom to direct his anger now. Only himself.

Tavy clamped a palm to her mouth and willed herself not to be ill. Why hadn't she remained in the nursery for a minute longer? Then she would not have seen him. *Her.* Him kissing her. Her hand upon his—

She pressed the heels of her palms into her eyes and willed away the image, throat thick.

She must not cry. Foolish girls cried. Foolish girls who believed a man's pretty words. And now she hadn't even pretty words. He had kissed her the day before, touched her, but never said he wanted her. Not this time. This time he had done it to hurt her.

The corridor was silent. They must be in her bedchamber now. Tavy's knees shook. She had been quick enough to steal back into the darkness of the adjacent corridor as soon as she glimpsed the tableau around the corner. But now she lacked the steadiness of nerves to move.

She must. She remembered so well her own cries when he had given her pleasure. She could not bear it now if she had to hear—

She shoved away from the wall, ran along the corridor and threw herself into a shadowed alcove. Sinking against the wall, she covered her face with her palms.

"What am I doing?" she whispered, wanting Lal's arms about her neck, his soft comforting croon in her ear. For years he had been her sole confidant, holding her secrets silently. Nearly seven years, since she began keeping secrets.

"What have I already done?" She should not have allowed the betrothal to last even these few days, not with her heart full of another man. Ben touched her and she came alive. He spoke and something profound and powerful inside her swelled. He caught her staring at him and she hadn't the strength to look away.

She pressed her face into her hands. She must escape him. Perhaps she could go to the countryside with Alethea. But St. John's work kept him in town. Perhaps a seaside cottage alone? She could hire a companion. Or back to India, four thousand miles away? Uncle George still lived in Calcutta.

All foolishness. No distance would suffice. It never had.

He was not the man she wanted to want. He took what he wished without regard for others, as he had done with her years ago. But she could not live the rest of her life in that shadow. Tomorrow she must end her betrothal. Then she would apologize to Alethea for abandoning her and Jacob, and she would leave.

Chapter 12

*To UNRIG a ship is to deprive her of the standing and
running rigging, &c.*
                        —Falconer's Dictionary of the Marine

Your beau seems distracted, Octavia." Lady Fitzwarren bit into a lemon biscuit. "Have you given
him his *congé?* That would explain it."

Tavy's hand jerked upon her teacup and tea splashed
onto her skirt. "His what?" Her voice cracked.

Alethea's head came up from her sewing.

"His rejection, dear girl," the dowager said.

Tavy set her thumbnail between her teeth then withdrew her hand and bit her lip instead. She glanced at her
sister. "I intended to this morning."

"You did?" Alethea sat forward, setting her work aside.

"Aha." The dowager's gaze sharpened. "Then why
haven't you yet?"

"He has made himself scarce."

"Nonsense. He was in the breakfast room and went out
shooting with the gentlemen after that."

"Scarce from me," Tavy specified.

"Perhaps he senses your intent. But more importantly, what brought you to this point?"

Alethea's soft gaze seemed to repeat Lady Fitzwarren's query.

"I cannot really say."

"No matter. Tomorrow we will all return to town and—"

"Tomorrow?" She wanted precisely this. But her stomach tightened.

"Tomorrow." Lady Fitzwarren drew out the word, peering at Tavy above her teacup. Her gaze shifted to the parlor doorway.

"There you are." Marcus entered. "I have been looking for you all over this cavernous place."

Tavy allowed him to take her hand but she withdrew it momentarily.

"You are dressed for riding. Are you leaving?" All morning her thoughts had been muddled, head heavy from lack of sleep. What had seemed such a practical plan in the middle of the night seemed like wretched cowardice in the light of day. Walking earlier with her sister and the baby had convinced her that she could not bear even the thought of deserting Alethea now.

Marcus bowed to Alethea. "Lady Pennworthy, your husband requested a tour of the estate after Lord Styles mentioned some old Roman ruins on it. Our host suggested we go upon horseback." His eyes smiled. "It seems Sir St. John hopes you will take the opportunity for fresh air, ma'am."

Alethea stood. "I was awake most of the night with Jacob. I suppose a ride would do me good. Come, Octavia, let us go change our clothes."

Tavy hesitated. "Perhaps I will remain here with Lady Fitzwarren and continue my—my . . ."

Everyone looked at her. Alethea's gaze was gentle, Marcus's curious, and the dowager's unrepentantly skeptical.

Tavy sucked in a breath. "A ride sounds lovely." She paused at the door. "Marcus, I should like the opportunity to speak with you privately while we are out, if it is possible."

"Of course, my dear."

Alethea asked her nothing as they climbed the stairs to their adjoined bedchambers. Entering the compartment, she squeezed Tavy's fingers.

"St. John and I fell in love over a cluster of ancient ruins." She smiled, but her gaze looked oddly intent.

"What on earth are you trying to say to me, Thea? That if I glance at a few moss-covered rocks with Lord Crispin my heart will finally be lost to him?"

Alethea lifted Tavy's hand and seemed to study her fingertips one at a time. She released them. "No," she said and crossed into her chamber. "Not him." She shut the door. Tavy stared at it for a hard minute then continued to her own chamber.

She met the others in the stable. The sun sparkled, still high enough to promise hours more of bright daylight, and the sky shone crisply blue with a skimming of clouds upon the horizon.

"What a lovely day for an outing." Lady Gosworth's black curls bounced about round cheeks.

"I understand Doreé has an excellent stable," her husband commented, peering into stalls. Tavy breathed in the earthy, comforting scent of the animals, and an arm stole through hers, slender and wrapped in cherry red velvet.

"You will ride my favorite mount here." Constance drew her forward, halting before a stall door. "He is so sweet and smooth, one barely knows one is galloping until the road has quite disappeared." The long-legged bay came forward to poke its head over the partition. "Isn't he perfect?"

"Perfect," Tavy rasped. Ben walked toward them along the row of stalls. In snug-fitting breeches and dark coat, hat and crop in hand, hair slightly tousled, and gaze fixed upon her, he stole her breath. Her thoughts. Her very rationality.

"Lady Constance has chosen well for you, Miss Pierce."

"Of course I have." Constance pursed her lips. "How could I have done otherwise?"

"Pray forgive me, madam." He bowed neatly. "I forgot myself."

"Never do it again."

"I shall endeavor not to, but I may fail miserably."

"No doubt." Constance's eyes twinkled.

Tavy's palms were damp. She had never spoken with them together. Only a thorough cad could maintain such a light mien, relaxed stance, and roguish perfidy all at once.

"Now go." Constance shooed him away. "Be off to mount your other guests as you see fit. Miss Pierce is mine."

His gaze flickered to Tavy. "I will see you upon the road shortly, then." He bowed once more and moved away. She looked after him. She could not seem to prevent it.

"Constance, I am glad I have come to know you this week."

"Dear me, I hope not only for this week. You sound as though you plan to depart for some foreign clime again shortly."

Tavy smiled and shifted her gaze back to the beauty. The red of Constance's hat, gold of her hair, and high white collar surrounded her lovely face like an intricate frame.

"Will you accept Lord Doreé if he asks for your hand?" She had to know. She could not bear another moment uncertain.

"As you have accepted Lord Crispin?" Constance's blue eyes widened innocently, but perception winked within them.

"No." Tavy could not lie outright. She had never been able to do so with any success, and this woman who had shown her only friendship did not deserve it. "Not like that."

Constance tilted her head.

"Miss." A groom appeared. "Milord bade me saddle up this one for you." He gestured to the gelding.

"I will fetch my mare and find you again upon the drive," Constance said lightly and disappeared. The moment was gone. Tavy could not ask again. Nor would she. The answer, after all, should not matter to her.

Once the entire party was mounted, they started along the drive toward the road. Beyond an orchard of apple trees, the grass beneath speckled with fruit, a grassy field stretched obliquely toward the river. Lord Gosworth, St. John, Alethea, and several others headed across it. Content to remain far behind the enigmatic presence of her host, Tavy allowed her smooth-gaited gelding to lope along with the ladies' rather more staid mounts until they slowed to a walk and entered upon the path across the field.

Lord Styles dropped back to bring his splendid white stallion alongside Constance's mare, and the marquess accompanied him.

"Lord Doreé," Lady Gosworth called, "this horse is delightful and your estate is ever so charming."

"I am pleased you are enjoying yourself, my lady." He pulled his big black horse back and favored the countess with a smile that turned Tavy's heart inside out. It did not seem to matter to that faulty organ that he had kissed another man's wife the night before, or another man's betrothed the day before that, no matter how much either lady had encouraged him. And Tavy had no doubt Priscilla Nathans welcomed his embraces as much as she did.

A megrim settled into the back of her skull and commenced creeping its way forward beneath her eyebrows. Her contrary gaze flickered to him and she bent her head to hide it beneath the brim of her hat, allowing herself to stare at him astride his muscular mount. Man and beast made a beautiful pair, just as the first time she had ever seen him.

"My lord," Lady Gosworth said, "my husband does all his business in East Indian trade, and he has been there twice, yet he refuses to tell me a jot about the place. He says he does not have a knack for telling travel stories. I would be so pleased to hear something of it from you if you would oblige us."

"It has been some time since I last visited there, ma'am. You might ask Miss Pierce, however. She only recently returned to England after quite a lengthy sojourn in the East Indies." His tone did not mock or tease. He sounded perfectly sincere. Tavy's throat dried up like the Arabian desert.

"How silly of me," Lady Gosworth exclaimed. "You are such a lovely girl, I had forgotten you spent so much time there." Her look grew avid. "They say you have a pet monkey."

Tavy nodded. "I do."

"How on earth did you come by him?"

"I found him in the market. He was a runt, brought from America," trapped in a horrid cage, half-starved and bleeding from unmentionable places. At sight of him, Tavy had nearly swooned, then rang a peel over the vendor's head and took the tiny urchin home. She left him uncaged, but he had never left her.

"I daresay he is quite like my pug," Lady Gosworth cooed. "A veritable darling."

"I daresay," Ben murmured.

Tavy's gaze shot to him. Her breath failed. His eyes shone with shared amusement.

"Precisely like your pug, my lady," she managed. "I have no doubt."

"Whatever did you name him?" the countess asked.

She chewed upon her thumbnail through the tip of her glove. "He is called Lal," she mumbled.

Ben's gaze shifted. Warmth spread deep through Tavy's middle. She should not allow it, but her body would not listen to her rational will.

"Lal." Lady Gosworth said thoughtfully. "I don't believe I have ever heard that name. It must be Hindustani."

"Sanskrit, actually."

"Whatever does it mean?"

Tavy's eyes apparently had a will of their own as well. "Oh, nothing of note," she replied, captive in his gaze. "D-Dear one," she lied, as always only when he inspired it. She had named Lal because of what still simmered in her memory, her very blood, after years. And somehow knowing that the monkey spent time each day in *his* house had comforted her.

For far too long she had allowed herself to be a fool.

Desire. Lal meant *desire*.

He must know it. His mouth curved up at one side, the crease appearing in his cheek that had once devastated Tavy. It still did. Her heart beat furiously. How could he smile at her now as though he had not been cruel only two days ago? As though he had not made love to Priscilla Nathans the previous night?

But Tavy's nature tended toward happiness—or it had years ago, before she tried to deny it. And precisely that look on his handsome face had always encouraged her. Her resolutions of the previous night in her bedchamber wavered. She smiled. His black eyes sparkled in the slanting afternoon sunlight.

Lady Nathans spoke, and Tavy's nascent, unwise pleasure abruptly died.

"You have given your horse a foreign name as well, haven't you, Lord Doreé?" She gestured toward the animal.

"She is Kali," he said simply. "The black one."

"Oh dear, my lord." Lady Gosworth giggled. "It seems you were not any more imaginative than Miss Pierce in choosing names."

Tavy glanced aside. "To the Hindus, my lady, Kali is a fierce, destructive goddess. Most often she is depicted with four arms, brandishing a sword and a severed head."

Lady Gosworth paled. "Good gracious."

"Is that what you think of women, my lord?" Lady Nathans asked silkily. "That they are destructive?"

"No, indeed," he replied without inflection, but he looked at Tavy.

She did not hold her tongue as she knew she ought. "Fierce, then?"

"If only it were so," he said quietly. "It might be easier then."

She knew they were watched. She could practically feel Lady Nathans's gaze upon them, and Lady Gosworth's curiosity. But she couldn't care. For a moment, a flicker of time, Tavy was lost and she had no wish to be found. Not just yet.

In truth, never.

"Doreé," Lord Styles called over. "Let's have a go at the river road, shall we? I challenged Crispin to it earlier and he is game."

Ben pressed his mount forward toward the baron.

"Must you?" Constance said. "That road is full of holes. You will lame a horse."

"Many thanks for your concern over our health as well," Lord Styles said with a laugh, and pushed into a canter. Ben glanced back, tipped his hat, and followed apace.

Priscilla Nathans made a rumbling sound in her throat. "That man is positively mouth-watering."

"Lady Nathans," Lady Gosworth admonished.

The baroness cast her an intolerant look.

The cherubic countess tipped up her chin. "Lord

Gosworth says that now that we have been here to Fellsbourne, we must receive Lord Doreé in town."

"I know where I would like to receive him," Lady Nathans murmured.

"It is a shame he is not accepted into so many houses
in society," one of the other wives nearby commented.
"I daresay dozens of mamas would like to marry their
daughters to a rich, handsome marquess."

"But one simply cannot endure the notion of all that
Oriental blood in one's grandchildren," another said with
a shake of her head.

"My butler says his valet goes about in a turban. And I
have heard that some lords tried to block his preferment
to the title despite his parents' marriage and his enormous
fortune."

"And I have heard that dusky men have enormous—"

"*Prissy Nathans*, control your tongue," Lady Gosworth
hissed. "There is an unmarried lady present."

Tavy's eyes widened. Lady Gosworth stared back.

"Well." The diminutive countess seemed to recollect
herself. "He is not all that exotic." She swiveled to the
lady riding behind. "After all, Doreé is a French name, or
it was at one time."

The other nodded. "But I understand his given name is
not Benjamin, as one would expect."

"Oh, really?"

"Apparently it is Benji—" Her brow wrinkled. "Oh, I
knew I would not remember it. It is very foreign sound-
ing. Hindustani, no doubt."

"Benjirou is a Japanese name."

Four sets of female eyes snapped to Tavy.

"His nurse was Japanese." She filled the silence. "The
family quite adored her. Her son saved his life when they
were children, and Lady Doreé named him in her honor.
They are an extraordinary family."

"I daresay." Lady Gosworth looked as though she had swallowed a fish whole. "Quite extraordinary."

"Benjirou means 'son of two tongues.' Naturally." Neck prickling with heat, Tavy pressed her heels into her mount's sides and caught up with her friend.

Constance's cheeks were nearly as red as her habit, her eyes overbright.

"Constance, are you unwell?"

"Oh." She dashed the back of a kid glove across her cheek. "I only wish those men would not be such fools. Look there, they will break their necks careening across that field, and all for foolish pride."

"Pride?" Tavy murmured, training her gaze to the distance. Upon the gradual slope toward the river several horses galloped close. Far afield, the other riders watched. Tavy stared at Lord Styles's white stallion, neck and neck with Ben's mount. "Perhaps it is rather competition."

Constance turned toward her. "Perhaps on Walker's side. He has always wanted what the Doreé men have." She seemed to study Tavy's face. Her gaze lowered. "Except, perhaps, some things."

Someone shouted from the other group. Marcus held the lead, his mount's tail streaming as he covered the field in giant strides.

But something was wrong. The riders upon the edge of the field broke toward the racers, but far behind. St. John waved his hat in frantic gestures. Another shout. The reins of Marcus's horse flickered about its neck, his hands gripped in its flowing mane. He sat far forward on the animal, reached to its head, then jolted back, barely keeping the saddle.

Tavy's breath caught. "He has lost the reins."

"No." Constance said. "They have broken."

"It has bolted." Tavy kneed her mount and it leapt forward. But Marcus and the others were nearly a quarter mile away, a drama unfolding against the green so swiftly she could not hope to catch it in time.

"No." Constance's voice sounded hollow as she came up beside Tavy. "Ben, don't."

Tavy's heart climbed into her throat. Far ahead, the black horse flew, tearing up sod as its paces stretched across the field, closing the lengths to the maddened animal. Ben made straight for his quarry's path to head it off. It was a fool's gamble. A wall of hedges rose directly in the sights of Marcus's horse, but the beast showed no sign of slowing in order to scale it.

"He will kill himself," Constance uttered. "He will—" She snapped her crop against her horse's flank and shot off. Tavy dug her heels into the gelding's flanks. Ben's horse neared the frightened beast. Then everyone seemed to be shouting. A woman screamed. The black horse surged forward. Marcus's mount broke to the side and came to a sudden halt.

Abruptly, it ended.

Tavy could see nothing through the haze of tears. She swiped a hand across her eyes.

Dismounted, Marcus leaned into Ben's horse, brow upon his arm, Ben beside him. The errant animal stood apart, sides heaving, its lathered neck hanging and broken reins trailing to the grass. Riders surrounded them and gentlemen dismounted. Everyone seemed to speak at once. Tavy dropped from the saddle, pressed the reins into someone's hands, and moved forward as fast as her heavy skirts allowed.

Ben saw her coming and stepped away. The irony of it weakened her. Her heart raced for him alone.

She touched Marcus's arm. He gripped her hands. His face looked pale, eyes peculiar. Not relieved. Frightened.

"The leathers snapped." His voice came forth unsteadily. "He bolted."

"You kept your seat commendably. Can you walk now?"

"I daresay my horse needs it. He is usually such a good-tempered fellow." He drew her toward the animal, and she wondered if he forgot that he held her hand. He released her to take the reins, turning back toward the house in the distance. Heavy clouds spread across the far horizon, presaging rain.

Alethea and St. John approached upon horseback.

"Will you walk or shall we call a carriage?" Alethea's eyes were warm.

Marcus went on as though he did not see them. Tavy mouthed *Walk* and continued at her betrothed's side across the bumpy terrain, silent as the riders spread out, heading back, ancient ruins forgotten now. She scanned the field. Not far distant, Ben and Constance stood close, her hand in his, his head bent and their brows nearly touching. His lips moved as he spoke words Tavy could not hear. Words of comfort, no doubt.

The fear in Constance's eyes had mirrored the terror in Tavy's heart. She understood perfectly the need for such comfort, and it hurt more than she could bear.

By the time she and Marcus reached the house and he handed his horse's ruined reins to a groom, the others had gone inside.

"I will check on my horse, Marcus. I don't even know where it got to." She pasted on a smile, but he did not return it.

"Of course, my dear."

Tavy looked into his hazel eyes and saw nothing she recognized. Without another word, he moved toward the house.

She paused in the stable doorway, listening, then went forward along the long passage. A groom tugged his cap as she passed the box with Marcus's horse. Stripped of saddle and bridle now, it hung its head low.

Ben stood just inside the tack room, leaning against the wall. The chamber smelled of leather and boot blacking. The saddle from Marcus's horse sat in the center of the floor, beside it the ruined reins and bridle.

Tavy halted in the door frame. Without acknowledging her, Ben lifted his fist and his fingers uncurled. Upon his palm rested a spiny chestnut burr.

"It was beneath the saddle, wasn't it?" she said.

"Under the blanket. Far forward, so as not to be a bother until the rider leaned into a gallop."

"And the snapped reins?"

"Old leather. Mere unfortunate coincidence."

Her heart felt odd in her chest, too large and heavy and empty at once.

Finally he met her gaze. His black eyes glinted in the remnants of daylight filtering through the window.

"Change your mind already? Not trying to do away with your fiancée before the vows are spoken, are you?"

"How can you jest about this?"

"I don't know that I am entirely jesting."

A shiver crept up her back, slow and bitter. "Why did you suspect foul play?"

"Because you told me to."

A moment of silence spread between them. Slowly, Tavy's eyes widened.

"When I came to your house in town?"

He nodded. Her heart turned about so hard she felt dizzy.

"You invented this shooting party because of what I asked you?"

"Clever idea, wasn't it?" He tossed the burr into a waste bin. "Skilled beaters always rouse sluggish birds."

Emotion boiled in her tight chest, everything she had felt since she saw him at the theater, every moment of confusion and anger, elation and hurt. She stepped into the room.

"Will you still deny to me who you are?"

He straightened, pushing away from the wall.

"I am a proprietor of the East India Company with an interest in maintaining peace and accord between my fellow proprietors and Parliament," he said with perfect ease.

"Do you know," she said, barely able to move her lips, "at times I think I could hate you."

His gaze returned to hers, half lidded, the languid dip of his eyes accentuated. "I have always admired your candidness. But I am encouraged by your use of the conditional. *Could* hate is a good deal better than simply hate."

Her throat tightened. "Can a person hate someone and want him at the same time?"

He regarded her steadily. "I should say so, when it is entirely possible, after all, to hate oneself." He moved to the door, pausing beside her. "It was meant only to frighten your betrothed. He is too fine a horseman for his mount's scare to have harmed him. If the leathers had not snapped, he would have brought the animal to heel on his own."

She breathed him in, his nearness and scent and warmth. Despite everything she knew of him, nothing seemed to matter but the longing he created within her.

"Why are you doing this?"

"Let us just say habit."

"You cannot prevent yourself from rescuing people."

He laughed, but there was no mirth in the sound. "Something like that." He lifted a hand between them, toward her shoulder. She closed her eyes, willing him to touch her again, even the slightest, most innocent contact. Aching for it. But none came, and when she opened her eyes he was gone.

Chapter 13

To TOUCH. When a ship's sails first begin to shiver, either occasioned by an alteration in the ship's course, or by a change of the wind.

—Falconer's Dictionary of the Marine

The gentlemen remained at the dinner table long after the ladies retired to the drawing room. When they finally appeared, the party lacked several lords. Tavy forced her gaze away from Ben and waited for Marcus to come through the doorway. But he did not.

"Thoroughly cup-shot by now, I'll merit," Lady Fitzwarren mumbled at Tavy's side on a satin sofa. "Not the ideal moment to cry off, my dear."

"Cup-shot?"

"He took four glasses of wine with dinner, two before, and port after. Not far ahead of the others, though. Must be a celebration of the final night of their holiday in the country in such grand style. Men of business take their leisure very seriously, don't you know." She selected a sugarcoated delicacy from the tea tray, poked it between her lips, and chewed thoughtfully. "Dear girl, you must begin to notice such mundane details or you will be lost in society. But I suppose you only ever had eyes for the wonderful and fascinating."

The wonderful and fascinating.

Tavy only had eyes for the Marquess of Doreé, and she was indeed lost. She tried to ignore the pounding in her blood, but at dinner she had only heard his voice amongst the many. She had eaten little, spoken less, and in general behaved like an absolute ninny.

He had invited all these people to Fellsbourne because he trusted in what she had told him at his house in town. He withheld the truth from her, made her feel like a fool, tempted her into indiscretion, and then treated her poorly. Her cheeks were hot, hands damp, tongue numb.

"Where do you suppose he has gone?"

"He is right over there, of course." The dowager gestured across the drawing room with a scented puce kerchief, directly at Ben.

Tavy's face flamed. She darted a glance about the chamber, but the others were all busy in conversations. Several of the gentlemen were indeed bleary-eyed. Lord Gosworth laughed too loudly. Even St. John wavered upon his feet. Tavy could not look at Ben to see if he was foxed too. She had clearly lost the knack of hiding her thoughts.

She stood like a top popping, upending her tea plate. "I will go check on Jacob and Alethea, and then retire." She set the plate back upon the table with a little clatter.

Lady Fitzwarren rolled her eyes upward, brows steepled. "My dear, tomorrow we depart."

Tavy hid her quivering hands in her skirt. "Yes, yes." She could practically feel Ben in the room with the tiny hairs on her skin, like some insect's antennae. It was unendurable.

Lady Fitzwarren examined Tavy's twisted skirt.

"Are you certain you wish to go up just yet?"

"Of course." She covered a pretended yawn with her palm, nerves jittering. "Today's events overset me rather more than I like." More than anything in years. Seven years. "I am perfectly fagged. Good night, Aunt Mellicent." She swung around and nearly smacked into Lady Constance.

"Octavia, dear, are you leaving us so soon?" Her lovely azure eyes seemed to ask more. Or perhaps Tavy's imagination invented it. Her head spun with guilt and confusion and edgy, unfocused anticipation.

"I am truly done in for the evening."

Constance grasped her hand. "But won't you remain and sing while I play for you, then we can end the holiday upon a more comfortable note, quite literally."

Tavy snatched her fingers away. "No. No, thank you. You play so beautifully I would only ruin it with my indifferent voice. Good night." She dipped a curtsy and fled.

Heart speeding and legs shaking, she hardly knew where to go. Her bedchamber loomed like a prison offering nothing but an endless night of pacing.

She hurried out through the parlor's terrace doors into the garden, to the pebbled path. Peeking from behind thick, black thunderclouds, a corpulent moon lit the formal beds and walkways, illuminating every leaf, petal, stone, and flower in silvery-blue brilliance. Tavy walked quickly, and far. Exertion would work the fidgets from her blood and clear her head.

She came to the covered trellis where Ben had kissed and touched her, and her labors fell to ruin. Standing within its shadow, she felt everything again, his heat, his intimate caresses, the pain from his words.

She whirled about and rushed back to the house.

Bed. She would go to bed and tomorrow she would be

free of his impossible presence again in her life. After that she would avoid places he might be, a simple enough task given the wives' gossip. He was not universally received in society. Tavy could manage her life perfectly well without ever encountering him again.

Windows were dark as she neared the house and entered through the parlor. She paused. Marcus sat hunched over in a chair near the sputtering fire, elbows on his knees, head in his hands. The terrace door snapped shut but he did not respond until she stood before him and spoke his name.

"Octavia?" His eyes were streaked with red, his aristocratic face pale, thick hair mussed from his fingers raking through it. Even his cravat was askew and crushed.

"Marcus, are you unwell?"

He grabbed her fingers.

"Stay with me. Do not leave." His voice was clotted, and the pungent scent of wine soaked the air.

She tugged at her hand but he held it fast.

"You are foxed, aren't you?"

"Yes." He released her abruptly and dropped his face into his palms. "Yes. Mauled, yet still without an idea of how to—" His head snapped up. "You mustn't cry off. You mustn't, Octavia."

Her eyes widened. "How do you know I intend that?"

"I always expected it, especially since— But you cannot."

"I cannot?" She backed up. "You are disguised and I did not wish to have this conversation with you in such a state. Frankly I hadn't any idea you could be in such a state. But I fear you have mistaken my measure."

He stood up, swaying a bit.

"I haven't mistaken it. I know you are clear-headed, forthright, and honest. I know you haven't the ability to be cruel and that you forgive easily."

"Good heavens. You know those things about me? Are you certain?"

He clamped her hand in his again. "Certain. You mustn't cry off."

"You said that already, twice. Marcus, I am at a complete loss. If I am clear-headed then allow me to state with perfect confidence that you are not in love with me."

He seemed to try to focus his gaze. "Do you require that your husband offers you such sentiments?"

She stared. "That is beside the point, which is that I cannot fathom why you are so attached to this betrothal. I will bring a suitable portion to a marriage, of course, but you are hardly impoverished, and you are handsome and charming. At least, usually. There must be a dozen young ladies with fine dowries who would marry you in the blink of an eye. Again I ask, why me?"

"Because I know I can trust you."

"That you have reason to need to trust me so desperately is ample reason for me not to return the favor." She pulled away again and moved swiftly across the chamber, then turned. "You are involved in illegal business dealings, aren't you?"

He began to shake his head, but instead his shoulders slumped.

"Marcus, I cannot marry you. I should thank you for the honor. I should be grateful you bestowed it upon me. But at this moment I cannot."

His brow lowered. "You must marry me. You haven't a choice now."

Tavy's spine stiffened. "Are you threatening me?"

"Only with my life if you cry off."

"No, that is foolishness." But memory of the chestnut burr halted her. "It makes no sense."

He pivoted away, covering his eyes with his palm again, then turned back around to face her.

"My life is in danger, Octavia. If you do not marry me yours may be as well. Perhaps even your family."

"How on earth—"

"I don't know!" His eyes were wild. "I don't, God help me." His voice weakened. "But you must marry me and it must be soon. Three weeks by the banns, or sooner if I can find a bishop that will sell me a special license."

"You cannot threaten me into marrying you." She fisted her shaking hands. "I will not do it."

He gripped her shoulders. "You must. You will. You will make it well." His fraught gaze bored into her, losing focus quickly as though the images behind his eyes were more powerful. Abruptly he released her and strode across the chamber, knocking against a table as he went. The door slammed behind him.

Knees like aspic, Tavy sank onto a chair and pressed her frigid hands between her thighs. She tried to breathe evenly, but the thickness in her throat and prickling behind her eyes would not abate. Through the darkened window, lightning flickered distantly. A tear slid down her cheek. Thunder rumbled, low and slow.

She stood, passed her palm across her damp face, and moved to the door. Sniffing hard, she pulled the panel open.

Precisely the person she expected to see stood in the corridor. In a house full of servants, this particular footman, the one she had seen first at Ben's London house, seemed to be nearly everywhere she went. His ubiquity reminded her of Abha.

"Pardon me." She cleared her throat.

"Miss?"

"Can you tell me where I might find your master now?"

"I believe my lord is without, miss. At the lake, if I'm not wrong."

She turned back into the parlor toward the terrace doors.

"May I fetch your wrap, miss?"

"No, thank you." She was hot enough already. Foolish and heedless of her better judgment as well. But her hands felt numb and tears still wobbled in the back of her throat.

She walked quickly, straight to the lake. Thunder rolled closer now, but the moonlight-dappled path still shone bright. A modest Greek folly graced the lake's bank, its Doric columns and limestone pediment austere above the silvery expanse. Ben stood at its edge, silhouetted by the glittering water.

He turned to her.

She did not break stride. If she slowed, her legs might not carry her the distance. He remained still as she ascended the shallow steps, heavy rumbles cascading over the treetops.

"I told Marcus I suspected him of dishonest business dealings and that I could not marry him." Her voice sounded hollow between stone and water. "He said I must, that his life depended upon it and possibly mine and my family's. He was foxed, but I believe he was quite serious." She dashed fresh tears from her cheek. This was not how it was supposed to be. This was all wrong, horridly so.

Lightning flickered. Ben moved to her and surrounded the side of her face with his hand. He tilted her chin up and scanned her features.

"Did he hurt you?" His voice was harsh. His warm skin against hers and the worry in his eyes slipped through her like spring water, washing away fear.

She shook her head.

"Then why are you crying?"

"I don't know. I suppose I do not like being threatened."

He released her but did not move away. "I have learned something. It concerns a ship and cargo. Illegal, as you guessed. But I haven't enough information yet. I must pursue another avenue first."

"I don't see how you have any time for that."

His brow furrowed. The moonlight, skittish now behind clouds, cast his features into carved relief. He was beautiful, and Tavy drank in the vision of him so close, like on that other night so many full moons ago.

"Well," she took a deep breath, "it seems to me that you spend a great deal of your time—" She bit her lip. "—otherwise engaged."

He stared at her mouth. "I would certainly like to."

Her heartbeat tripped. She lifted her chin. "I saw you with Lady Nathans last night. At her bedchamber door."

His gaze swept up to hers.

"So, you see," she continued, the crackle in her voice matching a sizzle of lightning close by, "I am somewhat skeptical of your dedication to this project."

"Lady Nathans was how I learned of the ship."

Tavy's mouth dropped open. "You—You were with her to—to . . . ?"

He held her gaze steadily.

"And she—she—"

"Enjoyed a brief sojourn into the exotic."

Tavy stared. And abruptly understood. Her heart turned over.

He looked, of all things, resigned. But beneath the surface in his eyes shone a hint of something quite different. Something she had seen there for an instant seven years earlier when Aunt Imene said those horrible words. Something of despair.

"Did— Does she know why?" she finally managed.

"Not entirely."

"Still, you must be quite an actor." She schooled her tone to nonchalance, her heart racing. "But I suppose she is very beautiful. It could not have been all that difficult for you to maintain the pretense. Or perhaps it was not pretense on your part. Not all, at least, despite your avowal of a surfeit of such women."

The slightest dent appeared in his cheek, but his eyes remained shadowed.

"Thoroughly direct, as always," he murmured. "The only pretense of that sort that I have engaged in lately is in making you believe I do not want you."

The breath whooshed out of her.

"Oh. Is that all?" she uttered.

"What more do you want?"

"A great deal more, I should say." She did not halt the words that rushed to her tongue. She could not. "I want what you gave Lady Nathans."

"Miss Pierce," he said as though he hadn't heard her, "it may be to your advantage now to go back to the house and lock yourself in your chamber."

She blinked, her breaths coming fast, the breeze stirring about them chill but her body hot as lit coals.

"Lock?"

"Octavia, go now," he said huskily. "Or you are going to get a great deal more than I gave her."

She recognized that husky quality in his voice. She craved it.

"Why do you keep telling me to go?"

"Because I find I cannot bring myself to."

"I want to stay."

"I don't think you know what you want. But I know what I want, and it is not what you are looking for."

She trembled from her lips to her toes. "Will you marry Lady Constance someday?"

His brow lowered again beneath satiny hair.

"Will you?" she repeated more firmly.

"No."

"Does she wish to?"

His eyes looked so strange, intense and somewhat confused. Then, abruptly, fierce.

"No," he growled, and dragged her to him. He covered

her mouth and there was no holding back and no reason to now—not Marcus or Constance—nothing but her fear of falling.

She cast the fear aside, sinking beneath the onslaught of his lips, his hands tangling in her hair, his hard body grazing hers as she twisted his waistcoat between her fingers to hold him close. She couldn't get close enough. She wanted him inside her, his heat. Needed him. But she could not lie to him. He kissed her as though he would not cease, but he had before. The memory of his cold words beneath the trellis pricked her.

She broke free and sucked in a breath, gripping his shirt. He kissed her throat, trailing hot caresses into her hair, his tongue slipping along her sensitive earlobe.

"What if—" She gasped, his big palm hot and heavy on her behind. "What if I want it for the same reason as Lady Nathans?"

His mouth captured hers and she met him because she could not resist.

"What if that?" she insisted.

His eyes swam like pools of midnight water, his chest moving hard beneath her hands. "I don't care anymore."

She twined her arms around his neck and gave herself up to him. He kissed her and she knew only his mouth and hands and that she never wanted this glorious madness to end. Rain pattered onto the marble steps and her cheeks, thick droplets heating beneath his palm cupping her face then curving down her neck. She drank him in, tasting him, water slipping off his skin and between her lips in tendrils like nectar. Ravenous, she closed her teeth around his jaw, seeking him with every part of her. He pulled her tight to him and his kiss consumed.

The storm broke above, splitting the black sky with strident light, but they were fused. Ben slid his hand between their mouths, separating them, and Tavy took his finger with her tongue and sucked on it. He groaned, gripped her hand and pulled her down the steps.

The rain lashed at them, wind whipping sheets of water at an angle against her skirts. He urged her ahead through the darkness and she ran, her gown clinging and legs light, her body filled with feeling, thoroughly alive. Behind her, he laughed and it was like heaven opening up. She turned mid-stride, tripped, and he grabbed her up, covered her smiling mouth and made love to her with his kiss. The rain washed them in a blanket of sound, pure and clean. He drew away from her lips, holding her face in strong hands, water streaming down his brow and cheeks, and she blinked through the downpour to see him. He found her hand again, then the small of her back, and pressed her forward through the deluge.

She ran so that she could be in his arms again that much sooner.

He pulled her toward a door at the rear corner of the house and they stumbled inside. Ben pushed the door shut against the wind and without pausing drew her swiftly along the passageway, his fingers wrapped around hers. They emerged onto a corridor near the dining chamber. The house was dark and silent now, the sounds of the storm beating on windows and walls outside muffling their quick progress.

He halted abruptly, his grip tightening. Footsteps sounded ahead, then male voices. The glow of a lamp bobbed around a corner, approaching. Tavy's heart hammered.

Ben dragged her across the corridor, opened a door and pulled her within. A single candle lit the billiards room furnished with only the broad flat table, chairs against the paneled walls, a rack of cues and a sideboard topped with crystal carafes. He turned the key in the lock, dropped her hand and moved silently to the opposite door to fix the bolt.

Shivering in her drenched clothes, Tavy pressed her palms and ear to the door and listened. The footsteps came close and halted. The doorknob rattled. Her pulse leapt. She did not dare breathe.

Lord Gosworth's voice resonated through the thick wood. "Locked already. Blast Doreé's Methodist butler, shutting all the best brandy away at the stroke of midnight Saturday."

"S'pose my wife's expecting me, in any case," his companion mumbled.

"Good for you, lad." A sound like a thwack upon wool. "Good for you."

The footsteps receded. When they faded entirely, Tavy released her breath, then sucked it in abruptly. Ben's hands covered hers pressed to the door, his body coming up against hers from behind. From shoulders to thighs he trapped her, hard and purposeful. He kissed her neck and she tilted her head to allow him, shivering with the pleasure. His fingers curled around her wrist, then along her arm, trailing to her breast. He stroked her through the sodden garments and her body tightened with prickling bursts.

Her breaths came humid against the door. She pushed into his palm and his touch grew firmer, his other hand smoothing to her waist and without hesitation between her legs. She caught up her breath. He caressed her in deep long strokes, kissing her throat and neck, her damp skin on fire beneath his mouth.

Tavy sighed, a sound heavy and foreign from the depths of her that he roused so easily. She wanted him, and she wanted this to go on forever, the delirium of his hands on her just like this, the sweet heaven of his male need pressing into her behind, startling but delicious. Where he caressed her, she ached. She tilted her forehead into the door and reached back to grip his hips and settle her body tighter to his.

He pulled her around, flattened her against him and kissed her hard, harder, until she could not breathe. Until she breathed only him.

Ben swept her up in his arms, took two strides and set her down upon the edge of the billiards table. His fevered gaze covered her, and beneath it, soaked to her skin, bedraggled like a street urchin, Tavy felt absolutely beautiful. He had always made her feel beautiful. Always.

Her skirts clung, but his hands upon her ankles and warm along her calves were sure. Petticoat, gown, and shift came up and she helped him, her fingers quivering, her body anticipating she didn't know what but she wanted it. Wanted him so much. Her thighs were pale beneath his warm hands, but when she lifted her gaze, he was looking at her face. She pulled him forward and kissed him, wrapping her legs around his waist and bringing her tender flesh against the front of his trousers. He curved his hands around her behind and held her to him. He was taut and her breath fled, on fire for him but not knowing what to do.

"Ben?" she barely breathed, pressing into him. He slid his hands up to her breasts and held her and she grew faint, whispering his name as she shifted herself against his hardness, seeking relief for the delicious throbbing.

Gently he pressed her back onto the table. Then he knelt upon one knee, pulled her hips to him, and began again a dance with her body that Tavy had been dreaming about for seven endless years.

He stroked gently at first, his tongue soft against her need, and she nearly jumped from her skin. But he grasped her thighs tight and covered her with his mouth. Time ceased, the storm outside a bare echo of reality. She could not be still, thunder rocking through her with each kiss, each moment of pure pleasure in which she became more his. She arched her back, moving her hips to meet his hot caresses that drew her under. He stroked faster, harder, his tongue upon her a divine torture. Briefly, he dipped inside her, teasing. She gasped and gripped the edges of the table, frantic with the need to feel completion, frantic for more of his tongue in her until her breaths shallowed and her vision clouded.

"Please," she groaned, straining against him. "*Please*, Ben."

He took her beyond what she remembered, beyond what she dreamt, stroking her into pleasure so sublime and complete her entire body shuddered, trembling as the heat spread. She gasped for air, sobbing, no tears, only rich, sublime convulsions that embraced her from the depths of where he kissed to her lips.

She shook, breathless as he pulled her up and into his arms and buried his face in her hair. She clung to him and willed him not to release her, not to allow anything to end what she never wanted ended.

"This—" Her voice came forth raspy. "This table is lovely. But I want to be in your bed now."

Wonderfully, he laughed. His hands spread then ran down her back, holding her firmly to his chest. He did not intend to release her, it seemed. It would not end. Not just yet.

"Can you stand?" he said roughly at her ear.

"Stand? At this time I believe I could fly."

Chapter 14

BLINK. That dazzling whiteness around the horizon.
　　　　　　　—*Falconer's* Dictionary of the Marine

Given the considerable size of the house, it seemed a rather quick trip to the master suite. But— lingering between sublime gratification and shimmering anticipation as Ben drew her swiftly and silently along dark passageways—Tavy could not entirely trust her judgment.

Within his bedchamber, she hadn't time to take in the details of the fire-lit space before he set to removing her soaked garments with remarkably deft fingers. She helped, focusing on the task. She did not care what his bedchamber looked like as long as she was in it. And she would not need any of her clothing for the time being. He had kissed her passionately, intimately. She had nothing left to hide from him.

Still, when finally she stood naked before him, she quailed.

"Don't," he said, grasping her hands as she tried to cover herself. He stretched her arms wide. "You are beautiful. So beautiful."

Beyond beautiful. Exquisite. And she was his now. Finally. For the night at least.

Ben drew in a long, unsteady breath. In his thirty years, he had done nothing to deserve this moment. But he would take it without question.

"I feel like Parvati, standing here naked with my arms wide. Except of course that I only have the two." She grinned. Then her cheeks flushed, her warm eyes twinkling.

Something deep and hot inside Ben turned over.

"What is it?" He could not look away from her lips despite the expanse of creamy skin and dusky pink temptation below.

"I was wondering what the Goddess of Love would do in a situation like this with her extra pair of arms." She fluttered her fingers like fans. "And hands."

Ben's mouth went dry. He released her wrists, slipped an arm around her slender waist and threaded his fingers into her rain-darkened hair. She turned her face up to him.

"Any ideas?" she asked lightly, but her breaths were rapid, her breasts rising against his chest.

"Perhaps," he murmured over her intoxicating lips. "But at this moment I require only the two. Put them around me."

She did as she was bidden and the sweetest smile curved her lips. He swallowed roughly and lowered his mouth to trace her pure beauty with the tip of his tongue, to taste her as he had tasted her womanhood. He'd needed to know that he had not dreamt her flavor, honey and musky, beguiling Octavia, as he needed to assure himself now that her mouth shaped to his as though made for his kisses. He spread his hand upon her soft, round behind, and she made a mewling sound of pleasure in her throat. Ben felt the sound everywhere, beneath his skin, in his chest, and through his aching cock. Her lips were sweet, the curve of her throat a delicate slope of perfection, the swell of her breasts tipped with lush peaks, all of her body his now, again, after too long.

He bent and circled a dusky aureole with his tongue. She sighed and he lingered, his erection straining at the fastenings of his trousers. Her fingers slid into his hair, her other palm flat on his shoulder. With his mouth he memorized her hot, soft feminine beauty. Such beauty, precious to him. She shifted her hips and a low groan escaped her.

"Ben." Her voice was scant. She arched into him with a little whimper, but her hand pressed hard against his shoulder. "Please stop."

He lifted his head, his chest abruptly tight.

She gripped his neck and pulled his mouth to hers, lips opening, kissing him with undiluted urgency like he fully intended to kiss every inch of her. She broke the kiss, her breaths fast and sharp.

"I want—" She pushed him away and stumbled back. Pink stained her cheeks and the stiff tips of her perfect breasts. "I think it is vastly unfair," she said, clearly struggling, "that I am standing here like Parvati while you are fully clothed."

For an instant Ben felt peculiarly light-headed.

He unwound his soggy cravat. His collar went next, waistcoat, and suspenders in short order.

She lifted her hand to stay him. "May I undress you?"

He barely breathed. "I wish you would."

Slender and agile, her fingers worked at the buttons at his shirt, pushing aside damp fabric and coming to rest upon him.

She drew in a deep breath. "Oh my."

Impatience lapped at Ben, the feathery burn of her fingertips driving heat everywhere. He pulled the shirt-tail free of his trousers and dragged the garment over his head.

Octavia's eyes went wider than he had ever seen them. Ben's muscles contracted, every single one of them. With effort he managed to loosen his grip on the shirt enough to drop it. She stared at his body, her gaze traveling from his shoulders to his waist then back. He hadn't ever known such torment.

"Octavia." His voice came forth far from steady.

"I never imagined," she whispered in a tone of utter awe, and her hand darted out then halted. Tentatively, as though reaching into fire, she placed her palm upon his chest. Ben sucked in air, her touch tightening him. She must be able to feel the hard thud of his heart. She leaned into his shoulder and inhaled, her uneven breaths soft upon his skin. He willed his arms to remain at his sides.

"You know," she said in that same tone, heady and thin, "Lal used to visit your house every day. The kitchen, I think. When he came home he always smelled of delicious things, spices and what have you."

"Please tell me you have not just now compared me to a monkey."

She laughed. "You always smelled so good, from the moment we met." She laid her lips beside her hand. "Like a man," she sighed against his skin.

"I should hope so." He spoke in a vain attempt to still the trembling within him at the velvet caress of her open mouth. Her hand curved around his arm and she sighed, smoothing across his ribs to his back. Her feet followed, the tips of her breasts brushing his arm as she circled him. Only the barest intake of breath, then its release against his shoulder blade, revealed her reaction to the scars upon his back. Fully behind him, her palms slid to his waist, then she came around to face him again. Lifting her gaze to meet his, she slipped her hand over his buttock. Her eyes shone.

He forced words through his lips. "Enjoy your tour?"

"Very much."

"Care to continue your previous occupation?"

"Yes, indeed."

The release of each trouser button seemed to Ben an eternity of redoubled torture. He gripped his fists at his sides.

"You must relax." Her voice hinted at her own high tension. "The veins in your arms are distressed." Her hand paused upon his trousers, then wrapped about his wrist. She bent and ran her damp tongue along the inside of his forearm. Ben choked on a surge of desire, her mouth so close now.

He grasped her shoulders, pulled her up against his chest and kissed her hard.

"Remove my blasted trousers now, or I will."

Her head bobbed but she said, "Perhaps you should. I— My hands are somewhat unsteady."

He released a taut breath. "Octavia, I beg your pardon—"

"Oh, *don't*." She drew him down again and pressed her lips to his. "Only be quick about it." Slender fingers grazed the waistband of his trousers, shaking slightly as they paused above the bulge of his erection. "I am very curious."

Curious, quivering, but eager and as impatient as he. She stared fixedly as he unfastened the remaining buttons, her color high. Ben hadn't any idea what to make of her. But he had never known a woman like Octavia Pierce in any other way. Why should she be like other women in this?

With his clothing gone finally, he had only one design:

to be between her legs and deep inside her. But she seemed to have another idea. Her slender hand stole to his waist then behind once more, her gaze traveling over him thoroughly.

"Good heavens, Ben, you are a beautiful man," she said breathily, but he could not respond. She stood so close he could feel the heat of her body upon his arousal. Her hand hovered. "May I?"

He could only nod jerkily.

She touched him, the lightest caress, and he was undone. He grasped her arms. "Octavia."

"Did she do this?" Her voice trembled.

Dear God.

"Who?" He could barely speak for the pain of pleasure.

"Her. Priscilla Nath—"

"I was with her all of five minutes."

Her gaze flickered up to his, uncertain. "You work fast."

"I did not make love to her. But unless you would prefer to discuss other matters first, I am going to make love to you. Right now."

She nodded quickly, her eyes wide. "Yes. Yes. Now would be good."

He swept her up and deposited her on his bed. Against the white linens, her skin was pale, her hair dark. Ben gazed upon her lovely arms, her long, shapely legs, the thatch of soft russet hair at their crux, her full breasts perfectly peaked, her eyes heated pools of anticipation. He had never seen anything so beautiful, never wanted anything so much.

He parted her knees and moved between them, bringing their bodies together. She gasped then moaned as he slid against her. Lightly he caressed her with his shaft, stirring her heat and driving himself mad. To touch her like this, to have her— It seemed as though he had waited all his life for this moment. Feeling her beneath him now, her silken thighs flanking his hips, her breathing heavy, might as well have been a thousand years of missed opportunity. Wasted time.

Time he must win back now.

He trailed his tongue along the slope of her neck and she gripped his shoulders, holding him, keeping him near, and Ben ached in the deepest part of him.

He whispered her name, touched her, and her body danced for him, supple woman asking for caresses he had longed to give her for years, reaching for more. Kissing her, he drowned in her flavor, her high, needy sighs, the captivating softness of her breasts and belly, and he grew hard beyond endurance. He could not touch her enough. Needing to feel her arousal in his mouth, he took her taut nipple with his tongue and she arched against him, thrusting her breasts upward, whimpering her hunger.

"Oh, Ben. *Yes*."

She squirmed beneath him, seeking satisfaction. He reached between their bodies and swept his fingers along her womanhood. She shifted against his palm, perfect, ready. He parted her, holding steady against her entrance though he shook with the effort of restraint. Her lashes fluttered, a sound of acquiescence stealing from her throat. In feral relief Ben pressed forward, she gripped him, wet, tight—*dear Kama*, so tight—and he entered a paradise he vowed never to leave.

Chapter 15

OCEAN. That vast collection of salt and navigable waters in which the two continents are enclosed like islands.
—*Falconer's* Dictionary of the Marine

Tavy clung to Ben's shoulders. Her whole body tingled, encompassed in his warm embrace, swimming in murky near-pleasure as she focused on the spot where he pressed inside her. It hurt a bit, but then she shifted her hips some and it started to feel good too, strange and stretched, and astounding and wonderful.

Then—abruptly—wrenchingly painful.

Ben's palm trapped her scream.

"Dear God," he uttered. His body went still as stone. But Tavy's was softening already, heat gathering around his presence within her, the delicious throbbing beginning again, but even deeper and hotter than before. She dropped her head and shoulders back, and his hand fell away from her mouth. He felt good inside her. Not strange any longer. Instead, perfect.

Then there seemed to be much less of him there.

"No! Don't go. Stop!" she exclaimed, locking her legs about his hips and gripping his shoulders.

The sinews in his neck stood out, his arms and chest muscles taut as he held himself immobile atop her.

"I could not stop now if I wished it," he replied quite convincingly, his jaw gorgeously tight and eyes entirely black.

"Then why aren't you moving?"

"Because, Octavia," his deep voice sounded strained, "your exquisite thighs have me in a death grip."

"Oh." She loosened her knees. *"Ohhh."* He sank into her, full and deep, and she moaned and at the same moment a sound of pleasure so profound came from his chest that she knew he told the truth about not being able to stop. He drew out almost completely then stroked in again, slowly. Then he did it again. And again, until she sighed with the sheer brilliance of it, understanding the rhythm and creating it with him.

Then, quite suddenly, there was no understanding. No thought. No intentionality. Only pleasure and intense need and a coiling ache so profound it seized her whole, lifting her and wrapping around her, them, so that they seemed one. She gripped him with her hands and, deliciously, inside. He took her hard and deep, deeper each time, caressing so far within it tickled and hurt and filled her up until she was thoroughly open, drowning in his driving thrusts. With her voice she begged him for more, words without shape, their skin sliding smooth and slick as they made passion. She sought him and he gave her his powerful body, kissing her mouth, caressing her breasts, blinding her with the frenzy of their intertwined need.

Desperate, she rose to him and he grabbed her hips, trapping her against the mattress, uttering urgently against her neck an oath in Hindi, then astoundingly tender, *"Madhuraa."*

Sweet one.

She came in a chaos of completion, repeating his name. It was an ecstasy so brilliant, so thorough and continuous, that as she took his release deep within her, she wept.

But only for a very brief moment.

Dragging air into her lungs, Tavy let her hands and knees slide away from him and turned her cheek to the mattress. She was ruined. A maiden no longer. Unfit to wed now. Ravished by the very man who had broken her heart.

Her lips split into an enormous smile. Never in her life of chasing adventures had she enjoyed one so utterly superb.

The co-architect of her ruination moved from between her legs to sit upon the edge of the bed. He rubbed a hand across his face, his head bent. His skin glistened with moisture, his tawny strength magnificent in the firelight. Tavy stared, and her breathing puttered.

"Why didn't you tell me?" he said quietly.

She shifted onto her side and pulled her knees up to her chest, languorous warmth curling through her.

"I didn't think you would do it if you knew. And you did not ask."

He turned to face her, his brow serious. His gaze scanned her whole body, lingering on her lips then rising to her eyes.

"Thank you for giving me that honor."

It was not what she expected him to say. And she could not respond with the truth, that she might very well have gone to the grave a virgin if he had not taken the honor.

For a long moment he continued watching her. Then he touched her ankle, smoothed his palm along her leg and leaned in to kiss her. His mouth was gentle, not like before but like the very first time he had ever kissed her. She wove her fingers through the short locks at the back of his neck. But she needed to touch him more, always, and she slipped her hand along his shoulders and back, and discovered again the scars.

She sat up and curled around him, her fingers going ahead. He remained still, allowing her exploration. Her breath stole out in rivulets. Across the center of his back, three rough, umber welts stretched, each a foot in length, two crisscrossing, the third dipping lower. They looked like the whip-marks one sometimes saw upon slaves in India. But Benjirou Doreé had always been a prince in that land.

"How did you come by these?"

He drew away and lay back onto the mattress.

"English schoolboys can occasionally be astounding brutes," he murmured.

Tavy's nostrils flared, her heartbeat suddenly fast again.

"What did your brothers do to the boys, to punish them?"

"Nothing."

Her eyes widened. *"Nothing?"*

"They never knew."

"You never—" She needn't finish. Clearly he had never told them.

She stared at him—at the handsome man who must have been a beautiful boy, at his graceful hands that played so lyrically surmounted by the fearsome fanged tiger, at his sensitive mouth and fathomless eyes like the deepest secrets of the continent where he had been born—and awe and sorrow crept into her heart so steadily she ceased breathing to allow them room.

She laid her cheek upon his chest, her hand on his waist. Soon, it seemed, he slept. But Tavy, her heart stalled, remained awake for a long time, feeling his breathing and the even rhythm of his heart and suspecting that she had just made the greatest mistake of her life.

* * *

She awoke alone in his big bed, on her side, linens tucked about her. Embers in the hearth touched the darkness with the faintest glow. Her gown and underclothes hung on the back of a chair.

She drew her hands from beneath her cheek and pushed up to sit, scanning the chamber. But he was behind her. She could feel his gaze upon her like a touch.

She looked over her shoulder. He sat by the curtained window, garbed in a dark dressing gown. Locks of satiny black hair fell over his eyes, the hollows of his cheeks defined by the dim light. As always, he was watching her.

"Why aren't you sleeping?" Her throat was dry and her voice sounded scratchy.

"I am engaged in a much more satisfying activity."

"Watching me sleep? That is ridiculous."

His delicious lips curved into a half smile. He stood and the dressing gown parted, the silk sliding over his glorious physique as he moved to the bed. Tavy drew in a quick, silent breath as he sat down beside her. The bedsheet had fallen to her waist. She knew it made her a goosecap at this point, but she felt exposed. He took her hand and stroked her palm with the pad of his thumb, and her nerves dissolved, replaced by another sensation entirely.

"It is nearly dawn." His voice remained quiet, enveloped in the dark.

"I do not see a clock."

"I do not require a clock."

"Why? Are you one of Lord Byron's vampyres?"

"Merchant ships depart early. I am often at the docks by this hour." His eyes glinted. "But if you prefer creatures of the night, I could look into it."

"Thank you, but that will not be necessary." She smiled, tingles besetting her belly, then—as his warm gaze dipped to her mouth—somewhat lower.

"The servants will soon be abroad." He did not move, nor did his gaze shift.

"Then I should dress and go." She threaded her fingers through his, bringing them palm-to-palm.

"Yes." His voice sounded quite low.

"But perhaps," she whispered, "you could kiss me first."

"I think that would be unwise. There isn't time."

"For a kiss?"

He lifted his gaze to hers. "Octavia, you are naked in my bed. I cannot simply kiss you and leave it at that."

For a moment she struggled for air.

She threw her arms about his neck, pressed her open mouth to his and let him bear her back into the mattress. Their mouths locked, Ben pushed the linens away and dragged her hips beneath his while she tore the dressing gown from his shoulders. Arms free, he banded them about her and his tongue swept between her lips. She twined her legs about him and reached between them, a wanton since the moment he first kissed her, for his touch alone. Her fingers wrapped around his spectacularly firm and silky man part.

He groaned, broke the kiss, and grabbed her hand.

"No." His voice was husky. "We cannot do this."

She shifted her needy flesh against his knuckles. "We can be quick. In fact I rather think I cannot be otherwise." The hot tension was already coiling inside her from his hand brushing the place where she was wonderfully sore.

His perfect lips hovered over hers for an instant. Then he released her and pulled away, off the bed. He drew on his dressing gown, tying the sash about his waist.

"Discovery is not the only consequence of concern here." He moved to the chair by the fireplace and withdrew her garments.

Tavy stared, uncovered and cold, her stomach sinking and pleasure dying to ash.

"What other consequence could there be?" She managed a credibly even tone.

"Come now." He laid her clothing upon the bed beside her. "Do not tell me that Imene Stack failed to educate her niece in all matters pertaining to adulthood."

Tavy fought to clear the hard lump from her throat. He sounded unlike him. She'd heard desire, laughter, anger, and scorn in his rich voice before. But never bitterness.

"Forgive me for stating the obvious," she did not touch her clothes, "but isn't it a bit late to be anxious on that particular account?"

His eyes were unreadable. "It is never too late for caution, and I should have taken greater care last night."

He could not have spoken words more surely calculated to devastate her. And she had been a much greater fool than she even anticipated. Tavy pressed down on the pain, years of practice at damping her unruly emotions coming to her aid. She reached for her shift.

"I will need assistance with my corset and gown, if you will." He had made short work of removing them the night before. She had no doubt he possessed sufficient experience with the opposite.

She tugged the chemise over her head and stood to don the rest. Settling the stays about her ribs, she turned her back to him. His fingers brushed hers as he laced. Before she could reach for the gown, he took it up and helped her into it as handily as any lady's maid, except that his height made it a great deal easier. Tavy's stomach hurt. Everything inside her hurt.

His hands stilled upon the fasteners, moved to her shoulders, and he drew her back against his chest. He inhaled deeply and she steeled herself against the swell of warmth within her. It was not real.

Gently he gathered her hair and pulled it aside, his breath tender upon her neck.

"Why did you ask me about Constance last night?"

"She is my friend. I did not wish to betray her."

He was silent a moment. "And yet—before—you had no qualms about your fiancée."

Tavy held her breath. He needn't know about the sham quality of the betrothal. It would only shame Marcus, and it would make no difference to Ben. He wanted her, but he would not have her for more than temporary enjoyment. Just as before. He had now made that perfectly clear once more.

He stepped back, leaving her cold again.

"Tell Crispin that you will marry him."

She pivoted around. *"What?"*

"Tell him your acceptance is conditional upon him divulging to you the blackmailer's name and purpose. Then, when he gives you that information, tell me."

She choked down her rising gorge. This could not be happening.

"You are who I thought. You are your uncle's heir."

He did not respond, his sober regard never wavering. Gone entirely was the tender man who had watched her while she slept.

"You would do anything to accomplish what you must, wouldn't you?"

For a moment he did not reply. Then he nodded. They stared at each other, Tavy's heartbeat labored.

Ben moved close again, lifted her chin with his fingertips and placed a soft, perfect kiss upon her lips. Then another, this time lingering. Perhaps a last kiss, but when he drew away his eyes were warm, gentle once more. Another of his pretenses, or truth, she had no idea.

"Now, go." His voice was low. "Go make amends with your betrothed."

Tavy wanted nothing else than to throw herself into his arms and beg him to never release her.

She straightened her shoulders, slid her feet into her slippers, and went to the door. No candle lit the corridor, but she did not need light to guide her way. She was lost, and no material illumination could help her now.

Ben stared at the closed door, numb to his marrow. He had done what he needed, as he always did, and he hated his dead uncle, his family, and every person across the seas that depended upon him, more than ever before.

But he had spoken the truth. He should have been more careful of her—of her virtue, then of the future. He'd told himself that a woman who welcomed a man's touch while betrothed to another could not be a maiden. A neat, believable excuse to take what he wanted, what he had wanted since nearly the first time he set eyes upon her. Then he had lost himself in her beyond the point of safety, easily, willingly. *Intentionally.* Because part of him wanted to bind her to him permanently, to make her his regardless of the consequences.

If she found herself increasing, he would wed her. But then he would never know the truth.

Distress had flashed in her lovely eyes when he had spoken of caution. She tried to mask it, but in this she was a poor dissembler. But perhaps that moment simply marked a quick shift in her approach to securing a titled husband. A rapid recalculation in the face of his resistance. Her honesty in passion told him he was wrong to believe it. But a woman who sought to dissemble was not after all entirely honest. When he instructed her regarding Crispin, her eyes had shone with astonishment, but also guilt. She had not told him everything about her arrangement with the baron.

Secrets. Dissembling. At one time he had thought Octavia Pierce incapable of such things. But that time had been brief, little longer than the night that had just passed in which she had given herself to him as to no other man. The blood on the bedclothes proved it just as his experience of her body did.

But before she had, she made certain he hadn't already chosen a bride.

He knew not what to believe, only that he wanted her more than air, more than the life he had been given. Now, with the sweetness of her hunger still upon his skin, he could no longer do what he should have done the moment she stepped out of his house in London: forget she ever existed. Whether by design or simple nature, she had ensnared him, and he was bound. It only remained for fate to play out his hand.

Ben had no delusions of winning. The riches of the world were already his, wealth and influence beyond what many kings enjoyed. That he only wanted one thing, the simplest and yet most impossible to assure for a man like him, was his own eternal folly.

Chapter 16

*BREAKERS. A name given by sailors to those billows
that break violently over rocks lying under the surface
of the sea.*

—*Falconer's* Dictionary of the Marine

At Sunday service in the chapel, Marcus appeared his usual self, all smiles and charm for the ladies and pleasantries for the gentlemen. But when the carriages arrived on the drive preparing to depart Fellsbourne, he came to Tavy with a sober brow. His eyes showed tiny rivulets of red and his skin seemed pale.

Tavy couldn't throw stones. It had taken every ounce of skill at her *toilette* to make herself appear little better than sepulchral. Two hours of sleep and turbulent emotions haggarded a woman horridly.

"I have business to attend to as soon as I return to town, but I will call upon you after that." Marcus took her arm as though he had the right to.

Tavy nearly snatched it away. But Ben stood nearby with

the Gosworths and her family. She did not owe Ben her assistance, and she didn't give a fig about Marcus's troubles any longer. But his threat against her loved ones hung over her.

Tavy told herself this was the only reason she would play this farce. But she knew the truth. She could no more deny Ben than she could fly to the moon on a magic carpet. He had asked for her aid, and she would give it to him.

"This evening, then?" Marcus looked hopeful.

"Tomorrow."

"I will take you driving." He patted her arm.

Standing between Ben and St. John, Alethea beckoned to her with a glance. Tavy must say an appropriately grateful goodbye to their host, just as all the Marquess of Doreé's other guests who had not spent the night making love to him.

Even as her throat went dry, hysteria wobbled in it. She went forward and made her curtsy.

"Thank you for your gracious welcome, my lord." Every exhausted mote of her blood was alive to him.

He bowed. "The pleasure was all mine, ma'am."

"You have a lovely home." From Greek folly to billiards room to master bedchamber.

"I am glad you approve of it."

"Octavia, you will ride with me." Lady Fitzwarren bustled between them. "Doreé, you are your father's son in the excellence of your hospitality. Your cook's curried sole is one of the finest I have tasted."

"I will convey to her your compliments, my lady."

"Oh, wait." Constance hurried over and grasped Tavy's hands. "I will call upon you in town the moment I return. We will make a plan to go shopping, or perhaps to the museum." Her grip was tight, her gaze peculiarly brittle.

"That would be lovely." Tavy returned the pressure of her fingers. Perhaps Ben did not know this woman's heart. Perhaps he was using Constance just as he was using her, with her full and enthusiastic consent.

"Come along, Octavia." Lady Fitzwarren drew her away.

She climbed into the dowager's carriage. Settling back upon the squabs, she lifted her fingers in parting to Alethea on the drive, and turned her gaze to the other window. The carriage pulled onto the straightaway flanked by masterful chestnuts, their fruit spilled upon the ground like loamy tears. She stared at the graceful slope of lawn toward the little Greek temple at the lake, trees nestled around its far flank. Everything sparkled after the night's heavy rain, clean washed and fresh with fall's golds, crimsons, and ochres on branches and carpeting the ground.

"That was a close run thing," the dowager exclaimed upon a relieved whorl of breath. "Thank heavens."

"Thank heavens?" Tavy's body drooped with weariness and something more.

"Thank heavens the two of you did not fall into each other's arms back there."

Tavy shrugged. "Lady Constance and I have become comfortable friends very swiftly, it is true. But sometimes a friendship will begin in such a manner."

"I was not speaking of Constance."

The landscape dropped away toward the road and Fellsbourne disappeared beyond an autumn-dappled copse. Slowly Tavy turned from the view to the dowager.

"Are you still betrothed to Crispin, child?"

"Yes." Marcus had showed no sign of accepting her refusal after all. And now she must renew her engagement in any case.

"I see."

"Aunt Mellicent, I should like it if you would host a party in town. Not a particularly large gathering, but sizable enough so that everybody is not in everybody else's pockets all evening long."

The dowager folded her hands atop her elegantly bulging midriff. "Should you like that?"

"Yes, quite a lot. I adore parties. And I should like it to be very soon, certainly no more than a fortnight from now but preferably before that."

"Is that so? And what else should you like, my dear?"

"For you to invite the Marquess of Doreé."

The dowager's lips pursed. "Anyone else?"

"No. Well, the usual sorts of people, that is. But no one else in particular." She could not very well make a habit of visiting his house in town alone, but she must have opportunity to share with him the information she learned when she accepted Marcus. Ben would not call upon her, of course. This was not courtship.

She folded her cold hands together as the dowager's gaze bore into her.

"Octavia Pierce," she finally said, "I will not throw a party so that you can engage in a clandestine tryst. It goes against my better judgment if not my natural inclination."

Tavy shook her head. "That is not my intention, Aunt Mellicent. I assure you."

Lady Fitzwarren studied her. "No. I can see from your face it is not." She smacked her hands upon her knees. "Well then, you shall have your party."

"How can you see anything from my face?"

"You are all demureness, to be sure, dear. You've nothing to fear from the gossips." She paused. "As long as they don't see the two of you together."

Marcus appeared the next morning, dapper in a gray coat and Hessians, looking fully restored to spirits. He handed her up into his phaeton.

"What an impressive carriage," Tavy commented.

"Only the best for you." He snapped the ribbons. "I took this pair off Lord Michaels yesterday. Fellow's down on his luck, you know. Doreé recommended them. He is a fine judge of horseflesh."

Tavy mumbled acknowledgment. It seemed a poor omen that Marcus would mention Ben so immediately. Or at all.

He guided them into the park. "I am glad to have the opportunity to speak privately."

"I expect you wish to apologize for your behavior two nights ago."

"Forgive me, Octavia. It was unpardonable—"

"You needn't elaborate. Gentlemen will drink spirits and say unwise things. One cannot wonder at it." One could also not help but wonder what Ben would say to her under the influence of strong drink.

"You are a treasure, Octavia." His smile seemed genuine.

"Thank you. You are overly fond of considering me in that light, I think." Was guilt to be her constant companion now?

He slowed the vehicle. "I cannot fathom how fortunate I am to know you."

"You are doing it a bit too brown, Marcus."

"No." He drew the horses in and turned to her as fully as the narrow seat would allow. "I am sincere in my praise, and in my affections. Octavia, you make me hope."

A sizzle of nerves worked its way through her middle. His brow was drawn.

"Hope?"

"I am within the grip of something I should not be. I am hoping that with you at my side I will be able to master it." He took a hard breath.

"Marcus, are you quite all right?"

"Not at all, I'm afraid."

"Has this anything to do with the blackmailer?"

He met her gaze squarely as though he would speak, then his fell away.

"Please tell me." She dove in. "You see, I was foolish the other night. Unthinking, really. I have been reconsidering your offer and I find that my feelings on the matter have altered."

His face lightened, the hope he'd spoken of clear upon it now.

"But on a condition," she added quickly. "I must know the particulars of this dangerous business in which you are engaged. If I am to be your wife, I need to understand why you, I, and possibly my family could be in danger."

He gripped her fingers, but not too tightly. Today he was sober, and although his hazel eyes now showed distress, he was in possession of himself again.

"I wish I could tell you."

"Yes, you have said that before. But if you expect me to be your wife you simply must. What is the blackmailer's name and what does he want of you?"

"To be forever bound to a preoccupation that I cannot like," he said with unusual vehemence.

"A preoccupation?"

"An obsession." His voice was low. "An influence from which I wish to free myself."

Tavy's stomach churned.

"Marcus, you haven't— What I mean to say is, you are not—"

"Am not master of my own mind in this?" He looked away to the treetops. "Yes."

"We are not speaking of opium, are we?" Plenty of English traders and soldiers in India practiced eastern pastimes, but she had never seen the signs of it upon him.

"I only wish we were."

"Then—" How could she ask it? But abruptly it made a great deal of sense. "Is it a-another man?"

His head came around sharply, eyes wide. *"Octavia."*

"Well, you are very mysterious and seem so thoroughly

distressed about this. And despite our long acquaintance you have kissed me only that once. What else am I to imagine?"

"You oughtn't to know about such things." But he did not sound particularly offended, and his eyes held a crisp appreciation she had not expected.

"But I do know. So, is that it?"

He put both hands around hers. "No, it is not. And I would like to kiss you again."

But he had not. Yet Ben had taken nearly every opportunity to do so.

"Tell me about the blackmailer and I will allow you to kiss me all you wish."

He said nothing for a minute. "You are accepting me upon that condition only?"

"Yes."

"Octavia, you must not seek out this man. He is a dangerous person."

"I do not intend to," she said with complete honesty. The lie came just as smoothly. "I only need to be assured that you are fully honest with me." Her lungs ached.

"His name is Sheeble."

The last mote of respect Tavy possessed for the baron of Crispin disintegrated. He should not have told her, no matter what she begged and no matter what conditions she placed upon it. Given her nature and persistence, he should know that she would not rest content with only a name. A man who cared for a woman would not put her in this danger. He had no true concern for her, only for acquiring what he wished.

Just like Ben.

"What is his business with you?"

"He wishes me to sign a bill of lading so that a ship can leave England without a full inspection."

"A ship with illegal cargo aboard?"

His Adam's apple jerked. "Yes."

"What sort of cargo?"

He shook his head.

She could not bear his touch any longer, even through her gloves. She drew her hands away and placed them in her lap.

"I accept your proposal of marriage, Marcus."

He took a breath, his shoulders rising then falling abruptly. "You will not be sorry. And I will be grateful to you for the remainder of our lives."

"I do not need gratitude. Only honesty."

"You have enough of the latter for the both of us, I daresay," he said with an uncomfortable chuckle. He took the ribbons in two hands again and clicked his tongue to set the horses in motion.

Oh, yes, she had loads of honesty, thoroughly tarnished now because of her weakness for a man who would never have her. Perhaps she had tired of seeking out adventures. This one was proving to be not so thrilling after all.

In front of her sister's house, Marcus handed her out of the phaeton and kissed the back of her hand. Tavy tried not to squirm. She declined his escort to the door.

Lal met her with a relieved chirp and leaped onto her shoulder. His tail curled around her arm in a caressing gesture, soft clucking sounds in the back of his mouth. Tavy removed her bonnet and placed her reticule on the table.

Abha stood in the corridor.

"He was not content in your absence." His comfortingly foreign rumble met her ears like warmth. Tavy missed hearing the music of Indian voices all about her. She missed the bazaar and the port overflowing with ships, and the heat, and her veranda. "You went away too soon after your return from the country. He did not understand."

Tavy studied her longtime companion.

"Abha, how are you getting along in London?"

"Well, *memsahib*."

"Really?"

He shrugged a heavy shoulder. "One city is like another." He wore the same loose cotton trousers, shirt, and tunic that he always wore in Madras. His beard and the small hat topping his hairless head were as neat as ever. He looked perfectly at ease.

"Not really," she said. "But you do not mind it here?"

"You do, *memsahib*."

Tavy chewed on her thumbnail, then plucked it out of her mouth and went to the foyer table. Lady Constance's calling card rested upon the silver tray.

"I enjoyed being in the country again," she murmured for Abha's benefit. Constance was back in town already, and calling upon her. If Lady Fitzwarren had seen something between Ben and her at Fellsbourne, then Constance must have as well. But if Constance cared for him in that way, she would not pursue their friendship in this manner.

"Abha, what do you know of the Marquess of Doreé?" She replaced the card on the salver. "I suspect you must know at least a bit more than everyone else in Madras, if not a great deal more. You always know everything."

"Not everything. I do not know why you ask me about him."

"Clever. Obviously I have just spent a week at his home, which—I note the extraordinary—shows absolutely no hint of India whatsoever." Not even his bedchamber. "Extraordinary, you know, when every Englishman I have met in London who has spent two days upon the subcontinent practically wears turbans and smokes the hookah. Isn't that a curiosity?"

Abha shrugged again. His usual taciturnity did not sit well with her now.

"You have not changed your clothes to look like one of the other servants here."

"I am not an English lord."

"He is a great deal more than an English lord, and you know it." Her cheeks were wretchedly warm. "And there is a very good chance that you and I are amongst the few residents of London who understand to what extent."

"Do you understand?" His deep-set eyes questioned. It was unusual for him, this man of few words and fewer queries.

"I spent the better part of seven years listening at knot-holes and cracks in the walls of bazaar stalls to find out. I should think I do."

His mouth curved into a grin.

Tavy chuckled. "You and Lady Fitzwarren are quite a lot alike." Her mood sobered. "Now I must write a note. I need you to deliver it to the marquess's house here in town. Please make certain that he receives it directly from your hands. If he has not yet returned to town, bring back the note and we will try again tomorrow."

His brow drew down, but he said, "Yes, *memsahib*. I will make certain."

"How do you like the new furnishings, Dorée? More lush than all those years ago when you came here as often as I." Styles waved his whiskey glass in a gesture that took in the entire dimly lit drawing room of Hauterive's. "Must be the elevated clientele these days. See over there the Duke of Avery, hoping to entice Abigail Carmichael into his bed. But she still has her cap set for you."

Ben had no interest in these sadly debauched members of the *beau monde*. Not in their *petites affaires du coeur*, in any case. Styles surely kept the conversation light for his benefit.

But Ben had had enough of this brief trek into his sordid past. He hadn't heard anything useful in hours of card play and drinking while Styles rambled on about the petty misbehaviors of his set. Nothing concerning Nathans or Crispin, and certainly nothing about that other matter he had kept in a corner of his mind over the past fortnight, the mystery Creighton had shown him.

"You've got that look like you are bored to death and past ready to leave," Styles said.

"Have I? How bothersomely transparent I must be to you."

"No, Ben, you are not your brother in that. I could always tell what Jack was thinking. Never made a fellow wonder." Styles's bright blue gaze met him fitfully. "But you don't like a man to know what you have going on. Do you?"

"You have had far too much to drink, Walker."

"Then tell me one of your secrets, Ben. Prove me wrong."

"If I must engage in such childishness to soothe your spirits. Perhaps you will give me your thoughts upon the matter."

Styles settled back in his chair.

Ben swiveled his brandy. "I purchased a ship recently from a Frenchman. A fine vessel, but with the most intriguing mystery attached."

"What sort of mystery?"

"The sort stuffed into a corner of the planking."

"Illegal goods?"

"Hair. A great deal of it."

Styles's brows rose. "Peculiar, rather than intriguing. Did you instruct your man to take it to market? Human hair takes an excellent price, of course."

"And those are the thoughts I sought from you? You have indeed drunk too much. Which suggests it is far past time I am going." Ben stood.

A heavy hand clamped onto his shoulder.

"Doreé, is that you?" The gentleman came around him,

releasing his grip only to take Ben's hand in a snug shake. "Is you, I'll be. They said you used to carry membership here. Never thought I'd see it. Glad to come across you like this, though." The man's eyes were glassy, but then, Fletcher James's eyes were nearly always glassy with some substance, at least in the past four years.

"Sir." Ben bowed. "I am just now on my way out. If you will excuse me."

"I'll go with. Got something to say to you, don't you know."

The burly footman gave them their effects and they stepped into the rustling, whistling midnight of London's hells. Music and light spilled from the gin house five doors down, the same to which Ben had fled the night after Lady Ashford's party. It seemed much more than a fortnight ago, before he had held Octavia in his arms again.

"Need a ride?" James gestured toward a hackney coach.

"Thank you, no. My horse is stabled across the street."

"But wait on there. Told you I'd something to say to you specifically." The man swayed, but his florid face looked earnest.

"Say on, sir."

He blinked hard. "S'not so easy now I've come to it, don't you know. Makes a fellow downright uncomfortable t'admit he was wrong."

"Ah. Of course."

"Got the notion of it, don't you?" His eyes narrowed. "Knew it was you that helped me out of the bind with that sharp three years ago." He shook his head. "Should've thanked you then, but didn't like the idea of it. Now I've got to."

"That sharp held your vowel on a cargo that rightfully belonged to me," Ben said mildly. "It was in my interest to see the situation rectified."

"You beat me at cards fair and square, cleared me with the sharp, and I thought you didn't deserve the time o' day. But when Sally told me—"

"You needn't continue."

"Damnation, let a fellow make an apology! Don't know if I'd do it if I weren't drunk as a David's sow, but now's the time." He nodded for emphasis. "When my wife told me how you asked her permission b'fore you stepped in, I was madder'n Old Nick that you'd gone to see her. But she brought me 'round to it, and I know now the fine thing you did."

"Your wife is gracious."

"Still dreams of dancing. Barely anyone calls now. Doesn't let it bother her too much, though. Busy enough with all those orphans. But it was a fine thing, you taking that business to her. Wasn't that tea you cared about, but that damned hospital. Didn't want Sally to lose it because of my bum luck, did you?"

"It was rather a question of whether your wife wished to lose it."

James's brow beetled. He peered at Ben for a moment, eyes abruptly keen.

"Know where a man's life is, don't you, Doreé?"

In Fletcher James's case, it was with his young wife upon her wheeled chair, her legs rendered useless by a carriage accident four years earlier that abruptly ended her days as a vivacious darling of the *ton*. That moment began her existence as the sole patron of a small but busy foundling hospital not two streets from where her husband now stood.

"I daresay," Ben murmured. "Good evening, then, James. Give my best to your wife."

"You could give it to her yourself," James said hesitantly, as though shy of being rebuffed, "if you care to call someday."

Ben crossed the street to the mews, his cravat peculiarly tight. So rarely he had involved himself in the minutiae of his businesses—public businesses and those belowboard alike. Occasionally, however, he hadn't been able to resist, as in the case of Sarah James, whose spirit he had understood merely by crossing the threshold of that hospital. He did not need her husband's gratitude, or even an invitation to call.

Her happiness, however . . . that was something else entirely.

It felt good.

Ben rode home with an unfamiliar sense of peace settling upon his shoulders. As he came into the foyer, Samuel met him.

"My lord, a certain person has been waiting some time to speak with you. He is in the blue parlor."

"Thank you." A brace of candles lit the corridor, but Ben had no need of light to know who awaited him. Samuel's unusual tolerance in allowing the visitor to remain needed no decrypting.

"Hello, Abha."

Towering half a head taller than Ben and thick about the neck and chest like the bales of cotton he had hauled as a youth, the man stood and came forward. He bowed deeply.

"My lord."

Ben's jaw flexed. "Cut line with the excessive formality. You are no longer in my employ."

"You honor me, *sahib*."

Ben repressed a scowl, his chest tight. Abha could only be here for one reason. "Have you a message for me?"

The hulking man produced a folded slip of foolscap from his tunic. Ben slid it into his waistcoat pocket. Abha did not move.

"Well?" Ben's voice sounded edgy. He'd known this

man his entire life, spent more of his childhood in Abha's company than any other human. Eighteen years had taken their lives far from the narrow alleyways of the Madras bazaar and the cotton fields around Mysore where Abha usually lived. But the clear intent in Abha's eyes was the same as it had been two decades ago.

"Good Lord, you haven't changed since you were fifteen," he said when Abha remained silent. "What is it? What do you wish to say to me now?"

"That which, out of honor, I could not say while you paid me for my service to you."

Ben waited.

"I say this, Benjirou. Once I saved your life. I can take it away as easily, or . . ." He paused. " . . . make you wish I would."

Chill slid through Ben's veins. "Son of my mother's brother," he said with intention the Japanese half-caste could not mistake, "your mother who suckled me, and mine who treated you as a son, would not look kindly upon such a deed."

"Son of my father's sister," his uncle's bastard replied, "your mother and mine would never know."

Silence stretched through the dark between them.

"Of what wrongdoing do you accuse me?"

"That which you paid me for seven years to prevent."

"I intend her no harm."

"Then leave her be."

Ben met his gaze straight. "I cannot."

Abha's heavy eyelids sank down. "Then tread carefully, my cousin."

Ben's spine unlocked. Abha would not call him that if he truly meant him ill. He had enormous respect for Abha's ability to carry through on a threat. It was the very reason he had hired his foster brother to watch over Octavia all those years ago. While Ben had returned to

England, Abha remained with her, the man Ben trusted most in the world to protect her.

After that, four times a year for seven years, Abha had punished him for that sublime arrogance by sending the same message across thousands of miles. Each time, three short words only: *She is well.*

Ben nodded. "I will take care."

Abha turned and without further words disappeared into the rear of the house, where he would depart by the servants' entrance.

Ben passed his palms across his face, took a deep breath, and went into the parlor. At the sideboard he poured three fingers of whiskey and carried his glass to a chair before the fire. He sat, set the crystal on the floor by his foot, and drew out her missive.

I am once more betrothed, and in possession of part of that which you desire.

It was unsigned. She must trust Abha as he did, but still she had not endangered herself by committing details to paper. She would tell him in person at Lady Fitzwarren's gathering.

He leaned back into the chair and stared at the fire. Flames licked at the coals, drawing life from the hard black chunks of dead matter. He tried to recapture the contentment of remembering Lady James and her hospital. But he could not. This business he had become involved with hadn't a shred of altruism to it. He did not deserve any gentle swell of satisfaction for now being on the verge of learning what he must to carry through. He deserved the terse diffidence in this single line of script.

He looked again at the words penned by her hand and closed his eyes. She hadn't any idea that she was already fully in possession of his single desire.

Chapter 17

ABACK. The situation of the sails of a ship when they are pressed against the masts by the force of the wind.
                 —*Falconer's* Dictionary of the Marine

Déjà vu.

Tavy sat before her dressing table gowned in white silk speckled with tiny pearls and sequins, hair arranged on the crown of her head threaded with white satin ribbon. The usual impossible orange lock stole from the arrangement to dangle over her brow. She smoothed it back but it popped right back down.

She drew in a steadying breath. Just like seven years ago, nerves twisted her belly. But unlike seven years ago, tonight he would actually come to the party. Through the front door.

Lady Ashford arrived early and took up a position by Tavy's side in the drawing room, from which she commented on each new arrival with wit enough to nearly distract Tavy from her fidgets. Nearly. The drawing room filled, and Tavy began to imagine herself back in Madras in 1814 once again, in a house full of people, yet she only wished to see one who was not present.

Marcus stepped through the door. Eyes wide, she turned to her hostess.

"You invited Lord Crispin?" she whispered.

"'Course I invited him. You are betrothed to him. Can't very well throw a party for you and neglect to include your fiancée, can I?"

"But everyone will imagine this is an engagement party."

"Daresay they will." The dowager's pinpoint eyes stared fixedly beneath yards of purple tulle wrapped into a turban. "You cannot have it both ways, my dear."

Tavy could not respond. She hadn't given Marcus a moment's thought for this evening, only that Ben would come and she could slake her thirst on the sight of him. And, of course, tell him her news.

"It is not what you think," she finally managed to utter as Constance appeared in the doorway. Heads turned her way, as always. She took Marcus's arm and they approached.

"You've said that before," Lady Fitzwarren murmured, "but I've yet to see evidence to prove it."

"Good evening, ladies." Marcus made an elegant leg.

"How lovely you are this evening, Octavia." Constance smiled fondly. "And you, Valerie. And what a marvelous house you have, Lady Fitzwarren." She looked about the chamber, furnished entirely in the Egyptian style. "This is quite nice, all the gold and red. And the austere white foyer with columns like a Greek temple. I hear that each chamber in your house is done up in a different style."

"Yes, yes. I have been enormously diverted redecorating this year. The second parlor is my favorite. Sumerian ziggurat, don't you know."

Constance clapped her gloved hands. "Oh, may I see it?"

" 'Course, my dear. Valerie, do join us and allow these lovebirds a moment's private conversation."

Valerie's dark gaze flashed between Tavy and Marcus, then to the door.

"You know how I adore your fabulous house, Mellicent. But I see Lord Doreé just arriving and I must have a word with him before others gobble him up. He goes about in society so infrequently, everyone is always especially keen to have his attention when he is present." With a bright smile she moved toward the door.

Tavy forced herself not to stare in Valerie's direction. The dowager and Constance walked away and Marcus stepped closer. Tavy halted herself from widening the distance between them.

"I hadn't the opportunity to speak with you before. I was quite busy at Leadenhall Street today. But you will be glad to know the announcement will appear in the journals in four days. Would you prefer to be married here in town or the country?"

Tavy struggled to breathe. It seemed all too real, and now imminent.

"I haven't given it a thought, truly, Marcus. I am sorry."

"Do so now. I am eager for the date." He smiled, nothing of the impatient lover in his look. But they stood in a chamber full of people. He could not very well express his desires in such a way. Although, according to Lady Fitzwarren, Ben had.

She could not resist. She cast her gaze to the doorway. He stood amongst a small group, Valerie at his side. The others laughed at something the viscountess said, he smiled, then looked across the chamber at Tavy.

Her insides seemed to collapse, heating and compressing as though he touched her. He returned his attention to the others and she dragged hers again to Marcus.

The baron's mouth was a line.

"Yes, Marcus. I will consider—"

"I told you not to encourage him, Octavia."

Her nerves stilled, a metallic flavor beneath her tongue. "Encourage?"

"You do not ask me which man?"

"You have only ever once given me such an order, Marcus. I cannot very well mistake it."

"I will not have my wife entertaining the company of other men."

Tavy could not reply. Marcus's accusatory look and her own duplicity turned her stomach. She deserved disapproval. Where had she gone? She'd told Lady Fitzwarren she was through with pretense, but that seemed to be all she knew now, and it rested poorly in her soul.

"Marcus, I cannot speak with you again tonight. I would not say anything either of us would like. But tomorrow I hope you will call."

"I will. Early." He grasped one of her hands. Tavy allowed it. No one would remark upon it. The announcement had not yet appeared in the journals, but gossip had assured that most present knew of their betrothal. "But do not leave it like this tonight. I beg your pardon for saying such a foolish thing." A spark of unease lit his gaze, but it was ill situated there. He was unaccustomed to begging.

She drew away and moved to a group of other guests.

For the next hour she barely knew of what she spoke, barely heard the violin trio Lady Fitzwarren had engaged for the occasion or the applause or her hostess's invitation for guests to enjoy refreshments in the adjoining chamber. Her preoccupation with avoiding her false fiancée and seeking opportunity to discharge her duty paralyzed her with tension. As the drawing room emptied and Ben came to her side by the pianoforte, she could hardly look at him.

He stood close but not remarkably so, hands clasped behind his back.

"I cannot do this." Her palms were damp. "I cannot lie like this. It turns me inside out."

"I am sorry for it."

"But I started it all, didn't I? I have no one to blame but myself for going to your house that day and asking for help. Nothing but"—*another lie*—"my foolish curiosity." She had only wished to see him again. To know him once more.

"Rather, your desire to help him."

The air went out of her. "The blackmailer's name is Sheeble. He is demanding that Marcus sign a document that will allow illegal cargo to leave port without detection by authorities."

The last of the guests left the drawing room. Only a footman remained at the doors to the foyer. Merry conversation emanated from the dining chamber. Tavy's elbow nudged a glass upon the piano, the pungent aroma of its contents lifting to her. She took up the glass and drank the liquid in a gulp, coughing on the fumes.

"It won't help," Ben said softly. "Believe me."

Her gaze snapped up. His eyes were so dark, so beautiful and intense despite their indolent dip. She could fall into them and never have the will to climb out again.

So she must not accidentally trip.

"It's best that I be the judge of that." She set down the glass with a jittering clack. A single black brow upon his handsome face rose. She pursed her lips and his gaze went to them. "Do not look at my mouth."

"I cannot seem to prevent myself from doing so."

"It makes me think things I should not."

"I would like quite a lot to hear what things in particular."

"I daresay you can imagine."

"I daresay. Still, hearing them upon your tongue would please me." From the brightness of his eyes, it seemed as though it would please him a great deal.

"It would put me to the blush. In any case, we should not be having this conversation."

"Perhaps not here. And your blush is very becoming. Everywhere it appears."

Tavy's breaths came fast. "I do not think this is—"

He covered her hand still gripping the glass, peeled her fingers loose, and her skin seemed to melt to his. Her entire body. She ought to have worn gloves tonight. She ought to have worn a whole suit of armor, for heaven's sake.

"I cannot stop thinking about you." His rough voice rumbled across her senses.

She breathed fast. "Are you for some reason obliged to?"

The crease appeared in his cheek. But he released her. She nearly grabbed him back again.

She straightened her shoulders. "I intend to tell Marcus tomorrow that our betrothal is at an end. Again."

He did not flicker a lash. "As you wish."

"You do not want me to obtain any further information through this method?"

"No."

Her insides crimped with panic. "Then I suppose we will not see one another again, since you go about in society so irregularly."

Furrows formed between his brows. The slightest shadow of the day's whiskers hinted about his jaw. Her body's memory felt that roughness again upon her neck and the insides of her thighs.

"I would like to call upon you," he said. "May I?"

"I have heard that request before. I do not quite believe it this second time."

Emotions crossed her face in rapid play. Surprise and doubt. But also hope. Ben's chest expanded, anticipation pressing against hot relief.

"Perhaps I do not deserve it," he said, "but allow me the honor. Please."

She hesitated a moment then nodded. Her gaze shifted to the dining chamber door. But Ben could not turn away from her. The candlelit angle of her jaw and the slope of her throat held him rapt.

"Octavia," Constance hissed across the chamber. "You are missed."

Without another word, Octavia moved around him and away. He leaned back against the piano, steadying himself. Constance took Octavia's arm and drew her into the dining chamber. Lady Fitzwarren replaced them in the doorway.

"Doreé, I must speak with you at once." She strode forward purposefully.

He bowed. "I am at your service, my lady."

"Don't play the pretty with me. You think you know what I have to say but you haven't the slightest idea." She halted before him, a swirl of violet perfume.

"I beg you to offer me enlightenment, ma'am." He had known Mellicent Fitzwarren since his days at Cambridge. Ashford's godmother, Lady March, had introduced him to the dowager. For what purpose, he hadn't been wise enough at the time to understand, but he had quickly come to. Lady Fitzwarren knew everyone in town and was as sharp as a tack. That she and Lady Ashford seemed to be Octavia's patronesses now was sheer . . . *coincidence.*

Ben did not believe in coincidence.

"That girl must marry soon," the lady stated, "and I do not mean Octavia Pierce. Not at the moment, rather."

No coincidences. Not in Ben's life.

"You refer to Lady Constance?"

"Intelligent man. Like your father." She snapped him on the chest with the tip of her furled fan. "Which is precisely to the point. I hoped to say this to you at Fellsbourne, but hadn't the opportunity. Those graves are no longer fresh but the mystery surrounding your father and brother's deaths still is. You must investigate it and put it to rest or that darling girl will never release herself from that tragic bond."

Ben allowed a moment's pause.

"I appreciate your concern, my lady. I am a great admirer of forthright speech."

"That is perfectly obvious to me." Her eyes glinted.

"I admit I had not previously considered the matter so urgent, nor so mysterious."

"Well, you will now. I had an interesting conversation with Abel Gosworth while at your country place, and discovered I'm not the only one who's got the notion that fire was no accident."

"Madam?"

"When the Tories pushed that bill through Parliament to put the Company in the hands of men who didn't know a damn thing about the East Indies, your father was spanking mad to overturn it."

"He believed the men best suited to controlling trade in the East were those who understood and worked hand in hand with the natives." Natives like Ben's uncle, who prized the back-and-forth sharing of cultures and married his sister to an Englishman, who did too.

The dowager's lips pursed. "I can see you don't believe me."

"Assassination is a heavy accusation, my lady. And, of course, my brother died as well in that fire. In matters of politics he was quite unlike my father."

"Jack didn't care a thing about Parliament, you mean. But others did, and that fire did not light itself. You haven't time to lose. That poor girl is on the edge of hysteria." She bustled away. "Now, come have something to eat," she threw over a shoulder draped with filmy purple fabric. "Your complexion is sallow and you are considerably more handsome when you have some color in you.

One must maintain appearances, after all, even when one is pining away."

Ben could not help but laugh. The unfamiliar sensation in his chest brought quick memory of the last time he had laughed, chasing after a beautiful woman in the midst of a thunderstorm, the rain washing away every doubt. Everything but the moment.

But Lady Fitzwarren's words spiked a disquiet he had ignored far too long. For Constance's sake he must now address it.

He strode toward the foyer. His hostess would not mind his abrupt departure, and he'd had enough tonight of the decadent torture of watching Octavia across a room and not being able to touch her. Her eyes had told him that her words were sincere. He had no doubt she despised lying, and he would not ask her to do so again. He was through with lies, through with subterfuge and mistrust. Tomorrow he would see her and try to discover if she was too.

Ben read through records at his house late into the night, then rose before dawn and rode to the docks. The sound of the Thames lapping at the wharf met him beyond the dock walls, and he knew the water would be black beneath shining gas lamps.

Despite Creighton's dedication to his work, his secretary never appeared before the sun. Ben let himself into the office on the second story of a building across from the gated entrance to the docks, and struck a flint to light a lamp. Then he unlocked a cabinet drawer and pulled forth a file. An hour later Creighton appeared, the gray of morning outlining him in the door frame.

Ben nodded a greeting. "Where is the ledger with the inventory taken of the hunting box after the fire?"

Creighton's stony face opened. Ben waited through his secretary's momentary astonishment with a patience he did not feel. He'd gone through every document relating to the incident, and, just as years ago, nothing suggested any mystery. The place had burned when a lit coal went astray from a grate when all were asleep. Any suspicions were unfounded. He was on a wild goose chase.

"I beg your pardon, my lord. It is still at the cottage. I considered it best left on the premises in case you should find use for it while there."

Ben stuffed the papers into the file.

"I will ride down there now. Send a message to Samuel to meet me at the inn with a bag. I do not need my valet. I will be gone only overnight." He went to the door and paused. "When is the *Eastern Promise* scheduled to sail?"

"A week Tuesday, sir."

"I have not forgotten about her peculiar cache."

"Of course you have not, my lord." Creighton sounded offended.

"Have the former quartermaster's report ready for me when I return. And look into a sailor named Sheeble, his business and close associates."

"Yes, sir."

Ben took the southeastern road toward Canterbury, but far before reaching it turned south into the woodland in the direction of Hastings, coming to his property swiftly. The modest pieces of land he owned in England all clustered about the same locale. Except for his father, the previous lords of Doreé had never strayed far from London or Paris.

He stabled his horse at the inn, greeting the tepid welcome of the locals with few words and plenty of coin. They resented him. Jack had been their favorite. In the months before the fire, he had spent all of his time at the lodge, moving in there permanently after Arthur's death. Jack had told him with a laugh of defeat that since he'd restored Fellsbourne, the lodge felt more like home—more like someplace Arthur had lived. Ben had agreed.

Then the hunting box burned, and Ben hadn't anyplace left that reminded him of either brother. His renovation of the house in Cavendish Square had as much to do with recapturing a sense of his half brothers' presence there as erasing his father's obsession with a land to which he never wished to return.

At the time, he hadn't any idea that eschewing India had everything to do with the woman he left there against his will. His anger and resentment had boiled far too thick to see that clearly. He hadn't seen clearly again until he looked upon her smile once more.

He left his horse at the inn and walked the path through the copse to the remains of the cottage. As he emerged from the stand of willowy ash and thick oak and pine, the sight met him as it always did, a leaden fist to his midriff. The broken piles of burnt stone looked forlorn, soot still clinging to the gray rock that had once been walls and foundations, square holes for crossbeams gaping like mouths bereft of tongues.

He moved toward the only structure still standing. Set apart from the cottage by thirty yards, the stable had escaped the flames. A groom escaped the tragedy as well, along with several horses. Afterward when Ben made the decision not to rebuild, he offered the fellow a place at Fellsbourne.

The stable had been converted to a storage room with a locked door and space enough for objects salvaged from the smoldering ruins. Ben pulled out the keys.

Within, dust motes stirred in the slits of sunlight chasing through the high-set window paned with thick glass and crossed with iron bars. He opened the door wide to allow in daylight. Ignoring the piles of miscellaneous charred debris of his father's and brother's life at the cottage, he unlocked the cabinet. A slim leather-bound volume rested within.

Creighton's neat script covered a hundred or so lines of the ledger's first few pages. He read it through, not bothering to cross-check the listed items with the objects stacked in the chamber; Creighton was as fastidious with his work as he was discreet. Ben closed the book and returned it to the cabinet. There was nothing of interest here, only partial memories and burnt dreams. Constance's dreams.

In the morning he would return to London and call upon her. Lady Fitzwarren was right. He had waited far too long to force Constance into this conversation. But enough time had passed now. Neither of them were the children they had been seven years ago. She must move on, just as he intended to.

Locking the stable door behind him, he pocketed the keys and walked in a pensive mood through the falling evening back to the inn. He took dinner in the taproom, checked on Samuel and his horse in the stable, and closed himself in his bedchamber.

He awoke into the darkness between midnight and dawn, his heart pattering in the cavity of his chest. Nothing stirred in his chamber, downstairs, or outside. The inn was quiet, the village asleep. But the alarm that woke Ben had not come from without.

He pulled on his clothing and took a lamp from the taproom. Dry leaves crackled beneath his boots along the short path through the wood to the ruins. He passed their uneven, black mass, cast in shadows by the waning moon, and went quickly toward the stable. His hands on the key and padlocks were steady. Preternaturally so. He unbolted the door and again went straight to the cabinet, his breath frosting.

The ledger rested cold in his palms, like the knife driving into his stomach as he read and reread a single line of the inventory.

Fowling piece, 46 in., single barrel, cherry(?) stock.

Ben knew only one man who used such an antiquated weapon, the single barrel fitted out with a special hard-wood for the buttstock.

Cherry. Walker Styles's favorite.

But Styles had not been at the hunting box when the fire took his best friend's life. He was in Sussex, checking up on matters at his family's estate. In fact, Walker had not been to the cottage for nearly a year before the fire. As crushed by Arthur's death at Waterloo as Jack and Ben had been, Walker avoided anywhere that reminded him of Arthur, including Fellsbourne.

Then Jack died, along with their father, and Ben abruptly came into the title and estate. Walker had been at his side through it all. A stalwart friend, grieving too, but ever present with advice and support to the younger son who had never expected to inherit an English lordship. Ben never suspected him of anything but intense loyalty and a mourning heart.

Suddenly craven, he could not bring himself to investigate the pile of carefully tagged items in the storeroom, to see the weapon for himself. He locked the ledger in the cabinet and returned to the inn. Three sleepless hours later he woke Samuel and told him to settle the bill and return to London.

Ben saddled Kali, strapped a pack containing a pistol and smallclothes behind him, and set off for Fellsbourne.

When he reached his estate he paused to tell his butler he had arrived for the afternoon only, and went to the stable. He found the old groom from the hunting box rubbing down a saddle horse's sweat-darkened coat.

"G'day, milord." The man unbent and tugged his cap. "This here's a fine fellow. Just had him out for a run up the hill. Got your blunt worth of this one, I'll wager."

"Yes, he has a smooth gait, doesn't he?" Ben moved into the stall. The gelding nickered, pressing his nose into Ben's palm, searching for treats. Octavia had ridden the animal not a fortnight earlier. Constance had chosen him for her.

Constance.

"Andy, I've a question for you."

"Milord?" The currycomb stalled on the gelding's flank. The man's brow puckered.

"Do not concern yourself," Ben reassured. "It has nothing to do with your work here. I am quite pleased."

"Thank you, milord." His skinny shoulders dropped.

"I wish to ask you something concerning the days prior to the fire at the hunting box."

"Don't know that I remember much about those days. 'While back."

"Yes, Andy. But you see, I have a most pressing need to know a particular detail, one I daresay you will recall without any effort." He spoke as though of the weather.

"I'll try to remember, milord."

"I will appreciate your effort. Do you recall, were my father or brother entertaining guests in those days just before the fire?"

"Well, no." The man shook his head. "I can't say as there was anybody about that week, with the rain like it'd been. Milord thought it poor shooting in rain, you know."

Ben's breath stole out of him slowly, relief slipping along his veins.

"Ah, yes. Of course. The rain." The very reason for the ample charred remains of the cottage. The rain had fallen hard and fast for nearly a week then let up. But as the cottage burned, the clouds let loose again, halting the fire's progress prematurely but still too late, leaving a ruin of lives in soggy puddles.

"'Cept milord Styles, course," Andy added. "But he weren't but family, at the box so often that year before the fire, specially after Master Arthur passed." The groom nodded thoughtfully. "Came to get me after he got out of the house. We stood there watching, both of us weeping like women. Didn't mind crying myself since he was, after all." He tugged his cap lower. "Th'other week when he were here he brought me a bottle, if you don't mind me saying, milord."

"Not at all," Ben murmured, limbs frozen, lungs in a vice grip.

"Drank it with me, in fact. Said it was for old times. For Lord Jack."

"Of course. Thank you, Andy. I had wondered. Now I know."

"Yessir."

Ben left the stable, dragging himself hard from the place his heart and mind pointed toward, a place he hadn't been in years, of such profound loss he shunned it because it hurt too much to linger there.

Styles had been there the night of the fire, yet he had never spoken of it. Moreover he lied about avoiding the box for so many months. Andy would have no reason to tell tales now. Already overwhelmed with taking up his new role in England so soon after his uncle's death, when the tragedy occurred Ben hadn't been in any right mind to interview the sole surviving member of the household, and Andy had not offered up any information voluntarily. Perhaps the local magistrate had questioned him, but Ben never knew.

Ben could only imagine one reason Styles would withhold such information from him.

The fire had been his fault.

His stomach clenched, his head spinning. The only man he had trusted since the death of his brothers and father, the single person who from the moment Ben acceded to the title accepted him without hesitation . . .

He strode up the drive beneath the lowering sun, struggling to hold the truth at bay. But it came, a tidal wave of pain and betrayal. He walked blindly through the front door of his house toward the parlor.

"Mr. Scott, I will be remaining the night." He shut the door, went to the sideboard and poured a drink. Somewhere within the second bottle he hazily recalled telling Octavia that alcohol would not help with her distress. He sloshed the remaining contents of the bottle into his glass and drank it down.

Ben remained at Fellsbourne for three days, most of those hours spent in the same parlor, draperies drawn to shut out the day, his assiduous servants making certain that the liquor never ran dry. On the third night he finally roused himself sufficiently to stumble to the master suite.

Still half disguised, he awoke shortly after dawn in the bed in which he had made love to Octavia not a fortnight earlier. He dragged himself up and to the window, drew the curtains aside and pressed open the pane. The gray, misty air smelled of moss and molded leaves and fresh hay, of life and death continuing in cycles as old as the birth of the continents and oceans, oblivious to the cruelties of their inhabitants.

He must return to London. He would confront Styles and hear his old friend's story. Perhaps he had it all wrong. Perhaps Andy remembered it poorly.

Perhaps.

But before he sought out Styles, he must pay another call, days overdue. His heart ached harder than it had in seven years, his world again turned upside down overnight. Now, finally, from one person at least, he needed the truth.

Chapter 18

LIGHT. That principle or thing by which objects are made perceptible to our sense of seeing, or the sensation occasioned in the mind by the view of luminous objects.
—*Falconer's* Dictionary of the Marine

Ben did not call. Tavy bit back the tears, gnawed on every one of her fingertips, and cursed her weakness for a black-eyed lord. Then she cursed him. Then she cursed the practice of lying. Then she cursed him again.

Dragging herself out of her morass of maledictions, she went to the museum with Alethea and Constance. After oohing and ahhing appropriately, she and Constance parted company with Tavy's sister and continued on to visit Lady Ashford. On the way they instructed the coachman to make a detour to Gunter's. They ate biscuits and ices, and—in contrast to their highbrow pursuits in the museum—aggressively pursued remarkably silly conversation about complete frivolities.

By the time the carriage drew to a halt before the viscountess's town house, Tavy had convinced herself that she felt nearly like a girl, with barely a care in the world, even as though she might not be required to flee back to India to escape the belly-deep pain of his presence in her life again. Her hands shook, even her lips quivered with the strain of pretense. But she was quite, *quite* proud of herself for not having succumbed to the desire to curl up in a miserable ball on the museum floor, or in her chair at the confectioner's shop, so she must consider it a small sort of victory.

She was laughing aloud with forced exuberance at one of Constance's witticisms when they entered the house and her gaze met Ben's. He stood arrested upon the third step of the staircase leading down from the second story, his hand on the rail. He wore riding breeches and his boots were streaked with dirt. His color was high.

"I have just been to your house," he said directly to her without preamble or any sort of greeting to either of them, and Tavy's fragile commitment to thorough indifference simply dissolved.

"Well, good day to you too, my lord." Constance made an exaggerated curtsy, brows tilted high.

He seemed to recall himself. "Good day, ladies." He bowed and glanced at her, but his gaze returned immediately to Tavy. "I hope you are well."

Tavy nodded and curtsied. She could manage no more. He looked perfect, and tired, and so handsome, and somewhat strange. Lines flanked his beautiful mouth, not of pleasure but tension.

"We have come to see Lady Ashford, as you will imagine," Constance said, taking Tavy's hand. "So if you will step aside we will be on our way up."

"Of course." He came down the stairs and Constance pulled her past him. "Will you return home after this visit?"

Her throat constricted. It should not be this difficult. But something in his eyes seemed odd. Constance drew to a halt halfway up the stairs, allowing her to respond.

"Yes." Brilliant. What a wit. What a composed, clever society ingenue.

He nodded, the brightness flickering into his gaze once more. Taking his hat and coat from the butler, he departed. Tavy forced air through her lungs.

In the parlor, Valerie sat amidst a chaos of open books, maps, writing paper, pen and ink.

"How lovely," she exclaimed, and drew them to a cluster of seats removed from the disarray. "I thought I would not see you until tonight at the ball."

"Whatever was Ben doing here?" Constance plopped down onto a satin ottoman, casting a glance at Valerie's abandoned project. "Are you insisting that handsome lords pay court to you while your own handsome lord is absent from town?"

Valerie chuckled, but her gentle gaze slipped to Tavy. "He was here seeking out Steven, of course."

"Are they well acquainted?" Tavy asked. She knew so little about the Marquess of Doreé, so little of what he did in London, how he spent his time and with whom he associated other than Baron Styles. He was, for all intents and purposes, a stranger still. She'd told herself that countless times over the past four days, but it had not made a dent in her unhappiness.

Valerie studied her for a moment. "Yes, they are. Quite well acquainted." She turned to Constance. "Now, Constance, I have it on excellent authority that your father is coming to town next month."

"Really? He has not told me. But he never bothers with that."

"Fathers can be trying, it's true," the viscountess agreed. Tavy stared at the door. She had nothing to tell him, no new information to impart, not even that she was no longer betrothed. The day after Lady Fitzwarren's party, Marcus sent her a note announcing that he was suddenly required to leave town to see to his property in the country. He had not contacted her since. Just like Ben.

"See? She is entirely unaware that we are speaking of her." Constance's voice came to her slowly.

Tavy righted her thoughts. "What are you saying, then?" She blinked. "Have I a smudge upon my face or some such thing?"

"No, you are lovely." The viscountess's eyes were kind. "Only a bit preoccupied, it seems."

"You should go home." Constance smiled, a light sweet look. "We have already had quite a day of it and I am perfectly fagged. You must be as well."

"If you wish." Tavy rose. Constance did not. "Well?"

"Oh, go along without me." Constance bussed her upon the cheek. "Valerie was telling me the most diverting tale while you were daydreaming and I must hear the end of it. I will call a chair when I have need."

"Well, I like that. It seems I am being dismissed."

Valerie chuckled. "Never. Now, go before you worry a hole in your reticule."

Tavy released the pressure of her fingers around her purse. "All right. Thank you, I think. But I was not daydreaming. I was merely—"

Constance's gaze dipped, hiding the expression in her azure eyes.

"—thinking," Tavy finished lamely.

"Go think at home." Constance looked up, her gaze uncustomarily vague. When Tavy hesitated, she waved her fingers, gesturing her away. Tavy gave Valerie a crooked smile and hurried to her carriage.

By the time she reached the house dusk had begun to fall. Too late for callers. Alethea and St. John had already departed for a dinner engagement. A footman was lighting lamps throughout the house. Tavy went to the nursery and looked in on her nephew, tiny, sleeping so peacefully, as yet wholly unaware of the tumult of life beyond the cradle. Lal crept across the chamber's threshold. Before he could make a noise, Tavy stole back into the corridor.

Restive, her skin oddly tight over her flesh, she descended to the parlor. A maid was lighting the fire. She bobbed a curtsy and went to the windows to draw the curtains against the falling night. When she left, Tavy moved to a table before the darkened window and touched the embossed leather cover of the book there. A thick volume, pages frayed from constant use, William Falconer's *Dictionary of the Marine* had been Tavy's bible for years. When her father first gave it to her, she was no more than fifteen, aching for adventure and travel, longing to follow her dreams.

She ran a palm over the book's smooth surface. She hadn't questioned why her father bought it for her, simply dove into it, learning and memorizing week after week. Finally he explained. Soon she would be making a lengthy journey by ship, he informed her, thumbs tucked in his waistcoat, chest puffed out with pride. He wished her to be ready for any eventuality she might meet with at sea over the course of this journey. She was—he finished with gravity suitable to the moment—going to the East Indies.

Of the few treasures Tavy took upon her voyage to remind her of home and the sister and father she missed especially dearly, the dictionary was her most beloved. She wrote in the margins, using it as a diary of sorts, commenting on the people she encountered, sights she saw, all of her marvelous experiences abroad.

Two years later, after Ben broke her heart, such childish fancies had abruptly seemed foolish. But she kept the dictionary. She'd no idea how it had ended up on the table in the parlor. It belonged on the shelf stacked with the other works of reference that St. John kept for his business.

Not, however, including its current contents.

Tavy opened the cover and turned back the pages. In the center crease, the yellowed journal clippings crackled softly as she touched her fingertips to them.

A footstep sounded behind her.

Her head came up as hands surrounded her upper arms, large and warm and achingly familiar. She drew in a quick breath, his scent tangling in her senses—linen and leather and that ineffable essence that was Ben alone.

He bent and touched his lips to her shoulder alongside the collar of her dress. Hot, wonderful shivers stole through her. She breathed in deep and his mouth lingered. He kissed the curve of her neck, then the hollow beneath her ear, stirring the tendrils of hair that had escaped pins. She stretched like a cat, arching to encourage the seduction of velvet caresses, and a sigh escaped her parted lips.

His hands slipped along her arms, then to her waist. His body almost touched hers, a tantalizing nearness that sought to unwind the knot of doubt and pain born of the past four days.

"Do you know who is kissing you?" His voice smiled, low and intimate, swelling a bubble of joy inside Tavy. He brushed his lips across her shoulder again.

"I daresay it does not matter," she replied, her grin feeling honest and so very good, "as long as he is quite, quite handsome and enormously wealthy."

He went still.

Cold passed along her skin where his mouth had been. She swiveled in his embrace and wrapped her arms around his neck.

"And you." She drank in the reality of him so close again, his strong hands upon her, his chest pressed against her breasts. That night at Fellsbourne had not been a dream. He was holding her now, again. But his eyes were troubled.

"I'm sorry." She twined her fingers in his cravat. "That was a poor jest. I told you a long time ago that I am not good at flirta—"

He caught her mouth with his and all thought halted, all regret, everything but the sublime joy of being in his arms again. Like water after a long thirst. He wanted her and she let herself drown in it, the pleasure and happiness tumbling through her now almost worth the pain of the previous four days.

Almost.

She retreated from the kiss reluctantly and he seemed just as unwilling to let her go.

"You did not come," she said. "I thought you would not."

"I was obliged to leave town. I did not intend to be gone over a day." He seemed to search her features, especially her eyes, lines forming between his brows.

"What?" She slid her palm along the edge of his cravat to feel his skin. He was so warm, his jaw rough with whiskers, the slant of his cheek smooth. She wanted to touch all of him again, to be free with his body as she had been during that brief moment at Fellsbourne. "You want to ask me something, I can see. What is it you wish to know?"

He shook his head. "I know too much already." He leaned in, brushing her lips then bringing their mouths together fully. It was a seeking caress, deeper with each stroke of his tongue along her lips and inside. He sought and Tavy offered, helpless against the pull within her that sought him in return, that burned to entwine everything of theirs together, mouths and bodies and hearts. He dragged her hips tight to him and covered her behind with his hand, fingers spread, owning her again so swiftly as she dreamed and feared. She tasted the desire in his mouth, his possessing hands. Nothing in his touch spoke of caution, only questing, questioning need.

She broke away abruptly this time, her breaths coming fast, fingers tangled in his hair.

"Ask me, Ben." It was the worst sort of heedlessness, but she could not halt her unruly tongue. "I am through with lying. Ask me what you wish and I will tell you."

His gaze retreated even as it swept across her face, and he did not speak.

Tavy's throat closed.

She had been right to mistrust again. He wanted only that part of her he could use briefly. She was unutterably foolish. *Again*. He had told her that night at the folly that he would not give her what she was looking for.

She backed out of his hold, and—the worst pain yet—he let her go.

"Why are you here now? I have no information for you, nothing of value in my possession."

He was silent a stretched moment. "I wished to see you."

She dashed her hand across her lips dampened by his kiss. "'See' is a broad term for you, apparently. My family is not at home tonight, as you clearly know. How did you come in here without a footman announcing you? Did you pay my brother-in-law's servants to assure privacy?"

"Your Indian manservant gave me your direction. I saw no others." An odd light glinted in his eyes. "But I came here earlier. I told you that."

"You wished to see me in the light of day?"

"There was a time when that did not surprise you."

Madras. The bazaar, beneath the sun's heat. The past that confused and contorted the present and would not seem to lay dormant.

"I was naïve then. I understand some matters a great deal better now."

"You understood then," he said with peculiar hesitancy. But his jaw seemed harder, his gaze withdrawing further.

"No, I suspect I was the only one who did not understand," she countered. "You certainly did. You knew all along. Everybody in the bazaar must have known, for pity's sake. Everyone except the foolish English girl who could not imagine—" She broke off. "I should have imagined. I hadn't any idea, and you led me to believe—"

"I did not intend to hurt you."

"Well, you did." Worse than she would ever let him discover. Just as now he was hurting her with the distance in his eyes.

"You were prepared." His voice was low. "You knew what you wanted."

"I knew nothing." Her breaths felt tight, aching again. "You nearly made love to me that night, and I wanted you to, but I hadn't any idea what was happening."

"You hadn't any idea?" Golden candlelight flashed in his eyes. "Do you expect me to believe that, when you were wearing so little? Your shift was translucent."

"It was ninety degrees at midnight. Of course I was wearing that little! And I never imagined any person other than my maid would see my shift. I was a complete innocent. I didn't know men wanted to undress women. I didn't know anything. I was hot!" As now, with his flame-touched gaze searing her. "And given that you made me twice as hot, I was happy I didn't have more clothing on. I did not know what could happen. What might have happened."

He stepped forward.

"Now you know." He bent to her, and Tavy went into his arms without resistance because, simply, she wanted him. She had wanted him since the moment she saw him and hadn't the strength to resist, no matter what his purpose.

But the kiss was not angry. He held her head in his broad palm and drank in her lips, then the sensitive tip of her tongue, his perfect mouth tracing a slow, luscious exploration of her flesh. He teased her, entering only enough to make her flushed below, remembering his tongue there, then tasting her in languorous strokes, drawing fire through her and making her breathless. She twined her arms about his shoulders and sank into him.

His fingers threaded through her hair, then curved along her neck to her shoulder, trailing a path of tender pleasure. She wanted him to touch her. Her breasts ached for it. Already the astounding sensation of opening stole between her thighs, born from his kiss and his strength so close. He separated their mouths then captured hers again as his hand at the small of her back fit her against him. She touched his face, the masterful planes of beauty beneath her fingertips as his lips moved to her throat.

"That night," she whispered, "you asked if you could touch me."

"Let me touch you." His voice was rough.

"Yes."

"You begged me to."

"Please, Ben."

"You needn't beg now, sweet *shalabha*. You needn't have then." He cupped her breasts and his caress was sublime and stunningly honest, as though he had never touched her more intimately. As though her body was something unique and precious to him to discover.

With his hands he transformed the barrier of her clothing into a tool of seduction, brushing the fabric across her nipples until she hurt with the need for him. The careful, steady strokes grew firmer, centered, and she pressed into his hands. His tongue swept between her parted lips, drew hers into him, and Tavy felt naked as though Ben had stripped her of every garment, like on that night in the garden swimming in heat, when he had given her pleasure but expected nothing in return, demanding no more than her gratification.

"I want to touch you now, everywhere I did that night," he said huskily. "Everywhere the moonlight caressed your skin."

But that night she had understood nothing, and yet everything at once, so naïve and so ready to fall. She was a different person now. Wiser.

"No," she whispered against his mouth. "No. *No.*" She grabbed his wrists and pulled his hands wide. He allowed it, and she held off this man with ten times her strength by his consent, his palms spread in a gesture like supplication. But her shaking fingers around his wrists felt the trembling in him too, and his eyes were dark.

"What do you want, Ben?"

He spoke without hesitation. "Sometimes I believe I could exist for nothing more than to bring you pleasure."

Her breath escaped upon a choking sigh. He shook her grip free and curved his hand around the back of her neck, pressing his lips to her brow.

"You thought I was like her. Like Priscilla Nathans."

"You were betrothed, Octavia, yet you allowed me to kiss you. You welcomed my kisses." His mouth curved into a rueful grin. "You also did a credible act of playing the indifferent society lady when you first came to my house here."

But she could not share his amusement. "Not in Madras. How could you have thought that of me then?"

"I did not know to expect anything else of English-women. I had never met a woman like you who spoke her thoughts, and all of them honest."

"You knew Constance."

He drew back and looked at her carefully. "Constance hides her own secrets."

"And you? Are you hiding secrets, Ben? Oh—" She released a sound like laughter but it was not. "Why do I bother asking? I know you have secrets. Your whole life is a secret." Where had he been for the past four days? He must have known she was waiting, as she had waited through the drenching monsoon for his return.

He gave her no answer, and she pressed her palm to his chest. Beneath wool and linen, his heart beat firm and swift like hers. It should be enough that he wanted her so much. But that alone would never be enough.

She moved several steps back.

"I am still betrothed to Marcus."

She said it for the worst of reasons, to test his response. She should simply ask him what he intended of her now that they had been lovers. In another age she might have. But she had changed in seven years, and now part of her feared his response. Part of her wanted to see it in his eyes only, so that his words would not forever after have power over her.

He gave her what she wished. His gaze did not alter, unreadable in the candlelight, and he did not speak.

Now she must make a choice, disentangle herself from his web of silences or remain within it indefinitely. Her head argued one side of the debate, her body the other. Her heart, that obstreperous organ, clearly believed it could hover in both camps.

Dropping her gaze, she went past him and across the chamber. She paused at the door, her knuckles white around the frame, and ducked her head. "This is your reminder."

"What reminder?" His voice sounded tight.

"You told me once to remind you to ask me for a warning. A warning when I would let you win." She looked over her shoulder. "The next time, Ben, I think you will win."

"I do not wish to win against you, Octavia."

"I don't know that you have any choice in the matter now." She left.

Ben stared at the empty doorway. He seemed to be fated now to watch her leave him, to see her walk away without giving him what he wanted most. The flavor of her lips upon his tongue worked like whiskey in his senses, dizzying him. He needed her, had come here tonight to know the truth, and yet he would leave again less satisfied than ever. Less certain.

She was still betrothed to Crispin. Still harboring secrets. Or ammunition?

He could not believe it of her. Nothing gave evidence of that except the battering weight of betrayal swirling through him now. Honesty came through her kiss and the touch of her hands, so foreign to him. More foreign than anything else he had known, and more so now.

He bent his head and passed his palm over his eyes. On the table beside him a heavy book lay open, its pages marked with pen along the margins.

Ben recognized the marine dictionary. He'd read it as a boy, and Creighton kept a copy of Falconer's book in the office at Blackwall. The hand in the margins was Octavia's, the same as the single line of script she had sent him days ago, neat and clean with a playful flare to the capitals. Her notes seemed scattered, some lengthier, most impressionistic, place names and brief descriptions of sites and people, sometimes quoted phrases.

Despite all, he smiled. It did not surprise him in the least that Octavia used this book in this manner. When he first met her she had been a girl full of life and freedom.

Now she was more subdued, but that spark of *vivant* still lit her warm eyes.

His fingers pressed back the journal clippings tucked in the crease to follow a note twining like a vine down the center of the page, then he halted. His name stared up at him.

He drew the three, yellowed scraps out, each from *The Times*.

The first clipping was painfully familiar. Only four days ago in his office he had read again his brother and father's obituary, alongside the notice of his own preferment to the title. The second was a snippet of a gossip column mentioning the completed renovations of his Cavendish Square house, and musing on when he would finally make his Scottish fiancée its mistress. The third, dated more than three years later, was an article from the Board of the Admiralty listing ship owners operating out of the Port of London, followed by a catalogue of vessels, highlighting one of his own as a particularly excellent example of mercantile craftsmanship.

Ben laid the clippings on the book and worked to draw air into his lungs. She had followed news of him more than three years after he left India. *Three years.*

His gaze shifted to the door again, and the hot, insistent certitude that she had spoken only truth washed up and against him, then through him—despite her betrothal, despite his fears—like a monsoon wind.

He moved across the chamber into the foyer and stood paralyzed at the base of the stairs, staring at the landing above. He could go after her. But he did not know if he would be able to discern the truth if he heard it now.

His hands fisted. When he had not found Octavia at home earlier, he went to see Ashford, to ask advice of the only person who might give him good counsel concerning Styles. But Steven was still abroad and Ben hadn't time to wait for him to return from Paris. He must confront Styles now. Then he would be free of this ache of doubt. And of obstructions.

Nearly free.

A presence stirred in the foyer behind him. He turned and met Abha's heavy gaze.

"I will ruin Crispin."

Abha smiled.

Chapter 19

Crispin could not be found. The doors of India House had closed for the day, and the baron was not at his club or his flat. Nor was Styles, but Ben knew where to find his old friend tonight. He rode home, scribbled a note to his secretary, and sent it off with Samuel.

His valet met his demand for formal attire with enthusiasm.

"Which pin would you prefer, my lord?" Singh stood with his hand poised eagerly over the dressing case as Ben folded his starched cravat into a simple arrangement. "The blue diamond, perhaps? Or the ruby crescent?" Singh's turban sported a tiny emerald, his loose cotton shirt fastened with freshwater pearl buttons. Ben suspected his valet spent a great deal more time with his jewels than he did.

He did not fault him for it. Old sailors loved swag, and Ben trusted Singh as he trusted Creighton, Samuel, and all his employees. A great deal more than he trusted his peers.

"The fire opal," he replied.

Singh produced an octagonal cut jewel the size of the flat of his callused thumb, of brilliant apricot shot through with golden strands, and affixed it within the fall of Ben's cravat. In the mirror, Ben stared at the jewel he had bought from a Mughal prince just before leaving India seven long years ago. Cut for a queen nine centuries earlier, the gem was precisely the shade of Octavia's hair.

"Off to Lord and Lady Savege's ball tonight, my lord?"

Ben nodded and headed toward the door.

"My lord?"

Ben paused.

Singh placed his palms together and bowed at the waist. "May the blessings of the universal god be upon you."

Ben lifted a brow. "Thank you, Singh. Any particular reason why today?" He could certainly use blessings at this point. His muscles were clenched, his stomach tight as though he anticipated a fencing match or horse race. Styles would be at the Saveges' fête.

"Upon this day five years ago, sir, you took me from that fearful galley and gave me freedom." The former slave bowed deep again and did not rise. "I am most grateful."

Ben stared at the top of his valet's linen-wrapped head, at Singh's hands rough and dark as earth. Something in him unwound. Across the chamber in the glass, a reflection of the shimmering jewel in his cravat winked.

"You are quite welcome, Singh." He turned and went from his house.

The Earl and Countess of Savege's home was not far.

Head full, Ben walked the distance without knowing the direction he took or the time elapsed. His hostess met him in the foyer.

"Lord Doreé, what a great pleasure to see you." She offered him a broad, generous-mouthed grin, her eyes sparkling as though she meant her welcome. It worked into Ben's fraught senses like Singh's words, with insidiously warm, familiar fingers.

The countess leaned toward him, grasping his hand as she had on that night five years earlier when she accosted him in an alleyway, seeking the truth as Ben did now. Then, he had known so little of himself.

He feared he still knew little. His world seemed to be turning around him, spinning more swiftly with each moment and each partially answered question. For years he had sought to trap the past behind him, locking its pain and turmoil behind bars. A quiet soul by nature, he had never sought the unrest his uncle thrust upon him, nor the hazards. Now they reached out to him, telling him they were his lot and he would be content with them. Not only content, but justified. Complete. Happy. If he could but understand whom to claim as allies, whom as foes.

"Lady Constance has been asking after you." Lady Savege's eyes shone with concern. "Perhaps you will seek her out and put her mind at rest?"

Ben moved into the crush of people packing the town house. He avoided such events even when welcome at them because he could not think in crowds. Born in India, the most populous land on earth, and all he had ever wanted was peace, the peace of common understanding and bone-deep joy he had found in the animated brown eyes of a freckle-nosed, long-legged English girl.

A crowd of young gentlemen surrounded Constance. Her mouth was wide with laughter and her eyes glittered far too brightly.

"She is fully in her element," Styles said at his shoulder.

Stillness streamed through Ben's veins like the ocean in a calm wind. "I do not think so. She much prefers her horses and the countryside."

Styles's regard slipped away. "And yet, she is at her most beautiful when surrounded by beaux, at her most lively and ebullient admired as she is at this moment."

"And your admiration, Walker? To what extent will you allow it to take you?" It was a gamble. Perhaps Constance had nothing to do with the fire. Styles had treated her with indifference so often. But Ben must probe his own open wound to discover the bullet within.

"I haven't an idea what you can mean."

"Did you envy Jack? Did you wish you were in his place?"

The baron chuckled uncomfortably. "If I had envied him then, don't you think I would have taken advantage of his absence by now?"

"Perhaps guilt has stood in your path."

Styles didn't miss a beat. "Guilt?"

"I understand you were a guest of my brother at the hunting box shortly before the fire." Long ago, when he was just a boy, his uncle taught him that the truth was often the hardest taunt for a dishonest man to bear. "I recently learned of this. Since you had not mentioned it to me before, I wondered why."

"I visited a time or two, but I never liked it." Styles spoke with measured calm. "After Arthur's death, in his absence, I found it . . . difficult."

"Yes. You told me then." Ben allowed that to sit. Constance had seen him, and every few moments her gaze flickered to him, then to Styles. A gentleman by her side bowed and proffered her a glass of champagne. She wrapped him upon the shoulder with her closed fan with a smack Ben heard yards away despite the orchestra. Her suitor's eyes went wide, but he smiled. Constance was a Diamond, and Ben had seen this before, pulling her away from such company just as many times as she wished.

"Haven't you any desire to separate her from her swains, then?" he asked casually, as though every cell of blood in his body weren't trained upon the reply.

"Not any more than you, I'll merit." Styles's gaze shifted across the ballroom. "Not given the present company."

Ben followed his attention. Octavia stood by the shallow stair ascending to the foyer. Her gown caressed her perfect curves with a gracious touch. Her soft skin lit with the chandelier's glow seemed pale, her eyes especially dark at the distance, her tempting mouth a straight line.

Ben met Styles's interested regard. The back of his neck prickled.

"The fair Miss Pierce still appeals, I see." The baron's blue eyes glinted.

"She is tolerably attractive." Ben forced a grin. "Why, my friend? Hanging out these days for fresher fare than the demi-reps at Hauterive's?"

Styles's eyes narrowed. "You know, just there for a moment you sounded like your old self again. Did our evening at the club last week have a positive effect on you after all?"

Ben thought of Fletcher James, of his lovely chair-ridden wife and the foundling hospital, of Singh and the knobby scars on his ankles and collar from where iron manacles had bound him to oar and bench, and he replied, "Yes."

Crystal shattered. Constance's brittle laugher cascaded above the crowd. One of her admirers produced a handkerchief with an elegant flourish. She snatched it from his fingers with a mock pout and dabbed at her skirts, champagne shimmering upon the floor at her feet.

Ben had seen enough. If he were another man he would cross the ballroom to the woman who captivated him, take her arm, and not release her for the remainder of the evening—at least not until he asked her about the journal clippings. And much more. But he was not that man. He was, in fact, finally beginning to understand precisely what sort of man he could be. Perhaps the man Octavia had waited for years ago.

From across the ballroom her warm gaze was trained on Constance, worry etching her brow.

"Good evening, Styles." He nodded farewell to his companion. He had sown the seeds. He must now allow them to germinate.

Constance met Ben's approach with wide eyes glistening with merriment upon the surface and distress beneath.

"Why, Lord Doreé," she tittered, "you have only now missed the opportunity to be covered in champagne like Mr. Anders and Lord Scott here." Her gaze circled her admirers. "But perhaps one of you kind gentlemen would supply me with another glass, and this time you can cast wagers upon whose shoes I will more thoroughly douse." She leaned toward Ben to speak sotto voice. "Wager on Lord Scott. His pumps are marvelously shiny, so I shall aim for him."

Lord Scott laughed, possibly as intoxicated as Constance, at least by her beauty and attention. Mr. Anders chuckled with less amusement, unhappy to be bested. Ben took Constance's hand and drew it through his arm.

"Come now, my lady. I will convey you home and you can throw all the champagne you wish onto your own shoes."

"You are ever so amusing, my lord," she giggled, but did not resist. "*Adieu*, gentlemen." She waved her fan in their direction. Ben pressed through the crowd. Her grip on his arm pinched. "What took you so long?" Her tone was entirely altered, her breath stained with wine. "I was wretched and you were not here."

"Hush," he murmured and drew her up the stair. Octavia stood there still, watching them.

"Darling Octavia." Constance grasped her friend's gloved hand. "I am sorry you did not arrive earlier. I should have had a much better time tonight if you and Ben had not both abandoned me." Tears teetered at the cusps of her eyes.

Octavia's gaze darted to Ben. "You are taking her home now, I hope?" she asked quietly. He nodded.

"He is rescuing me, you see. He *likes* to rescue people. He does it all the time, you know." A tear rolled over the spot of crimson on Constance's cheek.

"Yes. I do know." Octavia released her hand and looked at Ben again. "Go quickly now."

He bowed and drew Constance away and to her carriage. Once within, in the company of her hired companion, Mrs. Jacobs, his childhood friend sobbed into a handkerchief, speaking of her unhappiness only in tears. He held her hand and murmured words of comfort, but his thoughts swirled.

He had never told a soul who he truly was. His servants knew only what they must to perform their duties. Even Creighton, who kept Ben's books, did his correspondence, interviewed captains, and examined each ship upon arrival and departure, understood only a portion of the projects Ben's wealth and network of allies allowed. Ashford knew somewhat more, but still not all.

He wanted to tell Octavia. The longing rose in him quick and powerful as the carriage rocked along the dark London streets, an urging from deep within.

He could not. He would not put her in danger of being in possession of such information. And he had no assurance she would not tell her betrothed. Until he found

Marcus Crispin and forced him to come clean, Ben could not be certain of her. Even then he could not.

But now he was finally ready to discern how he might come to be certain. He was through with watching her walk away.

Tavy awoke to mid-morning sunlight slipping through cracks in the drapes, with no desire to be awake and less desire to do anything about it. She rolled over on the soft linen, tucked her face into the crook of her arm and squeezed her lids shut. But the image of Ben's eyes as he escorted Constance from the ball the previous night would not leave her. Tavy had only once before seen him appear so torn, just before he kissed her in the rain.

She forced her feet over the side of the bed and to the floor, then her body to the clothes press. Garbed in an unadorned walking gown, she went to the kitchen and requested a muffin and tea from the cook. She lingered belowstairs where Abha found her. Lal sat on his shoulder gnawing on an apple core. The monkey jumped to her arm and snatched the remains of the muffin from her fingers.

Abha's regard seemed to assess her. She tilted her weary head. "Good morning?"

"*Memsahib*, I have found Marcus Crispin."

"Found him? Has he returned to town?"

Abha shook his head.

Octavia put a hand to her brow. "I am afraid I will not be receptive to cryptic statements today. Please."

"He did not leave London."

"But why would he tell me he went to the country then remain in town?" she said, then understood. Marcus had lied to her. "Do you know where he is now?"

Her longtime companion nodded.

"Nowhere admirable," she guessed.

He nodded again.

"Take me there."

"No."

"Well then why did you tell me?"

"So that you would know."

"You must take me to him, Abha. You would not have told me otherwise."

"I will convey to him a message from you."

"All right." She went into the parlor to the writing table, scribbled a few lines, and handed the sealed paper to him. "Please request a reply."

Abha bowed and departed.

Tavy ran to the back of the house, digging into her pocket for a coin. The kitchen boy sat in a corner by the door, a scrap of a lad with bright eyes.

Tavy bent to him. "Mr. Abha is taking a walk now. Please follow him and if he goes inside a building return to me swiftly and tell me where he has gone." She pressed the silver into his hand. "There will be another just like it when you are finished."

He nodded and darted out the door. Ten minutes later Tavy was restlessly pacing the parlor when Abha reappeared, his hand gripping the kitchen boy's skinny shoulder.

"He saw me, mum." The lad shrugged. "Don't know how. Trailed him like me pap taught me, in the shadows an' corners."

"Mr. Abha is very clever," Tavy consoled him, directing a thin-lipped look at her old friend. She produced the promised second coin. The boy palmed it and scurried away.

Abha crossed his thick arms over his chest. "I will take you there."

Her eyes widened. "Do you think you ought?"

He shook his head. "But I do not like this man and you must not wed him."

"I will not wed him anyway, you know, whether I see him now or not."

"Still, I will take you." Warning weighed in his deep-set eyes.

"I will not like what I find there."

"No. But you will no longer allow any person to sway your judgment on the matter."

"Any person?"

"Come." He turned and went toward the front door. Tavy grabbed up her cloak and bonnet and hurried after.

The carriage halted before a respectable apartment building near Piccadilly. Tavy didn't know what she had expected, but something along the lines of a squalid alleyway near the docks seemed more in the line of a blackmailer's haunt. She produced a guinea for the doorman, but the fellow remained reluctant. Abha stepped into the foyer, arms crossed, head bare, and the doorman retreated behind a chair. Tavy gave him another coin and, as directed, she and her hulking bodyguard ascended three flights of stairs.

At the door to the flat, Abha did not knock. Instead he produced a small sack containing several tiny dowels of iron and fitted one into the lock. Tavy watched, oddly unsurprised. He turned the handle and the door swung wide.

The apartment's furnishings were sparse yet tasteful, a rug, a piecrust table, two chairs, and a small dining table still containing the remnants of breakfast. Two cups, two plates, two sets of flatware. A pair of doors let off from the small main chamber. Tavy moved toward one but turned at the sound of the opposite door clicking open.

Marcus stood in the aperture, wearing only breeches. Tavy gulped at sight of so much skin and hair covering pale albeit well-toned male flesh. She snapped her gaze upward.

"Octavia." His face was even paler, mouth agape. "What are you doing here?"

She found her tongue. "Rather, I should say, what are you doing here when you have told me you were in the country? And where is here? Although—" She scanned his barely clad person again. "I am rapidly beginning to see. Far too rapidly." She pivoted around. Abha stood like a statue blocking the door. "Let me past."

"Did he bring you here?" Marcus demanded.

"Let me past, Abha. This instant."

"Marcus?" A voice came from the chamber behind the baron, inflected with cockney. It was light, like a girl's. And trembling. "Who is it?"

Nausea swirled in Tavy's midsection. Marcus's brow was drawn, his eyes closed.

"Nothing to concern you, Tabitha." He opened his eyes to Octavia, and his look pleaded. "I hope."

Chapter 20

CARGO. The lading, or whole quantity of whatever species of merchandise a ship is freighted with.
> —*Falconer's* Dictionary of the Marine

By the time Creighton arrived with the former quartermaster's report from the *Eastern Promise* tucked beneath his arm, Ben had already spent hours aboard ship, lamp in hand, examining every crevice, plank, and coil of rope for imperfections. And clues. He found nothing except a perfectly ordered vessel ready to haul away as soon as its cargo came aboard.

"You've already done the inspection, my lord? Thank you, sir. I would have had to do it this afternoon after the loading, and what with the—"

Ben waved an impatient hand. Awake since before dawn, he had welcomed the distraction. He could not call upon Octavia this early, no matter his impatience.

"Show me the quartermaster's report."

"Yes, sir." Creighton pulled the papers from his stack.

"I'm sorry about not coming up with anything on that odd cache of hair, sir."

"I am as well. But I've—" At the bottom of the page, a scrawl of ink arrested his gaze. "Creighton, I cannot clearly read the quartermaster's name here. What is it?"

"Jonas Sheeble. I was about to mention that."

"And what did you discover of him in my absence?" Ben said with calm he did not feel. His extended foray at Fellsbourne into inebriated self-pity rose thick in his throat. If not for it, he could have known this days ago.

"He's a shady fellow, sir. Not much trusted around the docks, although quite well-to-do for a sailor."

"He sailed with this vessel to the East Indies, and returned with it?"

"Yes sir. Several times before the owner offered her up for sale, it seems."

"When, most recently?"

"She embarked nearly two years ago, made it to Madras and sailed right into Calais less than six months later, where our French contact purchased her."

Ben's gaze traveled across the deck he'd just studied so carefully, then to the hatchway to the hold. "Her cargo?"

"The usual. Printed cotton piece goods and tea imports. Woolen exports."

"Only wool?"

Creighton nodded. "According to Sheeble's report, the lading bill, and the port inspector's document." He drew the other papers from beneath his arm and proffered them to Ben.

"Has Sully checked in with you lately?"

"No, sir. He must not have found Lord Crispin yet."

"Send him to me as soon as he does, wherever I am. At any hour."

"Yes, my lord."

Ben's gaze shifted to the gangplank. A sailor in tattered clothing hung about the dock end, his face dirt-smudged, casting glances up at them. Creighton moved across deck. In the lightening hours the docks had come alive with activity, sailors and workers moving amongst carts and onto berthed ships, hauling cargo and tending to their vessels.

"You there," Creighton said across the gangway. "Have you business here?"

"Gots me a message for his lordship there," the fellow grumbled and tugged his filthy cap brim.

Creighton held out his palm. "Give it over, man."

The sailor plucked a square of paper from the brim of his cap and exchanged it for a coin, then scampered away. Creighton offered the missive to Ben. A single line crossed the scrap.

Take particular care of your loved ones.

The hand was bold and undisguised. Ben knew it as well as his own. Styles.

He stared at the scrawled line. Last night he had shown his hand, trying to force his old friend to tell the truth concerning the fire. Ben had not expected instant capitulation, but he had not expected threats either.

It smacked of guilt.

Guilt could drive a man to threats. But so could the fear of being revealed. Guilt for an accidental crime. Fear of being discovered for an intentional one.

Lady Fitzwarren's warnings tugged at Ben. Styles had always been active in Parliament, and had been openly critical of Ben's father's politics. But political differences did not necessarily translate to assassination, and he had loved Jack like a brother. He could not have wanted Jack dead.

"My lord?" Creighton's voice came to him as though through a tunnel.

"It is nothing," Ben forced through his lips, folding the

message and slipping it into his waistcoat pocket. Nothing but a threat meant to control him. If he pursued the matter of the fire any further, Styles would hurt Constance.

He moved toward the gangplank.

"My lord, I thought you would wish to know, this vessel partnered with another ship on its last voyage east, the *Sea Bird*. She is shortly to set to sea again."

"To Madras?"

"Apparently, sir."

"The original owner of this ship is the man who still owns the *Sea Bird*, I presume?"

"No." Creighton paused. "Lords Crispin and Nathans now hold the *Sea Bird*'s papers. They bought her several weeks before you purchased this vessel."

Crispin.

A strange, humming urgency threaded through Ben's veins.

"Creighton, from whom did Lords Nathans and Crispin and our French friend in Calais purchase these vessels?"

Creighton tilted his head in an oddly wary gesture. "I thought you might already know, sir. It's Lord Styles."

The wind seemed not to stir. It could not be coincidence. Or perhaps coincidence only in so far as the community of traders wealthy enough to purchase a ship with cash was quite modest. Modest enough so he would never have connected Crispin and Styles if Octavia had not made him aware of Crispin's troubles.

But perhaps he was looking for connections that did not exist. Crispin had kissed Octavia for Styles's benefit, and the burr beneath the saddle had not been an accident. But how could Styles have committed arson or even blackmail yet he hadn't an idea of it? Their friendship could not have been a lie. Not so many years of it.

"Creighton?" Ben's voice sounded peculiar in his own ears. Tinny.

"Yes, sir?"

"How difficult was it for you to discover that Lord Styles once owned these vessels?"

"Extraordinarily, sir," his secretary replied promptly. "The dockmaster's registers were incomplete. I went on something of a scavenger hunt before I found trace of the original owner. I was obliged to grease a dozen sailors' palms before I even knew where to start looking."

"Were you surprised at this difficulty?"

"Yes, my lord. In fact I was. But—" He halted, obviously reluctant to continue.

"But what?"

"You said it yourself, my lord. A man has no need to protect himself from prying eyes when he has nothing to hide."

"I will return later if I am able." Ben did not hear his secretary's response, or see the faces of the sailors he passed on his way to his horse. The morning was advancing. He had little time before Constance left home for the day on visits. And, as much as he wished only to see Octavia now, as much as he ached to bring the doubt-filled waiting to an end, he could not have this conversation in her presence.

At the Duke of Read's town house he sent his card up and paced the receiving room until Constance appeared. Her eyes were red. She did not come to him, or extend her hand as usual.

"Did I wake you?"

"Heavens, no." She pulled the bell rope, an unstable smile crossing her lips. "I was writing correspondence. I am not always a social butterfly."

"I know that."

"Of course you do, hypocrite." She did not meet his gaze.

"Constance, I would like you to go home."

Her eyes snapped up, strangely dull. "I drink a bit too much champagne at one party and you wish to exile me to Scotland?"

"I do not ask it because of last evening."

"Papa is coming to town soon. I would be silly for me to make the journey then turn around and immediately return."

"Then go elsewhere. Entertainments are thin now. Lady Fitzwarren may be willing to retire to her home at Stratford for the winter."

"Lady Fitzwarren? Good heavens, why on earth would you wish to exile her too?"

"She merely came to mind. You seem to be in her company frequently of late."

"I am in Octavia Pierce's company frequently as well but I doubt you wish her gone from town." Her slender brows knitted.

"Constance, listen to—"

"No. I will not go simply because you say so."

"You are in danger."

"I am not."

Her reply came too swiftly. Ben moved toward her. She seemed to force lightness into her eyes, the glint in them unnatural.

"You are a thorough widgeon, Ben. I am quite content and not at all in any sort of distress."

"I did not say distress. I said danger. And I did not realize that copious tears are evidence of happiness."

"I was foxed."

"Why?"

She turned away with a shrug. "Those gentlemen kept giving me champagne. They were enormously diverting." Her voice sounded edgy, the Scots burr rather stronger now.

"Constance, tell me."

She whirled around. "Why should I? You don't tell me anything. And there is nothing to tell. I am perfectly well and perfectly weary of you imagining you can dictate to me." Her gaze skittered away again.

"I have only your safety in mind."

"I do not doubt it," she said in a smaller voice. "But you are wrong this time." Her fingers pleated and repleated folds in her skirt. Ben's chest and limbs felt numb, the goodness of the past entirely lost, first his brothers, then Styles, now Constance. He went to the door.

"I am not the person you always expected me to be, Ben." Her voice broke. "I am not strong like you."

He left without a word.

Traffic was smooth beneath the unusually brilliant sky and he reached his destination in short time. He deposited Kali in the mews near Hauterive's. The entrance to the club was locked now, shutters closed. But Ben hadn't any interest in the place. He moved along the narrow, unpaved street, glaringly naked in the bright daylight, straw strewn about in the dirt. A filthy pie seller vended his fare, a pen of suckling pigs for sale squealing at his heels. A prostitute lolled in a doorway, glassy-eyed with the aftereffects of too much gin and too little sleep, her rouge from the previous night smeared.

A tiny coal-blackened sweep curled around a mutt sleeping across the gin house's threshold. Ben stepped over boy and dog and pushed the door open. His throat tightened at the odors of stale ale and unwashed bodies. God, but it was good he'd always been drunk when he had come here.

The tables seemed clean, though, which they never were when the tavern was fully occupied. A handful of patrons slumped upon benches, slack-jawed with drink though it was not yet noon. Given his three days at Fellsbourne, Ben withheld judgment.

Lil looked up from behind the tap. Her lips curved into a sloe-eyed smile.

"Well, look what the cat drug in so soon after the last visit." Her gaze traveled up and down him. "You look good enough to eat, duck. But I don't suppose that's in the cards for ol' Lily today, is it?" She winked. Her skin looked thin over tired bones, her hair combed but in the daylight garishly tinted.

"Thank you, Lil. I have come to speak with you."

"'Bout what, love?"

"The other night when I was here, my friend Lord Styles came in. Do you recall?"

She nodded, her mouth settling into a line.

"You seemed unhappy with him."

"Unhappy weren't the word, love." She tilted a mug beneath the tap and drew ale into it, and set it on the bar before him.

"Why, Lil?"

"Seeing him got me to thinking about the girls. Especially my Missy."

"The girls?"

"All them girls who went off at once."

Ben's grip tightened. "Who is Missy?"

"Not but a sweet little one. Used to stay with me when the gentlemen weren't, you know. Didn't want to get herself into my line o' work, see, but we was good friends still. I used to know her mother 'fore she drank her sorry hide into a hole in the ground."

"Do you still see Missy?"

She shook her head and placed her palms upon the bar's surface as though for support. "Just the one letter in two years."

"Why did she go?"

"Told her she shouldn't, of course. But she liked the idea. All them girls did, but they was too young to know.

And none of them ever came back, so I was right to worry, wasn't I?"

One letter in two years. Ben released the glass carefully.

"Do you still have Missy's letter?"

The doxy's gaze fixed firmly in his. "What would you want with a thing like that, duck?"

Ben held her regard. Lines fanned from the corners of her big eyes—eyes that had seen at least as much of the worst of the world as his.

"I wish to help," he said.

She studied him for a moment, then pushed away from the bar and went through a door behind. She returned with a folded envelope and proffered it.

"Here it is, love. Don't know what good it'll do you. Just a mess of tears and loneliness."

Ben's breathing stalled. It must have cost the girl a considerable sum to send the missive, perhaps all the wages she had earned since her departure from London. The mark of origin on the envelope indicated Fort St. George. Madras.

He unfolded the single page and read the spindly lines. This was no clerk's hand, nor a prostitute's. The girl, Missy, could write.

Tears and loneliness, indeed. Her horrifying shipboard experience. And a name: Sheeble.

Ben folded the page, slipped it inside the envelope and handed it back to Lil. Crispin would pay for this. And Styles . . .

"How many girls went with Missy, Lil?"

Lil shrugged. "A few score, I 'spect."

"Perhaps this Mr. Sheeble that Missy mentions will know." The Mr. Sheeble who, when girls died from sickness that ran rampant aboard ship during the ocean voyage, cut off a lock of hair from each before casting the bodies overboard. To record his captain's losses, according to Missy's account.

Lil reached for Ben's hand.

"You're a clever one, love." Her voice was uncustomarily thick. "D'you think they made my Missy into a tart like me after all? She didn't say, so I think p'raps they did and she was too ashamed to tell old Lily."

Ben curled his fingers around hers and squeezed. "If Missy is anything like you, Lil, then she is a finer person than most I know."

She pulled away, sniffing.

"Lil?"

"Duck?"

"Why did seeing Lord Styles the other night remind you of Missy?"

Her eyes went flinty again, like that evening in Ben's fogged memory when he had barely noticed anything outside of his mind and heart so wrapped around the woman who had come back into his life. Who had never left it, in truth.

"Before they went off, he came in here looking all spruced up like you now. Turning eyes down the street, making promises to everything in a skirt, including my Missy." Her lips tightened. "He's the one as got them girls to go."

Tavy struggled against the lump in her throat and met Abha's gaze. "Why did you bring me here?"

"Ask him."

She took a deep breath and turned fully around once more. Marcus had donned a shirt and was drawing the door shut behind. A small hand arrested his action, becoming an arm then an entire slender body. Tavy's breath escaped her slowly.

The girl was stunning—shining raven hair, ivory skin, wide deep eyes the color of evergreen leaves that matched her modest round gown. Only the barest hint of care-worn corners at her lips and on her brow revealed her mean origins. Nevertheless, she was most definitely a girl, not over seventeen. Tavy's nostrils flared. She could not meet Marcus's gaze.

"I am so pleased to meet you, Tabitha," she said, "and so enormously glad to have this final justification for not marrying your protector."

"Octavia—"

"Marcus, I really do not imagine there is anything you could say that would alter my opinion of this situation. Nevertheless, I must ask you for the particulars, however distasteful I suspect I will find them. You see, I trust Abha with rather more than my life, and he seems to have thought it important for me not only to know you have a mistress, but also why." She pressed her palms to her burning cheeks.

"Will she reveal us, Marcus?" The girl lifted an angel's gaze, filled with devotion. She shifted it to Tavy and whispered, "Please, miss, do not tell him."

"I daresay I should be affronted that there seems to be someone else to whom you would not wish this—" Tavy gestured about her. "—situation to be revealed."

"Octavia, I cannot beg your pardon enough."

"Do not beg anything, Marcus. Just tell me about the blackmailer."

"She knows Mr. Sheeble?" The girl clutched Marcus's arm, and real fear shone in her gorgeous eyes.

"Tabitha, I must speak with this lady alone." He disentangled her lily fingers and urged her back into the bedchamber. "I will be with you again shortly," he added softly.

The girl's gaze eased with a look of such honest affection, Tavy's breath caught. Marcus patted her hand and shut the door behind her.

"Allow me to don more fitting—"

"That will not be necessary," Tavy said hastily. "I have already seen quite a bit more than your feet, so the cow is already out of the barn, as it were. And frankly I do not wish to be here any longer than absolutely necessary."

He frowned. "What do you wish to know?"

"Who is Sheeble?"

"A sailor and thief. As I told you before, his business is in dirty cargo which he seeks to sell at great profit."

"What is this girl to him?"

His gaze skittered away.

"Marcus?"

Face stiff, he uttered, "His insurance."

"I do not know why the men of my acquaintance should be so fond today of speaking in riddles," Tavy said with an understated sigh.

"He has threatened to send her where he sends the others if I do not assist him as I have before. He insists that I continue to do his bidding whenever he wishes."

Tavy's stomach clenched. "The others?"

"Girls. English girls."

"Where does he send them, Marcus?"

"To the East Indies. Where else?"

Abha's soft shoes shifted upon the floor.

"You are aiding a man who sells English girls into prostitution so that you can retain hold of your own?" Tavy could not mask her disgust.

A spark lit in Marcus's eyes. "They are intended as wives for English soldiers and minor Company officials, so that the men will not resort to taking native brides. But—" He halted.

"But?"

He shook his head, his mouth an implacable line.

"You will not tell me more, I see, so I can only imagine the worst." Tavy folded her trembling hands. "Marcus, was I or my family ever in danger?"

He hesitated, then shook his head.

"Well then, I am sorry for you." She turned, and this time Abha stepped aside to allow her passage.

"She is not what you believe," Marcus said in a low voice. "I am not."

A dull ache lodged in Tavy's chest. Who was she to throw stones at him for loving the wrong person, or at the girl for imagining in him her rescuer? At Tabitha's age, she had done the same.

"No. I can see that," she said quietly. "Why don't you take her to safety? To the countryside?"

"Her mother and young sisters are here. She will not leave them."

"Even to be a lord's mistress with a house of her own?"

He nodded.

"Then you are fortunate to have met with such a loyal heart, I think."

Marcus's brow drew down. Tavy walked out of the flat. At the carriage, she finally met Abha's gaze.

"I am still not certain why you did this. I am both grateful and angry with you for it. But I wanted to know the truth, so I have no one to blame but myself. Still, I feel rather peculiar and think it would be best if we did not see each other again today."

He bowed and stepped back.

When Tavy reached home, she went to her bedchamber and instructed her maid that if asked, she was to say that her mistress had a megrim. She did have one, in any case, as well as a horrible suspicion as to the reason she had made a project of Marcus's blackmailer weeks earlier.

A knock came at the door and it opened.

"Octavia?" Alethea queried in a voice far too lively for Tavy's confused state at the present. "Lady Fitzwarren has arrived and— Oh, goodness, your face! What has happened?"

"Thank you, sister." Tavy returned to the view of the bright autumn day through the windowpane. "The next time I wish praise for my appearance, I shall certainly come to you."

"But you have been crying."

Tavy rubbed at the moisture on her cheek. "Have I?"

Alethea moved across the chamber and smoothed her hand along Tavy's arm.

"Lady Fitzwarren has come for luncheon as planned, but something is amiss and you have forgotten that, haven't you? I will tell her you are indisposed."

"No." Tavy sniffed forcefully, blinked away tears, and headed for the door. "Company will be just the thing to wrest me from my blue devils."

When Tavy entered the parlor, Lady Fitzwarren's face opened in a look of perfect awareness, proving Tavy's instinct horridly wrong. The dowager moved with rustling haste to grip her hands.

"What has he done?" she demanded.

"Oh, well." The tears prickled again, and she gulped them back. "It seems he has taken a mistress—a mere child, but a remarkably beautiful one—and is being blackmailed by a very bad man through this girl. He is obviously quite in love with her, however, and she with him. So who is to fault either of them?" she finished with an airy wave of her hand.

"Not D—" The dowager's fleshy lips snapped shut. "No, of course not." She dropped Tavy's hands and tilted back on her heels. "Then why are you crying, silly child?"

"Because I have just been thinking some tremendously uncomfortable thoughts and I am not quite certain how to proceed now."

"First things first. Have you broken off the engagement?"

"Well, yes. Of course."

"Oh, thank heavens," Alethea said upon a sizable exhalation, and sank against a chair.

"Yes, let us all sit and talk this through," the dowager said. "Your sister and I are consumed with relief and consequently somewhat shaken, so you must pour out the tea, Octavia."

Tavy obeyed, and since the activity prevented her from chewing on her fingertips she was grateful for it. When she finished she could not be still. She went to the window, needing to look out. Always, outward.

"I think I accepted Marcus, or rather even considered accepting him, because I somehow knew he loved someone else."

Neither of the other women spoke immediately. Then Alethea asked softly, "You do not wish for a love match, after all?"

"She does not believe she deserves one," Lady Fitzwarren stated.

"Whyever not?" Alethea sounded affronted.

"Because your mother is a selfish, airheaded widgeon. And your father, a kind but weak man, never had any idea what to do with a daughter as spirited as Octavia. To have sent her away to live with that cold woman and stickbrained man in the very prime of her young womanhood was a thorough travesty, I always said."

"You said that? To whom?"

"To them!"

Tavy turned away from the view. "You know, this is all very interesting, naturally, given that you are speaking of me, but I am still here in the room."

"Have I said anything with which you disagree?" the dowager demanded.

"No. Mama and Papa did not sympathize with my character in the least. I was terribly awkward, not at all pretty, and too plainspoken. I hadn't any of your feminine graces,

Thea, and I loved all the wrong things, like sea travel and adventure and India. As girls on the verge of their introduction into society go, I was a complete disaster. But he saw something in me that he liked, nevertheless."

"Not Marcus Crispin?"

"Octavia Pierce, for a young lady of impeccable honesty you have been wretchedly deceptive."

"Well, I don't know why I should have told anyone anything about it. I have always been traveling in some way or another, in my imagination even before I left England, dreaming of adventures, not content living within myself. Marcus seemed the perfect solution for continuing to live in that manner. He would not have asked anything of me that I would have found difficult to provide. And he never would have left me because he never would have given himself to me in the first place."

"Left you?" Alethea whispered.

Tavy met Lady Fitzwarren's gaze. Tears quivered on the rims of the dowager's baggy orbs.

"I am deceptive, Aunt Mellicent, to myself most of all."

The dowager nodded. "How do you feel now, child?" she said without a trace of sentimentality, despite the tears.

"Wretched." Her stomach hurt, as well as her brain and heart, in a wholly new and desolate manner. "I think I must go now and write a note." She crossed the chamber and returned to her bedchamber.

As she had requested, Abha was not to be found, and she still hadn't the desire to see him. So she put the missive into a footman's hands—a remarkably direct and open action that felt marvelously good—and waited.

After several hours, nerves strung, she asked the footman about his errand. He replied that he had given it to Lord Doreé's first footman.

Tavy continued waiting. The day waned and Ben did

not call or send a message. Perhaps she had been wrong about him. Perhaps she should have trusted her misgivings, as before.

But as dusk deepened into a purple-blue haze, her nerves twisted tighter, her stomach knotting in a continuous loop. She worried for herself. For Marcus and the girl who should not have to suffer even if they did not entirely deserve her help. And most of all for Ben. She could not make herself believe that he would not return her message if he were well. She simply could not have been that mistaken again.

She must see him, and she was finished with waiting for him to come to her. Seven years past finished with it. This time she had pressing business that could not wait.

Chapter 21

*BINDING-STRAKES. Two strakes of oak in the deck.
The design of them is to strengthen and bind the deck so
well together, as to prevent its drawing.*
                    —Falconer's Dictionary of the Marine

Ben went to Crispin's rooms. A bulky fellow with weathered skin stood on the street corner, leaning against a coal bin. One of Sully's men. He tugged his cap to Ben and shook his head. Crispin still had not returned home.

He went to Brooks's club, but none of Crispin's acquaintances had seen him, and Ben did not know why he bothered. For years he had expected his employees to take care of tasks without his intervention. And they always did. But the anger in his blood fueled by frustrated hopelessness and an urgency to bring it all to an end propelled him through London.

At Styles's house the butler shook his head apologetically. "His lordship left for the countryside this morning."

"When do you expect him to return?"

"He did not say, my lord. But his man said he took only a few items in his bag and did not require assistance for the journey."

Ben rode Kali to India House without entirely knowing where he guided her. At the door to the library, Lord Gosworth hailed him.

"How do you do, Doreé. Just the man I was hoping to find, actually."

Ben bowed. He hadn't the time or attention for discussing business. But he hadn't the clarity of mind for anything else. The only moments he'd had of true sanity since returning from Kent were those in which he held Octavia in his arms. But he would not allow himself that again until the rest was settled. He could not. He would not offer her a man who did not yet know himself.

"Nathans called upon me yesterday." The earl stepped close as a pair of gentlemen passed by. "Said Marcus Crispin's not been in touch with him for days now. Fellow was in a real taking. Recently sank a load of blunt in a vessel called the *Sea Bird* just about ready to sail. She's an impressive boat sitting at the export docks now, in fact."

"What is Lord Nathans's concern?"

"Says the goods haven't arrived from up north yet." He lowered his voice. "But Crispin signed the lading papers today. Ship is set to sail with an empty hold, and Nathans is in a pother over it. Wanted my confidential advice on how to handle a renegade partner." Gosworth's eyes narrowed. "I told him to ask you. Thought you might know something about it."

"With all due respect, you were mistaken, sir. I haven't an idea of the business. And never having had a partner myself, I am the least likely to be able to offer advice." Sheeble was probably holding the *Sea Bird*'s cargo— the girls—somewhere else in London. Possibly near the docks, at a brothel or several. But if he were taking them from the hells again, Lil would have known. This time Styles must be finding them elsewhere, perhaps in the country . . . where he had just gone to check up on his cargo?

Country-bred girls. Farm girls who could read and write. To become prostitutes in the Indies? It made no sense.

Gosworth's face sobered. "Doreé?"

"Sir?"

"I'm sure you're well able to assist Nathans and Crispin if you wish, of course," the older gentleman said. "But I've been meaning to say a word to you for some time now."

Ben waited.

"Your father was as fine a person as I've ever known." Gosworth clasped his arm. "You are his son, lad, through and through."

Throat dry, Ben returned his steady regard.

"Thank you."

He released Ben and bowed. "Good day, my lord."

"Good day, sir."

Ben called for Kali and rode home.

"My lord," Samuel said as he entered his house and pulled off his greatcoat, "a message arrived for you several hours ago."

"Sully?"

"No, sir."

Ben accepted the pile of correspondence from the footman and went to his study. Dropping the post onto his desk, he crossed to the sideboard and took up a carafe of brandy and filled a glass to the rim. One palm braced upon the sideboard, he drank the contents. But it did not serve to still the chaos in him.

Gosworth was a good man. And the men who worked

for Ben—Singh, Creighton, Sully, Samuel—gave him their loyalty and discretion without fail. He paid them well for it, but there was more. More to Lil's trust. More to Abha's iron-fisted faithfulness.

Yet the two people Ben had most cared about for years, most trusted like a brother and sister, were lying to him.

Styles's deception dug deep. Knowing more about it now only tore wider the wound of betrayal. But Constance's evasions were nearly as painful to bear. They had never been truly honest with each other, both hiding far too many secrets. But something distressed her greatly now, yet she did not trust him with it.

His gaze slewed to the desk. A modest ivory envelope topped the stack of letters. A lady's writing paper.

He poured another dram of liquor and carried it across the study. The fire remained unlit, lamps dark. Only bluish evening light filtering through the window illuminated his name on the envelope.

Not Constance's hand.

Octavia's.

He swallowed around the ache in his throat, set his glass on the desk, and took up the letter.

"You needn't read it. I am here now, so I can just as easily tell you."

She stood in the doorway, the dim light from the corridor casting her in silhouette. Samuel hovered behind, as though she had gotten in front of him unawares. Astounding. But Octavia Pierce had never been anything but.

"You are here," he said as though in a dream. But he did not trust dreams. He trusted in very little any longer. Except, perhaps, this woman.

She drew the door shut in Samuel's face and pressed her back against it.

"I realize this constitutes intruding upon you at home again." She spoke quickly. "But given everything, I thought perhaps that prohibition might be relaxed, although frankly it probably should not be for the sake of my reputation, especially at this late hour. I did come in a hackney, though."

"Octavia—"

"This must be tiresome for you."

He shook his head and barely managed the word, "Tiresome?"

"Well, I always seem to be coming to you in order to share some awful news and ask your help f—" She faltered. "—for another man."

"Is that why you are here now?"

"Yes. No. Yes. Perhaps. I don't know." Her eyes swam with the same distress as that night at Fellsbourne before the rain.

"I will help you if I can." He would, whether she still wanted Crispin or not. He simply could not prevent himself from doing so. "I will help."

She pushed away from the door and moved swiftly across the chamber. She halted a stride from him, seeming to balance upon the balls of her feet. Her gaze sought.

"Is this all right?" she whispered. "That I am here?"

"You must know it is."

She threw herself against his chest and he grabbed her up and wrapped his arms around her.

"I am miserable." Her words came muffled into his coat. "I want to laugh again. Please make me laugh. It used to be you always could."

"I did so to see you smile. But forgive me, *shalabha*, at present you do not seem in a jesting mood."

A half laugh, half sob stumbled from her throat. She grasped his waistcoat and pressed her body close.

"Then make me sigh. Make me weep with pleasure as you did in the country when I forgot about everything else. Now, Ben, please. I need you."

His hands rounded her back to fit her against him, his throat thick.

"Making you weep seems to be my specialty."

She groaned softly, a sound at once of unhappiness and release.

"No. Not in the manner you mean." Her face lifted. "Others did, occasionally. Perhaps even I did. But not you." She rose onto her toes and touched her lips to his chin, the sweetest caress that ran through his body like silvered water. "Except that once, of course, for about six months." Her eyes closed, her lips making a seductive exploration of his jaw, her hands stroking across his chest. Ben felt her, and his body followed his heart's aching.

"Six months." He barely breathed.

"Until I returned from Calcutta with my aunt and uncle and learned you had gone. I stopped weeping then. Tears, you know, are born of despair, but also of hope."

He kissed her open mouth, threading his fingers through her hair and holding her close. But she wanted more. Her hands sought, her tongue hot and her sublimely curved body restless against him. She kissed his neck, unwinding his cravat and unbuttoning his waistcoat with quick fingers.

"Will you again make me ask you to take me to your bed?"

"No. But Octavia, the servants—"

"Are like the king's Yeoman of the Guard. I have noticed this. And well they should be. But even if they were not I wouldn't care. I want to live as myself again, Ben. I want to feel happiness, and the last time I felt that I was naked and in your arms."

He picked her up and carried her to the stairs, taking them three at a time and pausing to kiss her at the top of the flight. She twined her arms about his neck, her breaths heavy.

"Go. Go quickly," she uttered with the same urgency pressing at him.

In his bedchamber the door slammed shut and their mouths locked, hands tearing at clothing until she wore only a thin shift. He pulled her to the bed, unfastening his trousers and dragging her down onto his lap. She straddled him and twisted to tug the chemise over her head, revealing her lissome beauty in a sensuous stretch that mounted the pounding in Ben's blood. His hands circled her waist, her butter-soft skin hot and flushed beneath his mouth as he kissed her belly, along each rib, caressing the undersides of her breasts with impatient fingers then sweeping his thumbs over their velvet centers. They rose to his touch. With his mouth he covered a tight pink peak, teased her arousal with his tongue, and she arched to bring him closer.

She was beautiful everywhere, the hearth light illuminating her skin to gilded ivory, her half-lidded eyes rich and sparkling with flame. He slipped his hand between her thighs and stroked her. She moaned, damp and taut to his touch, and pressed into him, impatience in the sensuous thrust of her hips.

"Ben." Her voice was thin. "I—" Her palms slipped to his face, turning him up to meet her fevered gaze. Tumbling from its pins, her hair like molten fire cascaded before her eyes now wide with passion but another urgency too. "I never accepted Marcus until you told me to. He offered, but I said I needed time to consider. He announced the betrothal at Fellsbourne without my consent."

Ben's heart racketed beneath his ribs. "Is this true?"

"Of course it is true. I cannot lie any longer."

"Why didn't you tell me this before?"

Her brows twisted. "Misplaced loyalty. And I believed it did not matter to you one way or the other."

"It mattered. It matters." He pulled her down and embedded himself deep in her, a groan breaking from his chest as she whimpered her body's acceptance. He held her to him, unmoving, breathing in her scent of roses and perfect woman and whispered, "It matters."

She trembled, shifting her hips, then sighing as she drew him out then into her again, her fingertips pressing into his shoulders.

"Oh," she sighed, "this is what I want. This."

He grasped her soft buttocks and guided her need, too hard and hot and surrounded by her not to take her harder with each stroke, to satisfy the desperate craving to have her in every way, beyond flesh. To make her his. But she needed no encouragement. She rode him faster, throwing back her shoulders and arching her neck. He spread his palm between her breasts and slid it to her throat, the vibrations of her moans a gift beneath his hand, then her tripping laughter.

"Thank you, Benjirou. Thank you for rescuing me again," she whispered upon a sigh like rippling tide, eyes closed, her smiling lips wide, and Ben lost his soul, finally, irrevocably. He sought her, heart spilling, body surging. Her brow knit and she bore down upon him, moaning as he pulled her tight, her laughter transformed into cries of pleasure, then astonishment, then ecstasy. With each fluid shudder she branded him, and he submitted. He buried his face in her hair, crushed her sweet, supple body to his chest, and came hard and complete inside her.

She broke his hold, her shimmering eyes flying wide. "What about caution?"

"I have never been cautious with you, Octavia Pierce. Never." He caught her hand and pressed his mouth to her palm. "I simply cannot be."

She said nothing, her lips parted as her breathing slowed, firelight dancing across her smooth cheeks and pert freckled nose. She drew her gaze away and dipped her head to his shoulder, her hands curving around his ribs. He encircled her slight body with one arm and stroked along the length of her tumbled hair.

Finally she slipped off his lap and pulled up a corner of the bed linens to wrap around her. She looked small and vulnerable in his bed, and he wanted to take her in his arms and hold her, this time more tightly so that she would not leave. But lines of tension creased her brow, and she remained withdrawn, as though uncertain.

"What is it?" he said quietly. "Do you wish to tell me the news that brought you here tonight?"

"You brought me here tonight." Her eyes were too wide. Wary. It stilled his heart.

"The other reason you came," he made himself say.

"I suppose I must. I don't wish to think about it, but until I tell you I will not be able to let it be." She glanced toward their clothing strewn upon the floor. "It is quite unpleasant. Perhaps we should be dressed for this conversation."

"Under no circumstances."

Hesitation entered her eyes. "Ben, I do not—"

"Octavia, you are not going anywhere any time soon."

"But—"

"You came here of your own volition. Pay the consequences of your folly." He could not help smiling.

Her lips twitched. But then she frowned. "This is very important. It is also very grim."

"I have been responsible for dealing with important and grim matters every day for the past seven years, and longer. That you are involved this time is my sole concern."

Her warm eyes questioned, pools of liquid hope.

"Tell me about your business," she whispered. "About what you do."

"My business is . . ." He drew a breath. " . . . broad."

She nodded, rapid little movements of her head, her cheeks flushed. A sensation filled Ben like a fist opening up, releasing years of regret and resentment.

"I pursue and halt those who seek to do harm to others."

"Halt them from doing harm in what manner exactly?"

"Enslaving people. Waging unjust war. Bankrolling tyranny."

"Good heavens." She released a breath, a soft swish of air. "Quite a bit broader than I had imagined." She seemed to consider it for a moment. "Tea and woolens serve as a cover for all of that?"

"Something must. Not everyone considers the activities of my organization in a positive light."

"I daresay. Where does all of this take place?"

"Wherever it is needed."

She said nothing in response. They sat for a moment like that, the flame-lit night holding them in its generous embrace. Finally she drew in a long breath.

"Marcus is being blackmailed by the Mr. Sheeble he spoke of before, to aid him in shipping poor girls to India to be wives for English soldiers and Company clerks. Apparently this supply of English girls is to prevent them from taking Indian brides."

It was the missing piece of the puzzle. Better than Ben had assumed for the girls who survived the voyage, but not by any means legal. And so many had died.

"Is that all?" he asked.

"Well, I dare say that is quite a bit of 'all' already. Although perhaps not to you, I suppose. But, no. There is a girl involved. Her safety is Marcus's greatest anxiety. It seems that something untoward is occurring, and he is unhappy about it. He is assisting with this next journey only in order to protect this particular girl from danger."

"They are being taken under false pretenses and are perishing on the voyage east."

"Dear Lord." Then her gaze sharpened. "You know about it already?"

"Some, but this completes the picture. How much did he tell you about the girl?"

Tavy held Ben's steady, warm, perfectly beautiful gaze that she could live inside forever.

"He did not tell me. I met her."

His regard did not alter, but a muscle ticked in his jaw. Her fingers itched to smooth it away, to uncurl his fists. She did not care about the girl or Marcus's faithlessness. Tavy understood better than she should why Marcus had treated her shabbily. She had lied to him as much as he had lied to her, both of them trying to escape what their hearts wanted most by using the other as a shield.

"It is all right," she assured. "Not about all those girls, of course. But about the one girl and Marcus."

The furrows between Ben's brows deepened.

"Truly." She dipped her gaze to his hands, which held the fates of so many people, and worked her fingertips along his palms until he released his grip. Strong hands, and beautiful. She loved the way he touched her, the way he looked at her. "I have been considering it all day, you know, and I think he imagined I could guide him away from his infatuation for this girl. Not that he would transfer his feelings for her to me, but that I would be a steadying influence on him. He actually said something like that once or twice. That I was steady."

Silence met her. Tavy looked up and her heart pirouetted. A half smile crooked Ben's mouth.

"What?" she breathed.

"He does not know you very well, does he?"

Throat dry, she shook her head.

"Not well at all," he murmured.

"You do?"

His grin slipped away.

"What if I have changed?" Her voice quavered like a silly girl. "What if I have decided that adventure is not exciting after all? You see, I think after this escapade, I am weary of it."

"Then," he said without a hint of levity, "you must forthwith live a quiet and staid existence. Perhaps take up stitchery or some such thing."

"Stitchery."

"Yes. Or is that what old spinster women do?"

Her heart thudded. "Spinster women?"

"No," he replied without a moment's lapse. "Stitchery would not do for you. Absolutely not." His voice was husky.

Tavy laughed and his eyes sparkled. A thrill of happiness scurried through her. Ben pulled her to him, wrapped his arms around her, and kissed her on the mouth, then on the brow and neck and everywhere in between. She slipped her hands along his sides to his waist, her heart expanding. Being with him felt so right. And yet it had felt this way before, in the country, when she was foolish enough to believe that making love with him meant something else. Something more.

She had felt it long before that too. Seven years ago.

But this time she knew better. This time she would not be so foolish.

"I should leave now."

"No." He spoke against her neck, his mouth delicious and hot upon her skin, making her tingly all over. "You will not."

"You are accustomed to people doing what you wish, I suspect. But would you hold me here against my will?"

He drew back, his eyes serious. "The temptation would be great. Do you wish to leave?"

She placed her hand on his chest. He covered it, flattening her palm to his firm muscle. His heart beat steady and fast, and hers tripped in reply.

She shook her head.

He drew her down into his arms. She curled against his body, the male beauty she still could not quite believe she could touch after all the years struggling not to dream of him. Her palm smoothed along his chest.

"I wanted for so long to put the past behind me, that time when I imagined the world was made for adventure," she whispered. "I have been trying to forget it for years. But, it's strange. Sometimes those memories feel a great deal more like reality than now."

"They are so vivid to you?"

"I daresay you have had such an exciting life since then you barely have any memory of that time at all. Except of course for the indecency of my shift." She smiled uncertainly against his shoulder.

He cupped her hand in his palm and ran the pad of his thumb along each of her fingers.

"To shade the sun, you carried a yellow parasol with white lace." He spoke softly just above her brow. "You wore your hair a great deal shorter, the ribbon of your bonnet tied to the side as though it constricted your throat to wear it otherwise. You spoke to merchants in the bazaar like you had known them your entire life, and they the same to you, despite your wretched Hindi. You laughed without inhibition. And you chewed on your nails."

Tavy struggled to draw breath. "I used to do quite a few things I no longer do."

"You still chew on your lip at times."

"A gentleman would not mention that."

"It makes this gentleman want to kiss you."

She lifted her head and met his gaze flecked with firelight. The intensity of the black depths was not at all in company with his teasing tone.

"*Shalabha,*" he only said.

"Why did you call me that?" she whispered.

He turned onto his side, hand slipping to her hip.

"Because, grasshopper, you were all legs."

"No."

"Yes." His fingertips traced a path up the inside of her calf and thigh, halting just shy of her tender crux, his palm warm. Tavy's breathing stuttered. He had just made love to her, yet his slight caress ignited her desire again, this time languorous but still so strong.

"And here I thought it was because I fluttered about your flame." She tried to sound amused, but her heart beat so hard he must feel it. *"Shalabha*, a moth, a plain insect unnoticed by everyone."

"A beautiful girl," he murmured, stroking. "Beautiful legs."

"All legs. And elbows, and—"

He moved atop her, pressing her knees apart. "Legs that my hands ached to explore." He reached beneath her knee and his fingertips dallied upon her skin, the barest touch licking across her like sunshine. "Legs I imagined myself between." He drew her thigh alongside his hip, his smooth, hard arousal coming against her. "Legs I wanted wrapped around me."

"You did?" she breathed. "Back *then*?"

"Yes. Cross your ankles."

She did so, sighing a long breath of mingled pleasure then mounting anticipation. Ben kissed her throat and she dropped her head back, already feeling him inside her even as she anticipated it.

But these were lover's words. She had been an awkward girl, the girl she often still felt like.

"I think I don't believe you," she said very quietly, so perhaps he would not hear it.

"I find that difficult to comprehend." He shifted his hips, caressing intimately. A sound of want stole from her throat, and she twined her fingers in his satiny hair.

"I mean about then. I was not— I was different."

The tip of his tongue traced her ear. "Before you desert the past, Octavia, know the truth of it," he whispered against her skin. "I imagined this. Having you. You wanting me."

She trembled, gripping his arms, and where he stroked her soft flesh she throbbed. She tilted her hips up to meet him more fully and he came into her in a fluid, possessing thrust. Her back arched, her body pleasured as he filled her so completely, stretching her and making her want everything. His palm circled her jaw and he bent his head and kissed her like he was drinking from her lips. She sighed, the past and present tangling together in her heart and body, doubts and certainty twisted so that one looked like the other.

"You might have had anyone you wanted," she said upon a sigh.

"I wanted you."

"I was no one."

"You were beautiful. Your smile, your laughter, the words upon your tongue." He made a sound deep in his chest as he stroked into her, his thrusts controlled, seducing, making her need him more with each slow invasion.

"Ben."

"Your eyes and glance," he murmured above her lips. "Your touch."

"I never touched you. Not until—"

"You often did. You did not know that you did." He kissed her, capturing her breaths as he moved in her, caressing her to a madness of helplessness, his body a masterpiece of giving that made her only want to give more until she was empty. He wrapped his hand around her hip and held her firmly to him, his voice deep and rough. "You were not afraid."

Never. Enthralled, as he had accused her weeks ago. Intoxicated. Beyond infatuated. But not afraid.

She turned her cheek to the pillow, dragging her gaze away, reveling in his thrusts, pulling him in as the sweet ache built alongside the pain of wanting him more than she could endure.

"Perhaps I should have been," she whispered, surrendering to him fully, finally, a sob of mingled relief and agony catching in her throat for the heart she was losing after so many years of holding onto it like life. But there was no life without him. She had known it then and nothing could change it. Not now. The moment she had met him—a naïve, wide-eyed girl seeking adventure—it was too late.

He touched her face and turned her to him.

"No," he said roughly. "You should have been mine."

Tears stole along her cheeks as their bodies sought, dancing with the beauty of skin and sighs. He touched her deep, and everywhere, making her his again and again with each caress, each breath drawn as one. And when the violence of her need grew too great, he touched her anew, deeper yet, and she came apart, crying out in blind, wordless ecstasy, then again when he found his pleasure in her.

He brushed the moisture from her cheeks as he had that night in the garden in Madras, and again at Fellsbourne. But he did not ask why she wept now because he must already know—although she did not really, whether she wept from joy or sorrow. She had given her heart once, had it destroyed, and held hard onto the remaining pieces for years since. This second giving away was anguish.

She stared into the fire, her vision blurring.

"Do not hurt me again, Ben." Her words were barely a whisper. "I think I would forget entirely how to be me."

His arms came around her and he gathered her to him,

lips pressed to her brow. Drawing back, he threaded his fingers through her hair and held her, his eyes lit with sparks from the flames full of wonder and longing.

"I will not. I could not."

Her lungs compacted.

"I—" she choked out. "I am so in love with you." Trembles shook her, of fear and fullness. "I have always been."

His throat worked, his eyes a storm of darkness. But he did not speak. Tavy's heart pounded, joined by an echo, a staccato rapping on the door.

"Milord?" The hushed voice came urgently from the other side of the panel. But in Tavy's heart another voice spoke, cold and sharp, Aunt Imene telling him to take his hands off her. The expression in his eyes now was the same as then, warmth rapidly withdrawing into distance.

He drew a hard breath. "Blast."

"An understatement, perhaps." She pulled out of his arms.

He grasped her wrist and with his other hand stroked back her hair. Then he released her, pulled on his trousers, and went to the door, closing it behind him.

Tavy tugged a bed linen around her body and sat motionless. She suspected his servants would not disturb him like this unless absolutely necessary. But her heart spun around the seven-year-old memory of waiting for a man who never returned. And he had not said he loved her.

The door opened and Ben came across to her. He bent, wrapped his hand around the side of her face and tilted her mouth up to his. The kiss was too sweet, too perfect, and far too brief.

"I must go out now." His voice was low.

"Now?"

"I must attend to a bit of business."

In the middle of the night. Business as only this man would have.

She managed to nod. "All right."

"I will return shortly. Don't leave."

"Don't—"

"Stay." He backed toward the dressing room door.

"Stay?"

The corner of his mouth lifted, the dent appearing in his cheek. "Stay." He went into the other chamber. He reappeared shortly, dressed with a careless elegance that stole Tavy's breath, and crossed to the door. He paused. Then he returned to her, scooped his hand around the back of her head and kissed her hard.

"Stay." He broke away and departed.

Tavy stared at the door. Finally she crawled up the bed to the pillows, lay down on her side and tucked her hands beneath her cheek. But without his body to heat her, she was chilled. She rose and went to the fire to stoke the coals. Their clothing lay scattered upon the floor. She draped her gown and undergarments over a chair.

With ridiculous shyness she gathered Ben's discarded clothes too. His chambers were understated and masculine, done in dark woods and jewel-toned fabrics. She glanced about, hoping to find hints of India, but it felt like prying to look too closely, so she laid his clothing on the dressing table. She hesitated, then took up his cravat and shirt again and pressed them to her face, breathing in deeply. Her legs got wobbly, of all things.

She set down the clothes, her fingers brushing over a stiff square in the pocket of his waistcoat. She yanked her hand away. If it was prying to look around his chambers, then it certainly would be a greater intrusion to dig into his pockets.

Instinct and something more than curiosity drove her. The note unfolded easily between her fingers. *Take particular care of your loved ones.*

The air of the chamber seemed to grow colder. Was

that where he had gone? Were his loved ones in trouble now, in the middle of the night? Who? Constance? Lord Styles?

Tavy stuffed the paper back into the pocket, her stomach sick and heart racing. She crossed the frigid chamber to the bed, climbed in and pulled the blankets up to her neck.

She did not sleep, eyes wide to the deepening black of night as the coals in the grate died to embers, then to ash, and still he did not return. Again. In the darkness, her body strung with mingled fulfillment and dread, Tavy began to understand about all those years ago and a beautiful young man who, perhaps, simply could not return to her. Who, with the world's troubles as his daily responsibility, might never be able to. Just as he might never be able to tell her everything she longed to know. Or, even, to love her.

Finally, she understood. And it made her feel very small indeed.

Chapter 22

DESERTION. The act of forsaking a ship or boat, or running without leave of absence.
— *Falconer's* Dictionary of the Marine

He's counting his last minutes, milord, or else I wouldn'ta bothered you like that." Sully's thick brow furrowed as he climbed aboard his cob.

"How long ago was he shot?" Ben pulled Kali around.

"An hour, I 'spect. Jimmy's watching him now, but he ain't no surgeon. If the bully-back kicks a'fore we get there, I wouldn't blame the lad for it."

Ben rode fast, pressing Kali through the dark streets, her hooves striking cobbles then hard-packed dirt when they accessed the narrower alleys. He pulled the mare to a halt before the mews in the most familiar street to him this side of Mayfair, threw the reins to the stable hand, and went inside. The scents of horses and gin met him in the chill air.

Sully pressed open a stall door. "In here, milord."

Beside a prone form, a hulking youth with half-lidded

eyes crouched against the wall. He stood and pulled the brim of his cap.

"Bloke's frightful bad off, milord."

"Thank you, Jimmy. That will be all." He gestured the men out then knelt in the straw beside Sheeble.

He was a small man, dark-whiskered, and wiry like most sailors. Now his weathered face shone ghostly pale in the lamplight, his lips gray.

"If ye've come to finish me off," he gurgled, barely moving his mouth, "then go 'head and do it right quick, yer lordship. I'd 'preciate it. I got me a nast—" He coughed and blood flecked onto his lips. "—nasty belly ache."

Ben drew back the blanket covering him. Crimson soaked Sheeble's shirt and waistcoat. His narrow body shook, the life losing force in his veins. Ben replaced the coverlet.

"Who did this to you?"

Sheeble's face screwed up. "His connivin', belly-stabbin' lordship."

"Lord Styles or Crispin?"

"'Tweren't Crispin. 'Fraid of his own shadow, that one." He coughed, sending another trickle of blood along his chin. Ben took up a corner of the blanket and wiped the stain away.

"Lord Styles hired you to load the girls aboard ship in secret here in London, then to make certain they arrived in the East Indies, is that correct?"

Sheeble's eyes closed.

"You may as well tell me," Ben said. "You will die very shortly anyway. A confession will place the blame where it is most merited. Lord Styles will be punished for murdering you."

The man's eyes slid open a crack, but it cost him effort.

"Went over there in 'nineteen."

"To Madras? Crispin met the girl on that trip?"

Sheeble's thin lips twisted. "Didn't know they was all below until halfway there. Then we had him."

No wonder so many girls had perished, stored in the hold like cargo aboard a slave ship.

"Why English girls? Why take them to India?"

"He don't like our boys consortin' with them womens over there. Got to keep 'em apart to rule 'em right. Ev'rybody knows that."

English brides for Company men and soldiers. No Indian wives like Ben's mother. No family connections. No . . . "advantage," as Styles had put it.

"Lord Styles was not on that journey to Madras two years ago. How exactly did he blackmail Lord Crispin?"

"My idea." Sheeble hacked again. This time he was silent for an extended minute. His eyes did not open when he spoke, and his voice rasped. "Thought his lordship'd give me half for finding a bloke to sign the shippin' papers, 'stead of him." He spoke with obvious difficulty. "Only gave me fi-five percent, the bum Turk."

"Why did he stab you tonight?"

"So's I wouldn't tell you what's I just did."

"You intended to tell me all of this before?"

"Crispin was gettin' cold feet." He coughed, a liquid sound. "Thought I'd get me another hundred before the game was up."

"You imagined that I would pay you for information. Why me?"

A weary leer curved Sheeble's gray lips. "Not too bright, are ye, gov'ner? That's bum coves for ye, struttin' around thinkin' nobody knows nothin' but them."

"Lord Styles hid his involvement in this trade behind Crispin's signature then ownership of the vessel, threatening loss of the girl then exposure to the authorities if Crispin refused."

Sheeble's brow puckered, his breathing labored.

"Have you access to documents that implicate Lord Styles in the business?"

"Nothin'. Kep'—" A jolt shook his chest. "Kep' them all hisself."

Which meant Ben could find them eventually. But he was not interested in turning his old friend over to the authorities. Not yet.

He placed his hand upon the sailor's arm.

"Jonas, you will indeed die very soon. What you have done now, telling me this, may go some way toward paving your path more fortuitously in the beyond. I hope so, for your sake. For mine, I thank you."

Sheeble's eyes opened again, filled with fear.

Ben waited, not removing his hand, for some time until the life eventually slid from the fretful eyes. Then he closed them, drew the blanket over Sheeble's brow, and left the stall.

Sully glanced around him curiously, peering into the stall. "'S he dead, sir?"

Ben nodded.

The former dockworker folded his arms across his bulky chest. "Gave him the thumbscrews before he knocked off, I'll wager."

"Not tonight, Sully. I am feeling merciful." Merciful. Staggered. Dizzy with certainty he could not yet fully comprehend. Humbled. And above all impatient to return to the woman who caused this unprecedented state in him. "If he has family, return him to them. If not—"

"The beggars' cemetery." Sully shook his head regretfully. "You be treating him better than he treated other folks in life."

"We can only hope to be judged not by our sins, but by our judges' compassion," Ben said quietly. She loved him. She had always loved him. And it made him want to be merciful, forgiving as she had been to him despite how he had hurt her, as even now she was still merciful to Marcus Crispin, who had used her.

Ben's shoulders prickled. He had learned a great deal from Octavia about honesty and the tragic futility of lies. He suspected he had quite a great deal more to learn of compassion. But he would not waste those lessons on her former fiancée.

"Have you found Lord Crispin yet?" he said, moving toward the exit to the street.

"Yessir," Sully replied. "He's back at his rooms. I was coming to tell you when this happened. Thought it might be more important."

"Fine. Maintain a watch on him." He would deal with Crispin soon. But tonight he had other business. He pushed open the door and crossed the street. Candlelight flickered through cracks in draperies in the upper windows of Hauterive's.

"Milord." A thick-muscled footman bowed and stepped back to allow him entry. From the gaming chamber a woman's laughter tripped—sultry, inebriated. But Styles would not be playing at the tables tonight, not after what he had just done. Ben turned toward the parlor.

Styles lounged in a chair by the hearth, an empty glass hanging from the tips of his fingers, his gaze upon Ben as he entered. Swathed in imported silks and brocades, the chamber boasted only a handful of patrons at this late hour. By now most had either gone to their beds, to someone else's, or upstairs. The décor may have altered, but the purpose of this club so many blocks from St. James's never did.

Ben moved across the parlor, gesturing for a footman to bring him a drink, and lowered to the chair opposite the baron.

"I stopped by your house today. Your people said you had gone into the country."

Styles twirled the glass between his fingers. "My business there was brief." He assessed Ben, his blue eyes clear. "What brings you here in the middle of the night, Ben? Does the fair Miss Pierce fail to please, after all?"

Ben's blood chilled. He pasted a confiding grin on his lips.

"Still following my flirtations, old friend? How curiously flattering."

"I saw you leaving her house the night before last, before that route at Savege's. Rather late for callers, I would say. And you seemed somewhat distracted."

Ben received the glass from the footman.

"I have business with St. John Pennworthy. Noisome arrangement." He lifted the brandy to his lips.

"Convenient, I should say, in your pursuit of the lady."

"No pursuit there. Merely appreciation of a beautiful woman." He sipped then set the glass on the table. "Now that the mystery of the fire at the hunting box is solved, I find I have more leisure to enjoy the simple pleasures of life—shooting on my property, admiring lovely females, sharing a moment of calm after midnight with an old friend."

"The fire?" Flame-light glinted off Styles's gilt hair and across his face, casting shifting shadows. "I did not know there was a mystery to be solved there."

Ben leaned forward and clasped his hands between his knees.

"At the time, I ignored the cause of the fire. I assumed it was an accident. But, do you know, Walker, I think it preyed upon me. I did not realize quite how greatly until I finally addressed it."

"And what did you find?"

"I spoke with Andy, the old groom at the cottage, the only survivor of that night. You would not remember that, of course." He looked into the fire. "But Andy did. We talked at some length and I am satisfied with what he told me. I feel I know everything I must now to move on." He brought his gaze back to Styles. The other man's face was hard.

"I am glad for you."

"Thank you." Ben stood.

"Leaving so soon?" Styles came to his feet. "Why not remain? Ladies Carmichael and Nathans are both in the drawing room now. Either one, I suspect, would be glad to see you here. After all, enjoying the simple pleasures does not preclude partaking of the more satisfying ones."

Ben grinned and shook his head. "Too complicated. I am not interested in becoming involved in that sort of game."

"Or perhaps you are simply too distracted elsewhere to appreciate such bounty? Are you certain the fair Miss Pierce does not command your attention more than you care to admit?"

Here it was upon a silver salver for Ben, a threat meant to make him fear, a pointed addendum to the anonymous note he had sent. Styles could no more than suspect his involvement with Octavia. But suspicion might be enough.

He must wait for his old friend to confess voluntarily. He could not risk making his own business public enough to assure Styles's public condemnation. But clearly Styles would not surrender easily. He still expected to win. Members of the old English aristocracy always did, no matter the odds.

"Why this encouragement, Walker? Haven't you faith in my initiative any longer?"

"Rather, a suspicion that you are limiting yourself unnecessarily." There was no warmth in his voice, no fellow feeling or raillery. They both knew of what they were speaking. Ben had only to wait out his rival, to not be the one to flinch first.

"A useful reminder," he said with a thoughtful nod.

"Thank you, my friend." He headed toward the drawing room, Styles behind him just as years ago when nights such as this had been both a game and a penance to Ben. Now it was neither, but the safety of the woman he loved. If Styles needed proof of his disinterest in Octavia, he would provide it. And tomorrow, when she no longer rested in the safety of his house, she would still be safe because Styles would no longer believe he could use her to hurt him.

He paused at the drawing room door. Priscilla Nathans's emerald gaze snapped up, sharp with instant calculation through the haze of cheroot smoke and insufficient candlelight. At another table, Abigail Carmichael hung upon the back of a gentleman's chair, her expensive dress revealing a deep bosom and her stunning face mottled with drink. Her fogged gaze rose to his. Ben lifted a hand and gestured, a mere indolent flick of his fingers. But the beautiful widow responded, moving to him without hesitation and tucking her hand around his arm.

"You called, my lord?" She batted thick lashes and clung. Her eyes did not focus.

Ben cast Styles a slight grin and drew the lady toward the stairs to the upper story. He did not look back to see if his ruse had the intended effect.

The retiring chambers had been redecorated in the past seven years too, but Ben noticed little save the paper and pen on the dressing table. He poured a glass of ruby liquid from a carafe and Lady Carmichael drank greedy mouthfuls while he undressed her to her shift. He laid her on the bed then turned to his more pressing task.

"Come now, Doreé," she slurred. "It has been far too long. No more making me wait."

"A moment, my dear." The brief note written, he went into the corridor and gave it into the hands of a footman along with a guinea.

"Make certain he has this before he leaves his house or

receives any callers in the morning, and you will be well rewarded."

"Yes, my lord." Face eager, the servant hurried off. Ben returned to the bedchamber. Sparing a glance for the unconscious figure sprawled atop the mattress, he went to the window. Within two hours it would be dawn. Before that he would be gone from this place of loneliness and unquenchable thirst and return to the woman who made all of it seem like a distant bad dream. He settled into the chair at the dressing table to wait.

When the darkness thinned sufficiently for Tavy to discern details of the bedchamber, she rose, drew on her clothing, and opened the door. In a chair against the opposite wall, a housemaid dozed. Tavy cleared her throat. The girl startled awake and leapt up.

"Is your master at home?"

"No, mum." The maid curtsied. "But he bade me assist with anything you might be wanting."

"Please have a carriage called for me, then return and help me dress properly."

The maid curtsied again and hurried off. Tavy moved back into Ben's bedchamber. It all seemed like a strange dream, stranger than her night with him at Fellsbourne. Then, she hadn't any reason to worry about his safety any more than she always had from thousands of miles away. Now someone threatened him. But perhaps he received this sort of threat every day. And perhaps women declared their love to him as frequently.

The maid returned, laced Tavy into her clothing, and pinned up her hair. In the corridor, the familiar footman met her and escorted her to the mansion's rear entrance. The morning had not yet come, and the gray of predawn lay thick about the alley. A closed carriage waited, enormously elegant, with shiny black panels and sparkling wheels, the pair drawing it gorgeous from braided manes to powerful haunches. No noble crest decorated the door. An anonymous vehicle for a clandestine departure.

"Did he tell you to bring me out through the tradesman's entrance?"

"No, miss," the footman said, handing her up into the carriage. "I took the liberty, thinking you would prefer it."

"What is your name?"

"Samuel, miss."

"Thank you, Samuel. I appreciate your consideration." She sat back.

"Miss?"

She studied his face framed in the doorway. He had an honest look about him, as all of Ben's servants did. Interesting quality for the employees of a man who lived a life of masquerade.

"Yes, Samuel?"

"If I may say, I don't think his lordship had the notion you'd be leaving a'tall."

"His lordship has never been an unmarried lady in London with only a single change of clothes." Or a sorely confused heart.

Crinkles formed about Samuel's eyes. He shut the door, spoke out a word to the coachman, and the carriage rumbled into action. Tavy leaned into the velvety squabs and closed her eyes.

She reached home in the first light of dawn and passed through the rear gate into the garden behind the town house. The back door was locked. Given to significant self-deception until mere hours earlier, Tavy had not thought of bringing a key the previous evening. The kitchen boy answered her knock.

"Mornin', mum," he grumbled, rubbing the sleep from his eyes. "Mistress's been up the night worryin' on you. Don't think she told the master, though."

"Thank you for the warning. What about Mr. Abha?"

"Went out last evenin'. Hain't seen him since."

"I am here, *memsahib*."

She turned as Abha came through the door behind her. "Where have you been?"

He did not respond.

"Did you follow me?"

He nodded. She folded her arms, shoulders drooping with weariness.

"Well, if you were going to spy on me you might have relieved my sister's worry by telling her where I was."

"I did."

"Oh. Thank you." She went directly up to Alethea's dressing chamber. Infant swaddled in her arms, her sister dozed upon a divan. Her eyelids flickered open and she released a long breath of relief.

"I am so sorry, Thea. Truly."

"Are you all right?"

"Yes. Mostly."

"Is he here?"

A sweet, sharp ripple passed through Tavy. She shook her head.

Alethea's brow knit. "What have you done?"

"Nothing that I have not done before." Except the part about declaring herself in no uncertain terms. But it had stumbled out of her overflowing heart and she could not regret it.

Her sister's eyes widened. "Before?"

Tavy waved her hand about. "At Fellsbourne." Her cheeks were hot. But she deserved this, although perhaps not the ache of uncertainty pouring through her every cell.

"While you were betrothed to Lord Crispin, or before?"

"After, actually. Or, well. Yes."

"Has he offered you marriage?"

"*Um* . . . Betrothed to another man until *yesterday*."

Or perhaps he had not offered simply because he did not wish to. But Alethea needn't know that, and Tavy did not think she could say it aloud in any case.

Alethea's expression remained unusually firm. "Be that as it may, now we must discuss this."

"Allow me to sleep first. I will be a great deal more rational after, I suspect."

Alethea nodded. Tavy went to her bedchamber and undressed. She crept under the bedclothes and tucked her hands beneath her cheek. A sleepy Lal crawled onto the pillow beside her and curled into a ball.

Upon awaking, she took only a cup of tea in her bedchamber then searched out her sister. St. John and Alethea sat in the parlor in which Ben had kissed her and made her forget everything but him. As he always did.

"I am sorry to have kept you from the office today, St. John. And sorry to have kept you awake through the night, Thea."

"St. John just came home for lunch, and I slept all morning as you did. It is past noon already, you know."

"Oh."

Silence descended.

"Well?" Tavy finally said. "You are not Mama and Papa, and you allowed me to do mostly whatever I wished for nearly five years in Madras, so you will not chastise me, I hope."

"Are you quite all right, Tavy?"

"Yes. But please, I truly do not wish to speak of the particulars."

"Octavia," St. John said, looking grim. "In the absence of your father from town at this time, do you wish me to call upon Lord Doreé and demand his obligation to you?"

"Oh, Lord, no. Please. But thank you for asking me. I appreciate you not taking the decision without my consent."

Alethea glanced at her husband. St. John withdrew a folded paper from his pocket and gave it to Tavy.

"I received this before I left here this morning."

Tavy took it with impressively steady hands that grew rapidly unsteady as she scanned the words.

Sir, Your confidence in matters of business at this time is appreciated. Upon my honor, Doreé

"What does it mean, Tavy?" Alethea asked.

"Your guess is quite as good as mine." She folded the message and gave it back to her brother-in-law.

"Lord Styles approached me at Leadenhall Street this morning concerning a rumor he heard of a project I am pursuing with the marquess," St. John said.

Tavy's heart stumbled. "What did you say to him?"

"I said that matters remain uncertain."

"*Are* you involved in business with the marquess?"

"I am not. Octavia, until this morning when Alethea informed me of your absence last night, from all I have known of Lord Doreé I have respected and trusted him. But one word from you, and I will pursue this."

"No. Do not." Ben must have good reason, especially if it involved lying to his closest friend. She could not imagine otherwise.

"At least his intent seems clear enough," Alethea said.

Yes, that he was perfectly capable of sending a message to her brother-in-law concerning a mysterious business matter but no message at all to her.

Tavy's heart thudded. This could not continue, swinging between misery and elation, hopelessness and the ecstasy of finally allowing herself to be completely in love with him again. But this time a great deal more so. Because now she understood much better what he did with his time, which he did not fritter away on fashionable activities and wicked women, and his wealth, which he did not reserve for expensive horses and cards. In truth she had known it all along, borne home intimately when he revealed to her his pursuit of Marcus's blackmailer.

But something about how he left her in the middle of the night drove the reality deeper. To him, helping people was not an adventure, not a project or diversion to escape discontent. He helped people because he simply could not do otherwise.

"He must be confident of your discretion, sister," Alethea said. "And, perhaps, of your feelings?"

"Possibly." *Quite.*

"Are you certain you do not wish St. John to speak with him?"

"And demand that he marry me? Yes, very certain. That sort of thing is nonsensical, except I suppose in the case of the obvious consequence." Due to lack of caution. Tavy's heart fluttered, her stomach twisting.

"What will you do now?" Alethea asked.

"Do?" She had not given it a single thought. She was living the greatest adventure of her life, yet she had no atlas, no dictionary, and no idea at all of how she would travel hereafter. For the first time ever, she was taking the moments as they passed. It was a state at once marvelous and terrifying.

A footman appeared at the door. "Lady Constance Read."

Constance's eyes were rimmed with red, her mouth unsmiling. Tavy took her hand.

"How kind of you to call." She drew her into the chamber. St. John bowed and Alethea smiled, stiff greetings. Of course, like the rest of society they had no reason to believe that Constance and Ben did not intend to marry. Tavy hadn't either, except Ben's assurance, gotten from him at a moment when some men might say anything.

But she'd had this conversation with herself a dozen times already, although not, of course, since she told him she loved him and he responded with silence. Rather, near silence. He had cursed.

"I must be returning to work." St. John offered Alethea his arm.

"Octavia, we will continue our conversation later," Alethea said, then nodded to Constance and departed with her husband. Tavy led Constance to a seat, but the duke's daughter only perched agitatedly upon the edge.

"They are quite good," she said upon a slight quaver. "Quite good to leave you to me."

"You are clearly distressed, Constance. How may I help you?"

Tears tumbled over the rims of her azure eyes onto her cheeks. She thrust her palms over her face.

"Oh, Octavia," she uttered, her shoulders slumping. "I have made such a horrid mistake."

"Dear me, I cannot believe it of you."

"But you should. I am a wretchedly selfish person and I often act first and think later. And this time I acted quite, quite unthinkingly."

Tavy tucked a handkerchief into her fingers but Constance seemed content with silent tears dribbling from her palms and soaking the lacy hem of her sleeve.

"You have not shown any wretched selfishness with me," she comforted, "only kindness since the moment we met."

"That is because I like you. But, you see. I have betrayed your friendship horridly, and you will never forgive me for it. And oh, Octavia, I must tell him, but I am afraid to."

Tavy blinked several times.

"Tell who?"

Constance lifted guilty eyes. "Ben. He persuaded me to

it, of course, but this will change everything. He will be furious with me, yet I cannot do anything about it now. I should have thought of the consequences. *He* should have." Constance dissolved into tears anew, one hand covering her trembling lips, the other curving over her belly.

Tavy stared at her friend's fingers clutching her abdomen and her breaths thinned.

The consequences.

"I cannot imagine him being furious with you for anything," she said without revealing a hint of the panic rising in her.

"I acted without caution, because I wanted him to—" She broke off, her eyes full of misery. "I cannot even say it. Not to you, of all people. I thought I could, but I cannot."

Tavy did not want to go where her thoughts rushed, and part of her could not believe it of him. But the other part—the part that had spent two nights in his bed without a promise of any sort whatsoever from him—told her she was still quite as foolish as she had always been when it came to Benjirou Doreé.

"Then do not say it to me." Her blood ran fast and jittery but her voice remained smooth. "Say it to him."

Constance's eyes flicked wide. "You are right. I must. But how can I?"

Tavy stood and drew her to her feet.

"I will take you, so you will not need the courage to make yourself go."

Fresh tears stained Constance's face. She resisted Tavy's attempts to draw her away from the couch. "I do not deserve your kindness, especially in this."

"Don't be silly. I suspect you would do the same were our positions reversed." It actually hurt to say the words. But Constance's gaze softened.

"No. I am not honest like you, Octavia. Or brave."

"If you knew how wretchedly dishonest I have been these past several weeks you would not be looking so admiringly at me." She would, however, award herself points for bravery at the moment. She tugged, and this time Constance came along.

She gave Constance's coachman their intended direction. They sat in the closed carriage in silence that grew thicker as the minutes passed and Tavy's heart thundered harder with each turn of the wheels. In front of Ben's house, a footman let down the steps and handed them out. Tavy guided Constance before her into the colonnaded foyer.

The butler bowed. "Good day, my lady, miss."

Constance did not speak. Her cheeks were pale, her full lips a bare breath of pinkish white. But at least she had ceased weeping. Tavy took her arm.

"Is your master at home?"

"Yes, miss. The footman has just—"

"Where is he? In his study?"

"Why, yes, but—"

Tavy pulled Constance along the corridor. Samuel passed them a moment before Ben appeared in the doorway of his study. His brows were drawn, his mouth hard. A sob broke from Constance and she pushed past him into the chamber.

Tavy stood paralyzed. Ben's gaze consumed her, but rather less like a lover than a prosecutor before an accused.

"What are you doing here?"

"Hm. Not precisely what I hoped or frankly expected to hear from you given that twelve hours ago you told me very definitely to stay."

"Yet you did not. Did you arrive in Constance's carriage?"

"Yes."

He released an audible breath. "Then you must depart in it now." He stepped into the corridor and grasped her arm to turn her around. Her throat tightened. She pulled free of his hold.

"But she wishes to speak with you. Or, she does not particularly wish it, but I think she must."

"She may remain. But you must go."

Tavy stared, jaw slack, and her heart began to splinter.

"I had not planned on remaining."

"Your usual approach, it seems."

"You are criticizing me for leaving at the same moment you are telling me to go?"

"Something like that." His eyes looked odd, silvery. He moved close again and lifted his hand as though to touch her, but seemed to think better of it and his arm fell to his side.

"I have something I must say to you," she managed with credible evenness.

"Say it." His voice was low. She wanted to imagine in his rich tones an echo of the intimacy they had shared. But with Constance only yards away weeping over having betrayed her and the prospect of telling him news of consequences he would not like, Tavy could not allow herself to live in dreams. No more lying in his arms while he whispered beautiful things to her. Oh, Lord, but she wanted that beyond reason. She wanted him so much and yet it seemed after all that she was not to have him.

In point of fact, she had nothing to say now, nothing that could change circumstances or turn back time. But if she did not speak, she would have to leave, and her body wanted to remain with him as though drawn by magnets. Her lips moved, and finally words emerged.

"Will you help them too?"

"Them?"

"Lord Crispin and the girl."

Creases formed between his brows. "Octavia, he is a criminal."

"And all of your activities are thoroughly licit, I'm certain."

"He committed acts that hurt people."

"Will you at least show them a little mercy?" she insisted.

"Mercy is not mine to show in this case. It is the law's."

"But—"

"No."

"Ben, he was blackmailed. He saved her from danger."

"He served his desires."

"They are *in love*."

His jaw hardened. "That is not sufficient justification for deserting one's conscience."

Her hands went cold, her chest contrarily hot. He was perfectly correct, of course. But it hurt quite a great deal in the pit of her stomach, and higher, beneath her ribs, to hear him say it. She knew not whether to rejoice that she had come to understand his character so well or to despair.

She forced herself to meet his gaze without flinching. "Marcus should pay for the wrongs he did. But if you save those other girls, you must save this one too. Choosing between them would make you no better than him."

"Perhaps." His black gaze scanned her face. "But allow me to select my particular variety of villainy if you will. Now, go."

"But you are not a villain, or at least I didn't think so until a few minutes ago when you began speaking to me like a cad."

"Do you wish to be bodily removed from this house? Because I am on the verge of—"

"Don't you dare threaten me." She turned away. "I feel

an overwhelming sense of déjà vu." She swung around to him again. "I cannot believe you are dismissing me again."

"Not dismissing, and it disturbs me no less." His voice was warm, but a hint of panic threaded through it, strange. She stared, nonplused. "Octavia, trust me. Go home and remain there, I beg you."

Beg?

"Trust you? How on earth do you imagine I can do that?"

"I am more than happy to explain how, but this is not the time or place for that conversation."

"Why, because of what Constance has come to tell you?"

"I haven't any idea what she has to say, but I have important business I must see to now." His hand came up again and this time he cupped it around her cheek. "By God you are too beautiful."

"Too beautiful for what? To address with a modicum of civility?"

"To resist. You must leave this instant." He released her and raised his voice. "Samuel, see Miss Pierce to Lady Constance's carriage and home."

"Yes, my lord."

"All right. I will leave." Too many parting statements barraged her head. *This is thoroughly unacceptable and I will not stand for it. Throw me out now but do not expect to see me ever again. Be gentle with her, you faithless rogue.* Or perhaps simply, *I will love you forever even though I will try very hard not to.* She could not choose. Heart aching and mind tangled, she left.

But she had no faith to break any longer. Not after such treatment. And not after Constance's revelation. Tavy went home as instructed, but she did not remain there long.

Chapter 23

CAST AWAY. The state of a ship, which is lost or wrecked on a lee-shore, bank, rock, &c.
—*Falconer's* Dictionary of the Marine

B en gripped the doorjamb to prevent himself from going after her. He had never been so inarticulate, so at a loss for reason, and so thoroughly split between what he wished to do and must do. Except seven years earlier, with her.

But Styles must not see her at his house. Ben had not spent the dawn hours deploying his employees throughout London to have his plans all come to nothing now.

He rubbed a hand across his face to clear his vision. Dear God, simply seeing her warm eyes and animated lips made caution fly. He'd wanted to drag her into a closet and make her listen to every word of truth until there were no more to tell, then to kiss her until she said she loved him again. He could hear it hundreds of times and still not have heard it enough.

In his study, Constance stood in the shadows beneath the painting of the tiger, staring up at it.

"It seems you have finally decided to tell me what has been distressing you these past weeks." He crossed the chamber to her.

"I did not want to. I went to Octavia to tell her instead, thinking that would be easier. But it proved impossible. I am such a coward."

He touched his fingers to her chin and tipped her face up.

"Not so cowardly. You are here now."

"I am only here because she brought me. She seemed to know I must tell you. She is v-very good."

"She is."

The tears spilled anew, drenching her cheeks and dripping from her chin. Ben pressed a handkerchief into her hand. She turned her face aside.

"Constance, have over with it."

"I have been unfaithful to you," she whispered.

"I am afraid, my dear, that you must make yourself much plainer than that, or I will begin to imagine that you are not in your right mind."

She pivoted away, covering her eyes with her hand.

"I told him everything he wished to know. I told him so that he would have me, and he said he would, but now—now he—" She lowered her hand to her mouth, her eyes frantic.

"Constance." She knew as little of Ben's real business as any member of the *ton*. There was nothing she could divulge to anyone of her acquaintance that everyone else would not know. "Perhaps we should begin with the identity of this man."

"You must know it." Her tone tightened. "You have encouraged me on his behalf any number of times."

Foreboding crept into him. "Styles?"

Her eyes widened.

"I never encouraged you toward him." But he had encouraged Styles to pursue Constance, because of her infatuation with him. At the time, he had trusted his friend.

"Perhaps not," she admitted. "Perhaps I misspoke. But you teased me about him."

"I did. Am I to regret it now?"

She nodded.

"Constance, what have you done?"

"What I should not have," she snapped, but her shoulders shook. "And he has played me false."

Ben drew in a slow breath. "What would you have me do now, call him out?"

"Oh, no. No." She came toward him swiftly and reached for his hand, but then snatched hers back. "I would never put you in danger to salvage my honor. But—But I think I may have put Octavia in danger instead. I do not know how, precisely, but this morning when he called— Oh, Ben, I think he means her no good."

"Constance, tell me now exactly why you believe this. Exactly."

She backed away a step, her eyes wide. "I—"

"Tell me."

Tears slid down her face as she spoke. "At Fellsbourne he wanted to know of your interests in ladies. It was merely idle conversation so I obliged. But today he asked if your flirtation with Octavia indicated anything more profound. He behaved so—so— I thought he was finally coming to be certain that you and I were not—" She stuttered. "I sought to assure him, so I told him what I believed concerning you and she."

"What do you believe?"

"That there is a great deal between the two of you that neither of you will speak of."

"What makes you believe he intends her harm?"

"He seemed satisfied that her betrothal to Lord Crispin was not based on anything more than the most superficial affection. You know that, don't you?"

"What else, Constance?" Dear God, how could he have been so blind?

"When I told him what I thought about you and she, h-his eyes seemed to light, as though I had given him the key to a puzzle. I thought it perhaps some sort of competition between the two of you. Octavia once said something about that—competition. I did not understand what she meant at the time, but after he reacted that way I thought perhaps he has designs on her and she is aware of it and sought to make you jealous. But that does not fit with her character in the least, so I discarded the idea. But then he left in such haste—" Her voice broke off. "Ben, please tell me what is going on."

"He is only interested insofar as harming her will hurt me."

"No." Her hand slipped over her mouth. "What have I done?"

A fist of fire lodged in his chest, and panic.

"I am sorry he did this to you, Constance." He could say nothing else to stem the confusion in her blue eyes. He went toward the door.

"But why would he wish to hurt you? You have been friends for so long. Like brothers."

"He killed Jack." The words struck the air like lead. "He set the fire that burned my brother and father and six other people in their beds that night. He murdered your betrothed then lied to us both about it for years."

She went immobile. Then her body seemed to crumple. Ben moved to her swiftly and took her up in his arms. She pressed her face to his chest.

"Why? He loved Jack as much as you did. Why would he do such a thing?"

"I am endeavoring to discover that now."

She loosened her grip, face awash in hopelessness.

"I am sorry, Ben. So sorry I have put Octavia in danger."

He shook his head. "You could not have known. But have you told me everything?"

She nodded, but her eyes spoke of grief he had not seen there in years.

"Remain here as long as you wish," he said gently, "or return to your home, but do not leave the house or accept callers until I tell you otherwise."

"He has had any number of occasions to harm me. He will not now."

"He already has. What he does not understand is that I will not abandon you because of it."

Her gaze retreated and she stepped back. "I will not ask the same friendship of you any longer, Ben. It would not be fair to Octavia."

He studied the lines across her brow, the sorrow in her eyes. Octavia had brought her here. She had not shied from Constance's distress or dependence on him. She had only sought to remedy the trouble, as she wished to do for Crispin and his lover. Her heart knew no subterfuge or jealousy. It only knew how to give.

Samuel appeared at the door. "My lord, Mr. Sully has sent word."

He must have located Crispin. "Have Kali saddled." But his conversation with Crispin must wait. Styles as well. He must see Octavia now and tell her everything. He should have done so earlier when she was standing before him, her eyes filled with intention and confusion at once. He should not have let her go without knowing about Styles. Now young Jimmy was keeping watch over her from the street, and surely Abha from within the house. But Ben could not entrust her safety to another man for an hour more. Never again. That was his job.

He paused on the threshold. Constance stood beneath the tiger portrait again in shadows, the great beast looming over her in an attitude of princely power.

"Will you be all right?"

She nodded. "Make it well again, please." Her voice was thin.

"I will."

"You always do."

Samuel met him at the front door with greatcoat and hat.

"Where is Lord Crispin?"

"At his club, sir, a quarter hour past."

"Is Mr. Sully still here?"

"No, sir. He's gone back to the office in the event that his boys send news, as you wished."

"Samuel."

"My lord?"

"Have that large painting in my study removed and remounted in the drawing room over the mantel." He started through the door. "It needs more light."

"Miss Pierce is not in, my lord."

"Not in?" Ben stood perfectly still in the foyer of St. John Pennworthy's house. "Did her manservant accompany her out?"

The butler stiffened. "I believe so."

But Abha had, after all, allowed her to meet Crispin's lover. And there was every likelihood that if she wanted to see Crispin now, Abha would take her to him again.

"Where did she go?"

The servant's face seemed to lengthen. "I haven't an idea of it, my lord."

Ben headed in the direction of St. James's Street. Above carriages and carts, horsemen and pedestrians, the November day hung heavy with coal dust and fog, the sort of chill-to-the-bone weather Ben had struggled for years to become accustomed to as a boy. That had been in the countryside, at Fellsbourne and Eton, where trees and green fields at least gentled the harsh transition from tropical heat to foggy gray.

But he had forced himself to adapt, molded himself into the perfect English boy despite the constant torment of his peers. At the time, he told himself it was for the best—for his family's honor, his uncle's needs, his own peace—a private peace in life he had always yearned for yet never achieved. She gave him that peace, with her unrehearsed touch and speech, her genuine smile and thirst for life. She had from the first.

Except at the present moment.

She could not go into a gentleman's club, but Ben would not put it beyond Octavia to wait on the sidewalk for Crispin to emerge. She had never been shy when she wanted something.

Despite his anxiety, he smiled.

But no beautiful minx with hair the color of fire opals stood on the block in front of Brooks's. Ben entered the club and scanned the chambers. Gentlemen peppered the subscription room, playing at cards, backgammon, and politics.

One man sat alone hunched over a corner table, hand on his brow, the other around an empty glass. Ben slid into the seat across from him. Crispin lifted his head and his face crumpled.

"No," he uttered and looked to the wall.

"What have you to tell me?" Ben asked quietly.

"Rather, how will you punish me? You needn't, you know. I have been punished sufficient for a lifetime."

"A somewhat melodramatic response, and not particularly lucid."

"Need I be more lucid?" He swung his head back around. "You are here on his errand or your own. Either way, I am thrice damned."

"Tell me of the first two damnations and I will offer you assurances concerning the last. Possibly."

"Do you truly believe you could make it any worse for me now?"

"Undoubtedly." Ben held his gaze. "My lord, my patience thins."

"You don't know?"

"Apparently not. Enlighten me."

"He took Tabitha." He lowered his brow into his palm once more, masking the gesture here amongst his peers in an attitude of weariness. Even in grief, the baron calculated his persona.

Ben's blood hummed with impatience.

"Tabitha is the girl you keep, I am to understand. The one for whom you sent dozens of others to their deaths?"

"Not all died," he muttered. "Sixty reached Madras in the last shipment."

"How many vessels have sailed with such precious cargo, Crispin?"

"Since I have been involved, only the one, nearly two years ago, and the ship setting off tomorrow." Disgust curled through his voice. "Before that, I don't know. Three, four perhaps."

"Why did you become involved? Easy income?"

His brow was dark. "What will you do if I tell you?"

"What do you imagine I will do?"

"Expect me to stand as witness against him."

"Would you?"

Crispin's genial eyes hardened. "It would ruin me."

"Undoubtedly."

"But you could protect me."

Ben shook his head. "I haven't so many friends in Parliament as my father did, or more importantly, as Lord Styles does now."

"But I suspect those few you have are the ones worth

having. And I don't think a vessel leaves port in London without you knowing what's in it and where it is bound."

"Clearly several have, or I would not be sitting with you here now."

Crispin's face pinched. "I took passage on Styles's ship two years ago merely because it was heading to Madras and that was my destination. I hadn't any idea it belonged to him or what cargo it carried. The master was a drunkard, the quartermaster Sheeble in charge."

"Sheeble bribed you with the girl?"

Crispin looked toward the wall again, as though he could find courage there. "When I discovered the girls, I threatened to make it known at the next port, and to have them sent back home. But by then it was too late."

Ben knew about too late. Nine years ago he learned that lesson when he rescued an English miss in a crowded marketplace.

Crispin dragged in a breath. "I did not sleep."

"Guilt for agreeing to keep the business secret and profiting from it?"

His eyes slewed back to Ben. "I never wished to profit from it, and I have not." His voice was hard. "Sheeble said that if I slept, he would put Tabitha overboard. I could do nothing. The crew anticipated their gold at the end of the cruise. None of them would help me, and they took my sword and pistol, even the lock on my door. I kept her with me and barely slept for two months until we reached port. Sheeble let me have her then, but he maintained a watch on us."

"I assume you smoothed the transfer into India of those girls who remained alive, without notice by the authorities. Why did you agree to sign the documents?"

His shoulders fell. "I was beyond myself. Ill. It was easier to do what he wished than to continue. I could not work and remain in society and protect her from Sheeble all at once. It was impossible."

In society in Madras at that time he had begun to court Octavia, an attempt to release himself from the grip his obsession had on him. But such a grip never released a man.

"Did Styles ever threaten you himself?"

Crispin's lip curled. "Sheeble always, until you so conveniently gathered us all at your estate."

"He allowed you to purchase the *Sea Bird*, making you believe that would be an end to the trade in girls."

"He lost a fortune in Nepal, but you must know that. I paid him twice what the ship was worth. I thought that would end it."

"But he warned you that was not to be." With a burr beneath a horse's saddle and an impromptu race. Ben should have known. But he hadn't known about the fire then. He had not yet learned to mistrust his old friend. "Will he bring the girls from the countryside this time?"

Crispin lifted his gaze again, abruptly sharp.

"Apparently you know everything already. Why are you here?"

"Take care now how you speak to me, sir," Ben said evenly. "I have been asked to show you more mercy than you deserve, but I am inclined otherwise."

Crispin's eyes flickered with something deep and disturbing. Dread.

"I deserve no mercy at all. Not from you."

Icy fingers stepped up Ben's spine. "Where did Styles take your Tabitha?"

"To the safe house with the new girls. But only for a night, to frighten me. He brought her back this morning. I have sent her to the country with my housekeeper."

"You no longer fear for her safety?"

Crispin shook his head, eyes swimming with guilt.

Ben's throat twisted. "Where," he said as steadily as he could, "is Miss Pierce?"

The baron looked like a man already upon the gallows.

"When he came to my rooms this morning," he said in a strangled voice, "he said he is finished with Tabitha. That she and I are no longer useful to him. You are his principal object."

"*Crispin*—"

"He has all the leverage he needs with Octavia."

Cold, hard purpose washed through Ben, submerging the panic fighting to break loose. "Where is he?"

Crispin shook his head, throwing his face into his palm, not masking his misery now. "In the countryside, or preparing the ship. I don't know. I don't know, for God's sake! I wish— I wish I had never—"

Ben stood and moved swiftly across the chamber and from the building, telling himself that Sully and Abha would not allow her to come to harm. That she was clever enough to recognize danger if it confronted her. That he was not upon the threshold of losing his life the moment he had gained it.

But as he pressed along London's leaden streets toward Blackwall where Sully's men would bring news to Creighton, he passed through a world of humanity that had become once again thoroughly alien.

Chapter 24

DISABLED. The state of a ship when, by the loss of her masts, sails, yards, or rigging, she is rendered incapable of prosecuting her voyage without great difficulty and danger.

—*Falconer's* Dictionary of the Marine

L al clung to Tavy's head with the grip of an animal three times his size.

"This will not do," she mumbled, peeling the monkey's tiny black fingers from her bonnet one by one only to have him reattach more firmly than ever.

"I told you this, *memsahib*. Your absences give him worry."

Tavy ceased her efforts, resigning herself to walking down St. James's Street with a capuchin monkey wrapped around her nape. Passersby gaped, stared, pointed, proper English gentlemen and ladies reduced to nursery behavior by the sight of the Original and her exotic pet. But Lal's behavior when she returned home from Ben's house had made it clear that he would have torn the house apart if Tavy left him again. And somehow she felt safer with him.

She scanned the upper windows of Brooks's gentlemen's club. She could not very well knock on the door and expect to enter. But Abha could give a note to the doorman. If only she had thought to write one.

"Miss Octavia Pierce, what a pleasant surprise." The female purr suggested precisely the opposite. Priscilla Nathans's violet pelisse perfectly complimented the emerald glint of her eyes. She was alone, followed only by a servant carrying an armload of parcels. Her ruby lips curled into a moue of distaste. "And what interesting headgear."

"Thank you, my lady. I will accept that as a compliment."

"I am sure you will."

Lal leaned over Tavy's shoulder and bared his teeth. Tavy moved toward the front door of Brooks's.

"Searching for anyone I know?"

Tavy looked over her shoulder. "As a matter of fact, yes. I don't suppose you have seen Lord Crispin today?" According to Abha, Marcus was no longer at either of his residences. But Tavy needed to find him and insist he turn himself in to the authorities. His actions had hurt people, even though he had not wished to. He simply did not have Ben's strength of character. Although, of course, Ben had hurt *her* perfectly well. But since she seemed to be the only person in humanity to have that honor, it must be for the best.

"Lost track of your fiancée? How diverting." Lady Nathans chuckled, a rippling sound of superiority. "Perhaps you have been too attentive elsewhere, hm?"

Lal's fingertips dug into Tavy's shoulder.

"I don't know what you mean, but I am certain it will not do me any good to find out." She stepped away.

"Abigail Carmichael had a lovely night with him. I've only just now come from calling upon her at home. She is exhausted, of course. Some gentlemen are not easily sated."

Octavia tasted sour milk.

"My lady, you obviously delight in speaking in riddles." Lal's fingertips pinched her earlobe, his whole little body jittering. "Unfortunately I am not so fond of deciphering them, especially since Lady Carmichael's nocturnal activities certainly have nothing to do with me."

"Don't be so coy, my dear. A person has only to see you glance at Doreé to know your feelings."

"Do you know, Lady Nathans, I believe you are—quite literally as well as figuratively—a green-eyed monster."

The monster's green eyes narrowed. "What on earth could I have of which to be envious?"

"What you imagine your good friend Lady Carmichael had." That which Tavy, whatever way she looked at it, could not possibly accept. Perhaps he had been with Constance under certain circumstances, although Tavy was already beginning to doubt it now that she'd had time to consider. But not another woman, and certainly not the previous night during the hours he had left her alone. Not the man she knew him to be now.

"I saw them with my own eyes, my dear, as did Lord Styles and the others. I needn't imagine a thing."

"Hm." Tavy's blood hummed. "Well then, imagine this: Imagine telling me the name of the ship your husband and Lord Crispin own which is shortly to set sail for the East Indies."

The demi-rep's gaze sharpened.

"Has Doreé cozened you into seeking out information for him?" Her purr sounded rather rough now. "How quaint you are to be so devoted."

"Then," Tavy continued as though the baroness had

not spoken, "if you do not tell me the name of the ship, imagine me telling Lady Carmichael exactly what did not happen in your bedchamber that night at Fellsbourne before your host left it."

Tavy almost laughed at the momentary panic that sluiced across the baroness's face. But the monster masked it quickly.

"You could not possibly know anything," she said smoothly.

"Oh, well then, if you have no anxiety upon that score, I will just call upon Lady Carmichael as soon as I am finished here."

"*Sea Bird*."

Tavy swiveled on her heels and met the baroness's gaze. "*Sea Bird*, you say? And which berth might she be lodged in?"

"I haven't any idea." Lady Nathans scowled. "What do you take me for, common gentry like yourself?"

"Oh, I would not take you for anything. In that, I believe Lord Doreé and I are quite alike." With a smile, she headed down the sidewalk, Lal hurling a string of staccato comments in their wake.

"Do you wish now to go to the ship?" Abha asked at her shoulder.

"Well, Lord Crispin is not at either of his flats. Do you think he might be there?"

"No."

Tavy peeled Lal's mitt from her chin and drew in a thick breath. "Why not?"

"He is behind you."

Tavy pivoted. Amidst the attractive traffic upon St. James's—ladies walking arm in arm, gentlemen dressed to the nines, tradesmen in neat trousers, even a flower girl in a fetching smock—Marcus looked horrible. Worse than she must have looked with the monkey on her shoulder. He strode straight to her at a hard pace, drawing stares.

"I hoped to find you before I left." His voice was hoarse, his face pale and eyes red as though he had been crying. He looked at Abha and his brow seemed relieved. "You are safe."

"I am." She shook her head. "Where are you going?"

"My house in the country. But first I must see Nathans, apologize to him for implicating him in this business. I needed his money to purchase the ship, but he is innocent, of course." His brow contorted, the thick lock of hair falling over it that she had once wished to brush away in a comforting gesture. His cravat was crushed, his coat wrinkled, and whiskers shadowed his jaw already at midday. He looked directly at her, for the first time since she had known him apparently unconcerned with what others might think of him. He seemed a man thoroughly beaten, and it was awful to behold.

"Marcus, you must turn yourself in. If not because it is right, then because you cannot go on like this."

"I will." His lids drooped until his eyes were half closed. "I promise, I will return and give my testimony. But now it is in Doreé's hands, where it should have been all along. He will see it to its end." His blurred gaze swept up to her face. "Do you know who he is, Octavia? Do you truly know?"

She stared, dumbstruck, and nodded.

His gaze slipped to Abha, then farther along the street. Tavy followed it to a young man, thick-set and garbed like a dockworker, leaning against the rear wheel of a parked hackney coach.

"I hope you know," Marcus whispered, returning to her face. He shook his head. "I beg your pardon, Octavia. A thousand pardons for putting you in danger."

"Danger? But you said that was a story you invented."

His eyes seemed to grow fraught again. "He did not tell you, then." His gaze slewed to the lumper down the block once more. "But he—"

"Tell me what, Marcus?"

He gripped her hands. "If he did not see fit to tell you, I cannot." He reached into his waistcoat and withdrew an envelope. He pressed it into her palm. "Give him this."

"Lord Doreé? What is it?"

"He will understand. Octavia, my dear, God bless you. And forgive me, please." He released her and swung away down the crowded sidewalk.

The crisp stationery shook in her fingers.

"Where do you wish to go now?" Abha asked.

"I hardly know." But she did. Ben had spoken with Marcus, clearly, but he hadn't told her. Still he kept secrets. But one secret she must learn the truth of finally. "I will call upon Lady Constance."

Abha nodded. Tavy strode toward the carriage. The young dockworker pushed away from the hackney, falling into her tracks.

"Abha, do you know that man?" Her gaze darted to the stranger as she climbed into the carriage.

"No, *memsahib*. I do not."

In the downstairs parlor of the Duke of Read's town house, Lady Fitzwarren sat ensconced in a gilt-and-white chair. She rose hastily and moved toward Tavy with a heavy exhalation.

"There you are, dear girl."

At the window, Constance whirled about and threw herself forward to grip Tavy's hands.

"Octavia darling, I went to your home but you were not there. Where did you go?"

Tavy's head spun, her heart tangled. The blue eyes glimmered with such affection and concern.

"Constance, I came here to— I—" How could she do it? "I have no way of asking this delicately, but are you increasing?"

The dowager sucked in an audible breath. Constance's brows dipped into a frown. She shook her head. But this was not sufficient answer for Tavy's heart.

"Yet you are clearly troubled. At the Savages' ball the other night—" She took a steadying breath. "Constance, I must know if you and Ben intend to marry. Please tell me now, without evasions."

Her blue eyes flickered with a hint of agitation. "We do not."

Tavy tried to control her quick breaths, but her lungs would not seem to function properly. She glanced at the dowager. Lady Fitzwarren's pinpoint eyes were direct. She nodded her head once, a spray of purple feathers fluttering upon her bandeau.

Tavy pulled her gaze away. "Did you—" Good heavens, this was equally difficult. "Were you ever lovers?"

"No. Never. Oh, look at me, Octavia." Constance gripped her fingers. "I said no."

Tavy jerked her hands away. "But why not? And why did you never marry?"

The beauty's lips curved into a sad smile. "No doubt it would have made things quite a bit easier for me if I could have convinced him to marry. But he would never agree to it."

Tavy stared into her friend's brilliant eyes. "Did you wish to?"

Constance twisted her slender shoulders in a movement that might have been a shrug or assent. "For companionship, yes. Safety and comfort."

"You never . . . ?"

"Desired him?" Her slim brows lifted. "I tried to kiss him once."

A lump clotted Tavy's throat. "And?"

"It was years ago, after that endless period of mourning. I needed to know if we would suit, if I could run away to him and not grow to regret it, or estrange my closest friend by forcing a faithfulness upon him he did not want."

"What happened?"

"He let me make a fool of myself." A rueful curve shaped her lips. "He was very kind at first in putting me off, then he said it was like kissing his sister, and I remember throwing something porcelain at him, or perhaps marble." Her grin crept into a private smile of memory. Then her gaze lifted to Tavy's. "But sometimes I have found myself wishing it were otherwise, when I look at him and see what you see."

"What do I see?" Tavy barely whispered.

"A beautiful man in every way. A man without equal upon this island or any other. Octavia, I have known him since he was thirteen and I have never seen him look at a woman the way he looks at you."

Tavy's heart ached so hard she was obliged to press a hand to her chest. "He is dishonest with me."

"His life is a masquerade. But you know that, don't you?"

"I thought— When you said you had betrayed me, I thought you meant with him." Her hands twisted in her lap. "I simply cannot go on like this, imagining and fearing and not trusting but wanting to trust. I am not fashioned for that."

Constance said softly, "I don't believe he is either." Her smile was gentle.

Raw hope battered Tavy's insides.

Constance reached for her hand. "You are more observant than you know. I have been so heartsore. But since I learned of his perfidy, I am more sorry for him than anything else."

"His perfidy?"

"His lies to Ben, to me, and everyone else."

"Whose lies?"

Constance shook her head. "Octavia, what—"

"Who lied to you and Ben? Marcus?"

"Lord Crispin? Why, no. It was Walker. I thought you understood—"

"Lord Styles? What did he lie to you about?"

Constance's eyes glistened. "About the fire at the hunting box seven years ago. Ben did not tell you?"

"No." But apparently he told everyone else everything.

"Walker set the fire." Her voice quivered. "The fire that killed Jack and their father."

"No. Oh." Tavy could say no more. Her heart ached far too much, for him and for herself. He had kept this from her. How long had he known? Surely this morning when he sent her away from his house. "Why did Lord Styles lie about it? Wasn't the fire an accident?"

"Ben does not know yet. He intends to discover the truth."

Tavy's breath caught, hot and sharp alarm darting through her. Her fingers scrabbled for her reticule and the envelope within.

"Marcus said that I was in danger, but that it was all in Ben's hands now." She pulled the letter from her reticule.

"He said you are in danger?" Constance's face blanched. "But how could Lord Crispin know that?"

"Lord Styles blackmailed him. Ben said he had important business to attend to today, but I was so—"

Icy fingers dug into hers.

"Octavia, I told Walker about you and Ben. I am so sorry."

"What did you tell him?" Tavy spoke to prevent herself from breaking for the door. She told herself she would know if he came to harm, that something inside her would feel it. But dread blotted out all else. He must have gone to confront Lord Styles.

"I told him of your mutual affection. Walker wishes to use you to hurt Ben."

"He didn't need you to tell him that," Lady Fitzwarren interjected. "Anybody can see it plain as day whenever they are around one another."

Tavy shook her head. "He let me believe it was only about that awful business, which is albeit quite an important matter, but—"

"What awful business?"

Tavy's fingers tore at Marcus's letter until the pages lay open in her hands. She consumed the words.

Dear Lord.

"Is it about the fire? It was arson, wasn't it?" Constance's voice was strained.

Tavy disentangled her fingers and patted her friend's hands, releasing a big breath and fixing a relieved look in her eyes.

"No. Not at all. I have figured it all out. This letter explains it." She waved Marcus's pages about. "There is nothing to worry about," she lied, as though she did it every day with perfect ease. It was not her news to tell, she understood now. And she could not share with her friend the panic sluicing through her, the weakening fear. Not unless she discovered concrete reason to.

But oh, God, it mustn't come to that.

She bussed Constance on the cheek and cast the dowager a bright look. "I must be off now."

"Octavia Pierce, before you take another step explain yourself."

"I will just make a quick call upon an acquaintance, Aunt Mellicent," she said airily, moving toward the door. "Then I will return here directly and fill you in on all the details." She flashed a quick smile and sailed out of the room.

Roiling stomach in her throat, she flew down the steps toward the carriage, gesturing for Abha to join her inside. The door closed behind them and she gasped in air. Her trembling fingers thrust the letter at him. Atop his shoulder, Lal clicked his tongue in agitation.

"Where would he go to confront Lord Styles? His house?" She stretched to wrap on the top panel. Abha stayed her hand, lifting his heavy gaze from the crumpled pages.

"To the ship. The noise. The privacy. He will lure him there." Abha leaned out the door and gave the coachman directions. Tavy could not breathe.

Privacy to do what? Noise to disguise what sounds?

Carts and horsemen clogged the streets through the City toward the East India Docks. The carriage crept along. Tavy's hands twisted in her skirts.

"Can we not go faster? This is unbearable. Quite as unbearable as anything I have experienced in seven years, only rather worse, actually. Why didn't he tell me?"

"It is not the first time he has wished to protect you, *memsahib*."

Her gaze snapped up. "Protect me?"

Abha's hooded eyes looked intent. "He did so for seven years."

She blinked. "I beg your pardon?"

"Upon your eighteenth birthday he hired me to watch guard over you."

"Upon my . . . ?" Her tongue failed, and her heartbeat, her brain's very functioning.

"Your uncle knew that he must take me in. He understood who Benjirou Doreé was, even if your aunt did not. Later, your brother-in-law suspected, but he asked nothing, although I never took payment from him. My service ended when we arrived in England."

Tavy could not move.

"That lad you asked me about earlier," he said when she remained silent. "All day he followed you. He works for him."

Tavy's lungs tightened. She turned her face away, but sobs formed in her throat, tears thick in her eyes. After an endless minute of strained silence, she pressed her fingers to the window and peered out.

"Is he in danger now?" She barely whispered the words. Her heart beat fiercely but she mustn't cry.

"Yes."

The sky was dark with sea-coal and cluttered with the masts and rigging of tall ships, the water of the Thames inky between vessels lined bow-to-stern in berths along the export basin. Tavy knew the place well. When her sister first married St. John, she had spent hours studying the sparkling new docks, warehouses, and offices, dreaming of one day traveling upon a great ship to distant, exotic lands.

Nine years later it looked different. The gatehouse and the wall surrounding the quays was the same, but the planks of the docks and quayside buildings were worn from constant use and soot, and even busier than when they had first opened. Sailors worked at lines and scrubbed decks, making ready to sail, while watermen rowed a galley alongside, patrolling for thieves. Dockworkers hauled cargo from laden carts aboard the closest ship, ropes squealing and three dozen men circling capstans like mules tied to a millstone, swinging the heaviest crates aboard over the rail.

With Lal clinging to her neck, Tavy dashed from the carriage and along the quay, Abha following in loping strides.

"How will we find him? How will we know which ship?" She fought back the fear.

"You already know which ship."

Of course. Priscilla Nathans.

"You are his equal, *memsahib*," Abha rumbled at her side, "as I have long known."

Chapter 25

CANNONADING. Used in a vessel of war to take, sink, or burn the ship of an enemy, or to drive it from its defenses ashore.

—*Falconer's* Dictionary of the Marine

The top deck of the *Sea Bird* stretched long and empty below skeletal masts and yardarms and the loosening clouds overhead. No barrels or crates stood about waiting to be hauled below. No sailors labored at pitch and planking, line or canvas. No dockworkers tread the gangplank, loaded down with cargo. Not even a guard stood at the rail, surety against thieves still common enough on the docks despite Company proprietors' efforts to halt such incursions into their profits.

Ben strode aboard and to the steps belowdecks. As a child in India he had learned the habits of snakes. They hid, waiting in the dark until their prey came to them.

Not bothering to quiet the clunk of his boots on the boards, he descended. The gun deck was low-ceilinged and dim, all but two gunwales at the far end closed to the daylight without. The air was close, warmer than above and stale, typical for a ship at dock.

A footstep sounded behind him. Ben turned. Styles stood in the doorway to the master's quarters.

"Ah," he drawled. "Come to finally speak to me directly, Ben? I wondered how long it would take you to muster the nerve."

No nerve. Rather, desperate fear. He forced his voice to remain even. "As long as it will take you to begin to feel guilt over what you have done to Constance."

Styles released a dramatic breath, audible across the deck empty of everything but three dozen cannon lined back-to-back along its length and still coils of rope.

"Constance?" He shook his head. "All you could say now, and you begin with her?"

Octavia could not be aboard this ship now. If Styles had her here, he would not delay in threatening. They had come too far for that now.

"Why did you do it, Walker? Why did you use Constance to get at me? You could have done so easily in any number of other ways. You have."

A thin smile curved his lips. "I took enormous satisfaction in having her, Ben. Having the woman you never had the courage to take."

Ben had never noticed before how Styles thrust out his chest when he spoke, like a fighting cock.

"Jack would despise you for what you have done to her. Even more so than because you murdered him."

Styles's eyes flickered darkly in the shadows, but he did not speak.

"You did not intend to kill him, did you? It was an accident, wasn't it?"

"Of course it was an accident."

The back of Ben's neck prickled, his muscles tensing.

Styles's voice had quivered upon the words, but his hand slipped into his coat pocket.

"But you give yourself too much credit, you know. I would have had Constance anyway. That it affected you poorly only sweetened the conquest."

"Misusing a woman already infatuated with you is not a conquest, Walker. It is selfish cruelty."

He pursed his lips. "Bitter words. Spoken from personal experience, Ben?" He leaned his shoulder against the doorpost as though perfectly at ease. "Now tell me the truth. We are hiding nothing from one another any longer, after all. Is the indifference on your part a show, or does the fair Miss Pierce have you as twisted about her little finger as you have her about yours?"

"If you harm her, Walker, I will hunt you down like an animal and kill you with my own hands."

"Ah. I suppose that does justice as an answer." He smiled. "But aren't you here now to kill me?"

Styles must not have her. Crispin's fears were yet unfounded. Ben drew in a steadying breath and shook his head. "I am not."

"Then you'd best get off this ship, because I, on the other hand, am quite prepared to kill you." He drew a pistol from his pocket. Decorated with silver and ivory about the butt, it gleamed in the dim light. Slowly, he pulled his thumb back and cocked it.

"I understand this ship belongs to Crispin and Nathans."

"Playing it a bit too cool, aren't you, Ben? I am quite sincere in my intentions, you know."

"You would have killed me years ago if you intended to, like you killed my father."

"You only became a true hindrance to me when you learned of this business." Styles waved the pistol, taking in the ship with the gesture. "And when I killed your father, I rid Britain of a dangerous man."

"Dangerous? My father was a gentleman-politician. He hadn't a dangerous bone in his body."

"Indian-lovers should not rule Britain's interests in the East, Ben. Jack knew that, despite your father's infatuation."

Ben stilled. So this was it. What he had suspected, now so clearly stated upon his old friend's twisted lips.

"Jack did not care about India, Walker. He was perfectly happy with his brandy and birding. Politics were the farthest thing from his interests."

Quiet descended in the space between them, the only sounds the creaking of boards and the lap of water against the hull, and the muted noise of commerce on the quay without.

"I could have influenced him." Styles's voice was gravelly. Alien.

"You murdered my father because you wished for greater control over his heir?"

"I brought a quick end to the greatest threat British interests in the East have seen in a century."

"You wished to halt him from pushing through Parliament the bill that would have put the Company back into the hands of traders who—"

"Who had gone native. Like your father and his cronies. Men like those are a danger to England. A danger to us all."

Ben stilled, certainty creeping through him like an opiate, twining in his limbs, numbing him.

"When did you begin this trade in humans, Walker?"

"A year after the fire."

"A year after you murdered your best friend, a man who loved you like a brother."

Styles's nostrils flared, his breath forced now. "I never meant to hurt Jack."

"Why didn't you save him?"

A pause. "I tried."

"Tell me how you tried. You owe me at least that."

Styles bared his teeth in a scowl, but Ben knew he would speak. He had loved Jack, and whatever he and Ben were to each other now, they had shared that love.

"I set the fire in your father's chamber, but it spread too rapidly. I pulled Jack from the bed. I dragged him." He looked away into the deep shadows. "He was drunk. He would not come. He kept saying he was on the field at Waterloo amidst cannon shot, with Arthur."

"So you left him to die, with my father and six innocent people."

His gaze slewed back, sharp and glittering. "I hated you for what I had done. For a time, I did wish to kill you."

"But then your arrogance overcame your grief. You thought you could influence me."

"But no one can, can they?" He laughed, a round sort of contempt. "It doesn't matter who you are, Ben, whatever it is you do with all those ships, or in that office. You are alone. You may hold a title, but you are not one of us. You will never be a true Englishman."

Ben shook his head. "How you must have railed against fate when I came into the title instead of Jack. *Me*, a living incarnation of what you most despised. I cannot imagine. Frustration? Fury? So you sought another method for controlling associations between natives and Englishmen, providing wives for all those sailors and Company officials miles away from home. But you did not ask the girls first if they liked the idea. And then you treated them like cargo."

Styles's eyes narrowed. "My way will win, Ben, and yours will be trampled under the feet of men whose boots a mongrel like you should not even be permitted to shine."

"Dirty words, Walker, and beneath you. But you have reached your end, and I think you know it or you would not have been waiting here for me like a snake under a rock. Fate has thwarted you at every turn and you are furious, not only that I discovered your crimes, but that I have never bowed to your natural superiority. You are an arrogant son of a bitch."

"More arrogant than a man who comes to meet his enemy unarmed? You are a fool, Ben."

Ben laughed, a dry, weary sound, an affectation perfected in a distant lifetime to depress the attentions of men and women he had used for information and no longer needed.

"What need have I of a weapon, Styles?"

Styles's eyes flickered with uncertainty. "You imagine that I fear you. I don't."

"Walker, the greatest difficulty I have had in these past days is in trying to imagine anything at all about your intentions and wishes." He regarded him steadily. "But you do fear me."

Styles said nothing. Then he pivoted, strode into the captain's cabin, and returned with a sword in either hand.

Ben shook his head. "Come now. You know I will win."

Styles threw a weapon forward. It skidded along the planking, jarring to a halt against Ben's boot. The tip shone sharp in the dim light.

"No, Walker."

"Fight me now, or I will shoot you." He shook the pistol. "I have been carrying this for days for precisely that purpose, you know. Of course you know." He laughed. "You know everything."

Ben retrieved the rapier and palmed the hilt. Styles set the pistol down and came forward swiftly. Ben raised his weapon and parried the first attack, metal snapping against metal in quick clicks, echoing across the low-slung space. Styles drew back momentarily, scanning Ben's easy stance with ever brightening eyes.

"Do you know, old friend," Ben said quietly, "despite your hatred, I think you are confused."

Styles came at him again, cheeks florid. Ben allowed him to advance, blades meeting in swift attack and parry, but Styles never pressed close enough for concern, and Ben did not riposte.

"You are a finer swordsman than this, Walker. You are not trying."

Styles struck out again, blades clashing then the slide of release as Ben deflected the blow and steel clanked against the heavy black flank of a cannon, close to the hilt. Styles's arm jerked aside and he grabbed his wrist with a strangled oath.

"Damn you, Doreé. You will not win."

"I have already won." He diverted another hit, pressing his opponent's sword arm wide. "You cannot hurt me."

"You are wrong." Styles paused, his breaths labored, eyes glittering with something more than anger. With emotion deep and pained. "You did not deserve a brother like Jack. Or Arthur. You did not deserve their title. You don't deserve any of it."

Ben lowered his weapon. "I will not kill you, Walker."

"Then I will kill you." His sword clattered to the planking. He reached into his pocket, yanked out the pistol and cocked it anew. "Decide now."

"I wonder." Ben allowed his gaze to slip along the length of the steel in his own hand. "Is it the fear of being discovered by your fellow lords as a criminal, or your consuming guilt that frightens you the most?"

"Crispin is running scared. He won't talk."

"Yes, you have cleaned house very nicely. Jonas Sheeble is dead and you do not even own this vessel any longer. And yet here you are. Interesting." He set the sword tip upon the floor. "The guilt will never fade, Walker. You know it won't." At the corner of his vision, movement stirred. On the stair rail, a tiny shape descended to the deck upon spindly legs, its long tail curled in an arc for balance.

Ben's breath stilled.

No.

No.

Styles raised the pistol. "You have no proof against me. Watch me win now."

Ben stepped forward, closing the distance between them slowly, every muscle tensed. "I could turn you in."

"I have more friends in Parliament than you ever will. You cannot touch me."

The monkey leapt off the stair rail onto the floor, then scampered atop a cannon. Styles's head jerked around. Ben's heart raced. Footsteps descended the steps and he nearly shouted, but the tread was heavy, the boots upon the boards a man's. Abha.

But if Abha were here, she might be as well.

"The pistol is cocked, Abha." Ben lifted his blade at the ready, gaze pinned to Styles as he moved away from the stair, dividing Styles's attention.

Walker cracked an astounded laugh. "You think your henchmen can subdue me?"

"Not his henchmen." Octavia's sweet voice rang across the deck, and Ben's heart twisted. "Only me."

"Ah, Miss Pierce, welcome to our party." He raised the barrel.

She paused on the lowest step, her bright gown like an exotic flower in the gloom. Only Abha's thick body stood between her and Styles's weapon, but her face was serene.

"Thank you, my lord," she said. "But I am afraid this is a party you will not enjoy very much. I have in my possession a document written by Lord Crispin admitting to his guilt and giving wonderfully precise details concerning your shared illegal business activities. Quite a few names, dates, and monetary amounts, it seems, although I admit to only scanning the latter. I haven't a head for figures, you know."

Ben nearly laughed. But the pistol still pointed over Abha's shoulder, and Styles seemed paralyzed.

"In your arrogance," Ben said quietly, "you never imagined he would turn on you, did you?"

"Lord Styles cannot be blamed, really. It is not to Lord Crispin's advantage to have done this." Octavia's tone seemed pensive. "But Marcus is not an evil man at heart. Simply a weak one, I think." She did not remove her gaze from Styles, but her lashes flickered.

"Show me the document," Styles said.

"I may not have a head for figures, my lord, but I am not a complete idiot. Do you think I would bring it here so that you could take it from me and destroy it? Really."

"Does she bluff like this with you, Ben?" he said in a peculiar voice, as though they were sitting across a table at the club together, glasses of brandy in their hands.

"No." Ben's grip tightened around the hilt of his sword. "Never."

Styles's shoulders moved up and down in a jerk of a breath. Silence streamed across deck.

"It is over, Walker," Ben finally said. "You know it is."

Styles's arm dropped. The pistol cock snapped closed, echoing in the close space, and Ben released his breath.

"Abha, relieve Lord Styles of his firearm."

The big man moved forward and took the pistol from the baron's open palm.

"Now, if you will, Abha, escort Miss Pierce off the ship."

"Yes, my lord."

Ben could feel Octavia's gaze on him as she ascended. Styles turned to him. Ben lowered his sword.

"So you will turn me in, will you?"

"I don't think so."

"Ah. You have something else planned for me."

"I want you to go, Walker."

"Go?" Fear flickered in the blue eyes. "Where?"

"Wherever you wish." Ben spoke slowly. "But go far. If I hear of you, I will let you know, and you will then be obliged to take to the road again." He paused. "And, Walker, I have ears in many lands. Unless you prefer a life of wandering, you would be best to choose from the outset a distant location. Perhaps even one in which the people are nothing like you, where you are the alien, foreign and mistrusted. Hated."

Styles stared at him, face white. "You cannot mean this."

Ben laughed and shook his head. "Of course I do, old friend."

"Isn't the knowledge that I will be humiliated before my equals sufficient for you? That I may rot in prison?"

"You said yourself you have friends in Parliament who would not allow that. It is no doubt the reason you did not use that pistol just now. You expect your friends will wrest you out of this. But, Walker, I don't want you to have friends ever again. I want you to know what it is to be stripped of everything you hold dear—title, status, wealth, authority over others. That is the humiliation I wish for you now because I know that will be worse for you than any other punishment."

"And if I refuse? Or if I go then return someday?"

"Then I will do what I must."

Boot steps sounded upon the overhead deck. Abha would have summoned help.

"Now it is your turn to decide. Choose, Walker."

"Let me go."

Ben nodded.

Young Jimmy and two of Sully's other men appeared on the steps.

"Take Lord Styles to my ship at the end of the dock, Jimmy, and see that he is introduced to the master. Let Captain Agrieve know that the baron will be paying his way to Tunis with labor, and that he should drop him at the port there."

Jimmy tugged his cap, eyes bright. "Yessir, milord."

"And, Jimmy, remain with the ship until it disembarks. We do not want Lord Styles to miss his boat, do we?"

Jimmy smiled. "No, sir."

Styles swung around to Ben, shock in his thick breaths. "You would not."

"What did you think, that I would allow you to return home and pack your trunks? Visit your bank?" Ben shook his head. "Go, Walker, and do not return. And remember, if I hear of you, I will take the law into my own hands, as you are so fond of doing."

They led him away, Styles's back rigid, his face a hard mask of pride, even now.

For several moments Ben stood motionless, allowing the truth to settle over him. The finality. He drew in a long, deep breath. A cleansing breath, steadying himself.

Then he vaulted up the stairs.

The afternoon had cleared and thin sunlight shafted through the rigging, casting shadows onto the dock. Sully, Creighton, and Abha stood at the end of the gangplank as though they lingered about together every day, appearing for all the world like they were studying the *Sea Bird*'s moorings. Octavia was not with them.

Ben crossed the bridge in long strides. "I told you to keep a watch on her. I told you not to allow her from your sight. I told you— *Where is she*?"

Sully's thick brows rose. Creighton drew the tip of a

pen out from between his teeth and pointed it down the dock.

"Right there, my lord."

Ben's heart halted, then stumbled to life anew. She stood beside the next vessel along the quay, looking up at its decks, her carriage erect, the hood of her cloak tossed back onto her shoulders. Sunlight poked through the loosening cloud cover, slanting across her face and form and rendering her almost ethereal.

But she was far from that. She was the single true reality Ben had ever known, the most precious, recklessly steadfast, and divinely beautiful creature imaginable. Even with a monkey perched on her shoulder.

The animal's head turned toward him. Octavia's gaze followed, lit with emotion. Ben moved forward.

"My lord." Creighton cleared his throat. "Your weapon?"

Ben grinned, shoved the sword into his secretary's hand, and headed toward the only past, present, and future he had ever wanted.

Chapter 26

HOMEWARD BOUND SHIP. A vessel when returning from a voyage to the place from whence she was fitted out.
—*Falconer's* Dictionary of the Marine

Tavy struggled for breath. Ben's face was flushed with life and so beautiful it hurt to look at him.

Lal jumped from her shoulder and skipped along the planking to meet him. With a gentle hand, Ben put the animal off him and halted before her. His gaze scanned her then came to her eyes. He smiled, and Tavy's heart opened, a blossom beneath sun.

"You rescued me," he said.

"I thought it was about time I returned the favor." They stared at one another. "He capitulated so easily. You did not really need rescuing, did you?"

"I think I have needed rescuing by you my entire life, Octavia Pierce."

"That is a very nice thing to say, but I don't imagine it

is true." She spoke to prevent herself from leaping into his arms, like the monkey.

"Is Crispin's confession real?"

She nodded.

"He gave it to you and you came here to help me. What did you imagine you would find?"

"I had no idea. I did not even know you would be here. But I had to come."

"Octavia, I am sorry."

"For what? Leaving me in the middle of the night to go carry on with another woman?"

He looked surprised for a moment, then his measured gaze said all.

"Priscilla Nathans told me," she said. "And, no, I did not believe her. Not for more than a minute, anyway."

"A minute." He seemed to consider the notion. "I suppose I should be glad for the brevity of your mistrust this time." His lips crept into another slight curve.

Octavia's heart turned over. "You were in danger because of what I asked. Because Lord Styles hoped to harm me. I do not want to be a liability to you, Ben. I could not bear it."

"Liability?" His voice deepened. "You are the reason those girls will not die on their way to India, the reason they are not being shipped away from home and into unwilling servitude. You are the reason I have put my father and brother's deaths to rest, that their murderer will finally pay for it. The reason Constance can now live her life as she should. I would not have done any of it had you not shown me."

"But I am not good at deception. I cannot play these games any longer."

"This is not a game, Octavia. This is my heart that you stole and I can no longer live without. I have done many things I do not like in service to others, and I finally understand why, and why I must continue. But I cannot if losing you again is the price."

She barely breathed. Words would not come. Remarkably.

"I am sorry, Octavia, not only for leaving you in the middle of the night but for leaving you seven years ago."

"S-Seven years ago?" she whispered.

"I was head over heels in love with you then. I still am, more and more each day." His mouth shaped a gentle smile, the flash of white teeth like that first day in the Madras market. "How could I not be?"

A sob of joy caught in her throat. The air all around seemed to shimmer, golden and dazzling in the criss-crossed shadows. She stared at his perfect face, his beloved face, and the present embraced the past in a sumptuous tangle. Early evening breeze rattled lines against spars, sailors called to one another across planking, a bell tolled and the scent of brine rose from the river, a cacophony of sensation Tavy melted into, every pore in her body opening fully to life again, finally.

"I know about Abha," she somehow managed to utter.

"He told you." Ben's shoulders seemed to relax.

"All these years from thousands of miles away you have been protecting me," she whispered. "Why didn't you tell me?"

He stepped close, his black eyes glimmering in the setting sun, vulnerable, his soul crystal clear through them. "Because until last night I was not certain the news would be welcome to you. Put me out of my misery finally, *shalabha*. Accept me. I am yours, as I always have been. I need you to be mine."

"Oh, Ben." She rested a palm upon his chest, then her brow. "I feel weak all over."

He drew in a deep breath, touched his fingers beneath her chin and lifted her face to meet his gaze, wrapping his arm about her. "Then allow me to hold you until you regain your strength."

"Rescuing me again?" A quivering smile. "You know, it is very difficult for a woman to resist a man who rescues her so many times."

"I suspected that." He pulled her to him tight and his heart beat hard and steady beneath her fingertips. "I love you, Octavia," he murmured against her cheek. "I love you." He captured her lips and kissed her so sweetly and with such sublime seduction of heart and body that she could only surrender willingly, happily, as she had at the beginning with him, when the world was wide and love could be plucked from the heavens if one were adventuresome enough to reach for it.

Her smile was radiant. "Take me home, Ben."

"Where to? Madras or Kent?"

"Wherever you are."

"You have my promise, *shalabha*. Forever."

Epilogue

The marchioness leaned into the main deck rail and loosened the ribbons on her bonnet, setting a flurry of gold-red locks free. Sea spray and smoke from the Madras manufactories ahead tangled in the tropical air and in her nostrils, beckoning. Sprawled in a comfortable pale mass on the East Indian coast, Fort St. George commanded the harbor, surrounded by palm trees and town houses and screened by dozens of ships. She loved this sight, the sight she craved and that held her spellbound now, as on that first time she sailed toward it a decade ago.

She sensed her husband's approach from behind. He slipped his hands around her waist, then his arms, and she leaned back into his warmth.

"So, we arrive." His voice was peaceful.

"I have been thinking," she said, months of shipboard contentedness now transformed into jittery anticipation. "What if you are unhappy here? What if it all seems horridly alien to you after so many years?" She turned from the scene of tropical heaven before her to an even more intoxicating sight.

His eyes sparkled beneath the equatorial sun, his expression pacific. "Then you will remind me and it will become familiar once again."

She studied his face. "You are not sorry to have come?"

"No." He sounded certain. "It is time. I stayed away too long."

"You must have come back someday. Your family is here, and India is in your blood."

His arms tightened. "You are in my blood."

"I know you did this because I wanted to, and you are a prince for it." She smiled. "But it will be good for the business, even such a brief visit."

"Six months is sufficient time." He bent to touch his lips to the side of her mouth, then again to the other side. Sweetness coiled through her at the light caress, the need he always roused in her rising full-bodied and soul deep. She wound her arms about his neck. The sailors were accustomed to these displays of affection by now, and if anybody complained, Abha would glower them into submission, or Lal would scold.

Welcoming her husband's kisses, she struggled to order her thoughts. "Sufficient time to reestablish allies and make new contacts?"

"Sufficient time to make love to you in every place I once imagined doing so."

"You did? Where?"

His hands slipped to her lower back and he pulled her flush to him. "Everywhere." His voice was husky, the evidence of the vitality of his imagination delightfully tangible against her.

"In the garden, I suppose." She lifted her lips.

"Yes." He kissed the corner of her mouth. She shifted to meet him, but he teased, turning his attention to her lower lip with tantalizing little bites.

She sighed, a throaty sound of sheer bliss. "Where else? Never tell me the bazaar."

"Yes."

"The *bazaar*?" She gasped, the tip of his tongue turning her joints to jelly. "And the park?"

"Yes." He kissed her full upon the mouth.

"The cotton fields?" She laughed in sheer happiness. "Company headquarters? Or, no—my aunt and uncle's drawing room?"

"Yes. But mostly your bedchamber. I fantasized about you in your bedchamber."

She smoothed her palms across his chest. The apricot-colored gem on her ring finger glittered alongside the gold embroidery of his waistcoat.

"I have a bedchamber here aboard ship, you know." She took her lower lip between her teeth. "A rather fine cabin, actually. I know the owner, you see."

"Do you?" His hands rounded her waist again. "And do you think he would mind if I used you quite thoroughly in that cabin momentarily?"

"I daresay he would not mind it at all. He is a generous sort." Her voice came forth breathy. Silly for a woman married so many months, but there it was. His gaze and words did things to her inside. Very fine things.

He brushed his lips across her palm. "You will not regret missing our approach?"

His mouth did things as well. Even finer things.

"I have already seen the view." Her pulse was quite rapid. "And we will not dock for another hour, will we?"

One black brow lifted. "About an hour."

"Oh, then." She grinned and gripped his hand to pull him toward the stair. "No time to waste."

He laughed, the sun shone hot and delicious upon her skin, and she was home.

Author's Note

Mughal princes in India decorated their palaces with pictures and sculptures of tigers to show their supreme power. This symbolism caught the imagination of the English who subjugated these native rulers through treaties and warfare. They imagined India as a tiger, a great fearsome beast that only the mightiest foe could vanquish—the regal lion, England as conqueror.

When England lost its colonies in North America to revolution in 1783, full attention turned toward its eastern prize. Sparkling like a familiar yet ever-mysterious jewel upon the threshold of the Far East, India was replete with riches and opportunity beyond imagining. Through steady conquest of the subcontinent and the sea routes around it, England gained enormous wealth that enabled not only its strength in the war against Napoleon but also the decadence of the Regency period.

A small note on one not-so-throwaway comment by

Tavy: Although attributed to Byron upon its 1819 publication, *The Vampyre* was written by Byron's physician, John Polidori. While Polidori's elegant, enigmatic vampire did not shy from the daylight per se, he enacted wicked deeds upon innocent females, most certainly at night.

My humble thanks go to my university colleagues for research guidance on the East India Trade Company, to Dr. Joel Dubois for assistance with Hindi and Sanskrit, and to Gordon Frye for his vast knowledge of firearms. Special thanks also to Marcia Abercrombie, Elizabeth Amber, Anne Calhoun, and Sheetal Trivedi. Finally, many thanks to Faith Bodley for her fabulous trilogy title, Rogues of the Sea.

Keep reading
for a sneak peek at
WHEN A SCOT LOVES A LADY
The first book in
Katharine Ashe's new series
Coming in 2012
from Avon Books

Prologue

A lady endowed with grace of person and elevation of mind ought not to stare. At two-and-twenty and already an exquisite in taste and refinement, she ought not to feel the pressing need to crane her neck so that she might see past a corpulent Louis XIV flirting with a buxom Cleopatra.

But a lady like Katherine Savege—with a tarnished reputation and a noble family inured to society's barbed censure—might on occasion indulge in such minor indiscretions.

The Queen of the Nile shifted, and Kitty caught another glimpse of the masculine figure at the ballroom's threshold.

"Mama, who is that gentleman?" Her smooth voice, only a whisper, held no crude note of puerile curiosity. Like satin she spoke, like waves upon a gentle shore she moved, and like a nightingale she sang. Or so her suitors flattered.

Actually, no longer singing like a nightingale. Or any other bird, for that matter. Not since she had lost her virtue to a Bad Man and subsequently set her course upon revenge. Vengeance and sweet song did not mesh well within the soul.

As for the suitors, now she was obliged to endure more gropes and propositions than declarations of sincere devotion. And for that she had none to blame but herself—and her ruiner, of course.

"The tall gentleman," she specified. "With the dog."

"*Dog?* At a ball?" The Dowager Countess of Savege tilted her head, her silver-shot hair and coronet of gem-encrusted gold glimmering in the light of a hundred chandelier candles. An Elizabethan ruff hugged her severe cheeks, inhibiting movement. But her soft, shrewd brown eyes followed her daughter's gaze across the crowd. "Who would dare?"

"Precisely." Kitty suppressed the urge to peer once again toward the door. Of necessity. If she leaned too far to the side she might lose her gown, an immodest slip of a confection resembling a Grecian goddess' garb that her mother ought never have permitted her to don let alone go out in. But after thirty years of marriage to a man that publicly flaunted his mistress, and with an eldest son who'd long been an unrepentant libertine, the dowager countess was no slave to propriety. Thus Kitty's attendance at a masquerade ball teetering perilously on the edge of scandalous. Truly she should not be here; it only confirmed gossip.

Still, she had begged to come, though she spared her mother the reason: the guest list included Lambert Poole.

"Aha." The dowager's penciled brows lifted in surprise. "It is Blackwood."

To Kitty's left a nymph whispered to a Musketeer, their attention likewise directed toward the tall gentleman in the doorway. Behind her Maid Marion tittered to a swarthy Blackbeard. Snippets of whispers came to Kitty's sharp ears.

"—returned from the East Indies—"

"—two years abroad—"

"—could not bear to remain after his bride's tragic drowning—"

"—infant son left motherless—"

"—a veritable beauty—"

"—those Scots are tremendously loyal—"

"—vowed to never again marry—"

Louis XIV kissed Cleopatra's hand and sauntered off, leaving Kitty with an unimpeded view of the doorway. Garbed in homespun, a limp kerchief tied about his neck, a crooked staff in hand, and a beard that looked as though it were actually growing from his cheeks rather than pasted on, he clearly meant to pass himself off as a shepherd. At his side stood an enormous dog, shaggy quite like its master, and gray.

The ladies that surrounded him, however, paid no heed to the beast. Hanging upon his arm, Queen Isabella of Spain batted her eyelids and Little Miss Muffet appeared right at home dimpling up at the man who, beneath his whiskers, was not unattractive.

Quite the opposite.

Kitty dragged her attention away. "Are you acquainted with him, then?"

"He and your brother, Alexander, hunted together at Beaufort years ago. Why, my dear? Would you like an introduction?" The dowager purloined a glass of champagne from a passing footman with all elegance, but her eyes narrowed.

"And risk covering my gown in dog hair? Good heavens, no."

"Kitty, I am your mother. I have seen you sing at the top of your lungs while dancing through puddles. This hauteur you have lately adopted does not impress me."

"Forgive me, Mama." Kitty lowered her lashes. The hauteur had, however, saved Kitty from a great deal of pain. Pretending hauteur, she allowed herself to nearly believe she did not care about the ever-decreasing invitations and calls, the cuts direct, the occasional slip on the shoulder. "Naturally I meant to say 'Please do make me an introduction, for I am hanging out for an unkempt gentleman with whiskers the length of Piccadilly to sit at my feet and recite poetry about his sheep.'"

"Don't be vulgar, dear. The poor man is in costume, as we all are."

As they all were. Kitty most especially. A costume that had nothing to do with her Athenian dress. Music cavorted about the overheated chamber, twining into Kitty's senses like the two glasses of wine she had already taken. Foolishly. She was not here to imbibe, or even to enjoy, and certainly not to indecorously ogle a barbaric Scottish lord.

She had a project to see to.

As at every society event, she sought out Lambert in the crowd. He lounged against a pilaster, an open box of snuff on his palm, his wrist draped with frothy lace suitable to his Shakespearean persona.

"Mama, will you go to the card room tonight?" She could never bear playing toady to Lambert with her mother nearby.

"No introduction to Lord Blackwood, then?"

"*Mama.*"

"Katherine, you are an unrepentant snob." She touched Kitty's chin with two fingertips and smiled gently. "But you are still my dear girl."

Her *dear girl*. At moments like this, Kitty could almost believe her mother did not know the truth of her lost virtue. At moments like this she longed quite desperately to throw herself into her mother's arms and wish that it all go back to the way it was before, when her heart was still hopeful and not already weary from the wicked game she now played.

The dowager released her. "Now I shall be off. Chance and Drake each took a hundred guineas from me last week and I intend to win it all back. Kiss my cheek for luck."

"I will join you shortly." Kitty watched her mother go in a cascade of skirts, then turned to her quarry.

Lambert met her gaze. His high, aristocratic brow and burnished bronze hair caught the candlelight dramatically. But two years had passed since the sight of him afforded her any emotion but determination—since he had taken her innocence and not offered his name in return—since he had broken her heart and roused her eternal ire.

She went toward him.

"Quite a bit of skin showing tonight, my dear." His voice was a thin drawl. "You must be chilled. Come to have a bit of warming up, have you?" He sniffed tobacco from the back of his hand.

"You are ever so droll, my lord." Her unfaltering smile masked the bile in her throat. She had once admired this display of aristocratic ignobility, a naïve girl seeking love from the first gentleman who paid attention to her. Now she only sought information, the sort that a vain, proud man in his cups occasionally let slip when she cajoled him sufficiently, pretending continued adoration in the face of his teasing.

That pretense, however, had excellent effect. Through months of painstaking observation, Kitty had discovered that Lord Lambert Poole practiced politics quite outside the bounds of legal government. Once she'd found papers in his waistcoat with names of ministry officials and figures, numbers with pound markings. She required little more information to make his life in society quite uncomfortable were she to reveal him.

But heat gathered between her exposed shoulders, and a prickly discomfort. Where plotting revenge had once seemed so sweet, now it chafed. And within her, the spirit of the girl who had sung at the top of her lungs while dashing through puddles wished to sing instead of weep. Tonight she did not care for hanging on his sleeve and playing her secret game, not even to further her goal.

"Come on, Kit." His gaze slipped along her bodice. "There's bound to be a dark corner somewhere no one's using yet."

She suppressed a shudder. "Of course I deserve that."

"Precedent, my dear."

She forced herself to step closer. "I have told you before, I—"

Something swished against her hip, a mass of gray fur, and she jolted aside. A steadying hand came around her bare arm.

"Thare nou, lass. Tis anely a dug." A warm voice, and deep. Wonderfully warm and deep like his skin against hers, that made her insides tickle.

But tickling insides notwithstanding, Kitty's tastes tended decidedly toward men who combed their hair. A thin white streak ran through Lord Blackwood's, from his temple tangled amidst the overly long, dark auburn locks.

And beneath the careless thatch across his brow he had very beautiful eyes.

"Lady Katherine." Lambert's drawl interrupted her bemusement. "I present to you the Earl of Blackwood, lately returned from the East Indies. Blackwood, this is Savege's sister."

"Ma'am." He nodded by way of bowing, she supposed.

Drawing her arm from his hold, she curtsied. "I do not mind the dog, my lord. But—" She gestured toward his costume. "—isn't it rather large for chasing sheep about? I daresay wolves would suit it better."

"Aye, maleddy. But things be no always whit thay seem."

Now she could not help but stare. Behind the beautifully dark, hooded eyes, something glinted. A hint of steel.

Then, like a thorough barbarian, without another word he moved away.

But she must be a little drunk after all; she followed him with her gaze.

In the shadows at the edge of the ballroom, a satyr with a matted chest of hair and a hand wrapped around a half-filled goblet leered over a maid—not a costumed guest but an actual maid. A tray of glasses weighed down her narrow shoulders. The satyr pawed. The girl backed into the wall, using her dish as a shield.

Lord Blackwood stepped casually between the two.

"Weel nou, sir," he said in a rough voice that carried above the music and conversation. "Did yer mither nae teach ye better as tae bother a lass when she's haurd at wirk?" His brow furrowed. "Be aff wi' ye, man, or A'll be giving ye a lesson in manners nou."

The satyr seemed to size him up, but the earl's measure was clear. Shepherd's garb could not disguise a man in the prime of his life.

"She's going to waste working on her feet," the satyr snarled, but he stumbled away.

"Ah," Lambert murmured at Kitty's shoulder. "A champion of the working class. How affecting."

At the touch of his breath upon her cheek, her skin crawled.

Lord Blackwood spoke quietly to the maid now and Kitty could not hear him. The girl's eyes widened and she nodded, her face filled with trust. As though she expected it, she allowed him to relieve her of the tray of glasses. Then she dipped her head and disappeared into the crowd.

Lambert's hand came around Kitty's elbow.

"Don't bother, Kit." His blue eyes glittered. "Since his wife died, Blackwood's not the marrying type, either." His grin was cruel.

He enjoyed imagining she was unhappy because he would not marry her. Years ago, ruining her had been entirely about insulting her brothers whom he despised. But now Kitty knew he simply liked to think she pined for him. Indeed she had pretended gorgeously, allowing him liberties to keep him close. Because she believed she needed to see him suffer as she had. First when he refused her marriage. Then when he proved to her that she was barren.

She looked back toward the man who had lost his young wife years earlier yet who still remained faithful to her. A rough-hewn man who in the middle of a society crush rescued a serving girl from abuse.

From the shadows the Earl of Blackwood met her regard. A flicker of hardness once more lit the dark warmth of his eyes.

Things were not always what they seemed.

But Kitty already knew that better than anybody.

1

London, 1816

Fellow Subjects of Britain,

How delinquent is Government if it distributes the sorely depleted Treasury of our Noble Kingdom hither and yon without recourse to prudence, justice, or reason?

Gravely so.

Irresponsibly so.

Villainously so!

As you know, I have made it my crusade to make public all such spendthrift waste. This month I offer yet another example: #14½ Dover Street.

What use has Society of an exclusive gentlemen's club if no gentlemen are ever seen to pass through its door? — that white-painted panel graced with an intimidating knocker, a Bird of Prey. But the door never opens. Do the exalted members of this club ever use their fashionable clubhouse?

It appears not.

Information has recently come to me through perilous channels I swim solely for your benefit, Fellow Subjects. It appears that without proper debate Lords has approved by Secret Ballot an allotment to the Home Office designated for this so-called club. And yet for what purpose does the club exist but to pamper the indolent rich for whom such establishments are already Legion? There can be no good in this Rash Expenditure.

I vow to uncover this concealed squandering of our kingdom's Wealth. I will discover the names of each member of this club, and what business or play passes behind its imposing knocker. Then, dear readers, I will reveal it to you.

— *Lady Justice*

Sir,

I regretfully notify you that agents Eagle, Sea Hawk, Raven, and Sparrow have withdrawn from service, termination effective immediately. The Falcon Club, it appears, is disbanded. I of course shall remain until all outstanding cases are settled.

Additionally, I draw your attention to the pamphlet of 10 December 1816, produced by Brittle & Sons, Printers, enclosed. Poor old girl is doomed to disappointment.

Yours, &c.,
Peregrine

Avon Books is proud to support the Ovarian Cancer National Alliance.

September is National Ovarian Cancer Awareness month, and Avon Books is urging our authors and readers to learn about the symptoms of ovarian cancer, and to help spread the "**K.I.S.S. and Teal**" message to friends and family.

Ovarian cancer was long thought to be a silent killer, but now we know it isn't silent at all. The Ovarian Cancer National Alliance works to spread a life-affirming message that this disease doesn't have to be fatal if women **K**now the **I**mportant **S**igns and **S**ymptoms.

Avon Books has made an initial donation of $25,000 to the Alliance. And—with your help—Avon Books has also committed to donating 25¢ from the sale of each book, physical and e-book, in the "K.I.S.S. and Teal" promotion between 8/30/2011 and 2/28/2012, up to an additional $25,000 toward programs that support ovarian cancer patients and their families.

So, help us spread the word and reach our goal of **$50,000**, which will benefit all the women in our lives.

Log on to ***www.kissandteal.com*** to learn how you can further help the cause and donate.

A portion of the sales from each of these September 2011 titles will be donated to the

Ovarian Cancer National Alliance:

VISCOUNT BRECKENRIDGE TO THE RESCUE
Stephanie Laurens

THE SEDUCTION OF SCANDAL
Cathy Maxwell

THE DEED
Lynsay Sands

A NIGHT TO SURRENDER
Tessa Dare

IN THE ARMS OF A MARQUESS
Katharine Ashe

ONE NIGHT IN LONDON
Caroline Linden

STAR CROSSED SEDUCTION
Jenny Brown

A V O N

An imprint of HarperCollins Publishers
www.avonromance.com

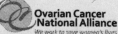

Ovarian Cancer National Alliance
We work to save women's lives

www.ovariancancer.org

KT2 0911

This September,
the Ovarian
Cancer National
Alliance and Avon
Books urge you to
K.I.S.S. and Teal:

**Know the
Important
Signs and
Symptoms**

Ovarian cancer is the deadliest gynecologic cancer
and a leading cause of cancer deaths for women.

There is no early detection test, but women with
the disease have the following symptoms:

- **Bloating**
- **Pelvic and abdominal pain**
- **Difficulty eating or feeling full quickly**
- **Urinary symptoms (urgency or frequency)**

Learn the symptoms and tell other women about them!

Log on to *www.kissandteal.com* for a downloadable teal
ribbon—teal is the color for ovarian cancer awareness.

The Ovarian Cancer National Alliance
is the foremost advocate for women with ovarian
cancer in the United States.

Learn more at www.ovariancancer.org

KT3 0911